Lost Kingdom

ALSO BY MATT MYKLUSCH

The Jack Blank Adventures

The Accidental Hero

The Secret War

The End of Infinity

Order of the Majestic Book 1

ORDER OF THE MAJESTIC

Lost Kingdom

MATT MYKLUSCH

ALADDIN

NEW YORK   LONDON   TORONTO   SYDNEY   NEW DELHI

This book is a work of fiction. Any references to historical events, real people,
or real places are used fictitiously. Other names, characters, places, and events
are products of the author's imagination, and any resemblance to actual events or
places or persons, living or dead, is entirely coincidental.

ALADDIN

An imprint of Simon & Schuster Children's Publishing Division
1230 Avenue of the Americas, New York, NY 10020
First Aladdin hardcover edition May 2020
Text copyright © 2020 by Matt Myklusch
Jacket illustration copyright © 2020 by Owen Richardson
All rights reserved, including the right of reproduction in whole or in part in any form.
ALADDIN is a trademark of Simon & Schuster, Inc., and related logo
is a registered trademark of Simon & Schuster, Inc.
For information about special discounts for bulk purchases, please contact
Simon & Schuster Special Sales at 1-866-506-1949 or business@simonandschuster.com.
The Simon & Schuster Speakers Bureau can bring authors to your live event.
For more information or to book an event contact the Simon & Schuster Speakers Bureau
at 1-866-248-3049 or visit our website at www.simonspeakers.com.
Jacket designed by Karin Paprocki
Interior designed by Mike Rosamilia
The text of this book was set in Goudy Old Style.
Manufactured in the United States of America 0520 BVG
2 4 6 8 10 9 7 5 3 1
Library of Congress Cataloging-in-Publication Data
Names: Myklusch, Matt, author.
Title: Lost kingdom / Matt Myklusch.
Description: New York : Aladdin, 2020. | Series: Order of the Majestic ; [2] |
Summary: When Fate puts the Secret Map of the World into Joey Kopecky's, Shazad's, and Leanora's hands,
they set out to find a lost kingdom that could hold the key to a new age of magic.
Identifiers: LCCN 2019050028 (print) | LCCN 2019050029 (eBook) |
ISBN 9781534424906 (hardcover) | ISBN 9781534424920 (eBook)
Subjects: CYAC: Magic—Fiction. | Adventure and adventurers—Fiction. | Voyages and travels—Fiction.
Classification: LCC PZ7.M994 Lm 2020 (print) | LCC PZ7.M994 (eBook) | DDC [Fic]—dc23
LC record available at https://lccn.loc.gov/2019050028
LC eBook record available at https://lccn.loc.gov/2019050029

FOR REBECCA, JACK, AND DEAN.
YOU GUYS ARE MY WHOLE WORLD.

Contents

Chapter 1	ASSAULT ON THE MAJESTIC	1
Chapter 2	GREEN ENERGY	33
Chapter 3	PROTECT THIS HOUSE	66
Chapter 4	THREE WITCHES	85
Chapter 5	ON TOP OF THE WORLD	103
Chapter 6	OUT OF THE FRYING PAN	121
Chapter 7	THE ROAD TO JORAKO	137
Chapter 8	FAMILY MEETING	164
Chapter 9	THE DEVIL'S TEETH	195
Chapter 10	VAMPIRE TOURISM	207
Chapter 11	TO THE BATCAVE	236
Chapter 12	PAINTED INTO A CORNER	265
Chapter 13	WHERE THE RIVER GOES	298
Chapter 14	STAR MAPS	311
Chapter 15	END OF THE ROAD	328
Chapter 16	THE IMAGINARY VORTEX	357
Chapter 17	EYE OF THE TIGER	374
Chapter 18	GO THE DISTANCE	392
Chapter 19	THE LOST KINGDOM	403
Chapter 20	THE SECRET HISTORY OF THE WORLD	414
Chapter 21	THE JOURNEY CONTINUES	437

1

Assault on the Majestic

"They're coming."

Joey stood in the lobby of the Majestic Theatre with his face pressed up against the glass door. He had one hand cupped over his eyes to block out the sun and get a better view of the building across the street. "I see them."

"What are they doing?" Shazad asked from right behind him. "Don't tell me they're coming here . . . already?" There was a pained tone in Shazad's voice that Joey understood completely. Joey wasn't ready for another fight, either. It had been less than twenty-four hours since their duel with Grayson Manchester. He needed a break. They all did.

"How many of them are there?" Leanora asked, moving in next to Joey to see for herself.

"I only see two. Over there by the door. That's them."

On the other side of the street, a man called Ledger DeMayne, sometimes known as Mr. Black, had just exited the corporate headquarters of the National Association of Tests and Limits. The NATL was the world's leading producer of standardized tests, servicing every school in America and quietly deciding the futures of children everywhere. The organization was actually a front for a secret society called the Invisible Hand. From what Joey understood, it was one of many. DeMayne had been introduced to Joey as the chief administrator of the NATL, but his real job was something more sinister than grading tests. The Invisible Hand enforced an unyielding measure of control over the world's limited supply of magic, and DeMayne was their leader. At least, that was the impression Joey got during their brief, standoffish conversation earlier that morning. Joey wasn't entirely sure if the man across the street was old enough to lead a Machiavellian cabal of evil magicians that dated back to the age of Merlin, but if Joey's introduction to magic had taught him anything, it was that looks could be deceiving. DeMayne was a young man with thick blond hair, handsome features, and excellent taste in clothing. Dressed in what was clearly a very expensive suit, he had stepped out onto the sidewalk like he owned it.

DeMayne looked good enough to grace the cover of a magazine, and the same could be said for the young woman who accompanied him. She wore a stylish bright red overcoat with a dark red ruby brooch pinned to her lapel. Joey wondered what her name was. The few members of the Invisible Hand he had met so far all used simple, color-based aliases. Mr. Black, Mr. Gray . . . As far as Joey could tell, it was an inside joke mocking the nonmagical "norms" of the world, who were easily fooled by magicians and their tricks. Joey figured he was getting his first look at Ms. Red. Something about her gave him the chills. Deep crimson hair fell down around her shoulders, framing an attractive, but cold and unfriendly, face. Her eyes were hidden behind dark sunglasses. DeMayne was talking and she was hanging on every word, which seemed to support Joey's theory about who was in charge. As DeMayne spoke, he gestured across the street toward the Majestic Theatre and paused midsentence. Looking over the hoods of passing cars and peering in between pedestrians, he made eye contact with Joey and gave him an "I see you" wave.

Joey backed away from the door. DeMayne was taunting him. Something was about to go down; Joey could feel it. It was the reason he had raced to the theater from his school, which was on the Upper West Side of Manhattan, more than twenty blocks away. He had wanted to warn Leanora and Shazad what was coming, but now that Joey had done that, he didn't know what to do next. Everything was happening so fast. He felt like it was only yesterday that he had first met Redondo the Magnificent and found out magic was real. But that wasn't yesterday. It was two days ago. Yesterday was the day Redondo died. He had sacrificed himself to save Joey and his friends.

The events of the last week flashed through Joey's mind. Meeting Redondo, he had discovered that the world was a bigger, more extraordinary place than he had ever imagined possible. Magic was real—but only if you believed in it. Joey had learned about the Order of the Majestic, whose duty it was to keep magic alive and free. At least, it had been until they disbanded some twenty years ago. He had also learned about the Invisible Hand, who selfishly fought to keep the world's magic to themselves. Unfortunately, they hadn't disbanded. Without the Order of the Majestic around to check their influence, the Invisible Hand had worked tirelessly to confiscate the world's remaining magical items and consolidate power. It was an extreme case of magicians not revealing their secrets. The Invisible Hand was like a group of spoiled children who didn't want anyone else playing with their toys.

Joey had been caught off guard when DeMayne had invited him to join their twisted little club, but he hadn't extended the offer out of the goodness of his heart. At the time, DeMayne was under the impression that Joey was still in possession of the world's most powerful magical artifact . . . Harry Houdini's wand.

Joey only wished he still had it. He had been master of the wand for such a short period of time. Before Redondo died, he had arranged a contest between Joey, Leonora, and Shazad to determine who should inherit the wand. In the end, Joey won it—and immediately lost it—but he'd managed to keep the wand away from the Invisible Hand. It was a minor victory, but a victory nonetheless. However, there was more at stake than just the wand. The Majestic Theatre was filled with magical artifacts big and small, and at the moment it was all but defenseless. Redondo was gone, the wand was gone, and the theater was back in New York. For twenty long years Redondo had hid the Majestic and its many treasures in an alternate dimension that *he* had created using the power of Houdini's wand. With him gone, the theater was back in the normal world. It was vulnerable.

Redondo's warning about the extent of the Invisible Hand's greed echoed in Joey's ears:

There is nothing I have here . . . nothing I could give you so trivial that the Invisible Hand does not wish to obtain it.

Looking at DeMayne and the lady in red, Joey felt like a pig in a straw house up against the Big Bad Wolf. "They didn't get the wand, but they're not done with us. Whatever else Redondo kept in this theater . . . They're coming for it. All of it."

"I knew they would eventually," said Shazad. "I just hoped we'd have more time."

"No such luck," Joey said. Across the street, Ledger DeMayne beckoned with his hands, telling Joey and the others to come out.

"I guess we'd better go out there," Leanora said.

"I guess so," Joey agreed.

Leanora pulled the door open and they went outside. As the theater door closed behind Joey, with his nerves dialed up to eleven, he felt like a character in a movie. He and his friends stood on one side of the street with their enemies on the other. It was like a high-noon showdown in an old Western. A harsh wind blew sheets of newspaper down the sidewalk like rolling tumbleweeds. The magical gunslingers sized each other up in silence. DeMayne spoke first.

"Joey, what are you doing here? Shouldn't you be in school right now?" His voice was crisp and clear, as if they were separated by a dinner table rather than a busy street. "What would your parents say about you cutting class on the first day?" He clicked his tongue in disapproval.

"I'm not cutting anything," Joey said. "I don't have a class schedule yet. Dr. Cho gave me the day off while they figure out what to do with me."

"I see. You're welcome for that, by the way," DeMayne replied. He turned to the lady in red, adding, "You know he never even thanked me for giving him a leg up at school? I don't think it even crossed his mind."

"Ugh," she grunted in a judgmental tone. "That's the problem with everyone his age. So entitled."

"Generation Z," DeMayne agreed. "They're even worse than millennials."

Joey took offense at that exchange, coming as it was from people who thought they were entitled to all the world's remaining magical artifacts, but he had bigger problems than the Invisible Hand's hypocrisy.

"What are they talking about?" Shazad asked Joey. "What did he do for you?"

"Later," Joey said. "It's not important right now."

"True," DeMayne agreed. "Why don't we talk about something that *is* important?" He motioned to the grand and newly restored Majestic Theatre. "Redondo kept a store of magical artifacts here. We've come to collect them. Understand this—it's going to happen. You can't stop us. However, we don't have to be at odds with one another. There's no need for violence. In fact, there's no need for any of you to be here at all. It's a lovely day. I would advise the three of you to take a walk. Perhaps you could visit the park. Or, if that doesn't interest you, there are plenty of other theaters around here. . . . Why not take in a matinee? Doesn't that sound more interesting than this conversation? Don't you feel like you have somewhere else you want to be right now?"

Joey scrunched up his face. "What are you talking about?" He looked at Shazad and Leonora, baffled. "Is he serious? Take in a matinee?"

"He's doing something," Shazad said. "Look around—the block's clearing out."

Joey turned his head, looking up and down the street.

Shazad was right. The sidewalks were getting emptier. People passed by in each direction, but once they were gone, no one else followed behind them. No new cars turned onto the street, either. At both ends of the block, everyone and everything just kept going, up one avenue and down the other. Before Joey knew it, they had the street all to themselves. "What's going on?" he asked. "Where'd everybody go?"

"It's him," Shazad said. "Or her. They must have some kind of warding object or obfuscation charm working."

"A *what?*"

"It's a good one," Leanora said. "Fast acting."

"What are you guys talking about?" Joey asked.

"Think of it as a big, magic 'keep out' sign," Shazad explained. "I'll bet right now everyone in this city is feeling a sudden urge to avoid this street. Even people who have business here are probably remembering something else they have to do, or some other place they need to be. They're deciding to turn down the next block instead of this one for no reason at all. . . . You get the idea."

Joey nodded, grateful for Shazad's and Leanora's magical knowledge, especially now that Redondo was gone. Shazad had been raised in a secret magical country where his family watched over magical artifacts and kept them safe. Leanora was part of a traveling family of magicians called the Nomadiks, who traveled the world, putting on shows and hiding magic in plain sight. Joey felt safer with them at his side, but he was still worried. What did the Invisible Hand have planned that was so explosive they had to clear out the civilians before they got started?

"If their magic's so strong, how come it's not working on us?" Joey asked.

"Because I'm wearing a mental-fortification charm." Leanora located a blue crystal amulet mixed in among the many enchanted pendants she wore around her neck. "My grandmother gave me this to guard against hypnosis and magical suggestion. A girl can't be too careful. Lucky for us, you two are standing close enough to fall within its range." Leanora lifted the necklace chain with two fingers and held it out, dangling the charm in front of her. "Touch the stone. I can lend you some of its power."

"For how long?" Shazad asked as he and Joey felt at the crystal.

"Long enough," Leanora said.

The lady in red barked out a derisive laugh. "Long enough

for what?" she asked. "Congratulations. You can stay. That doesn't mean you should. Better you leave willingly than hold your ground and try to put off the inevitable. Don't be stubborn, children. Walk away. Otherwise, we can't be responsible for what happens to you."

"We're not going anywhere," Leanora said. "And you're not coming into our theater."

"*Your* theater?" DeMayne asked.

"Redondo left it to us," Joey said. "We're the new Order of the Majestic," he added. His voice sounded flimsy and weak.

DeMayne and the lady in red looked at each other, quietly processing Joey's statement. A second later they erupted with laughter, making a real show of it. The lady in red had to lean on DeMayne's shoulder for support as she carried on. He had a hand pressed to his side, ready to bust a gut. Evidently, Joey's half-hearted declaration was so funny it hurt. DeMayne's and the lady in red's hysterics chipped away at Joey's confidence, mainly because he couldn't blame them for laughing. The words had felt ridiculous coming out of his mouth. Who was he kidding? They weren't the Order of the Majestic. They were three kids up against fully grown magicians who took what they wanted, did as they pleased, and didn't care who got hurt in the process. Joey was grateful there were only two of them, but he couldn't take much comfort in that. For all he knew, DeMayne had a legion of reinforcements waiting inside the NATL building. Also, depending on what kind of magical items they were carrying, two of them would be plenty. Maybe too much.

"We should get started," said the lady in red.

DeMayne nodded in agreement. "We've got a busy day ahead of us. Out of the way, children. You've been warned."

"So have you," Leanora replied. "Stay on your side of the street."

As DeMayne stepped off the sidewalk undeterred, Leanora tapped her right heel twice and a tiny pair of wings appeared on the ankle of her boot. She tapped her other foot two times and a matching pair of wings materialized there. Joey was about to ask what was going on when he saw that she was charging up her firestone pendant. Leanora used one hand to grip an orange stone that hung around her neck. Her other hand was lighting up with reddish-orange energy like smoldering wood. Joey watched as an amber wave traveled past her wrist until her entire forearm glowed with power. He never even saw her move her feet. At most, Joey saw Leanora shift her weight. A second later she was across the street, throwing a flaming elbow into DeMayne's chest. His body sailed back and slammed into the wall of the NATL building. Joey blinked, and Leanora was standing next to him again.

"Whoa!" he blurted out, impressed. "Where'd you get those boots?"

"Inside the theater," she said with a smile. "They were listed in Redondo's ledger—the Winged Boots of Fleetfoot, whoever that was." She twisted her foot to show off the fluttering wings. "They're elven made. Superfast and completely silent." She pounded her foot on the pavement with inaudible stomps. "They can run three steps in the air at a time, too. Pretty cool, huh?"

"Pretty cool," Joey agreed, wishing he had something similar on his person. He wondered what else Redondo had inside the theater and worried he'd never get the chance to find out. Redondo had left Joey, Leanora, and Shazad more than the building when he died. Also included in his final bequest was a ledger describing all the magical artifacts he was entrusting them with. They were items he knew the

Invisible Hand would want, and they had to be protected, because there were precious few things like them left in the world. For Joey, they were his only link to magic now that Houdini's wand was gone. Redondo had told Joey that once upon a time magic had flowed through the air like the breeze, accessible to everyone who believed. Today it was different. At some point in history (no one knew exactly when), magic had gotten lost. Locked away. Now it took more than belief to tap into its power; it took magical items. Ancient artifacts, created for extraordinary purposes, that retained varying degrees of magical energy. Leanora's new boots, her firestone, and her fortification charm all qualified. The transfiguration cape that Shazad wore around his shoulders was another example, and there were others inside the theater. Leanora and Shazad had spent the morning going through Redondo's ledger while Joey was at school. When he'd arrived at the Majestic, they weren't even halfway through the treasure trove of magical artifacts. The Invisible Hand hadn't given them enough time to go through everything, but they had apparently had enough time to grab a few things to help defend the theater—and themselves. Joey, on the other hand, was unarmed. All he had was Redondo's magic deck of cards. Redondo used to pull three at a time and get cryptic insights on what was happening in the moment and nebulous hints about future. Joey didn't feel like drawing any cards at the moment. He was afraid what his fortune might be.

"So much for diplomacy," the lady in red said, helping DeMayne to his feet.

"Looks like we're going to have to do this the hard way," he agreed, dusting himself off. "Time for an object lesson. Speaking of which . . ." He slid back the cuff of his sleeve to reveal a bulky, shiny metal watch. Even at a distance, Joey could tell it probably cost more than the average car. "I didn't expect I'd have to use this today, but that's why I keep it with me. To iron out unexpected problems."

"Emphasis on *iron*," said the lady in red.

DeMayne smiled and pointed an aiming finger at her. "That's good. I like that. Let me just shake off this glamour. . . ." He shook his wrist, and the watch became a plain black metal bracelet. He flexed his fingers, forming a fist, and the wristband morphed into an iron gauntlet covering his whole hand. It didn't stop there. DeMayne bent his arm forward as the black iron climbed upward, eventually covering his entire body in a hulking suit of armor. The last piece that fell into place was a helmet, which grew around his head. "Last chance, children," he said with the visor up, looking like something out of *Game of Thrones*. "I promise you, if we go down this road, it won't end well."

Joey gulped. He and his friends traded uneasy glances. "Shazad, tell me you took something useful out of the theater too."

"Yeah, I got some stuff," Shazad said. He went into his pocket and took out a small cube the size of a golf ball. It had a cloudy white, quartzlike quality and gilded details that lined the edges of each face of the cube. "Here goes nothing." Shazad clutched the cube tight in his hand, and a wave of white energy swirled around him. He vanished from sight and reappeared standing next to DeMayne. Shazad touched his armored shoulder, and the two of them vanished in another swirl of magical light. They reappeared up in the air, twenty feet above the ground. A split second later, Shazad vanished again, returning to Joey's and Leanora's side. DeMayne dropped like a stone and hit the street with a crash, cracking the pavement.

"What happened?" Joey asked. "What'd you do?"

"What is that?" Leanora added, indicating the cube.

Shazad held the cube in an open palm. A soft glow at its center was fading down to nothing. "Redondo's book called it Kadabra's Cube. It's a magical transport item. Teleportation," he clarified. "One catch. You can only go as far as you can see."

"Ouch," Joey said, gawking at DeMayne's body sprawled out on the ground. "That was hard-core."

Unfortunately, it wasn't hard enough. DeMayne picked himself up, no worse for wear. "Now I'm starting to get annoyed," he said, rising to his feet. "Do you have any idea what this is? What I'm wearing?" He slapped his iron breastplate with an open hand. "This is the Armor of the Ages. Nothing can harm it, not even the passage of time. The older it gets, the stronger it gets, and it's over a thousand years old. You could drop me from orbit and it wouldn't make a dent. I told you, you can't stop me. The best you can hope to do is slow me down, so if that's all you've got, you might as well give up now. Before I have to hurt you."

Shazad took out a small, polished piece of black wood, the size and shape of a rolled-up diploma. "That's not all I've got." He twirled the stick around, transforming it into a full-size bo staff. "The Staff of Sorcero," he said to Joey.

"Right. The Staff of Sorcero," Joey repeated, as if everyone knew what that was.

Leanora took the firestone pendant off her neck and tied it around her left hand. "Joey, I think we're going to have to team up against the Black Knight here. Can you hold off the red lady?"

"With what? Card tricks?"

"Try this." Leanora handed him a familiar length of thick, maritime rope.

Joey took the Gordian rope reluctantly. He had not had great success with it in the past. "I'll try."

"Try hard," Leanora said. With that, she and Shazad went off to fight DeMayne. Shazad took the lead, charging in first. Just before he reached DeMayne, he activated Kadabra's Cube and disappeared. DeMayne swung hard, trying to punch him, but his fist found nothing but air. Meanwhile, Shazad reappeared behind DeMayne, swinging the staff. Sparks flew as he connected with the side of DeMayne's helmet. It was a jarring blow, amplified by magical energy. DeMayne stumbled a step, but he recovered quickly, sweeping an armored hand around at Shazad, who backpedaled, spinning the staff in front of him defensively. At the same time, Leanora was running up through the air, getting into position over DeMayne. Golden discs lit up under her feet with each step she took. One, two, three—and she threw a fiery punch into the back of DeMayne's neck, driving him to his knees. Shazad followed that up with a hard strike across his faceplate. DeMayne fell backward, landing with his feet up in the air. Leanora moved in for another firestone-charged punch. DeMayne rolled fast—way faster than Joey would have thought possible in that armor. He dodged her blow, sprang up, and caught Shazad by the cape. The next thing Joey knew, DeMayne was swinging Shazad around like a mace, right at Leanora. She got out of the way with time to spare, thanks to her magic boots. DeMayne let Shazad go, and he tumbled through the air, but he vanished and reappeared, landing safely on his feet thanks to his magic cube. While they were busy saving themselves, DeMayne marched on the theater. He didn't have far to go. Just the width of the street. Shazad and Leanora paused for a quick conference.

"You go high, I'll go low?" she asked.

"That works."

This time Leanora went in first. As she approached, DeMayne shot a hand out at her like a football player trying to stiff-arm an opponent. She slid under that and delivered a crushing blow to the side of his knee. It probably would have crippled him if he wasn't armored up, but with the protections he had, she succeeded only in throwing him off-balance. As DeMayne bent over, steadying himself, Shazad leapfrogged him. When his hands hit DeMayne's armor, Kadabra's Cube whisked them both away, moving them back to the door of the NATL building, effectively hitting a reset button on the fight.

Joey and the lady in red stood transfixed, watching the battle begin again. She shook her head as it went on. "They're wasting their time. This is only going to make him angry. That's not going to be good for anyone." Joey didn't think a happy Ledger DeMayne was good for anyone, either, but that went without saying. The lady in red took off her sunglasses and fixed Joey with a penetrating gaze. "You're the one who wielded Houdini's wand. Is it true you threw it into a black hole?" Joey said nothing. She took his silence as confirmation. "What were you thinking?"

"I was thinking about keeping it away from people like you. And I did."

"For now." She let out a condescending sigh. "Such a lack of imagination. I don't have that problem. I'm an artist. You can call me Scarlett."

Joey tensed up as Scarlett opened her coat. She had holsters for several long paintbrushes sewn into the lining of each side. "Have you ever studied art? Really studied it? You should. It's a magic all its own." She inspected her brushes, tapping the bristles, trying to decide which one to use. "Think about it. . . . Making something out of nothing? The infinite possibility of the canvas? What's more magical than that?" She chose a paint-splattered brush from the right-hand side of her coat. "Lately I've been on something of a pop-art kick. Warhol, Lichtenstein, Haring . . . Are you familiar with their work? No?"

Joey stared at Scarlett with a blank expression. He found it odd that she wanted to have a discussion about famous artists while their friends duked it out five feet away.

"Never mind. I'll show you." Scarlett turned away from Joey to address the wall of the NATL building. Working quickly with what was clearly a magical brush, she re-created several images Joey recognized from a recent class trip to the Museum of Modern Art. There were multiple-exposure images of Elvis Presley and Marilyn Monroe, handsome men and women who looked like the romantic leads of a fifties-era comic strip, and colorful, clean-lined, faceless figures with rounded heads and hands. "See? You recognize it. I can tell. It's one thing to hear the names, but when you experience the art up close, that's when it comes alive."

She patted the wall, and the figures she had painted started moving. No longer content to be two-dimensional images, they stepped out of the wall, leaving person-shaped holes in the concrete. Joey backed away as they advanced on him. Scarlett scoffed at Joey's lack of art appreciation. "What are you doing? Don't run away. Pop art is supposed to be less intimidating, more relatable. That's the whole idea. Don't be afraid, Joey. Embrace it. Open your mind!" The artwork chased Joey through the street, swinging heavy stone fists that would literally open Joey's mind if he wasn't careful. He kept moving as iconic pulp images tried to smash him into a pulp. Marilyn Monroe in particular had never looked so dangerous. Once again, Joey wished he hadn't thrown away Houdini's wand.

Across the street, Leanora and Shazad were still fighting DeMayne, but they couldn't stop him. Shazad was teleporting and Leanora was speeding. Their attacks hit hard and looked painful, but their magical weapons had no lasting effect. Joey's friends were getting tired. Meanwhile, DeMayne hadn't lost a step.

Joey wanted to help them, but he had his own problems to deal with. Elvis, Marilyn, and the others had him cornered with his back up against the theater wall. Hopelessly outnumbered, Joey had one chance—the Gordian rope. As they closed in on him, Joey let the rope go. It shot out, springing to life like an out-of-control fire hose. Joey hugged the wall as the rope grew impossibly long, running circles around his attackers, weaving in and out of gaps between their arms and legs, around torsos, over shoulders, and then pulling itself tight to draw them all close together. After the rope had the stone figures tied up, it kept going—and growing—until they were all trapped at the center of a giant, impenetrable knot.

"I can see this is lost on you," Scarlett said. "Pearls before swine." Frowning, she waved her brush like a wand, and her living homage to the pop-art movement stopped struggling. Paint dripped away like melted ice cream and pooled on the street. The concrete figures crumbled into dust and returned to the wall behind Scarlett, leaving no trace they had ever left it. "Let's try something else." Scarlett put the pop-art brush away and selected another. "What do you know about abstract expressionism? Ever hear of Jackson Pollock?" She came around the tangled mess of now empty rope and shook the new brush at Joey, firing splotches of paint like bullets. Joey dove behind a parked car just in time. Scarlett kept up her assault, pelting the car with paint. It splattered everywhere in a mix of colors, hitting hard enough to dent the doors and shatter the passenger-side windows.

Keeping as much of his body behind the car as possible, Joey peeked his head around the rear bumper. The Gordian rope lay in a tangled heap, three feet away. If Joey could reach it, he could turn it loose on Scarlett, but he wasn't close enough. More paint struck the car, smashing the taillights. Joey pulled himself back behind the car, but an idea popped into his head. He couldn't get to the rope, but maybe the rope could get to him. He stuck a hand under the car, mentally asking the rope to slither into his hand, and most important, believing it would listen. Sure enough, the rope did as it was told, but as soon as he had it, a well-aimed shot of paint tagged him in the shoulder. It ripped through his shirt, hitting him with the force of a thrown brick. "Ahh!" He fell backward, losing his grip on the rope—and his only chance at defending himself. "Guys, I'm hit!" he called out. He had no feeling in his right arm. "A little help here?"

Shazad and Leanora were in no position to help anyone. They were too busy fighting an invulnerable enemy who hadn't even busted out his big guns. "Enough," DeMayne said, drawing out half a sword. "This ends now."

Shazad froze in place. "Is that . . . ?"

"The Tempest Blade," DeMayne said, flipping up his visor with his free hand. "Also known as the Sword of Storms," he added, holding up a broken sword that cut off in a jagged line a foot from the hilt. "Do you understand now? We're armed with the most powerful items of magical antiquity. You can't hope to defeat us." DeMayne turned to Joey, who was lying on the street, covered in paint. "You chose the wrong side."

DeMayne pointed the sword at Leanora and Shazad, and tornado winds lifted them off their feet. Gripping the Tempest Blade with both hands, and struggling to hold on, DeMayne turned, blowing Leanora and Shazad over to

25

where Joey was. As he angled the sword down to deposit them on the street, Joey thought the winds might drive him into the pavement. Scarlett turned her shoulder to the wind and found shelter behind the same paint-splattered car that Joey had used for cover. Even that was no good, as Joey saw two of its wheels lift off the street. The car was about to flip. "Ledger! Turn it off!" Scarlett shouted over the roaring gale.

DeMayne nodded in reply. His arms were shaking. A large vein appeared in his forehead, and he tightened his jaw as he worked to get the blade's wild magic under control. Judging by the strained look on his face, it was a hard-fought effort, but he stopped the wind before he blew everyone away. It cut off suddenly, as if someone had turned off a giant fan. Grateful, Joey let out a deep breath. His ears were ringing. He couldn't sit up just yet.

"There we are," DeMayne said, spinning the sword in his hand with a dramatic flair. He cocked his head and smirked at Scarlett, amused. "Look at your face. You were worried."

Scarlett tucked her paintbrush away and put her sunglasses back on. "I hate that thing," she said, pouting.

DeMayne gave a shrug and sheathed the Sword of Storms in a scabbard at his waist. "What can I tell you? It had more finesse back when it was whole." He tapped his wrist, and the Armor of the Ages retracted into his gauntlet, which shrank into an armband, then turned back into a watch. He swept an arm out, presenting the theater to Scarlett and stepping aside in a gallant motion. "Shall we?" he asked.

Her dour face brightened. "We shall."

Joey propped himself up on his elbows and watched DeMayne and Scarlett approach the door. Leanora and Shazad did the same. There was nothing they could do to stop them. They had given it their all, but it wasn't enough. The Invisible Hand was going to loot the theater and do what they had already done to the world at large—rob it of its magic.

But first they had to get inside. When Scarlett touched the handle of the Majestic's front door, Joey heard a loud *boom*, like a cannon going off. Time slowed down as a concussive force rippled out from underneath the theater marquee. Something happened to the air. It turned thick and took on a viscous, gel-like quality. Joey actually saw the shock wave spiral out of the theater in slow motion, focused entirely on DeMayne and Scarlett. The intruders went tumbling back onto the street, settling next to Joey and his friends, completely unconscious.

Joey rubbed his head as time sped back up and the air returned to normal. He staggered to his feet in a state of shock. "What just happened?" He nudged DeMayne's body with his toe. Leanora checked Scarlett. "They're out cold, both of them."

"They couldn't get in," Shazad said in a daze. He got up slowly. They were all struggling to process the Invisible Hand's sudden reversal of fortune.

"What stopped them?" asked Joey. "Did you leave something in the lobby? A last line of defense?"

Leanora and Shazad exchanged curious looks, asking each other the same question with their eyes. "It wasn't us," Leanora said. "Maybe Redondo?"

"I don't think so," Joey said. Redondo was gone. They were on their own now. Weren't they? "What if it was the theater?"

"You think the Majestic defended itself?" Shazad asked.

"Stranger things have happened," Joey said. "They happened right here." He gestured to the street where they had just had a bombastic magic duel unbeknownst to the rest of the city.

"I guess it is possible," Shazad admitted.

They all looked at Redondo's former stronghold in awe. "I wish I'd known that was going to happen," Leanora said. "We could have saved ourselves a lot of trouble."

"I would have stayed in school," Joey said. "Is that it, then? The theater's safe? It's over?"

"No way," Shazad said. "They're not going to give up that easy. Especially now that they've seen a bit of what we've got here. This is just this beginning."

One Month Later

2

Green Energy

Joey's mom and dad dropped him off outside Exemplar Academy. Normally, Joey rode the PATH train in from Hoboken with his father and took the subway by himself from there. Today both his parents were with him, and they'd taken a car into the city. Door to door service. Joey's mother had said it was because Joey had a big bag to carry, but he knew his luggage wasn't the reason they drove in. It was because she wanted to put off his actual departure as much as possible. He wasn't just going to school for the day; he was going away for the week on a school trip. His mom was more anxious about it than anyone else was.

"Are you sure you're going to be okay?"

"Mom, it's no big deal. Really. I'm thirteen years old, don't forget."

Joey's mother looked at him. "Is that supposed to make me feel better?"

"Come on, honey," Joey's father said, putting an arm around his mother. "He's a very mature thirteen. He's not going to get into any trouble."

"I know that." She pulled Joey into a group hug. "I still worry. I don't like the idea of you traveling by yourself, all alone on the plane."

Joey thought his mother was being overly dramatic. "You don't have to worry. After everything I've been through in the last month, a little plane ride is nothing. Besides, I won't be alone. I'll be with Janelle."

"I know," Joey's mother said again. She gave him one last squeeze before letting go. "That's the only reason I'm okay with it." Janelle Thomas was a fellow student at Exemplar Academy. She was Joey's age and also from Hoboken, but the similarities between them ended there. Janelle was a legitimate genius—a child prodigy in the field of physics. She was Joey's best friend at school and the only "normal" person in his life who knew that magic was real. His parents didn't have any idea.

"He's going to be fine," Joey's father said. "If Joey can handle going to school here, he can handle anything."

Joey smiled. There was a time when the thought of enroll-ing at a school like Exemplar Academy had been enough to freak him out. Discovering magic and the conflict between the Order of the Majestic and the Invisible Hand had put life's little challenges in perspective for him.

"Okay, okay," his mother said, putting her hands up in surrender. "What do you want me to say? I'm his mother. I can't help worrying. It's my job." She looked at Joey like she didn't want to let him leave. "You've never been away from us this long. And it's a big trip! California. You've never been that far from home before."

Joey smiled innocently. "First time for everything." The truth was, he had once traveled as far as Siberia to visit a friend of Leanora's family, and there no way to quantify the distance he had traveled to the alternate dimension Redondo had created to hide the Majestic Theatre. His par-ents knew nothing about that and probably never would. They couldn't handle the truth. His mother could hardly handle California. "It could be worse," Joey said. "Janelle's staying in LA for a month."

"Oh!" Joey's mom made a noise like such a thing was unthinkable. "Don't tell me that."

"Remember?" Joey asked. "Janelle told us about it the first day we came here."

"He's right, she did," Joey's father said. One of the first things they had learned about Janelle was her upcoming trip to the California Institute of Technology to work on a cutting-edge renewable-energy project.

"I remember," Joey's mother said. "I was very impressed. I still am. I just didn't think you'd be going with Janelle. I don't know how her parents do it. A month?"

"They're going out there next week to visit," Joey said.

"Maybe we should do that too," Joey's mother suggested. "Make a vacation out of it?"

"You know I can't," Joey's father said, apologetic. "With the company getting acquired, I'm swamped at work. It's the worst possible time." He was a partner at a small accounting firm that was in the process of being swallowed up by a big one. Long term it was going to be a good thing for Joey's dad career-wise, and a good thing for the family financially, but in the short term it meant a lot of work and a lot of late nights. "When this is over, I promise we'll do a real family vacation. Something big. Hawaii maybe. Trust me, I'll need it more than anyone."

"Sounds good to me," Joey said. "I'll be all right," he reassured his mother. "Really."

His mother made a "hmmph" sound. "Sure, *you'll* be fine. What about me?" She opened her arms. "One more hug." Joey groaned, but he leaned in like a good son and his mother wrapped him up tight. "You're growing up so fast."

"In a good way, though," Joey said.

"That's true," his mother admitted. "I'm really proud of the work you guys are doing. Who knows? Maybe you can get us off fossil fuels by Wednesday and come home early."

Joey chuckled. "We'll do our best."

"Got everything you need in here?" his father asked, tapping the top of Joey's rolling luggage.

"Just about." Joey flipped his lucky coin—formerly his father's lucky coin—into the air and caught it. Added to the long list of things his parents didn't know was the fact that the coin was a magical item, enchanted by Redondo to help recruit children into the Order of the Majestic. His father didn't remember it fully, but he had gotten the call back when he was Joey's age. Unfortunately, Grayson Manchester had seen to it that he never got the chance. Joey didn't know how much magic was left in the coin, but he kept it for sentimental reasons. It was one of the two magical artifacts he had with him at all times, the other being Redondo's deck of cards.

"Call us when you land," his father said.

"I'll text you."

"Call us," Joey's mother stressed. "Every night."

"We're going to be working crazy hours," Joey said, doing a little bargaining. "I'll call you, sure, but sometimes we can just text each other too, right?"

"I want to talk to you at least once a day," his mother said.

Joey backed away toward the school entrance without committing to anything. "I better get in there. Bye, guys!" He waved, a big smile on his face. "Love you!"

"I'm serious, Joey," his mother called after him. As Joey turned around to pull his bag through the door, he saw his mother miming a telephone, holding up her hand with her pinkie and thumb extended.

Joey returned the gesture with a slight tweak. Pretending not to understand, he shook his hand with his thumb and pinkie stuck out in a Hawaiian, "hang loose" kind of way. "That's the spirit, Mom! Aloha!"

"Not funny!" his mother said, trying to suppress a grin. Joey's father did the same, with less success.

Inside, Joey made a quick stop at the school cafeteria and picked up breakfast to go. One of the things he liked about going to school at Exemplar Academy was that they had the best of everything. State-of-the-art facilities, brilliant teachers, top-of-the-line lab equipment, and even the food was great. Every morning there was a big buffet set up with an omelet station, waffles, pancakes, fruit, fresh-baked muffins, and more. Joey grabbed some bagels and went up to a laser science lab on the fourth floor, where he found Janelle hard at work, as usual.

"Where've you been?" she asked as he came in.

Struggling with the door, his backpack, luggage, and a carry-out bag from the cafeteria, Joey checked his watch. "It's nine o'clock. You didn't stay here again last night, did you?"

"No, I came in early," Janelle said as she checked the connections on some wires. "You think my parents would let me pull an all-nighter right before I go away for a month? Not a chance. And it's 9:06, by the way."

"Sorry, Professor," Joey said, making light of Janelle's minor scolding. "I brought food."

Janelle's eyes brightened as Joey held up the bag of bagels. "Cinnamon raisin?"

"Toasted with cream cheese." Joey knew that Janelle often got so lost in her work that she forgot to eat. One time she had gone eighteen hours in the lab with nothing but water and some Altoids.

"I guess we can take a break," Janelle said, pretending that Joey was twisting her arm.

"Let's eat it over here," Joey said, dumping out the contents of the bag at an empty workstation. "Suhash won't like us eating anywhere near his laser. Especially now that he's finally got it working again."

"That's not his laser," Janelle said, joining Joey at the table. She peeled off the tinfoil he had used to wrap her bagel and took a bite. "Suhash's laser is over there under the tarp." She pointed to a separate lab station in the corner of the room. "I replicated his design over the weekend."

"What?" Joey put his breakfast down and went to the back of the lab. Sure enough, there was another laser apparatus there, identical to the one Janelle had just been working on. "You built another laser?"

"Just in case ours doesn't work," Janelle explained in a

tone that said it was no big deal. "I don't want to wreck Suhash's project if this thing blows up in our faces. Also, I want to be able to take everything with us to Caltech if it *does* work."

Joey looked back and forth between the two lasers in disbelief. "I don't understand how you did this over the weekend. It took Suhash a month to rebuild this thing after the last one melted down."

"That's true, but it's not a fair comparison really. I didn't have to come up with the design. I just followed the instructions on his blueprints."

"In that case, forget it. I'm not impressed," Joey said sarcastically. "It's just like a fancy Lego set." Joey put the tarp back in place and returned to his bagel, wondering why he was even surprised that Janelle had done something incredible. She was exactly the kind of person Exemplar Academy was created for. It was a school for supergeniuses, where every kid had their own individual curriculum based on their personal area of expertise. Joey's classmates displayed a wide range of talents, including robotics, math, laser science, physics, art, athletics, music, and more. Everyone at Exemplar excelled at something specific and spent their school days getting better at it—making *their* brand of magic. Joey didn't have a clear specialty like the other students. Ledger DeMayne had arranged for his placement tests to state that he could do anything he wanted. That was the way the Invisible Hand went through life. DeMayne had said it could be that way for Joey, too. It had been part of his sales pitch to get Joey to join up with them.

Joey had told him to get lost.

At the moment, Joey's school schedule was to sample a wide range of subjects, tagging alongside every student and doing everything they did. His favorite study partner, for a couple reasons, was Janelle. First of all, she was awesome, and second, she knew what his *secret* specialty was. Her ideas about how to use it were exciting, too. Together they made a great team—magic and science joining forces. Shazad and Leanora didn't think the two could work together, but Joey had a different opinion. He wasn't entirely sure where magic ended and science began. The way he saw it, both scientists and magicians had the potential to do the impossible. He had seen it up close. After all, it was Janelle's science project that had saved everyone's life a month ago.

Shazad and Leanora had first met Janelle when Joey got

the idea to use her mini Hadron collider—and the Frisbee-size black hole it had created—to dispose of Grayson Manchester. Shazad and Leanora had taken Janelle for a fellow magician that night, and she had been working to prove them right ever since. Rather than breaking down when faced with the fact that magic rendered the laws of physics obsolete, Janelle embraced the challenge of learning something new and incorporating it into her research. That was her way, relentlessly optimistic in the face of any challenge. A passionate environmentalist, Janelle's project at Caltech revolved around sustainability and clean energy sources. In her mind, magic had the potential to be the biggest scientific breakthrough of all time. It was the definition of alternative energy. That was what she and Joey were working on that morning. Figuring out how to use magic to change the world.

"What time are Leanora and Shazad coming?" Janelle asked. "Did you talk to them this morning?"

"We talked yesterday."

"Why don't you text them? Tell them you're here."

"They don't text." Joey finished eating and gathered up the remnants of his breakfast. "Don't worry, they're coming." Just then there was a specific knock at the lab door.

The first half of a simple but memorable rhythm. "What'd I tell you?"

Joey went to the door and gave the return knock, finishing the tune and signaling that he and Janelle were alone. They had to take precautions like that whenever they used magic in public, just in case anyone was watching. Leanora and Shazad were using the same door Joey had used to enter the lab, but they weren't coming from the same place. Only after Joey had given the "all clear" did the door open to reveal the two young magicians.

"I don't think I'll ever get used to seeing stuff like that," Janelle said, shaking her head in wonder.

Joey stepped back to take in the impossible sight. Through a lab window on the wall, they could see the school's conventional, nondescript hallway on the other side of the glass. Through the open doorway a foot to the left of the window was not the hallway, but the Majestic Theatre's grand lobby. Leanora and Shazad said hello and stepped across the threshold, trading plush red carpeting, crystal chandeliers, and palatial decor for linoleum, fluorescent lights, and clinical functionality.

"It is pretty wild," Joey agreed as Leanora reached back

into the Majestic to collect a golden doorknob with a red ruby handle from the other side of the door. It had been in her family for years, and enabled her to go wherever she pleased, turning any door into a supernatural gateway. It was an extraordinary magical object that bent reality to her will, but even more extraordinary was the fact that, for Joey, seeing it in action was starting to feel normal. Commonplace even. He was grateful Janelle was there to share these "magic moments" with him. She kept him grounded, reminding him to appreciate the miracles he witnessed on a daily basis and not take them for granted.

As the friends greeted each other, Joey couldn't help but feel that Janelle met Leanora and Shazad's arrival with more enthusiasm than she had his own. Sure, he saw her every day, but still. "How come you don't ask them why they're late?" Joey asked.

"They're allowed. They come bearing gifts."

"I brought bagels," Joey said in his defense. "You guys hungry?" he asked Leanora and Shazad.

"I could eat," Leanora said.

Joey slid the bag across the table. "Help yourself. I got enough for everyone."

"No thanks," Shazad said, passing on the food. "And I wouldn't exactly call this a gift." He held up something wrapped in a blue quilted silk blanket. He guarded it closely, cradling it in one arm like a football with his free hand covering it on top.

"It's just an expression," Joey assured Shazad. "We know the deal."

Janelle held out her hands. "Can I see?"

Shazad looked at Joey as if he had reservations about handing the bundle over, which was funny considering it was the reason he was there.

"Dude, we talked about this," Joey said. "You're doing the overprotective thing again."

"Is something wrong?" asked Janelle.

"Don't take it personal," Leanora told Janelle. "He's always like this. You've got to learn to let go," she told Shazad, patting him on the shoulder.

Shazad grimaced, but he gave in. "I can't help it. It's how I was raised. Be very careful," he said, passing the wrapped object to Janelle as if it were a delicate newborn baby.

"I promise," Janelle said.

Leanora toasted Shazad with her bagel. "I'm proud of you."

"Me too," Joey said, hoping the gesture was a symbol of things to come and that Shazad would be open to more creative uses of the magic items they had going forward. If today's experiment went well, it would certainly help with that.

Janelle set the bundle down on a lab table and carefully unwrapped it. "Wow. Look at that."

Inside the blanket was a hand-carved stone mask the size of a hardcover book. It was forest green, streaked with white marbling, and had a smooth, polished texture. A few chips and scratches aside, the mask showed no physical signs of age, but it clearly belonged to another time. A lost time. There was something about it . . . an energy it gave off . . . an aura. Everyone felt it. Joey was convinced that even if he had not known that magic was real, he would have sensed it. He wouldn't have understood it, but he would have had a funny feeling about the mask. The face carved into the mysterious green mineral was formidable. More than human. Most likely it was the image of an ancient deity. The idol of some forgotten, vengeful god. Joey felt like it was the kind of thing Indiana Jones would try to find before the bad guys did.

"What's it called?" Janelle asked. Joey had told her about a variety of magical items, such as the Staff of Sorcero, the

Winged Boots of Fleetfoot, Kadabra's Cube, and more. "Does it have a name?"

"Redondo's ledger listed it as the Finale Mask," said Shazad.

"Spooky, huh?" Joey said.

"What does it mean?" Janelle asked.

"We don't know," Leanora replied.

"Have any of you tried it on?"

Joey, Shazad, and Leanora looked at one another. No one had been willing to test out the mask on their own face without knowing what would happen. Redondo hadn't put it down as an entry in his book for nothing.

"I don't think it was meant to be worn on the face," Joey said. "At least not by the living." He pointed out that neither the eyes nor the mouth had cutouts to see or breathe through. "I did a little research. Turns out, the Metropolitan Museum of Art has a similar piece on display." He brought up the browser on his phone and checked a web page for details. "Theirs is made of jadeite, a rare form of jade, which is what I think this mask is made of too. The Met traced their mask back to 1500 BC. They think it was a ceremonial item used in funerals."

"Funerals." Shazad grunted. "Sounds promising. Can you explain to me what we are doing here again?"

Janelle clapped her hands together. "I'd love to." She laid out the experiment she had planned, trying to fire the laser using the mask as a power source. Her theory was that magic could revolutionize the energy industry and change the way the world worked from top to bottom. "Solar and wind power are great and all, but magic is a game changer—if we can figure out how to harness it at scale."

Joey touched a hand to the mask. It lit up with green energy. "We know this artifact is an enchanted mineral, like Leanora's firestone. Obviously, it's larger and potentially more powerful. We want to see how powerful."

"And what we can use that power for," Janelle added. She was clearly excited. If this worked, it would be a huge breakthrough for her renewable-energy project. The test with the mask was a dry run before the trip to Caltech. She had hinted at a major breakthrough in her conversations with the faculty there, but her "magic bullet" solution to climate change had to make the grade at home before she could even think about bringing it out West. The California Institute of Technology was one of the best universities in the world and home to some of the greatest minds in the fields of science and engineering—in other words, Janelle's peers. She didn't want to introduce any radical ideas she couldn't fully explain if she didn't know for sure they were going to work.

"And this isn't going to damage the mask in any way?" Shazad probed. "You're sure about that?"

"We're sure," Janelle said.

"Pretty sure," Joey hedged.

That comment earned Joey a minor groan from Shazad and a harsh look from Janelle. "Here," she said, thrusting a set of wires with sticky gel nodes into Joey's hands. "Start putting these on the mask."

Joey stuck the puttylike nodes on the forehead and cheeks of the jadeite mask, and Janelle plugged the other ends into various ports on the laser. Leanora looked back over her shoulder at the lab window and unlocked door. "What's our story if one of your teachers comes to check on you? How do we explain who we are and what we're doing here?"

"You're my guests," Joey said, finishing with the mask. "A couple friends dropping by to say hi, that's all. I just had you do the secret knock so no one would see you using the magic doorknob to get here. Now that you're in the lab, we're fine."

"What about that?" Leonora asked, indicating the unconventional science project on the table. She had a point. An experimental laser hooked up to an ancient artifact from a lost civilization would be difficult to explain.

"Don't worry," Janelle said. "No one's coming to check on us. They treat kids like adults here." Joey nodded, backing up Janelle's statement. It was especially true where she was concerned. Dr. Cho and the rest of the teachers gave Janelle a ton of autonomy, drawing the line only at her mini Hadron collider experiment (which she had gone ahead and built anyway). The truth was, the scientists that Exemplar brought in to work with Janelle had a hard time keeping up with her. Also, they knew she was flying out to California today and didn't expect to see her in the lab.

"Almost ready to go," Janelle said, checking the connections one last time as Joey set up a cinder block target in front of the laser. Janelle gave everyone a pair of goggles and asked them to go stand behind a pane of safety glass before she fired the laser.

"You really think this is going to work?" Leanora asked, putting on her goggles.

"I wouldn't get my hopes up," Shazad said.

"Too late," Joey said.

"Too late for a lot of things." Janelle joined the group behind the glass and opened the laser control program on her laptop computer. "It has to work. We're running out of time. The world has about twelve years before we pass the point of no return on climate change. If we don't do something, we're going to cause irreversible damage to the planet. Rising sea levels, food shortages, drought, wildfires . . . not that we don't have all that stuff right now, but it's going to get worse. Everyone just argues about it like it's a political issue. . . . We have an opportunity to change that. Magic is clean, renewable energy. Maybe limitless energy. If we can tap into it? We could literally save the world."

"It's worth a shot," Joey said, meeting Leanora's and Shazad's doubts with optimism. Janelle's passion was infectious, and he was fully on board. The school motto at Exemplar Academy was "Our Students Change the World." Joey had previously thought it was ridiculous to expect such a thing of children, but here they were on the verge of actually doing it.

Janelle typed in a keystroke command on the laptop, turning on the laser. Out on the table, it powered up with a rising hum. "Here we go," Janelle announced. "Activation in three . . . two . . . one!"

The laser made a noise like a car that wouldn't start. It was the strained, whining sound of an engine that refused to turn over for lack of fuel.

"Hang on," Janelle said, not giving up just yet. She typed in fresh commands on the keyboard, adjusting the power levels for a second attempt. "Okay. Firing laser in three, two, one . . . go." She hit the enter key hard. Nothing happened. The mask didn't light up and the laser didn't fire. Not even a fizzling spark. She slumped her shoulders and stared at the idle laser. "I don't understand."

To their credit, neither Leanora nor Shazad said "I told you so" after Janelle's anticlimactic countdown.

"I'm sorry," Shazad said, trying to be supportive. "It was a good effort."

"A good effort and an . . . interesting idea," Leanora added, searching for something positive to say.

"Maybe one of the wires came loose?" Janelle wondered aloud, speaking more to herself than to anyone else. She came out from behind the safety glass to do a manual systems check on the laser.

"I don't think that's the problem," Leonora said, following her out. "It's technology, Janelle. Technology is the opposite of magic. They don't mix well."

"No." Janelle shook her head. "I don't believe that. Magic is just science we don't understand yet."

Shazad disagreed. "Magic isn't science. It's more nuanced than that. It's an art."

Joey's nose wrinkled involuntarily. The mention of art had made him think of Scarlett and her paintbrushes. He hadn't run into her or DeMayne since the fight outside the Majestic a month ago, but they were still out there, and the thought of them gave him the chills.

"You want art? I could show you algorithms that qualify as works of art," Janelle said. "Don't sleep on science, you guys. Any sufficiently advanced technology is indistinguishable from magic. Clarke's Third Law."

"Clarke's what?" Shazad furrowed his brow. "Who's Clarke?"

"Arthur C. Clarke. He was a British science-fiction writer and inventor. He co-wrote *2001: A Space Odyssey*."

"Is that a book?" Shazad asked, a blank expression on his face.

"A movie," Joey said.

Shazad shook his head. "I never saw it."

"It's not one of my favorites," Joey said. "I know, it's a classic," he added, heading off a rebuke from Janelle. He turned back to Shazad and Leanora. "Stanley Kubrick directed the movie. Everybody says he's a genius, but I don't know. If you ask me, it's kind of slow."

Janelle rubbed her temples as if she had a headache brewing. "Joey, can we focus? The point is, if you went back in time two hundred years and showed someone my computer or smartphone, they'd think it was magic. Would they be wrong?"

"Yes," Leanora said. "They would."

"I don't know," Joey said. "If you go back far enough people probably thought magnets were magic. Or rainbows and fireflies. Just because we have a scientific explanation for those things . . . that doesn't make them any less magical."

"Magnets?" Leanora said. "Really?"

"Redondo told us magic exists in every breath we take," Joey said. "We can find it everywhere, even here." He gestured to the lab and the laser. "Don't forget, Janelle's technology saved our butts from Manchester last month. And he was tracking me through my phone before that."

"What's that got to do with anything?" Shazad asked.

"I'm just saying, maybe magic and science aren't opposites. They seem more complementary to me. The Invisible Hand uses tech. Maybe we should too." Joey touched a hand to the jadeite mask, and the laser operated perfectly. Blinding green light shot out of its barrel, burning a hole in the cinder block target at the end of the table.

"Whoa!" Janelle shouted, throwing her arms up in front of Leanora and Shazad to keep them back. "Turn it off! Turn it off!"

Joey lifted his hand away and the light show stopped. Janelle hit him in the shoulder. "Don't do that!"

"What?" Joey said, not understanding what the problem was.

"Joey! We're supposed to stand behind the glass when this thing fires. What if I were leaning over the table? You could have burned my hand off."

"Hey, I'm on your side. I just proved this thing works."

"Sure, when you do it like *that*." Janelle ushered everyone back behind the safety glass and keyed in the firing sequence one more time. "Hit enter," she told Joey, stepping back from the computer.

Joey did as he was told, and the laser fired again.

Janelle's eyes bulged. "What the—" She moved Joey out of the way and tried to replicate what he had done, growing increasingly frustrated when she could not fire the laser. "Why does it work for you and not for me?" She opened a new window on the screen to check the test-fire data. "The mask obviously has plenty of power. Everything's hooked up properly; it should have worked."

"It definitely works," Leanora admitted, staring at the simmering hole in the target. "I can't argue with that. But it didn't work because you hit a few keys on a keyboard. The mask is a magic object. It needs help to find its power."

"You have to believe," Joey clarified. "It's like *Peter Pan*."

Janelle squinted at Joey. "What?"

"You know, the Disney movie?"

Janelle cast her eyes up at the ceiling. "I'm aware of *Peter*

Pan. It was a book before it was a movie, by the way. And a play before that."

"Whatever," Joey said, not really caring about the origins of Neverland's favorite son. "In the story, Peter, Wendy, and the others . . . They couldn't fly without Tinker Bell's help, right? They needed her pixie dust, but that wasn't enough to get them off the ground. You can't rely on magic for the whole trick. You've got to do the heavy lifting yourself."

Janelle stared at Joey. "You're saying I have to think happy thoughts?"

Joey shrugged. "It doesn't hurt."

"You can't doubt," Shazad said, adding helpful specifics. "Nothing kills magic dead like doubt. You can't be afraid of what's going to happen. You can't be afraid it won't work. You can't be afraid what will happen to you. You just have to believe."

"I did believe," Janelle protested.

"You have to be all in," Joey said. "A hundred and ten percent."

"It's impossible to have a hundred and ten percent of anything," the scientist in Janelle said automatically, but she saw the look on Joey's face and realized her mistake. After everything she had seen of magic, the word "impossible" should have been deleted from her vocabulary. That was the problem. Ever since she was a little girl, Janelle had been driven to redefine reality, but always through scientific and technological innovation. She had other tools at her disposal now and no experience using them. She was still constrained by the limits of the world as she had always understood it.

Joey had expected the laser to work using the mask as a power source, but he'd hung back and let Janelle make the initial attempt. First of all, it was her experiment, but second, he wanted to see if someone who wasn't a bona fide magician could pull it off. Janelle's inability to fire the laser powered by magical energy was a setback, but it wasn't a reason to stop trying. Joey had had his own issues making magic happen when he'd started out too. He believed Janelle would get there eventually, but it was harder for her. Joey and Janelle both had big imaginations, but they used them differently. Growing up, Joey had studied comic books, Star Wars, and Marvel movies. Janelle had studied actual textbooks. Joey's heroes were people who made things up. Janelle idolized people who made things real. His mindset was more open to magic. Her superior understanding of natural science, math, and things like the laws of matter and energy was harder to dislodge. It was holding Janelle back.

"This is a little off topic, but can I ask why you wanted to make a weapon?" Shazad inquired.

"What's wrong with making a weapon?" Leonora asked.

"It isn't a weapon," Janelle said. "This was just an experiment to measure how much power could potentially be drawn from a magical artifact. And the answer is . . ." She scanned the readout from Joey's laser demonstration and did a double take at the number at the bottom. "You've got to be kidding me."

"What is it?" Joey asked.

"1.21 gigawatts."

"Giga . . . whats?" Leonora repeated.

"Is that good?" Shazad asked.

"Good enough for time travel," Joey said.

"No, but it is good enough to provide energy for almost a million homes," Janelle explained. She typed away on her keyboard, checking and rechecking the stats on the laser output. "This is incredible. So much power generated in an instant—like it was nothing! Zero waste, no pollution, totally efficient . . . What we have here in this lab could power half of New York City. A roomful of these could run the world!"

"Too bad," Shazad said, drawing confused expressions from the rest of the group. "Even if this device could be operated by anybody—which it can't—you'd still need a plan to deal with the *people* who run the world," he explained. "The Invisible Hand would never let you take magic mainstream like this."

"That's why you need a weapon," Leanora said, raising a finger in the air.

"Let's not get ahead of ourselves," Joey said. "First we have to figure out how to replace fossil fuels with alternative energy sources that work only if you're in a good mood."

"I don't think you can," Shazad said. "Not enough people believe in magic for that."

"So we make them believe," Janelle said. "How do we do that?"

Joey grimaced, daunted by the enormity of the task. "That's the real trick, isn't it?" The Order of the Majestic was supposed to keep magic alive and keep people believing. It was their duty. The Order used to put on incredible magic shows that inspired wonder in the world and made good things happen. They shared magic by hiding it in plain sight, but they took a major hit after Houdini died. Redondo tried to pick up where Houdini left off, but he got taken out of the picture too. The world had become a darker place without them in it, one with no room for magic. Now it was up to Joey and his friends to reignite faith in magical possibility, but they had no idea where to start or what the best way to go about it was.

"Can't we just show people what we have here?" asked Janelle. "Start there?"

"You're not ready yet." Leanora motioned to the laser. "This isn't ready. A trick has to work every time if you want other people to believe in the magic behind it."

"It works for Joey," Janelle argued.

"Only because I believed it was magic making it work," Joey said. "We can't just tell people to believe in magic and expect to get anywhere when their default state is not to believe. We have to create an environment where they believe on their own."

Janelle thought about that. "You're saying we can't change the world by making people believe in magic. We have to make people believe in magic so that we can change the world."

"Pretty much," Joey said.

Janelle looked at Joey. "How?" she asked again.

"I wish I knew," Joey said. "Even you didn't believe enough to fire the laser, and you've seen magic in action. Plenty of times."

"I know." Janelle looked away, disappointed in her performance. "Sometimes I still can't wrap my head around it. I want to be 'all in' like you guys, but it's just so much to accept. I thought I was going crazy the first time I saw you using that wand."

"Occupational hazard," Joey said. "Magic can make you question your sanity. You took it better than most people would have. Way better. You'll crack it."

Janelle looked up. "I know that," she said, shaking off the minor funk she was in. Janelle was not the type to waste time moping. "We'll crack this, too," she added, pointing to the laser. "I'm not giving up. Not by a long shot."

"That's the spirit," Joey said. Janelle went around the safety glass and disconnected the mask from the laser. She picked it up in her hands, trying to make it glow as Joey had done. Joey and the others stayed where they were. There was a brief, awkward silence that Shazad eventually broke:

"You didn't tell her."

Joey looked straight ahead, focused on Janelle and her ongoing attempts to illuminate the mask. "Tell her what? We haven't decided anything yet."

"That's the problem," Shazad said. "We can't keep putting this off. I kept an open mind, but I'm sorry, Joey. I didn't see anything here today to convince me this is the way to go."

"Neither did I," Leanora agreed. Her voice, like Shazad's, was sympathetic.

Joey sighed. "We just need a little more time."

"We don't have it," Shazad said. "We're pushing our luck as it is. We've got to get the relics out of the theater. All of them."

"This Invisible Hand came by again this morning," Leanora told Joey. "Just before dawn."

Joey's head turned. "Was it Scarlett again?"

"She's the most likely suspect," Shazad said. "There's fresh paint on the theater door."

Joey frowned. The marks on the theater door were strange. Joey couldn't explain it, but he got the same weird vibe off them that he got when he looked at the Finale

Mask. There was magic at work there, he was sure of it. They all were. "All right," Joey said reluctantly. "Janelle and I fly out this afternoon. Let us have the rest of the morning to tinker with the mask and I'll bring it back. I'll meet you guys at the Majestic before my flight, and we'll talk. We'll figure out a plan for this stuff before it's too late."

3

Protect This House

Joey got to the Majestic around noon. As he came down the street with his backpack slung over his shoulder, he scanned the faces of nearby pedestrians for possible threats and checked to make sure he wasn't being followed. He didn't see anyone, but that didn't mean they weren't there. Joey slowed his pace as he approached his destination. His heartbeat sped up, and part of him wished he had gone with Shazad and Leonora instead of walking to the theater by himself. The reason behind his jitters was right across the street.

Even in broad daylight, the NATL building bothered Joey. It loomed large in his mind, a Dark Tower worthy of Stephen King or J.R.R. Tolkien. Joey kept his distance from the building, wondering if Ledger DeMayne and his cronies were inside watching him. If they were, they didn't make their presence known. He reached the front door untouched. Just as Shazad had said, the entrance had been tagged with graffiti again. Despite his nerves, Joey paused to get a good look before he went inside. A succession of curious symbols had been routinely spray-painted on the theater door ever since the magical street fight with DeMayne and Scarlett. This was number five in a series. The marks would appear, then grow fainter day by day until they faded away completely, only to be replaced by freshly painted designs at the start of each new week. The old tag was now gone, and the new one had arrived right on schedule. Joey stared at the odd curved letters on the door. He didn't recognize the characters and could only guess at their meaning, but they felt to him like a bad omen. No other buildings on the block had been targeted by the mystery artist, which made Joey and his friends all the more certain it was Scarlett's handiwork. She had moved on from pop art to street art. Was she telling them to leave? Warning them not to come back to the theater? Joey wondered why she was being so cryptic and understated about it. That didn't strike him as her style. Shazad suspected the markings were part of a spell. He thought the weekly tags represented attempts by the Invisible Hand to breach the theater's defenses. The good news was, their efforts had not yet proved successful. So far Joey, Shazad, and Leanora were the only ones who could get inside the Majestic. Somehow, the theater and the magical artifacts within it were safe from the Invisible Hand. The question was, for how long?

Everybody worried the magical barriers around the theater wouldn't last, and rightly so. After all, if the Invisible Hand couldn't physically enter the Majestic, why had Redondo felt it necessary to whisk the theater away to an alternate dimension, the strange place he had affectionately referred to as "Off-Broadway?" It didn't make sense that he would go to such lengths to keep the theater safe unless he had to. Joey wished they could ask Redondo about it. He didn't understand the nature of the protected status he and his friends currently enjoyed, and it was hard—even for a talented young magician—to trust what he didn't fully understand. His concerns were compounded by the fact that the Invisible Hand wouldn't ever stop trying to force their way in. They had spent twenty years going after Redondo. Could Joey and his friends realistically expect to hold out that long? He hoped they wouldn't have to, but he felt that pressure weighing down on him. He lived with it every day.

On the way over, Joey thought he saw Scarlett trailing him. It wasn't the first time he'd had that feeling, either. There were multiple occasions over the course of the last month when Joey had thought he spotted her in a crowd, spying on him. On the subway. At the movies. Outside his apartment building. He was never sure if she was really there or if she was just in his head. She was like a phantom haunting him. He couldn't escape her. Every now and then Joey even thought he was still covered with the paint she had hit him with during their fight. He would be getting dressed in the morning and catch a glimpse of himself in the mirror with a mixture of paint splattered on his shoulder. He'd blink and look again, but it would be gone. The same thing happened whenever he saw Scarlett out in the world. He never knew if it was really happening or not, but the Invisible Hand was constantly on his mind. He saw danger around every corner and worried they might come after him or his family. Joey had told Janelle a side effect of magic was that it sometimes made you question your sanity. He could have said it made you paranoid, too, but it's not paranoia if there really are powerful forces conspiring against you.

Joey didn't feel safe until he was inside the theater. He shut the door behind him and checked to make sure it was locked. After that, he breathed a little easier. The opulent lobby was bathed in a warm, comforting light. It was a far cry from the dark, run-down and ruined space Joey had been introduced to the first time he'd visited the Majestic. Redondo's final act had been to restore the theater to its former glory. It was once again brimming with magical possibility, not to mention an abundance of magical objects. The question was, what to do with them? Despite countless debates, Joey and his friends had yet to come to an agreement.

Joey found the others in Redondo's old office. Shazad was seated at the desk. He was going through Redondo's big leather-bound book of magical items and checking the entries against an inventory he had made in a pocket-size notebook. Leanora was practicing fight moves with the Staff of Sorcero in the middle of the room. "What's up, guys?" Joey said on his way in. Leanora lifted her chin, wordlessly greeting Joey as she worked her way through a routine that resembled a martial arts kata. Her form was smooth and graceful.

"Did you bring the mask back?" Shazad asked, briefly looking up from his work. Joey held up his backpack in reply. Shazad gave a nod and returned to his books. Joey plopped himself down on the office couch, setting the bag on his lap.

Leanora finished her training exercises and spun the staff around, hand over hand, returning it to a more compact size. "You see the mark on the door outside?"

Joey nodded. "It was pretty hard to miss."

"Even harder to ignore, I hope," Shazad said, closing up the ledger and putting away his notebook.

"Anyone see Scarlett painting it?" Joey asked.

"No, but we have to assume it was her," Shazad said. "It's only prudent. I know you two like to joke about me being overly cautious, but I have to put my foot down here. We've got to do something before the Invisible Hand finds a way to break in and clean us out."

"I hear you," Joey said.

"We've been lucky so far, but we can't count on that. Hoping for the best isn't a strategy," Shazad stressed. "We can't put this off any longer," he added, getting a little worked up.

"Shazad," Leanora said. "No one's arguing with you."

Shazad's expression softened. He smiled playfully. "I wish. If that were true, we wouldn't be having this conversation. *Again.*"

"Fair enough," Leanora replied, returning the smile. "Where should we start this time?"

Everyone agreed the magical items in the theater were at risk of being stolen by the Invisible Hand. Unfortunately, the agreements ended there, as Joey, Shazad, and Leanora each had their own ideas about the best way to deal with the problem. Shazad wanted to take the magical artifacts back to his home in Jorako for safekeeping, and Leanora wanted to put the artifacts under her family's protection. She wanted Joey and Shazad to take their show on the road, performing with her and the other Nomadiks. Together, they could tour the world, inspiring audiences to believe in magic, helping people in need, and fighting back against the Invisible Hand. Shazad thought that sounded like a good way to lose everything, and Joey wasn't ready to drop out of school to become a full-time magician just yet. Not when he and Janelle were so close to solving the world's energy crisis. In the past, Shazad and Leanora had made their cases to Joey, asking him to be the swing vote and help convince the other person their plan was the right way to go. No doubt they assumed he was finally ready to abandon his own ambitions after the poor showing in the lab that morning. They were going to be disappointed there. Joey thought Leanora's and Shazad's ideas had their merits, but he also thought they gave up too much control. He hoped they could meet somewhere in the middle.

Had it been possible for anyone's parents to get into the theater, the matter would have been decided a month ago. The grown-ups would have taken control of the situation and settled it themselves, but there were no grown-ups in the room. For better or for worse, Joey, Shazad, and Leanora had exclusive access to the Majestic Theatre. They had promised each other that no one would take any magical artifacts out of the theater unless all three of them agreed to it, and so far everyone had stuck to that deal.

"Let's start with the fact that we've narrowed our choices down to two options instead of three," Shazad announced, confirming Joey's expectations. "That's some progress at least," Shazad added hopefully.

Joey kept his head down, still mixing his cards. He didn't say anything.

"We gave your way a chance, Joey. We kept an open mind, Leanora and I. You can't say we didn't. You and Janelle had weeks to get your experiment sorted out, but we tried it in the lab this morning, and it didn't work. I'm sorry, but it's time to move on."

"It's time," Leanora agreed. "Joey?" she asked, prodding him to go along.

Joey scratched at his neck uncomfortably. "Yeah, about that . . ." He winced, preparing to say something no one in the room wanted to hear. "I'm not ready to give up just yet."

Shazad sat up straight and looked at Joey like someone who had just reneged on a bet. "You've got to be kidding."

"Technically, our experiment worked," Joey argued, putting his hands up in defense. "You saw the data. 1.21 gigawatts. That's nothing to sneeze at."

Shazad let out a mighty "*AH-CHOO!*"

"You were saying?" Leanora asked.

"Come on," Joey said. "That was a fake sneeze."

"I'll give you that," Shazad admitted. "But I won't say your experiment worked. It only worked for you."

"How many gigawatts did you generate when Janelle tried

to use the mask?" Leanora asked, piling on. "I'm pretty sure it was zero."

"She's close," Joey said. "I can feel it. And if she can do it, other people can too."

"But she couldn't do it," Shazad said.

"She would have done it today if she'd had more time with the mask."

"You had a month," Leanora said.

"Did we really?" Joey asked. "Janelle never saw the Finale Mask before today. She couldn't come here to practice with it because she can't get into the theater. And you guys wouldn't let me bring any artifacts to her for more than a couple hours at a time. She's used to pulling all-nighters when she works on a project. She couldn't do that with this. It's no wonder she hit a wall."

"So you don't just want more time. You want to keep the mask at your school," Shazad said.

"That's only part of the plan," Joey said.

"There's more?" Shazad scoffed at the notion. "Forget it. If the Invisible Hand finds out the mask is there, it's as good as gone. Exemplar Academy doesn't have any kind of protection over it."

"We'll keep it quiet. We're good at secrets, aren't we?"

"No way." Shazad wasn't having it. "There are only two places we know the Invisible Hand can't get into. One of them is this theater and the other is Jorako. This place has been safe for a month. Jorako has been safe for generations. That's where these things belong," he said, patting Redondo's big book of magical artifacts. "All of them."

"My family's traveling showcase is safe too," Leanora said, unwilling to concede Shazad's point about Jorako being the only sensible option. "We have strength in numbers, something the three of us lack here. We go all around the world putting on magic shows with real magic, and it's always been fine because we keep moving. The Invisible Hand has yet to take anything away from us."

"The operative word being *yet*," Shazad said.

"You can say that about anything," Joey cut in. "Even Jorako."

"We don't take unnecessary risks in Jorako," Shazad countered.

"Some things are worth the risk," Leanora replied. "We're supposed to be the Order of the Majestic. We should be out there like Houdini and Redondo used to be, inspiring people to believe. We should follow in their footsteps."

"More like we'll follow them into an early grave," Shazad groused.

"That's your parents talking," Leanora said.

"It sure is. There are bad people out there, Leanora. Way worse than Grayson Manchester. My parents—my whole family—have kept more dangerous magical items out of their hands than you can imagine. I'm just being responsible. Sometimes it feels like I'm the only one."

"I thought you were willing to stand up to the Invisible Hand now," Joey said. "You fought Manchester and you fought to protect this theater. What changed?"

"Nothing changed. I fought because we had no other choice," Shazad said. "Personally, I'd rather we avoid confrontations like that. I don't like having my back up against the wall."

"Neither do I, but we can't just sit on this stuff. What good does that do anybody?" Joey asked. "Here's my idea— we split the difference. Shazad, you take the big-ticket items back with you to Jorako. The large magical artifacts. Things that are difficult to transport. You want to keep them safe?

Do it. I'm worried about the long-term security of this place too. Don't think I'm not. I'm all about getting help from the people in your family—yours too," he added, turning to Leanora. "You take the smaller items."

"Why the smaller items?" she asked, frowning.

"Not the less-powerful items. Just the things that are easier to travel with. Easier to conceal. Your family can use them in their act and whatever else they do, but here's the thing—we don't surrender rights to any of it."

Leanora squinted at Joey. "What do you mean?"

"I mean I want to keep experimenting with the magical artifacts Redondo left us. We've had them for a month. That's hardly any time at all. I'm still learning about most of them. I want to use them. I want to master them. And I'm happy to share them with your families as long as everybody understands that's what we're doing. Sharing. We should be able to get any one of those magical artifacts back here just by asking, easy as borrowing a library book. What do you say? Think your parents would agree to that?"

Shazad looked like he had a stomachache. "You're not being reasonable."

"I think I'm being very reasonable considering I've never been invited to Jorako or seen the Nomadiks perform."

Shazad and Leanora grew quiet. Their families were both irked about being denied entrance to the Majestic, and they had responded by making their own guest lists equally exclusive. Joey and Leanora weren't allowed to travel with Shazad to Jorako. Likewise, Shazad and Joey couldn't visit Leanora and watch the Nomadiks' show. Joey thought the adults on both sides were behaving like children. He could have taken their actions as an insult, and he would have been justified in his feelings, but he knew that wasn't helpful. Joey could only imagine the pressure Shazad and Leanora were getting at home. He didn't want to add to that. At the same time, he couldn't just roll over and go along with their parents' demands. He wanted to have a say in what happened to the magical items inside the theater too. He'd earned that.

"Do you really need to keep going with your project?" Leanora asked Joey. "It didn't work for Janelle and she's *seen* magic."

"That doesn't mean it can't work," Joey said. "Ledger DeMayne told me there's no room left for magic in the world. He said people don't believe like they used to because they *can't* believe anymore. I don't buy that. I believed. Redondo left us this place and everything in it for a reason. He brought us together for a reason. It wasn't just so we could give it all away to other people."

"Other people?" Leanora repeated. "These aren't strangers. You're talking about our families."

"They're strangers to me," Joey said. "What about us? What are we going to do? I may not know how to use magic to change the world, but I have a good idea. That's a start."

"Ideas are easy," Leanora said. "It's the execution that makes them matter. Redondo told us that."

"He also told us there's magic to be found in figuring things out," Joey countered. "The magic gets mixed in during the process. Why don't you guys help me and Janelle? If we all worked together, we could do this."

"We're not the problem," Shazad said. "The problem is, like it or not, DeMayne's right. There isn't enough magic left in the world to get those machines of yours working for everybody. Enchanted items like the mask . . . they don't hold their power indefinitely. They were infused with magic long ago, but it's not an infinite supply. That mask in your bag is going to run out of energy one day. What do you do then? It's not like you can swap in a replacement like a new set of batteries. You'd just be trading one energy crisis for another."

Joey said nothing. He had no answer for that.

"It doesn't matter anyway," Shazad continued. "People don't believe in magic anymore. Modern life is too scientific, too data-heavy and analytical for that."

"But we can change that," Leanora said. "We can change people's minds, one audience at a time."

"That would take forever," Shazad complained. "And better magicians than us—Redondo and Houdini—have tried that already. They got taken out by the Invisible Hand before they could make any difference in the world. How are we supposed to protect ourselves from the same fate?"

"Together," Leanora said. "What's the alternative? If we went with your plan and shipped everything off to Jorako, what's left for us? What would we do with ourselves?"

"We could go looking for the wand," Shazad suggested. Shazad leaned back in his chair and folded his arms. "Maybe I'd feel different about all this if we still had it, but we don't. You're forgetting that."

Joey felt himself shrink an inch. It always came back to

this. Sacrificing Houdini's wand had been his rash decision and he still regretted it. He wished he had been able to think of some other way to get rid of Grayson Manchester.

"I'm not trying to make you feel bad, Joey," Shazad said. "The Invisible Hand doesn't have the wand either. That's a good thing. But if what DeMayne told you is true, it's still out there somewhere. We should focus our efforts on finding it before they do."

Joey had a hard time arguing with that. He didn't trust Ledger DeMayne to tell him the correct time of day, but he had believed him when he'd said Houdini's wand was still up for grabs. What he didn't know was where to start looking for it. "Find it how?" Joey asked. "What are we supposed to do? Ask Janelle to make us another black hole and dive in after it?"

"We'll figure something out," Shazad said. "There's magic to be found in figuring things out," he added, reviving Redondo's words in service of his own argument.

Joey let out a sigh. He went back to shuffling his cards, feeling thwarted. A quest to recover Houdini's missing wand was not the cause he had hoped to rally his friends around. As much as he knew the wand was important and regretted its loss, he was also relieved to be absolved of the responsibility that had come with it. Torn by complex and contradictory emotions, Joey didn't know how to explain what he was feeling any more than he knew how to help his friends find common ground. He thought his compromise solution would satisfy everybody, but they were still at an impasse, and they were drifting farther apart.

"Let's set the wand aside for now," Shazad said. "Before we even think about going after it, we need to defend what we have here. We have to protect this house and the magic items we were entrusted with. That's paramount. I've been through everything Redondo left us. The thought of losing even one of these items is unacceptable. I vote we take everything to Jorako. No strings attached."

"You want to vote now?" Leanora asked. "We haven't made any progress. It's just going to be another stalemate."

"How else are we supposed to settle this?" Shazad asked.

Joey grimaced, mixing up his cards. That was the million-dollar question. He wished Redondo were there to tell them what to do, but he was gone. It was just the three of them in the theater . . . or was it?

Joey heard something outside the room. He leaned

forward slightly, turning his ear toward the office door. "You guys hear that?"

Shazad and Leanora sat up a little straighter. Leanora put a finger to her lips, signaling for everyone to be quiet. In the heavy silence that followed, a faint melodic sound in the distance was clearly audible. Leanora nodded slowly, her eyes alive with confusion and alarm. "It sounds like . . ."

"Singing?" Shazad finished.

"I thought I was imagining it," Joey said.

"There's someone in the theater," Shazad said, getting up. "I think our luck just ran out."

4

Three Witches

Leanora double tapped her heels and her magic boots once again flapped their wings. The next thing Joey knew, she was at the door. "You two wait here," she said. "I'll find out what's going on."

"Wait! We should go together," Shazad called after her, but she was already gone. Grumbling, he picked up the Staff of Sorcero, which Leanora had left behind on Redondo's desk. "This is what I'm talking about. Unnecessary risks. She didn't even arm herself."

"She's got her medallions," Joey said, getting up.

"Let's hope our guest doesn't have something stronger," Shazad said, coming around the desk. "We'd better get down there."

"Right." Joey had to hand it to Shazad. He didn't like

to fight, but he was no coward. When the situation called for action, he was there for it. You could always count on Shazad to have your back. Joey followed him out the door. In the hallway outside Redondo's office, the singing was louder, but still far away. A woman's voice drifted through the theater, originating somewhere near the stage.

As Joey and Shazad crept down the hall, Joey tried to identify the voice, and failing that, the song. He couldn't get a handle on either. The tune had an off-key, eerie quality that was somehow both unnerving and captivating. Joey had never heard anything like it. It didn't sound like English. He wished he could make out the words.

A door slammed somewhere in the theater and the singing stopped. Joey and Shazad froze at the top of the lobby's grand staircase. They looked at each other in the silence and waited. Joey's eyes were wide. He raised a hand to the side of his face, as if to help guide the slightest of echoes toward his ear. Nothing came.

"I don't hear it anymore," Shazad said. "You?"

Joey listened close. "Nothing. Maybe they're gone?" As soon as he said the words, he was seized with concern for Leanora and hoped that she had not gone with whoever it was that had been singing. "Lea?" he shouted. "Are you okay?"

No one answered.

"Leanora!" Shazad called out. "Are you there?"

More silence.

Gripped by fears that their friend had just been taken by the Invisible Hand, Joey and Shazad went racing down the steps as fast as they could go. Halfway down they crashed into someone and gravity took over. Joey didn't know who it was that had hit them, but they hit hard, knocking the wind out of him. He thought of DeMayne and his enchanted armor as they tumbled down, head over heels, and landed on the lobby floor in a tangled heap. Shazad was on his feet in a flash. He sprang up, spun the Staff of Sorcero around until it was full size, and stood ready to strike.

"Stop!" Leanora said, putting her hands up. "Shazad, it's me. It's okay."

Shazad exhaled and relaxed his stance, lowering the staff to his side.

"Thank goodness," Joey said. "We were worried about you."

"I'm fine," she said. "Nothing to worry about."

"Nothing to worry about?" Shazad scoffed. "That's debatable." He offered Leanora his hand. "That was reckless, running off by yourself like that," he said, helping her up on her feet. "What happened? Who was here?"

"Was it her?" Joey tacked on. "Was it Scarlett?"

Leanora nodded. "I think so. I can't say for sure, though. I didn't see her."

"She's gone, then?" Joey asked. "Already?"

"Looks like," Leanora said, dusting herself off. "I took a lap around the theater. As far as I can tell, we're the only ones inside."

Joey wiped his brow. "That's a relief."

"Not for me it's not," Shazad said. "I want to know how she got in. Also, what was she doing here? Did she take anything?"

"I don't know," Leanora said. "We should check."

"If she was going to steal something, she would have gone about it more quietly, don't you think?" Joey said. "Maybe she was just snooping around." He ran the back of his thumb across his lower lip, turning the matter over in his mind. Then he dropped his hand and shook his head, walking back the statement. "No. Even then, it doesn't make any sense. Why would she be singing? It's like she wanted us to know she was here. I don't get it."

"Could be she wanted to rattle us," Leanora suggested.

"Sure, but why stop there?" Joey asked. "Scarlett's been trying to get in here for weeks. You're telling me she finally succeeds, and all she does is pop in and pop back out?"

"We're assuming it was Scarlett," Shazad said. "We don't know that."

"I think we do." Leanora opened the doors to the main auditorium and motioned for the others to follow her in. "There's something you guys ought to see."

She led them down the aisle, up onstage, and behind the curtain, all the way back to the service entrance in the rear of the theater. The good news was, it was closed. The bad news was, it had been covered with a sloppy coat of white paint. Thick drips oozed down the front of the door like Elmer's glue. There was paint inside the doorframe, going through to the other side. From the looks of things, Scarlett's failed attempts to bypass the theater's front door had met with greater success in the back.

"Where does this door go?" Shazad asked.

Joey turned. "You don't know? We've been here a month."

89

"I don't use a door to get here," Shazad said.

"Fair enough," Joey said, noting that he had no idea how Shazad traveled to and from the theater.

"I do," Leanora said. "Just not any of these doors."

"This one doesn't go anywhere," Joey explained. "There's a back alley with a dumpster. That's it."

"Hang on," Shazad cut in, tensing up. "Listen."

Everyone held their breath and inched toward the door, getting as close as they could without bumping up against wet paint. The mysterious singing had faded down to muted humming, but it was the same odd song, and it was coming from the other side of the door.

"She's in the alley," Joey said, his stomach constricting.

"If it's her," Shazad said.

"Who else would it be?" Leanora asked.

The humming on the other side of the door continued.

"What's she up to?" Shazad asked. "Is she taunting us? Trying to lure us out?"

"I don't know what she's doing," Leanora said.

As the two of them speculated on Scarlett's possible motives, Joey took out Redondo's magic deck of cards and drew three off the top. He was hoping for a clue. As usual, he ended up with a trio of cards he'd never seen before and didn't understand. This time, it was three women who looked like witches. The first was a young woman with a spool of thread labeled THE MAIDEN. The second was a middle-aged woman knitting, labeled THE MOTHER. The last was an ancient woman holding a pair of shears. The name written below her picture read THE CRONE. The names and images were strangely familiar to Joey, but not enough to jog a specific memory. He didn't know who or what was waiting behind the door, but as he looked at the cards, something inside Joey told him he had to find out. He put the cards away and reached for the knob.

"What are you doing?" Shazad asked.

"It's okay," he replied, surprised to hear the words coming out of his mouth.

"Joey, don't!" Leanora called out.

She clutched his arm, but it was too late. He was already past her. Joey's heart galloped in his chest, but his hand was steady. He gripped the doorknob as if compelled to do so. He didn't know what he was thinking, but he did it before anyone could stop him. Shazad and Leanora gasped as Joey threw the door open. Across the threshold was not the alleyway, but the interior of a small cottage. Joey breathed a little easier when he saw it. The impossibility of the scene didn't faze him. He had seen doors like this one open up with Siberia on the other side. He had seen walls fall away and transport him from his bedroom into alternate dimensions. Magical gateways were a fact of life for Joey these days, so the phenomenon laid out before him was not unbelievable. Just unexpected. Likewise, Leanora and Shazad were not taken aback at the sight of the portal as much as they were taken by surprise.

The room on the other side of the door was inviting, full of amber light and warmth, both of which came from a large, central fireplace. There was a woman there, putting wood on the fire, but it wasn't Scarlett. She looked like the maiden on Joey's card, dressed in black robes with long blond hair. She glanced back over her shoulder, and they got a good look at her face. She was young, beautiful, and not terribly surprised to see Joey and his friends. She nodded, taking note of their presence at the door, but said nothing. The woman turned back around, stoking the fire and humming away.

Joey took a tentative step forward. "You want to talk about

reckless," Leonora muttered as Joey edged his way into the cottage.

"I didn't think it was possible a second ago, but he's got you beat," Shazad replied.

"C'mon, guys," Joey said, moving forward inch by inch. "We have to find out what's going on here, don't we?" His voice was shaky. He couldn't be certain that his actions weren't being driven by something stronger than mere curiosity, but he pressed on, crossing into the room. He found the mystery woman impossible to resist, despite the fact that she seemed perfectly content to ignore him.

Inside, the cottage was like something out of an old fairy tale or fable. Handcrafted from stone and wood, it had crooked walls that met at odd angles. All around there were shelves packed tight with bottles and jars of varying shapes and sizes. Joey couldn't tell what was in them, but ingredients for magic potions felt like a safe bet. In the corner, there was an antique cast-iron stove with a long black pipe that ran up into the ceiling. Next to that sat an empty cauldron, and in the center of the room, a rustic wooden table covered with assorted roots and herbs, a mortar, pestle, and several mixing bowls.

Once Joey was all the way inside the room, he was struck by the odd design of the fireplace, which had a mustache instead of a mantel. The stone wall around it had been sculpted in the shape of a bearded man's face, and the fire blazed inside its large, gaping mouth. As the blond woman put another log on the fireplace hearth, it gave new meaning to the phrase "feeding the fire." Joey felt like the stone face in the wall was staring at him. Its expression was intense, its eyes judgmental, and yet Joey wasn't afraid. The scene inside the cottage was odd but not unsettling. There was powerful magic at work in the room, and Joey couldn't explain it, but at that moment he felt like he was exactly where he was supposed to be. The others must have felt it too, because they followed him in, checking their reluctance at the door.

"What is this place?" Leanora asked, looking around.

"And who's she?" Shazad added in a whisper.

"I don't know," Joey whispered back. "Maybe we should ask her."

Shazad gave a nod and dove in. "Hello?" he asked, trying to get the woman's attention with a nonthreatening wave. "How did you get in here? No one can get in here but us."

The woman abandoned the fire and turned to face them.

"Is that what you think?" The corners of her mouth turned up in amusement. "Look again. I'm not in your home. You're in mine."

Shazad glanced about the cottage. She had him there. "I'm talking about before this," he said. "You were in the theater. It had to be you. We heard—"

"You should ask your questions one at a time," the woman said, raising her voice to talk over Shazad. "And it's better if you don't interrupt." She wagged a finger, and Shazad clammed up. "I go where I need to go when the time comes for me to go there. That includes Redondo's theater just now, this morning, and long before that. I knew Redondo before he was Redondo. I'm the one who gave him those cards you have in your pocket," she added, pointing at Joey. Her eyes flicked back to Shazad. "That's one."

Joey squinted at the woman. *One what?* he wondered as she turned back to the fire and held a thin stick of wood in the flame. Once the end of the taper was lit, she carried it to a small household shrine in the corner of the room. It was little more than a side table with a group of candles set on top. They were all burned down to the base save for one, which had not been touched. She lit that candle and stuck the burning stick of wood into a jar of sand on the floor. As she moved away from the shrine, Joey moved in for a closer look. The newly lit candle was tall and wide. It was inscribed with markings and rested on an ink-brush painting that bore a striking resemblance to the graffiti tag he had seen on the Majestic Theatre entrance. Joey stared at the image, telling himself it couldn't be. Then he looked underneath the burned-out candles surrounding the fresh one. They had melted away to nothing. Spent wax had hardened in globby drips that covered the table and more ink-brush paintings. Joey recognized the designs as the tags that had previously graced the Majestic's front door. The ones that had disappeared, week after week.

As Joey pondered the shrine's mysterious connection to the theater, Leanora stood in the open doorway behind him, inspecting the cottage's physical connection. "We're in *your* home . . . ," she said, trying to figure out how they got there. "It's the paint," she decided, touching a finger to the wet paint inside the doorframe. "I've never seen a gateway like this before. You used magic paint to bind this place to the theater?"

The fire in the stone face flickered as if a gust of wind

had blown through the room. The flames died down half-way, the room grew darker, and just like that, the blond woman aged thirty years. At first Joey thought it was because of the bad lighting, but a second look removed all doubt in his mind. Her blond hair had turned partially gray. Her face was fuller, with creases around the eyes and mouth. Joey, Shazad, and Leanora shared very startled looks. The woman smiled sweetly, oblivious to her change in appearance.

"The magic gets mixed in, child. The paint on the door-way contains a blend of plants, herbs, and oils that can still be found in the world—provided you know where to look." The woman crossed to the table in the center of the room, dropped a few roots and leaves into a bowl of orange paint, and started mixing. "If you've got the right recipe, you can use it for a great many things. For example, attaching my home to the theater and extending my protections with a symbol on the door. Maybe you recognize it? I think your friend here does." She nodded toward Joey, who was still standing at the shrine. "Those candles are infused with the same essence as the paint and marked in an ancient lan-guage. Something long forgotten." She clasped her hands in front of her and smiled again, this time with an air of sadness. "That's two."

"Hey, guys, over here." Joey motioned for the others to join him at the shrine. "Get a load of this."

Leanora and Shazad joined Joey in front of the candles. Armed with their host's explanation, they realized right away what they were looking at. "These are protective charms," Leanora said. "Four dead candles, one per week . . . That covers the last month."

"With a fresh one starting up today," Joey said.

Shazad nodded, piecing it together. "The candles burn out, the paint fades on the theater door. . . ."

"So she marks the door with a new symbol and lights a new candle," Leanora said, finishing his thought.

"It's *her*," Joey agreed. "She's the one tagging the door, not Scarlett. These marks aren't break-in attempts. She's been helping us. You're helping us!" he repeated, spinning around to face the woman at the table. "Not that I'm complaining, but . . . why?"

Woosh. Another phantom wind came through to put the dying fire out of its misery. Nothing but embers and smoldering ash remained. Joey and his friends were left with the light of a lone candle and whatever light came in through the open door. It took a few seconds for Joey's eyes to adjust. Once they did, he saw the woman was now ancient. Her transformation shouldn't have surprised him so much the second time around, but it did because it was so drastic. She was suddenly a hundred years old or more. Her gray hair was now stark white and stringy. The fine lines on her face became deep-set wrinkles, and she stood a foot shorter with a posture that was painfully hunched. Joey thought of the cards he had drawn, Maiden, Mother, and Crone. He wondered if the woman was aging, or if she was somehow all three women at the same time.

"I've been helping you," the old lady began in a creaky voice, "because I've been waiting for you three a very long time. I gave you this time alone in your theater so you wouldn't have everyone telling you what to do. Choosing your path for you. You have to follow your own hearts, dearies. I bought you time to find your way, but you haven't done it. You're still lost, and time is running out." She pointed to the shrine. "This candle here is the last one I'll light."

"The last one?" said Shazad. "What happens when it burns out?"

Joey held his breath. The woman had grown older each time they had asked her a question. If it happened again, she was going to turn into a skeleton. Fortunately, Shazad's words had no effect on her. "Sorry," the old lady said. "That's three."

"Three? Three what?" asked Leanora.

Leanora's question was ignored as well. The old lady smiled to herself as she hobbled to the wall and picked up a cane. Joey understood what she meant, much to his chagrin. "We only get three questions," he said. "You could have told us that when we came in."

The old lady shook her head, tittering. "You asked the wrong questions. Don't blame me. I could have told you about the Lost Kingdom. The Caliburn Shield. The Imaginary Vortex!" She turned up her empty, withered hands. "I'm afraid you'll have to find out on your own."

"What are you talking about?" Joey asked. "Who are you?" He knew it was pointless to ask, but he couldn't help it.

The old lady wagged a finger at Joey. "If I tell you everything, you won't learn anything." She pulled a scroll of parchment from a shelf on the wall and pressed it into Shazad's hands. "You have to find your own way."

"What's that?" asked Joey. "What did she give you?"

"I don't know," Shazad said, feeling flustered. The scroll was tied up with a string and double knotted. He put the Staff of Sorcero down for a moment and tried to pry the knot loose with his fingernails as the old lady pushed past him, hobbling toward the door.

"Where's she going?" Leanora asked. "Hey, where are you going? Don't leave," she pleaded.

The old lady left without another word and shut the door behind her, eliminating the theater as a light source. It had not been especially bright before, but without the Majestic's backstage lights, the cottage was nearly pitch-black. Leanora hurried to the door, no doubt hoping to bring the old lady back and coax more information out of her. She wrenched the door open. Blinding light and cold air poured into the cottage.

"What the . . . ?" Joey said, turning around as a chill sliced through his body. The light was so strong he had to shield his eyes.

Shazad did the same, holding up a hand and squinting. "Now what?" He stopped fumbling with the scroll and went with Joey to find out what was happening inside the theater—but the theater wasn't there anymore.

Joey's heart jumped up into his throat once he reached the door. He couldn't speak—he could hardly breathe—when he saw that the cottage was no longer "attached" to the Majestic. It was on a cliffside road, halfway up a snowy mountain, high above the clouds.

"Watch your step, boys," Leonora said, putting her arm out to block the exit. "We're not in Midtown anymore."

5

On Top of the World

The view outside gave Joey vertigo. His hand instinctively went to the door to steady him as he gazed out upon the tips of snow-capped mountains, and a rolling landscape of clouds stretched thin over a perilous drop. Joey's fingers tightened around the wood frame, tacky with wet paint, as he craned his neck to look up at the frozen peak a thousand feet above him. The cottage rested on a narrow ledge, set inside a sheer rock face at the end of a frosted, white path. The unforgiving rock wall that enveloped the cottage was beyond steep—beyond vertical even. Its incline was inverted, angling out over Joey's head. He withdrew into the relative safety of the cottage, wondering why anyone would ever build a house in such a terrible place, and for that matter, how? The winding trail that led to the cottage door was rocky and uneven, ten feet wide in some places and little more than two feet across in others. The ground broke off sharply past the edge of the trail, giving way to a long steep slope riddled with jagged speed bumps. One wrong step and it was human toboggan time, scraping over the mountain's sharp teeth on the way to a very sticky end. Joey tried to imagine someone hiking up the mountain, weighed down with building materials and all the contents of the cottage. He couldn't picture himself doing it. Ever. The idea of being out there under any circumstances sent a shiver up his spine, but maybe that was just the wind.

Joey took another step away from the door. He wasn't a big fan of heights and he liked the cold even less, but this wasn't just cold. This was icy death. The harsh wind that came off the mountain was like nothing Joey had ever felt before. If he had bundled up for an arctic expedition it would have still been tough to take, and he was dressed for springtime in New York. A wave of snow swept into the room. Joey put a hand up as tiny ice particles whipped into his face like frozen grains of sand. Through his fingers, he saw someone way down at the end of the trail. Someone dressed in red.

Joey tried to say something, but the words got stuck in his throat. He felt as if the air in his lungs had frozen into ice crystals. He dropped his hand and darted outside without thinking. The wind cut right through him, but he stood there and took it, scanning the mountain for Scarlett. He didn't see her.

"Shut the door!" Shazad called out.

Leanora pulled Joey back inside, closed the door and latched it, fighting hard against the wind the whole way. She turned around and put her back to the door, breathing heavy.

"What were you doing going out there like that?" Shazad asked him. "Not cold enough for you in here?"

"Sorry," Joey said. "I thought I saw someone on the trail."

"What?" Leanora said. "I didn't see anyone."

She went to open the door back up, but Joey shook her off. "Don't. It's nothing. There's no one." Joey told himself he was being paranoid. He always thought he saw Scarlett, and nothing ever happened. She couldn't have possibly followed him up here.

"Anyone else feel like they've got an anvil on their chest?" Shazad asked. "Or is it just me?"

Joey nodded. He was panting himself. "We're too high up. Our bodies aren't acclimated."

"Acclimated?" Leanora repeated, squinting at Joey.

"To the altitude," Joey explained. "The air's thinner up here. The actual air molecules are farther apart than what we normally breathe. Our bodies need time to adjust and make more red blood cells to carry more oxygen."

"How much time?" asked Shazad.

"The kind of time we don't have. It takes mountain climbers weeks to acclimate. We didn't do that. We just kind of showed up here."

"I feel tired," Shazad said, looking for a place to sit down.

"If we were any higher up, we'd pass out in a couple minutes." The room darkened for a moment, then returned to normal. Joey realized he was feeling light-headed. "We still might," he said. "Lea, let's get out of here. Use your doorknob."

"I'd love to," Leanora said. "Too bad it's back in Redondo's office."

"What?" Shazad said.

"You don't have it with you?" Joey asked, his voice rising with panic.

Leanora held out her arms, physically stating the obvious. Her hands were empty and the bag of tricks she usually carried was nowhere in sight. Joey's stomach turned.

"That's going to be a problem," Shazad said.

Joey grimaced. It certainly was. He took out his phone to see if he could use it to call for help, but that was another problem. Even if the phone worked, who was he going to call? What was he going to say? He tried reaching Janelle first. Joey didn't fully expect the call to go through, but he tried to catch a signal anyway.

"The phone again?" Leanora asked, scrunching up her face. "Really?"

"Don't worry. I've got location services turned off," Joey said, noting the feature that Grayson Manchester had previously used to track him. "I learned my lesson."

"You're not going to get any service up here," Shazad said.

"You never know. I saw a documentary on Everest one time. That's how I learned about acclimation and stuff."

"And?" Shazad probed.

"And, believe it or not, they had Wi-Fi at base camp, more than five thousand feet above sea level."

"This isn't exactly base camp," Leanora said.

"It isn't Mount Everest, either," Joey replied. "I hope," he added under his breath. The call failed, as expected. "Maybe I can send a text," he said, typing away with his thumb. He hit send, casting the text out into the ether like a digital message in a bottle. Joey held his breath, praying it would somehow reach the shore. "Ha!" Joey blurted out. "It's working! It went through!"

"Thank goodness. We're saved," Shazad said without feeling.

"Can she call someone for us?" Leanora asked in a more hopeful tone. "Someone who can help?"

"Call who?" Shazad countered. "What's she going to tell them? We don't even know where we are."

As if on cue, Janelle texted to ask Joey where he was and what time he was coming back. They were supposed to leave for the airport soon.

Joey grimaced, realizing his phone would not be the lifeline that he and his friends needed. Even if he could tell Janelle their exact location, it would take hours for a search-and-rescue team to find them. He rubbed his head, feeling woozy. They didn't have that kind of time.

"Shazad's right. This is no good." He fired off another text telling Janelle he'd meet her in California (he hoped) and put the phone away. "There has to be some magic way off this mountain. That old lady, or ladies . . . they were helping us. They wouldn't just leave us here to die."

"What did she give you?" Leanora asked Shazad.

"I don't know," Shazad said, turning his attention back to the scroll the old lady had pressed into his hands. "Let's see." He undid the knot and spread the golden-brown parchment out on the floor, hoping for written instructions on how to get home. "It's a map," he said, disappointed.

"A map? Of what?" Leanora asked, coming over for a look. "The mountain?"

"No," Shazad said. "The world."

Joey cleared a space on the table to lay the map out flat and used a cup and a bowl as weights to hold it down. It was an old atlas of the seven continents, hand painted with a colorful, ornate border and intricate details that modern mapmakers didn't bother with. Sea serpents surfaced off coastlines, and clouds with faces blew strong winds from the four corners of the earth. Set inside a gilded crest in the lower-right-hand corner of the map were the words "The Secret Map of the World."

"This looks like something out of a pirate adventure,"

Leonora said, joining Joey at the table. "Look here. X marks the spot." She pointed to a thick black X drawn somewhere in South Asia.

"I don't think that's buried treasure," Shazad said, noting the mountain range near the X.

"Shazad's right," Joey agreed. "It's probably our location. The Himalayas. Wonderful." He studied the map closer. It was crisscrossed with bright red lines connecting cities all over the world, some of them spanning great distances. Joey traced a few of the routes with his finger, growing intrigued by the names he came across. "Some of the places on this map . . . I've never heard of them. But the ones I have . . ." Joey trailed off, astonished. "Look at this: Transylvania, Waywayanda, Caloo-Calay, Celestia . . . Jorako?"

"What? Let me see that." Shazad nearly knocked over the bowl of orange paint as he leaned in for a closer look. "That isn't possible. We have charms in place. Jorako can't appear on any map!" He stared hard at the map, scrutinizing a little black dot in the middle of Egypt. Joey could have sworn he was trying to will it out of existence. When that didn't happen, Shazad let out a sigh. "I don't understand," he said, deflated.

"I guess Jorako's easier to find than you thought," Leanora told him.

Shazad straightened up in a hurry, eager—as ever—to contest that point. "Let's not go there," Joey said, jumping in before Shazad dove into a monologue about the impenetrable nature of Jorako. "First things first. Let's get out of here before it's too late." Joey felt the room whirl on him. He gripped the edge of the table as his legs wobbled. Fatigue was setting in. *We must be really high up to feel it this fast*, Joey thought. "There's got to be a way back," he said. "It's got to have something to do with this map. Otherwise, why give it to us?"

"Why do any of this?" Leanora asked. "You're assuming there has to be a logical explanation. I hate to say it, but maybe we're not here for a reason. Maybe we just messed up."

"There's got to be a reason," Shazad said. "Whoever that was in here . . . she clearly wants us to keep the magic we've got safe from the Invisible Hand, but she wants us to do it our way." He pressed two fingers to his temple and closed his eyes, making a face like he had a headache. "I don't know what that means. We don't have a way. That's our whole problem. We have three ways and no plans."

"I think she was telling us to change that," Joey said. "She said she knew Redondo. I believe it. Remember he told us a woman gave him these cards?" Joey took out Redondo's deck of cards, nearly fumbling them all over the table. His reflexes were going. He grumbled and put the cards away carefully. "Redondo said the woman told him he'd inspire a new age of magic."

"I remember that," Leanora said. "That's our job now. Redondo did his part. He inspired us."

"So we," Shazad began, "the people without a plan, are somehow part of this old lady's plan to inspire a new age of magic?" He grunted, passing judgment on that notion. "It would have been nice if she told us how to do that. I don't have any ideas, except–"

"Don't say the wand," Joey cut in.

Shazad put his hands up. "I didn't say anything."

"Neither did the old lady," Leanora said. "She couldn't say anything." Leanora paused, the wheels in her head turning. "Three questions. That was all we got. It seemed like a rule. Maybe she got around it by telling us what she *couldn't* tell us. You know what I mean?"

Joey blinked at Leanora. "Huh?" Her voice sounded far away, soft and dreamlike. He was getting foggy.

Joey could tell Leanora felt it too. Her eyes swam in their sockets for a second, but she took a breath and blinked them clear. "Think about it. What if . . . ? What if when she said she couldn't tell us anything, she was really trying to tell us something?"

"Okay," Joey said, trying hard to concentrate. "I get it. What *didn't* she tell us, then? Specifically? She said we asked the wrong questions, otherwise she could have told us about—"

"The Lost Kingdom," Leanora said. "That was one of them."

"The Caliburn Shield," Shazad said next. "That was another. What was the third one again?"

Joey thought for a second. "The Imaginary Vortex!" he said, raising a proud finger in the air. Unfortunately, he had no idea what to do with that information. "Any of that mean anything to you guys?" he asked Shazad and Leanora, but they were just as lost as he was.

"You think she gave us the map to find those things?" Shazad asked.

"How does that help us get out of here?" Leanora replied.

"I don't . . . I don't thinkit doez," Joey said. He was

113

slurring his speech, getting more and more tired. Leanora looked sleepy too. Joey shook his head to wake himself up, and the room shook with it. His arms felt like they had weights tied to them. He wanted to sit down on the floor and rest for a moment, but he stopped himself from following that impulse. He knew what was happening to his body. The warning signs were clear. "Lizzen guys . . ." Joey paused and slowed down his speech, trying to get the words out clearly. "If we don't get out of here soon, we're going to die. We've got hypoxia. Oxygen deficiency. It's going to make you tired, but don't close your eyes. Don't sleep. We won't make it dressed like this." They needed parkas, hats, gloves, goggles, face masks, boots, and long underwear. That was just the bare minimum, and they didn't have any of it. The closest thing they had to a jacket was Shazad's cape. "Up here at these temperatures . . . without protection? Sleep equals death. Everybody got it?" Shazad and Leanora nodded, their faces grim and weary. "Okay. Glad we got that straight." Joey shivered. "So, how do we get out of here?" he asked again, as if for the first time.

"Don't ask me," Leanora said.

Shazad gave a listless shrug. "I've got nothing."

Joey looked around the room, hoping to spot an answer. He was scared, but his thoughts were too jumbled for the fear to hit him properly. His eyes settled on the fireplace that was carved in the shape of a face. It was still staring at him. "How about you?" he asked it. "Any ideas?"

"I have some thoughts," said the fireplace. "It's bad luck to go in one door and out another. You should always leave a house the same way that you came in."

Joey nearly fell over. He looked back and forth between the fireplace and his friends, sending the room into a spin. After that he did fall over. Being on the floor felt better than standing, so Joey decided to get comfortable. He sat up and slid over to lean his back against the wall. "Is it just my oxygen-deprived brain, or did the fireplace speak?"

The fireplace grunted. "Obviously I can speak." Its voice was deep and haughty.

Joey stared at the fireplace in disbelief. "Obviously," he deadpanned. This was next-level weirdness, even for someone who was used to seeing magic in action.

"Why didn't you talk before?" Shazad asked the fireplace.

"With a fire going?" the fireplace scoffed. "Didn't anyone ever tell you not to talk with your mouth full?"

"Of course. What was I thinking?" Shazad asked sarcastically.

"Manners make the fireplace," Leanora said with a dazed smile. "The fire-*face*," she added, chuckling to herself.

Uh-oh, Joey thought. *She's getting loopy.* Then he realized he was laughing at her joke. He was getting loopy too. Fortunately, Shazad seemed to be keeping it together. For now.

"What's going on?" he demanded. "What are you? Who was that old lady? Or ladies? Whatever! Why are we here?"

The fireplace chuckled. "It doesn't matter."

"Why not?"

"Because you can't stay."

Shazad threw his hands up. "Who said we want to stay? We want to go home! Why is everyone talking in riddles?"

"No choice," said the fireplace. "Old rules. Old magic. The sisters did what they could, but it's up to you to choose your path. Time is running out."

"I picked up on that," Joey said, his eyelids drooping.

"Don't go to sleep, Joey," warned the fireplace. "You've got hypoxia. Next comes hypothermia. You don't want that."

"No, I don't," Joey agreed, his mind wandering. "That's too many hypos. Not good." He squinted at the fireplace.

"How do you know about this stuff? Did you watch that documentary too?" He was making himself laugh now. "That's funny. The fireplace likes documentaries. . . ." Joey leaned back a little too fast and bonked his head against the wall, but it didn't bother him. He felt numb. He stared up at the ceiling of the cottage, his thoughts a muddled mess. Across the room, Leanora was fading fast.

"I'm just going to close my eyes for a minute," she said.

Joey wanted to tell her not to do it, but he couldn't find the strength to say the words out loud. He understood how she felt. His head lolled. Keeping his chin up and his eyes open was a struggle. He wanted to rest too. Just for a minute. That's all.

Shazad tried to shake Joey awake. He was saying something, but it was hard to make out. His voice was a quavering echo with the speed and pitch turned way down. "JOey, DoN'T SLeeP," Shazad ordered in a disorienting warble. "SLeeP EqUAls DEATH, ReMEMber?"

Joey rubbed his eyes. He was drifting off. He couldn't help it. He pushed Shazad away, getting white paint on his shirt in the process. Joey rubbed his fingers together, feeling the wet paint. Then he looked at the paint on the cottage door, dripping in around the doorframe where he had touched it. He couldn't believe it was going to end this way, but he didn't know how to stop it. They had painted themselves into a corner by coming to this place.

Wait a minute.

A jolt of energy ran through Joey. He sat up straight, temporarily revived by the power of an idea. "That's it! Shazad, I've got it!"

Shazad turned in surprise, stumbling back toward Joey. "Got what? What's *it*?"

"The paint!" Joey exclaimed, showing Shazad his fingertips. "We painted ourselves into a corner. We can paint our way out! Look on the table; she was mixing up a new batch. She said if you know how to use it . . . She was showing us but not telling us. We've got to go out the same way we came in!"

Shazad looked confused. Joey knew he wasn't explaining it properly. He tried to get up and show Shazad what he was talking about, but he couldn't move. The burst of energy was gone. Spent. He could only hope Shazad had understood what he was saying and had enough strength left to do what was needed.

The next minute passed for Joey in snippets, viewed as he went in and out of consciousness, fighting the urge to sleep. He saw Shazad staggering over to the table, knocking herbs and roots to the floor. His vision blurred and came back. Shazad now had the bowl of paint cradled under his arm as he searched the room for a brush. The next thing Joey knew, Shazad was painting the door with frantic strokes, splattering it with a bright orange hue. The job complete, he threw the paint away and pushed the door open. Joey couldn't see what was on the other side. Not from where he was sitting. But he saw Shazad pick up Leanora and shove her out of the cottage. That gave him hope.

Joey was up next. Shazad lurched over to him with clumsy, awkward steps. Joey could tell he was drained from lack of oxygen and ready to drop. He had no idea how Shazad was still standing. The way he soldiered on was nothing short of heroic. Joey pushed with his legs, trying hard to do his part as Shazad dragged him to his feet. "Hold on to your bag," Shazad told him. "The mask is in there, right?"

"Got it," Joey mumbled as they shuffled across the floor together. "Did it work?" he asked. "The paint?"

Shazad grunted, straining hard. "It worked."

119

"Where are we going?"

"Somewhere safe."

"Oh," Joey said, delirious. "That's nice. Don't forget the map."

"The map!" Shazad exclaimed, turning around quickly. It was still on the table. Joey's knees turned into jelly and he collapsed onto Shazad. They tumbled through the open doorway together. A blast of hot air hit Joey in the face as he passed through the portal. The world went white and he shut his eyes, falling forward into the abyss. It felt like he fell forever. And then he didn't feel anything at all.

6

Out of the Frying Pan

Joey came to with the back of his neck burning and his nose in a pile of sand. He worked up the strength to roll over and immediately wished he hadn't. The heat was so overwhelming and the sun's glare was so intense, it felt like it was two inches away from his face. Joey threw his hands up to cover his eyes. For a second he thought he was on the beach, but he didn't hear the ocean, and the birds he saw circling overhead . . . they weren't seagulls. Looking up through his fingers, Joey had a sinking feeling they were vultures.

He groaned and pushed himself into a sitting position, spitting out grains of sand that were stuck to his lips. His head was throbbing. Joey massaged his temples, trying to wake up and remember what had happened. Flashes of the cottage and the three women ran through his mind. He remembered passing out from oxygen deprivation some-where in the Himalayas. Most likely, it had been high up Mount Everest, based on how quickly hypoxia had set in. *Guess I can scratch that place off my bucket list,* he thought, amusing himself. *There you go. Way to look on the bright side.* He brushed his face clean, still feeling a little punchy. Check-ing his surroundings, he saw nothing but bright side, every-where he looked. He was in a desert.

How did I get here? Joey wondered.

Even as he asked himself the question, foggy memories solidified to answer it. He remembered Shazad pulling him up and shouldering his weight as they stumbled through the cottage door. The mental fog lifted, and Joey's mind was suddenly sharp again. He spun around in the sand, jolted back to clarity by concern for his friends. "Nnngh!" Joey felt a shooting pain behind his eyeballs. He had spun around too fast, amplifying his headache. He winced and waited for it to subside.

The good news was, Leanora and Shazad were both there with him, lying unconscious in the sand. Joey breathed a heavy sigh of relief. They had all made it out. As Joey grappled with the fact that he and his friends had almost died on the mountain, it dawned on him that their current situation was not much of an improvement. He scanned the desert landscape slowly. Nothing but sand dunes as far as the eye could see.

"This keeps getting better and better."

A few of the birds swooped down, landing next to Shazad and Leanora. The birds nudged them with their beaks, testing to see if they were dead or alive. Joey's friends began to stir, and Joey crawled over to shoo the birds away. "Hey!" he called out. "Leave them alone. Go on. Get out of here. Go!" He flicked sand at the birds, running them off as his friends woke up.

"You guys okay?" Joey asked his friends as they came around.

Leanora gave an unconvincing nod. Shazad couldn't even muster that. He tried to sit up but quit before he got that far. "Ow." He lay back down and covered his eyes with the meaty part of his forearm. Shazad and Leanora both looked about as good as Joey felt.

"I'm all right," Shazad croaked after a short silence. "I've got the headache of a lifetime, but I'll live." A persistent bird pecked at his side. He swatted it away. "You hear that? Find something else to eat." The bird squawked and flew away as Shazad propped himself up on his elbows. "Egyptian vultures," he said, frowning. "Tough little buggers. Too smart for their own good." He looked around, squinting in surprise. "How'd we end up here?"

"It was you," Joey said. "You saved us."

Shazad's eyebrows went up. "I did?"

"Yeah." Joey nodded. "Big-time."

"What happened?" asked Leanora.

They talked through the events that preceded their arrival in the desert. It took only the slightest mention of anything to crystalize the memories in everyone's brain. Soon Shazad was sitting up and telling the story, filling in the gaps for Joey and Leanora. Apparently, Shazad had nearly dropped the bucket of paint, spilling it everywhere before he reached the cottage door. That would have been a disaster. He thought he was going to collapse before he got Joey out too. Then Joey collapsed onto him as he turned around to get the map.

"The map!" Joey blurted out. The last thing he remembered, it was still on the table. "Did you save the map?"

Shazad cocked his head slightly, thinking back. "I don't know. I think so." He shook out the folds of his cape and checked to see if he was sitting on it, but found nothing. He didn't have the map on him.

"What about the staff?" Leonora asked him. Everybody got up and looked around. There was nothing but sand as far as the eye could see.

"They're not here," Joey said, deflated.

"There!" Leonora said, pointing behind Shazad. "Look!"

"What is it?" Shazad asked, turning his head. "Which one?"

Joey scanned the desert, hoping it would be the map. Sure enough, there it was, a few feet off, half buried in the sand.

The wind picked up, catching the free end of the map and threatening to lift it into the sky. "Get it!" Joey said, gawking at the fluttering parchment. "Before it blows away!"

All three of them sprinted across the sand as best they could, slipping and bumping into each other as they went. Their bodies ached, their legs were weary, and they moved like zombies with their shoelaces tied together. By the time they reached the map, it was already airborne. They chased after it as it floated on the breeze, landing ten feet away. Joey got there first and dove for the map, his fingers just missing it as the wind sent it skittering across the sand once more. This comedy of errors repeated dune after dune. Every time they closed in on the map, the wind would carry it off before they caught it. They weren't fast enough, and once the wind really got going, they weren't tall enough, either. Soon the map was flying in the air like a kite, totally out of reach.

"That's it, then," Shazad said, hunched over as the map swirled twenty feet above their heads. "We need wings to catch that thing now."

Leanora turned. "Shazad, you're a genius."

Shazad looked up. "How's that?"

"Your cape," Leanora said, shaking the shiny fabric on his back. "Give me wings! Make me a bird." She pointed up at the vultures who were currently sharing the sky with the map. "One of those birds."

"Can you do that?" Joey asked.

"Of course he can do it," Leanora said. "He turned a wolf into a bunny in Siberia, remember? Tell him, Shazad. You can do it."

Shazad nodded reluctantly. "Yes, I can do it, but . . ."

"But what?"

"Have you ever *been* a bird before?"

Leanora scrunched up her face. "What kind of question is that? I'll figure it out. Quick, before it's too far away!"

Joey turned his back against the wind as it picked up steam. The map climbed higher and higher. It was sure to land a hundred feet away when it finally came back down. "I don't know what else we can do, but whatever we do, we better hurry."

Shazad shrugged and pulled off his Cape of Transfiguration. "All right." The cape was no bigger than a bath mat, shiny black on one side and gold on the other. He gave it a hard shake and suddenly it was as big as a king-size bedsheet. "Here goes . . ." He threw the cape over Leanora, covering her from head to toe. A second later, he whisked the cape away with a lightning-fast motion. It was as if he were pulling a tablecloth out from under a set of glassware and dishes that had been placed on a dining room table. When the cape was thrown aside, Joey looked and saw a bird strutting about where Leanora had once stood. She was the size of a chicken.

"Leanora?" Joey asked. She had dusty white feathers with spiky tan plumage around her neck and a garish red-orange face that terminated in a horned beak. She looked up at Joey and Shazad with black eyes and cawed at them, making a sound that Joey took to mean "Yes, it's me." She spread her wings, which were tipped with black feathers, and flapped them without skill or grace. Joey thought she was going to tip over as she turned around on a clawed foot and tried to fly. She took off awkwardly, rising and falling in the air, following an erratic path.

"What's she doing?" Joey asked.

"Learning to fly," Shazad replied.

"It's like she's got two left wings."

"She'll pick it up," Shazad told him. "Eventually. That's not what I'm worried about." Before Joey could ask Shazad what he *was* worried about, the other vultures took notice of Leanora and flew in for a closer look. They cawed back and forth to each other, calling more birds over to where she was. "There. What'd I tell you? Too smart for their own good."

Joey noted how close the other vultures were flying to Leanora. How interested they were in her poor flying. "They can tell she's not one of them?" he guessed.

"They can tell something's not right about her," Shazad

confirmed. "Animals don't like what they don't understand. They're a lot like people that way."

Leanora found her groove flying and resumed the hunt for the map, which was drifting even farther away. Unfortunately, by then the other vultures in the sky were hunting her. Out of nowhere, one of them dive-bombed Leanora, knocking her off course as she pursued the map. Joey could tell the move had caught Leanora completely off guard. She dropped like a stone, falling ten feet in the blink of an eye. Joey worried she might crash into a mountain of sand, but at the last second she opened up her wings and glided back to safety. More birds came in to continue the attack, screeching and pecking. They swarmed Leanora, relentless in their attempt to drive her out of the sky.

"They're trying to kill her," Joey said.

"Looks like," Shazad agreed, his face grim.

They watched, helpless as the aerial battle went on high above their heads. Leanora tried to swoop away, but the other vultures wouldn't give her any room to maneuver. They penned her in, flapping their wings and shrieking wildly. It was as if they were challenging her—daring her to do something. When Leanora didn't fight back, they hit her again, sending her tumbling through the air. "C'mon, Lea," Shazad said. "You're not gonna take that, are you?" He told Joey this was why he had asked Leanora if she'd ever been a bird before. Apparently, if you know how to handle yourself as an animal, you could fake it and fool other animals around you. However, if you couldn't walk the walk, things got tricky. Some animals could spot a fake a mile away. They sensed something unnatural and reacted, either by shunning the pretender as an outsider or by lashing out violently. "It should be me up there," Shazad said, cursing himself as Leanora tried to escape the vulture flock's wrath. "I've flown with vultures before. I've even run with wild dogs out here. I would have gone up, but neither of you have ever used my cape. Who would have changed me into a vulture? Who would have changed me back?"

"You could have warned her," Joey said, his eyes glued to the bird fight up above.

Shazad dismissed that. "I didn't want to put the idea in her head. There was a fifty-fifty chance they'd just leave her alone. Besides, it's Lea. You honestly think it would have made any difference?"

Joey grimaced. Shazad had a point. "You're right," he said. "It's Lea. She can hack it. She's a fighter."

"Come on, Lea!" Shazad yelled up at the dueling birds. "Don't let them push you around!" Leanora didn't need to be told twice—or even once, really. By the time Joey and Shazad starting cheering her on from the ground, she had run out of patience with the vultures and grown comfortable enough with her wings to fight back effectively. Leanora angled her beak toward the earth and broke off in a wide sweeping arc that first took her away from her tormentors and then swooped up high above them. Next she dove back down and reared up with her talons, clawing the wing of the first bird that had hit her. Feathers flew and the bird slunk off, flying badly with one lame wing.

"YES!" Joey shouted. "That's how you do it!"

Leanora clashed with another vulture, biting at it with her beak and pushing it away with her feet. She whirled on the rest of the flock, thrashing her wings and screeching like a pteranodon. She was angry and her message was clear—get the flock away from me. The birds did the smart thing and backed off, giving Leanora the space she needed to reacquire the map. It was so far away by then it wasn't much bigger than a postage stamp, but after her battle with the vultures, chasing down the map was easy. Leanora flew off to retrieve it and returned with the parchment clasped tight in her beak. She touched down on the sand at Joey's and Shazad's feet and spit it out. Shazad picked it up and threw his cape over Leanora. When he pulled it away, she was human again and the map was back in their possession. Mission accomplished.

"Well," Leanora said, inspecting a claw mark on her arm. "That was an experience."

"Nice work," Joey said. "You showed them who's boss."

"Lucky for us they're scavengers and not birds of prey," Shazad said.

"Hey," Leanora said, pushing back. "Bring 'em on. I'll take them either way."

Shazad smiled. "I bet you would."

"Okay, now what?" Joey asked. "Let's get down to business. Where are we?"

"Let's see," Shazad said, checking the map. As soon as he looked at it, his face fell. "Oh no . . . I didn't." He closed his eyes and let out a self-admonishing breath.

"What is it?" Leanora asked.

"I was afraid of this," Shazad said.

"Afraid of what?" Joey asked. "Are we in trouble?"

Shazad let out a terse laugh. "*You're* not."

Joey leaned in to look at the map, but just for confirmation. The look on Shazad's face said it all. "You took us to Jorako, didn't you?"

"Pretty much," Shazad said, his expression grim. "This isn't Jorako right here." He waved at the empty horizon. "But it's close."

"How close?" The X that marked their location on the map had moved from the Himalayas to North Africa, somewhere in Egypt. That meant they were stranded in the Sahara—the largest desert in the world. Joey looked around for some sign of a nearby town or village. There was nothing in sight. The place looked like Tatooine. "It's just over the next sand dune, right?"

Shazad scratched his head, thinking. "It's hard to say. If I had to guess?" He brushed some sand off the map and something happened to break his concentration. The images on the parchment moved slightly out of position and then snapped back into place on the page. "Whoa." Shazad repeated the motion, slower and more deliberately, dragging the continents around inside the map using the pads of his fingers. "What the?"

"Let me try something," Joey said, reaching in. He placed his thumb and pointer finger near the X and spread them apart slowly. Sure enough, the simple action magnified the view of where they were. It was like a paper version of a digital map. "This is amazing," Joey marveled. "We can pinch and zoom this map like a touchscreen!" He kept going, blowing up the image until the X and Jorako where the only two things they could see.

"At least we don't have to guess how far away we are," Leanora said. "Or which way to go." Like most maps, the Secret Map of the World had a legend with a scale bar for miles and kilometers. Unlike most maps, it had a compass rose that spun around on the page, presumably always pointing north. Shazad approximated the distance to Jorako and estimated the time it would take them to complete the journey on foot. They were a full day's travel away.

"A whole day?" Joey asked, hoping he had heard wrong. "In this heat? It's got to be 120 degrees out here."

"We'll die," Leanora said matter-of-factly. "Dehydration."

"Maybe not," Joey said, wiping sweat from his brow. "We might melt."

Shazad cracked a cynical smile at Joey's gallows humor. "It's funny 'cause it's true," he deadpanned. Joey knew Shazad didn't like this any more than they did. His friend was trapped with no good options. Shazad wasn't supposed to take anyone back to Jorako, but what else could he do? They had no water, no supplies, and no way to call for help. Joey didn't even bother with his cell phone this time.

"At least if we can make it to Jorako, you can get us back to the theater, right?" Leanora asked.

Shazad nodded.

"Then what?" Joey asked.

"Then we have work to do," Leanora replied. "If we do the math on the shrine we saw back in the cottage, I'd say we've got about a week until the protection charms on the Majestic run out."

"One week to get everything out of there," Shazad said.

"Or to get a new charm in place," Leanora countered.

"Like the shield the old lady mentioned?" Joey suggested. "Anyone know what that is? The Caliburn Shield?"

Everyone looked at each other. No one had any idea. "I'll look it up when I get home," Shazad said. "Of course, we have to survive the desert first."

"*Can* we make it to Jorako?" Joey asked, dreading the trip ahead of them.

"I don't think so," Shazad replied. "Not like this." He held up the cape. "We'll have to make a few adjustments."

7

The Road to Jorako

"I can't believe I'm doing this," Joey said.

"Don't say that," Shazad told him. "You have to believe. This doesn't work any other way."

"I don't mean it like that," Joey said. "I believe it'll *work*. That's not the problem."

"What's the problem, then?"

"I don't know." Joey felt ridiculous complaining, but he felt ridiculous going along with the plan, too. "This whole thing, it's just a little . . ."

"Undignified?" Shazad said, zeroing in on his objection.

Joey snapped his fingers. "Exactly." He was grateful that Shazad had said it, because it meant he didn't have to. Deep down he knew he was being childish.

"You don't like this, we can always die in the desert and

end up as food for the vultures. That's what's going to happen if we try this on foot, you know."

"Technically, I'm doing it on foot either way."

"True," Shazad admitted. "But if we do it my way, you'll have four feet." He held up his cape, prepared to transform Joey. "Ready?"

"Do I have to be a *camel*?" Joey complained.

Leanora stifled a laugh. "Don't think of it as being a camel, Joey. Think of it as being a team player."

"That's easy for you to say. You get to be a vulture again. You get to fly."

"If you want to duke it out with the vultures up there, be my guest," Leanora told him. "I'll switch with you."

"No one's switching," Shazad said. "We've been over this already."

"I know." Joey sulked. There wasn't any point in going through it again. He knew the plan made the most sense the way it was. Shazad would change Leanora into a vulture so she could fly to Jorako. He'd transform Joey into a camel and would ride on Joey's back. Shazad didn't want to ask Leanora to carry him across the desert on her back. He thought it was ungentlemanly and felt that he and Joey ought to be more chivalrous. That led to a whole conversation about gender roles, with Leanora asserting that she was perfectly capable of carrying Shazad if she wanted to. Joey asked her if she *did* want to, and she quickly replied that no, she did not. Eager to change the subject, Shazad reminded Joey that Leanora had already established herself with the vultures and would now be able to fly without incident. Joey, on the other hand, wouldn't have to fight for the right to be a camel. Camels were gentle creatures who only ever showed aggression if they were treated badly, and there weren't any other camels around for miles anyway. Using the Cape of Transfiguration would allow Joey and Leanora to cross the desert as animals that were specially adapted to the intense, dry heat, and it would allow Shazad to appear to be alone when they arrived at Jorako. That was important, since no one but his family was allowed to be there. If he was going to sneak them in, this was the best way. Maybe the only way.

"The good news is you'll be the least thirsty out of all of us," Leanora told Joey.

"There is that," Joey said. He took off his backpack, emptied his pockets, and gave everything to Shazad. "You gotta change me back by tonight, okay? I'm supposed to text my parents when I land in California."

"Don't worry," Shazad reassured him. "You'll be yourself again before you know it. I promise."

Joey gave a nod. He was all out of excuses. "All right, let's do it." He stiffened up like a reluctant skydiver getting ready to jump out of a perfectly good airplane. "For the record, I'm doing this under protest."

Shazad threw the cape over Joey's head. "Join the club."

It was an odd sensation being a camel. Joey couldn't talk, but he kept his sense of self and his ability to think as a human, despite the fact that his body wasn't human anymore. The transformation itself was painless. Even better than that, it was instantaneous. One second Joey was himself, and a second later he was a camel. He didn't feel anything except relief. His camel body seemed to deal with the heat much better, which made sense when Joey thought about it. *Maybe this isn't such a bad deal,* he thought.

Shazad pulled the cape off Leanora, changing her into a vulture again. With that accomplished, he asked Joey to sit down so he could climb up on his back. Joey hadn't noticed, but as a camel he towered over Shazad, who was usually a foot taller than he was. Joey made a noise that sounded like Chewbacca complaining about a broken hyperdrive. What he was trying to say was "Give me a second to figure this out." The same way Leanora had to teach herself how to fly, Joey had to teach himself how to sit down. His body was big, unwieldy, and very heavy. If he did it wrong and lost his balance, he'd break a leg at best and crush Shazad underneath him at worst. Joey took it slowly, bending his front legs and dropping to his knees one at a time. Then he folded his front legs underneath his body. After that he did the same with his back legs, tucking them under his butt. *There we go,* Joey thought, proud of his accomplishment. *That wasn't so hard.*

Joey grunted as Shazad got into position on his back, but it wasn't hard carrying him up there, either. When he stood up with Shazad on his hump, he hardly felt any extra weight at all.

They struck off, heading north, in the direction of Jorako. As the journey progressed, Joey found the benefits of being a camel went beyond a strong back. He also had surer feet, perfect for walking on soft sand. For some reason, Joey had always thought of camels as having hooves. Instead, he had large two-toed feet with thick, callused pads that kept him from getting burned by the searing desert sands. If Joey had been in human form, the sand would have surely been murder on his bare feet. As he walked, it occurred to him that his transformation into a camel had done away with his shoes. All his clothes, in fact, were gone. He thought about Leanora's metamorphosis and realized it had been the same with her. Everything, including the magical pendants she wore, had vanished when she changed, and returned when she changed back. Joey wondered if Shazad's cape made for such a seamless transition naturally, or if the elegance of the transformation was due to his mastery of the artifact. Either way, Joey was thankful that he wouldn't be naked when he changed back.

They walked for hours through the desert, completely alone. It was an incredible experience. Joey found the stark, barren environment undeniably beautiful. A sea of dunes rose and fell before him like waves, their golden contours perfectly smooth, touched only by the wind. Oddly, the scorched landscape made Joey think of winter scenes—rolling hills hidden beneath a pristine blanket of snow without a single footprint in sight. Growing up in Hoboken, Joey had never seen an unblemished, snowy countryside except in Christmas cards, and he'd never seen anything like the Sahara except in movies. Now he was not only seeing it in person, but he was seeing it as something other than a person. It was a unique perspective, to say the least. Had Joey been himself, his thoughts might have been plagued by fear that he and his friends would not survive the journey, but instead he was at peace. Despite the long trek, he was not exhausted, and he was not thirsty, either. Joey remembered learning that a camel can lose up to 35 percent of the water in its body and still be just fine. Joey expected Leanora was doing fine also. She alternated between flying ahead and coming back to rest on Joey's hump. He felt her weight up there even less than he did Shazad's. Joey couldn't see Shazad and hoped he was holding up all right under the heat. He realized now that by staying human, Shazad had given himself the most difficult post. He was the one taking a hit for the team, not Joey. Thinking about it made Joey feel foolish for making a fuss about being turned into a camel. He tried to say so, but it came out as more Wookiee-speak.

"We'll be there soon," Shazad replied, patting his back. "We're close."

Joey grunted out a camel laugh. Shazad had apparently thought he was asking something along the lines of "Are we there yet?" His apology had been lost in translation. Joey made a mental note to thank Shazad later and tell him he didn't mind walking. It was a good thing he didn't mind, too, because it turned out they weren't close to Jorako. Not at all. Many more hours passed as they marched in silence. Soon the sun was going down, a sharp yellow cutout in a bright orange sky. Joey was mesmerized by the beauty of the sunset. He stared at it, unblinking, until something even more breathtaking caught his eye. An oasis emerged far off in the distance where the sun's glare met the horizon. It was a large enclosure of tall palm trees and lush greenery that stood in stark contrast to the water-starved landscape that surrounded it. The tantalizing vision wavered in the heat that even at day's end rose up off the sand in waves. And then, as quickly as the vision appeared, it was gone.

Joey blinked hard. If he could have rubbed his eyes, he would have, but camels weren't built that way. At first Joey wondered if the walk was finally getting to him. He wasn't thirsty, but he *was* hungry. At that point he had to admit he was a little bit tired, too, but that didn't mean he was seeing things. Joey stared hard at the space where the oasis had been, albeit briefly. His eyes grew weary, his vision blurred, and there it was again: a green, leafy paradise growing up out of the sand. It was like something out of a dream, and much like a dream, it dissolved before Joey could focus on it, disappearing once again. He grunted in confusion and stopped to look around. What was he dealing with here? A mirage?

He felt a strong urge to strike off in another direction and find the oasis again, but as he began to turn, Shazad leaned forward, pointing straight ahead.

"No, Joey," he said. "This way. It's there. Trust me."

Joey gave a skeptical grunt, but he stayed the course and did as he was told. It was a struggle. He trusted that Shazad knew what he was talking about—especially when it came to finding Jorako—but he couldn't help feeling he was going the wrong way. There was nothing in front of him. Nothing but sand.

Leanora swung around overhead, cawing at Joey and Shazad. She swooped down, getting right in their faces. She was flapping her wings and squawking, getting very animated. Clearly she thought they were on the wrong track too. Joey felt vindicated, but Shazad seemed to feel the same way.

"Good. You saw it too," he said. "Stay close. Stay with me." Shazad held out his forearm to Leanora. She unleashed a high-pitched, fiery retort, going as far as to fly into his extended arm, pushing it away. "Leanora, I can't understand you, but I know you can understand me." Shazad's voice was calm and even. "I know what I'm doing. Stay with me and Joey. We'll get there together. You'll see."

Leanora thought it over a few more seconds, but ultimately relented and landed on Shazad's arm. "Ah, your talons are sharp," Joey heard Shazad say. "I'm going to set you down here if it's all right with everybody." Joey felt Shazad's weight shift as he twisted around to deposit Leanora behind him. Joey felt Leanora's talons transfer onto his back, but as before, it didn't bother his camel hide. "There we are," Shazad said. "Joey, just keep moving forward. Trust that what you saw was real and that it hasn't moved. It's still in the same place you first saw it."

Joey grunted in the affirmative and carried his friends on toward the setting sun. He wanted to ask if the oasis was Jorako and when he'd be able to see it again, but he wasn't capable of speech. He made the most inquisitive noise he was capable of and hoped Shazad would understand. Fortunately, Shazad took the hint and explained everything.

"Remember the magic DeMayne and Scarlett used to clear the streets before our fight outside the Majestic? We have something similar in Jorako. Powerful magic objects that ward off anyone who approaches. You can't see Jorako from the outside. You can glimpse it for only a fraction of a second at a time, but you have to be looking right at it, and even then, it's there for you only if you believe it's there. You can't reach Jorako unless you believe in it, and that's not easy to do. The closer we get, the more magical protections come into play. Soon you'll both forget what we're even doing out here. You'll feel the urge to wander off, going back the way we came. Resist that impulse. It won't be long now."

As they closed in on their hidden destination, Joey's thoughts bore out the truth of Shazad's words. He was gripped by a strong desire to seek out the oasis elsewhere, anywhere besides the path to nowhere he was currently following. Lost and confused, he began to wonder what twist of fate had deposited him in the desert and turned him into a camel in the first place. He wasn't supposed to be there.

He was supposed to be in seat 14B, flying to California with Janelle. Over and over, he tried to turn around. Shazad urged him on each time, and called Leanora back. Several times Shazad was forced to remind his friends where they were going and why they were there. His reassurances helped redirect Joey and the disoriented feeling soon passed, but Joey did not see Jorako again. However, he did see a puff of sand kick up on the horizon as a rider materialized in the distance.

Joey took someone coming out to greet them as a good sign, but Shazad's reaction told him otherwise. "Wonderful," he said, clearly meaning the opposite. "I should have known we couldn't just slip in quietly. I'm late, and I never come back this way."

Leanora screeched out a question.

"It's my brother, Ali," Shazad replied, assuming she had asked him who was out there. He patted Joey's side. "It's a good thing I didn't make you a horse. You wouldn't fool his mount for a second. Night Wind can be . . . difficult," he said, searching for the right word. "Ali can be a handful too sometimes—not that he means to be." Shazad threw in the bit about Ali as an afterthought. Joey barely heard him say it. He was more concerned with Ali's horse. Joey thought about how Leanora had to fight off the vultures and worried that he wouldn't fare half as well against a horse's thundering hooves. Shazad seemed to sense his trepidation. "Don't worry. Horses are proud creatures by nature. Night Wind isn't going to strike up a conversation with you. You're a camel. Just keep your distance as best you can and try to act oblivious to what's going on. I doubt he'll pay you any mind. You, on the other hand," he added to Leanora. "A vulture will be harder to explain. You'll have to fly from here. Don't worry if you can't see Jorako. Just follow me all the way in. Your mental protection charm should help you stay on course. Wait with Joey while I deal with my family. I'll change you both back as soon as I can." Leanora squawked a short chirp, signaling that she understood. Shazad's brother was almost upon them. "Off you go, before he gets here." She spread her wings and flew away.

Less than a minute later, Shazad's brother arrived in a cloud of sand and dust. "Shazad, what are you doing out here? Are you all right? What's going on?" Ali's voice was higher than Shazad's. Joey put his age at somewhere around ten years old.

"It's fine, Ali. Everything's fine." Shazad addressed his younger brother with an air of weariness. "I'm just coming home at the end of a very long day."

"Yes, but why are you riding a camel? Why didn't you use—"

"I need water," Shazad interrupted, cutting his brother off before he revealed how he normally traveled to and from Jorako. "Have you got any with you?"

"Water? Oh, right," Ali said, momentarily embarrassed that he had not offered his brother anything.

"I haven't had anything to drink all day," Shazad rasped.

"I didn't realize you didn't have anything with you." Ali held up an empty flask the size of a thermos. He shook it, and the flask filled itself with crystal-clear water. Shazad took the water and chugged it down in one gulp. He repeated Ali's motion, filling the flask and drinking the water again. Ali took stock of his brother as he drank. "What's in the bag?" he asked, eyeing his backpack.

"Not water," Shazad replied, avoiding the question.

Ali's face lit up as he drew his own conclusions. "Don't tell me you're finally bringing back some of Redondo's things. . . ." He gave his brother a congratulatory clap on the

His thoughts were interrupted when Jorako revealed itself
him at last. The long walk, seemingly toward nothing,
ded abruptly. Joey had put one foot down on coarse sand,
d the next footstep landed on a thick, soft bed of grass.
ey's mouth fell open as the oasis materialized around him,
ming with life. It was the size of a football stadium, lined
th a forest of fifty-foot palm trees. Inside the dense ring
trees was a fertile garden, filled with short, stocky palms,
bust shrubberies, and bright pink and white flowers. A
t of color bloomed throughout the oasis, all of it per-
tly placed around a wide lake with a bubbling spring. It
ked like paradise, but the stunning natural beauty of the
ounds was nothing compared to the awe-inspiring sight of
azad's home.

Joey had assumed Jorako would be grandiose, and it was,
t not in the way he had expected. He had envisioned
mething out of *1,001 Arabian Nights*: a magnificent palace,
mplete with pillars, arches, and domes. Surprisingly, the
namental details that exemplified classic Islamic architec-
re were nowhere to be found. There were no jewel-like,
corative tiles. No intricate, kaleidoscopic mosaics or pat-
rned brickwork. The massive structure at the heart of the

back. "That's fantastic! Father's going to be thrilled. Did you
have to sneak them out of the theater? Is that why you're out
here like this? What have you got?"

"Nothing," Shazad said, appalled. "I didn't sneak anything out. I wouldn't do that. Stop being so nosy."

Ali was visibly let down by his brother's reply. "Still nothing? Father's not going to like that."

"I know. I'm working on it."

"What's taking so long? You should hear him every day
after you leave." Ali lowered his voice, imitating their father:
"It's been a month! When are Shazad's friends going to listen to reason? It's bad enough one of them lost Houdini's
wand. He's going to lose the rest if he drags this out any
longer."

Joey grunted and spit on the sand near the feet of Ali's
horse. He didn't mean to do it. Houdini's wand was a sore
subject with Joey and camels were known to spit. It was just
something they did. Night Wind snorted and stamped in
place, very much offended.

"That's enough," Shazad said, speaking to Night Wind,
Joey, and his brother all at once. His words fell on deaf ears.
Joey backed away from Night Wind, but the muscular, feisty

stallion followed after him, leaning into his space as Ali continued to update Shazad on their father's current mood: "I'm just saying he's running out of patience, is all."

Shazad let out a mirthless laugh. "Tell me something I don't know."

"He told me today he should have sent me to win the wand."

"He didn't say that," Shazad replied, sounding wounded. "Did he?" The question came a beat later, with less confidence than Joey was used to hearing in Shazad's voice.

Ali shrugged sympathetically. "It's not fair, I know. It's not your fault your friend threw away Houdini's wand. That was his stupidity, not yours."

Joey blurted out an indignant cry, trying in vain to defend himself. Ali wasn't being fair. He wasn't stupid. He was inexperienced! "Who's to say you wouldn't have done the same thing in my place?" Joey asked in an unintelligible, gargling groan.

Night Wind reared up, affronted that Joey had the gall to insert himself into the conversation a second time. He whinnied to Ali as if to say, *Are you hearing this?*

Ali got Night Wind under control, but he frowned

at Joey. "My horse doesn't seem to like much."

"No, he doesn't." Shazad gave Joey a ligh telling him to zip it. "We'd better separate as well ride ahead and tell Father I'm con handed. Again." He gave back the empty fl for the water. I'll see you at home."

Ali gave a nod and took up Night Wind ted Shazad on the shoulder and departed Shazad said nothing. He just watched his br after that, Leanora returned, but the remain ney passed in silence. Joey kept his head do He felt foolish for nearly provoking a con Ali's horse. He also felt bad that the wand the theater had become a source of friction his father. That was one benefit of not comi cal family. Joey didn't have any pressure fror bring home magical items. He would, howe explaining to do if he didn't get to Califor of the day. Joey did some quick math in his about the time zones and how long he had l was supposed to land in Los Angeles.

152

153

oasis was a futuristic fortress that was so at odds with its environment, it might as well have been an alien spaceship.

Joey could hardly believe his eyes. The giant building stood over the lake, crafted from thousands of crystalline cubes. They came in many different sizes, some of them as big as a house. They were stacked on top of each other like Lego bricks, packed tight in a complex, dazzling arrangement. Glass cubes jutted out on every surface, rising and falling in squared-off peaks like a geometric mountain range. As the sun disappeared over the horizon, individual cubes lit up, illuminating the building with a scattered checkerboard of golden-yellow and soft-white lights. It was a stunning display of beauty, completely unique. The more Joey looked at it, the more he realized the geometric precision of the permutated cubes and the unspoiled flora and fauna of the oasis didn't clash at all. The juxtaposition of the two styles was what made it special. Jorako was a wonder unlike anything Joey had ever seen before, and that was saying something.

Leanora took to the sky and flew a short lap around the immediate area, making a fuss the whole way. Joey let out a bewildered cry that sounded like a hound dog trying to sing opera.

"Easy, you two," Shazad said quietly. "You're supposed to be simple animals, remember? This shouldn't be that exciting for you."

Joey and Leanora quieted down and tried to play it cool as Shazad dismounted and walked them in. Dozens of people greeted Shazad on his way in, speaking in what Joey assumed was a Jorakan dialect. He couldn't understand the words, but their meaning was clear enough. Everyone was glad to see Shazad. He was well known and well liked. Joey wondered if everyone there was part of his family. They passed through a small outdoor market and walked down a pleasant garden path toward the lake. Families were finishing up picnics on the grass and stepping into midair portals that appeared to lead to different corners of the oasis. Joey tried not to stare, either at the magical doorways scattered through the area or at the giant crystal fortress that was Shazad's home. The entrance was out over the lake. An irregular staircase made up of the same glass cubes as the rest of the building zigzagged its way from the front door down to the water's edge. As they approached, Joey could see silhouettes of people milling about inside the building. Jorako was already big enough to fit half his neighborhood back in Hoboken, and he had a feeling its borders stretched beyond what he could see. Up ahead, the road split, with one path continuing on toward the lake and the other leading off in the direction of the house. Crystal lanterns lit an empty lane that led to the base of the staircase.

"I can't bring you in," Shazad said once they got there. "I'm sorry. I have to go find my parents first. They'll be expecting me inside. We need to act like everything is normal. Just keep your heads down and rest here by the water. I'll try not to be too long." Joey tried to reply, but Shazad shushed him, pressing a finger to his lips and reminding him to stay in character. He promised to return as soon as he could, and went up the steps to the house alone.

Once he was gone, Joey and Leanora looked at each other and tried their best to communicate in animal form. Leanora gave a kind of *what now?* shrug with her wings. Joey grunted in reply as if to say, *I guess we wait.* He looked at the lake and suddenly felt thirsty. The next thing he knew he had his face in the water and was drinking enough to last him for a week. Fully quenched, he found a comfortable place to sit down and lowered himself to the ground. He was an expert on that now. Joey wanted to explore the oasis, but he was too tired. Also, he spotted Night Wind close by and didn't trust himself not to do anything that would arouse suspicion. He had messed up enough already. The best thing he could do was follow Shazad's advice and get some rest.

When Joey woke up he was human again. Shazad was standing over him, having just pulled the cape off Joey's body like a blanket. Joey rolled over on his back and looked up at the night sky. The stars were out and shining bright. He sat up with a jolt. "What time is it? How long was I asleep?"

"A while," Leanora said, putting out a hand to help him up. She had been changed back as well. "It's late."

Joey got up and dusted himself off. He ran his tongue around his mouth, making a sour face. "My mouth tastes like pond water. Yuck."

"This should help with that." Shazad held up a small basket filled with thick pieces of pita bread, cookies topped with almonds, and honey-glazed golden nuggets. "Eat something. You must be hungry."

Joey dug in, going straight for the sweets. "Shazad, you're a lifesaver."

"Don't just eat the ghorayebah and zalabya," Shazad told Joey as he stuffed his face. "The aish baladi's fresh."

Joey paused. "Which is which?" he asked with his mouth full.

Shazad gave Joey and Leanora a quick rundown of the food he had smuggled out of the house. The butter cookies that had practically melted in Joey's mouth were ghorayebah, and the sticky treats that reminded him of doughnut holes were zalabya. Shazad took special pride in the bread, or aish baladi. It had just come out of the oven and warmed Joey's insides. "This might be the best bread I've ever had. Either that, or I'm starving. Or both."

"It should go with hummus or something to dip it in, but we have to eat and run, so I just grabbed something quick. This was the best I could do on short notice. Here, in case you're thirsty," Shazad added, producing a jug of water to go with the food. "Sorry it took me so long to get back here."

"Forget it," Joey said, taking a big swig of water to wash down the food. "It felt like five minutes to me. I passed out quick."

Leanora nodded in agreement and helped herself to more

cookies. "I figured you'd have to wait for your parents to fall asleep before you could come find us."

"Wait a minute . . . parents." Joey checked his pockets for his phone. "It must be the middle of the night," he said with his mouth full. "I'm supposed to call my parents."

"Don't worry." Shazad held up Joey's phone, displaying the text screen. "I took care of that. They kept trying to reach you, so I texted them back."

"I get reception out here?" Joey asked, astonished. He took the phone and read the message Shazad had sent his parents:

Hey guys—sorry I'm checking in so late. Flight got delayed, but we made it (eventually). Supertired though . . . gonna crash now. Talk more tomorrow?

Joey blinked at the screen. "That actually sounds like me," he said, impressed. He scrolled down and saw that his father had replied, writing that he was glad Joey had made it to California in one piece and told him to get some rest. Joey's mom seconded that but added that she expected an actual phone call from him in the morning. Replying as Joey, Shazad had sent back a sleeping emoji, effectively ending the conversation.

"Not bad," Joey said. He powered down the phone to preserve its battery and put it in his pocket.

"I read through the text history with your parents to get the right tone," Shazad explained. "Hope you don't mind."

"Not at all. You nailed it. Thanks again."

"How did it go with your parents?" Leanora asked Shazad.

Shazad grimaced. "About as well as it's been going for the last month, which is to say, not great. I don't have to tell you my parents aren't big fans of us keeping the magic items we have in the theater all this time. I didn't tell them I lost the Staff of Sorcero, either," he added, upset with himself. "Do me a favor and don't mention that when the time comes that you finally meet them."

"What's the Staff of Sorcero?" Joey asked, playing along.

"Never heard of it," Leanora said, doing the same.

The staff was a major loss, but no one could fault Shazad for not being able to save it. After all, he had saved them and the map, too, which was now rolled up in a tube-shaped container on his shoulder. "Don't worry. I'll take better care of this," Shazad said, tapping the map.

"Did you get a chance to research the shield?" Joey asked.

"I'll come back and do it after we get out of here," said

Shazad. "You're not supposed to be in Jorako, either one of you. If my parents found out about this . . ." He paused, thinking about what would happen if he got caught sneaking his friends into the oasis. "Let's just say it wouldn't go over well. I only brought you in because we can all go home from here. We should do that. Now."

"Absolutely," Leanora said, ready to go. "Lead the way. Let's leave before you get in trouble with your family."

"Before *we* get in trouble with my family," Shazad corrected.

Just then there was rustling in the bushes nearby. Joey had a sinking feeling they were being watched. He nodded in the direction the noise had come from and asked, "What if we're already in trouble?"

Joey, Shazad, and Leanora all turned to look at the bushes. Ali stood up behind them. Everyone gasped, but Ali appeared to be more shocked than anyone else. "Shazad?" he asked in a brittle voice, stepping out into the open. He looked crushed. Betrayed. "What is this? Who . . . ? What are they doing here?"

"We were just leaving," Joey said quickly.

Shazad put a hand up, hissing at Joey to let him deal with this. Chastened, Joey buttoned his lips. Shazad's eyes were locked on his brother. "This isn't what it looks like," he told Ali. His voice was calm and reassuring, but his words rang hollow. They didn't line up with the reality of the situation.

Ali was clearly stunned by his brother's actions. "It looks like you snuck your friends into Jorako."

Shazad's shoulders slumped. "Okay, it's exactly what it looks like, but it's not what you think. You don't know what we've been through today. I'll tell you everything, but first I have to ask you, please . . . don't tell Dad about this."

"I'm sorry, Shazad. I can't help you."

"What do you mean? Why not?"

Ali held up an orange-colored jewel. It was the size of a silver dollar and glowed brightly in the night. Joey saw an eye staring out from its largest facet.

"It's not Dad you have to worry about. It's Mom, and she already knows."

8

Family Meeting

"I didn't mean to get you in trouble," Ali told Shazad. "I didn't *want* to spy on you. It wasn't my idea!"

Shazad trudged up the steps to the cubist, crystal-rock palace, ignoring his brother's pleading voice. He didn't look angry. He looked beaten, like a criminal who had just been arrested and was on his way to the big house. Joey, Leanora, and Ali followed after him, trailing a few steps behind.

"It wasn't my idea," Ali said again, this time to Joey and Leanora. He was looking for absolution anywhere he could find it. "Our mother thought Shazad was acting strange," he explained. "She told me to find out if there was anything going on out here she should know about. What was I supposed to do? I didn't have a choice."

"It's not your fault, Ali," Leanora sympathized, walking beside him. "We're the ones who broke the rules, not you."

"What was he thinking, sneaking you in like this? Why'd you come here?"

"We didn't plan it," Leanora said. "We didn't have a choice, either."

Ali gave Leanora a weak smile, full of pity. Joey got the feeling they'd have to come up with a better explanation than that, and soon. "Which one of you was the camel?" Ali asked as they climbed the staircase.

Joey gave a little wave. "That was me." He figured he might as well come clean. "Not very convincing, I take it?"

Ali gave a shrug. "I did get the feeling you were listening in on our conversation."

Joey nodded. "It was hard not to."

"Because I was wearing this." Ali held up his hand, which was marked with an intricate symbol. "The Lingua Franca. It's a universal translator that works perfectly for people, and it works pretty well on animals. My parents wouldn't let me ride Night Wind without it. I use it to get him to listen better. You seemed to understand us a little too well. That was suspect. Other than that, you looked the part—except for the paint," he added, surprising Joey.

"The paint?" Joey looked at his fingers, which still carried traces of white from the cottage door. "What paint, this?"

Ali squinted at Joey's fingertips. "I don't think so. It didn't look like that. It was more colorful, and it wasn't on your hands—or your feet. It was splattered all over the side of your neck."

"What?" Joey tugged at his collar, checking his neck for paint. He turned toward Leanora, asking her with his eyes if she saw anything. She told him there was nothing there.

"That was the strange part," Ali said. "One second it was there, and the next, it was gone. If you saw that, you'd wonder what was going on too."

Joey massaged his shoulder, wondering the same thing. The spot where Scarlett had tagged him was still tender a month later. Joey had seen splotches of paint come and go around his neck, just as Ali had described, but he had always told himself the paint splatter and the soreness in his shoulder was all in his head. If Ali had seen it on him when he was a camel . . . Joey didn't know what that meant, but he didn't like it.

Shazad stopped at the top of the staircase and turned around. "Where's Mom right now?" he asked Ali. "Check the Tiger's Eye."

Ali peered into the large orange gemstone. "She's in the library."

"How does she look? Let me see." Ali handed Shazad the jewel. He held it up to his own eye. What he saw there did nothing to lift his spirits. "She's going to kill me."

"She's not going to *kill* you," Leanora said. "Is she?"

Shazad said nothing.

Leanora turned to Ali, who shook his head with a somber look. "No one's ever messed up this bad before. Not ever."

"Is there anything we can do?" Joey asked.

"You can say as little as possible," Shazad said. "Let me do the talking. I'm in enough trouble already. Let's not make it any worse." Joey and Leanora agreed to follow Shazad's lead and wished him luck with his mom. They all went inside together.

Joey was blown away by the interior of Shazad's home. The entryway led into a vast, open-air courtyard with a small pool in the center and a giant moving sculpture floating above it. The sculpture was a formation of crystal cubes, seemingly identical to the ones that made up the rest of the building, except they were in constant motion. Hovering in midair, they unfolded continuously from a central point like fireworks exploding over and over again. They didn't pause to form any recognizable shape, but rather kept revolving in a random, hypnotic, and fluid movement. Joey managed to pry his eyes away from the sculpture long enough to take in the rest of the expansive space. It was filled with comfortable furniture, potted plants, and even trees that rose out of the floor to help shade the courtyard during the day. The interior walls of the house towered over the group, lined with windows and railed walkways, but no one was looking down at them. All was quiet and still. Every surface was gray and bluish white, and smooth and flat as a sheet of ice. On the floors, a row of glowing crystal cubes ran out from the pool and the floating sculpture, lighting the way to covered passageways on the left and right and more stairs up ahead.

Joey whistled low. "And I thought this place was impressive on the outside."

"Did your family build all this?" Leanora asked Shazad, looking around, clearly impressed.

"We grew it," Shazad replied. "Everything you see here

started out with a crystal seed no larger than a sugar cube. My ancestors planted it here a thousand years ago. As our family got bigger, so did our home."

"How many people live here?" Joey asked.

"It depends on how you look at it," Shazad replied. "Jorako is more than one oasis. There's a whole network of them placed throughout the desert. Ours is just the main hub."

Joey thought about the people he saw disappearing into portals earlier that evening, which made more sense now. The idea that there were more hidden, magical places like this in the world blew him away. As they made their way up the steps onto a wide concourse, Shazad explained the number of people living in his house varied but that at any given time there could be up to a hundred members of his family there.

"It's so quiet." Joey heard only his sneakers squeaking as they walked down the dark, empty hallway. "Where is everybody?"

"It's a big house," Ali reminded him. "Also, it *is* the middle of the night."

"Good point," Joey said, lowering his voice.

"Some people are sleeping, but luckily, most of the family

isn't here right now," Shazad whispered. "We have people all over the world, all the time."

"Doing what?" Leonora asked. "They're not working as magicians."

"No," Shazad confirmed. "Most of them are historians. Researching lost civilizations is a good way to find magical artifacts. That's what we do here." Shazad gestured to a gallery outside the library, which was just up ahead. "Have a look."

Joey and Leonora approached the items on display in silent reverence. Even the spectacle of Shazad's home had not prepared them for this. It was like a museum exhibit filled with magical objects, all of them much older than anything Redondo had left behind. They were not the kind of things Redondo would have used onstage to hide magic in plain sight. They were more like pieces of history. Joey saw a Greek soldier's helmet labeled the HELM OF DARKNESS. He recognized the name. Joey remembered reading about it in a myth about the Greek hero Perseus. Wearing the helmet had rendered Perseus invisible so he could escape Medusa's sisters after slaying her. If the helmet was real, did that mean the story was true? He examined everything with endless fascination, finding more relics of Greek, Norse, Celtic, and Egyptian mythology. Despite everything Joey knew about magic, these were things he had never believed in. He had certainly never expected to see them in person. "Shazad, are these things for real?"

"Of course they are," Shazad said. "We wouldn't keep them here otherwise."

Joey wandered around the room, rattling off an impossible inventory: "A magic carpet, Aladdin's lamp, the Hand of Midas . . ."

"You don't want to touch that," advised Ali.

Joey nodded and kept going, reading as he went. "Freyja's cloak . . . wasn't Freyja Thor's mother? You don't have Mjolnir on a shelf somewhere, do you? Mjolnir was Thor's hammer," Joey added to Leanora. She gave him a look that made it clear she didn't need to be told. "These things . . . they're are all from ancient myths and legends," Joey said in wonder.

"Not myths," Shazad said. "Just old stories. People used to think they were gifts from 'the Gods,' but really, they were just magic."

"*Just* magic, right," said Joey ironically.

"How did you get all these?" Leanora asked.

"My family found them. We saved them. Brought them here."

"This is incredible," Joey said, marveling at the collection. "You're like magic archaeologists."

"Shouldn't these things be locked up in a vault somewhere?" Leanora asked.

"We don't need to lock it up," Ali replied. "Only our family is allowed here. If you can't trust your family, who can you trust?"

"I was about to ask your brother the same thing."

The voice came from a woman at the edge of the gallery. It was Shazad's mother. She was dressed in her nightclothes: a robe, silk pajamas, and slippers. She had one hand firmly planted on her hip and a steaming teacup in the other. When Joey saw the look on her face, he froze as if petrified by a spell. He knew that look. Every kid in the world knew that look. Mothers everywhere had a natural ability to deliver a lecture with their eyes, and Shazad's mom was no exception. The stony expression on her face asked a hundred questions, chief among them, "Do you have any idea how much trouble you're in?" Shazad appeared to turn green as his mother glared at him.

"Hi, Mom," he said, sounding dejected.

That comment earned Shazad another pointed look. His mother tilted her head to the side and crooked an eyebrow in a way that said, "Don't 'Hi, Mom' me." She pointed over her shoulder into the library. "Inside. Now. And keep your voice down."

A few minutes later Shazad and his mother were seated in the library. Joey and Leanora hung back at the doorway with Ali. Shazad's mother had held up a hand signaling for them to stay put while she dealt with her eldest son in private. It was a conversation Joey was happy to stay out of. As he waited by the door, Joey took stock of the library. The room had the same glass walls and flooring as everything else he had seen in Jorako, but the library was special. Nearly every flat surface, including the ceiling, had built-in shelves packed tight with books. Joey looked up and saw a sea of titles defying gravity above him, waiting to be taken down and read. Modern bestsellers and historical texts were up there, side by side with ancient tomes that Joey could only assume were lost books of magic, fables, and folklore. Joey would have liked to leaf through a few of them and learn their secrets, but he knew better than that. He wasn't going to touch the books. They were in enough trouble already.

Shazad and his mother were seated across from each other in a quiet reading area. At the moment it was very quiet. Shazad's mother had yet to say anything to him. Joey figured she was too angry to speak. She was looking at her son the same way Joey's own mother had looked at him back when he was seven years old and had drawn on the carpet with a Sharpie. Shazad stared at his shoes, waiting for his lecture and punishment. It was an awkward thing to witness, even from a distance.

"What have you done?" Shazad's mother asked at last. She spoke in a harsh whisper, but her voice carried across the quiet library just the same. Joey was grateful she wasn't screaming, but he had a feeling that for Shazad, the cutting disappointment in his mother's voice was worse than being yelled at.

Shazad looked up. "I can explain."

"Can you?" His mother pounced, sounding intrigued. "Oh, good. That makes me feel better. I'm glad you have an 'explanation' for breaking the single most important rule we have in our family. This place is a refuge for magic, Shazad.

That's a sacred responsibility. No one comes here without permission. *No one.* You know that."

Shazad slumped, his eyes turning back toward the floor. "I know that."

"Even the best security measures are only as good as the people who enforce them. Our vigilance protects us from the Invisible Hand. If they could find us, they would come for us. They'd try to take everything we have—everything we've worked so hard to save." Shazad's mother waved at the gallery outside the library. "In the long history of Jorako, no one has ever snuck anyone in like this, and the first one to do it is my son?" She turned away. "No! You're no son of mine."

Ouch, Joey thought.

The words were like a sharp pencil poking Shazad in the ribs. "Are you going to tell Dad about this?" he asked in a tiny voice.

"Your father and I don't keep secrets from each other," his mother replied matter-of-factly. "Is there any reason he shouldn't know? Any reason the entire family shouldn't know? Other than my own everlasting embarrassment, that is."

"I didn't mean to come here," Shazad said. "It wasn't my intention. Everything just happened so fast."

"You told your father you hiked through the desert for hours this afternoon. You had all day to think about what you were doing."

"That was after we'd already landed here. After that, I didn't know what else to do."

Shazad's mother narrowed her eyes and drank the last of her tea. She set the cup down on a side table next to her chair. "I'm not sure I understand, but I can't wait to hear what led you to believe that violating the security of our home was your only option." Shazad opened his mouth to explain, but his mother shushed him, pushing a sharp burst of air through her teeth. She glanced at Joey and Leanora by the doorway and sighed. "First things first. We don't often entertain guests at this hour, but that doesn't mean we forget our manners. I'm not sure if people who smuggle themselves into our home posing as animals *count* as guests, but regardless of invitation, I am their host. Did you offer your friends *shai*?"

"No," Shazad reluctantly admitted. His mother seemed oddly stunned by this apparent breach of etiquette.

"He gave us ghorayebah and zalabya," Joey called out from the door.

Shazad's mother closed her eyes and pinched the bridge of her nose. "What kind of a Hassan are you, Shazad?"

Shazad moved his hand back and forth in a cut-off motion beneath his chin, telling Joey to stop helping.

"*Shai* is tea," Ali said, translating for Joey.

"Sometimes known as 'duty,'" his mother said, getting up. "As in the bare minimum a host is obligated to offer visitors." She crossed the room toward an ornate tea set that was laid out on a nearby tray. "Come in. Sit," she said with a grudging edge in her voice, even as she poured tea for Joey and Leanora. "However you came to this oasis . . . whatever your negative influence on my son, you are in my home. And the most basic rules of hospitality will not be ignored in this place." She turned around a moment later, holding a hot cup of tea in each hand. "Speaking of which . . . Shazad, are you planning to introduce me to your friends at some point?"

Shazad grimaced and looked at Joey and Leanora. "Guys, this is my mother, Kamilah Hassan." Turning back to his mother, he gestured to Leanora. "Mom, this is—"

"Leanora Valkov," his mother cut in. "Of the Nomadik traveling clan of magicians."

"Formerly of Freedonya," Leanora added as Shazad's mother handed her a teacup. "Thank you."

Shazad's mother nodded. "I'm familiar with the story of Freedonya, and your family. I believe your people are somewhere in England right now?"

Leanora blinked, thrown by the fact that Shazad's mother was privy to such information. "Yes, that's . . . that's right," she stammered.

Shazad's mother had a knowing smile. "We like to keep tabs on the world's remaining free magic when and where we can. Although I often wonder how much longer the Nomadiks will qualify, going around putting on shows . . . drawing attention to themselves."

"No one's caught us yet," Leanora said, taking a seat next to Shazad.

"No, not yet," Shazad's mother agreed. "Does your family know you are here?"

"I didn't even know I'd be here until this morning," Leanora replied.

Shazad's mother made a face, accepting the answer as

satisfactory. "Your people knew where to find us long ago, but they haven't come back. The Nomadiks know how to keep a secret. I'm not worried about you." Shazad's mother shifted her focus to Joey. "You, on the other hand . . . ," she began, handing him his tea.

"This is Joey," Shazad said.

"Joey Kopecky." Shazad's mother said Joey's name in a "we meet at last" kind of way.

Joey raised his teacup, as if toasting Shazad's mother. "It's nice to meet you." He was nervous and the words came out sounding more like a question. "I've heard a lot about you," he added, trying to recover.

"I've heard about you, too. You're the one who doesn't want to let us keep the Majestic Theatre's relics here in Jorako."

Joey took a seat, not knowing how to respond. He didn't want to say anything else to escalate the situation. It was bad enough without any help from him. The way Shazad's mom was looking at Joey made him wish he had an invisibility cloak. He'd nearly opened up his backpack to give her the Finale Mask as a peace offering, when Leanora spoke up in his defense.

"It's not just Joey," she said. "We all have to agree."

"So I'm told," his mother replied. "You all think it's not enough to just save these items. We have to do something with them as well. Remind me, how did that work out with Houdini's wand?" A quick sideways glance at Shazad admonished him for not being the one to win the wand from Redondo, but Shazad's mother saved her true contempt for what Joey had done with the wand in her son's place. "You're the one who lost the wand, aren't you? The greatest and most powerful known magical artifact, lost because of your lack of imagination. And yet you think you know better what to do with magical items than people who have researched, uncovered, and protected them for hundreds of years. Why are you here? Did you come to test our magic? To see if Jorako is worthy of safeguarding the relics Redondo left you?" She looked pointedly at Shazad. "You let your friends talk you into this?"

"No one talked me into anything," Shazad said.

"What *did* happen, then? What's this about?"

Joey's heart went out to Shazad as he watched him wilt under his mother's stern gaze. "It's hard to explain," he said.

"Actually, it's not," Leanora cut in. "It's just a long story."

"Lea, let me—"

"The short version is, it was this place or death," Leanora said, cutting across Shazad. "Those were our two options. We're here because Shazad saved our lives."

That got Shazad's mother's attention. Joey actually thought he saw a touch of pride creep into her face, softening her expression slightly. She leaned back in her chair and tented her fingers. "Go on."

With momentum on her side, Leanora jumped into the story before anyone else could say anything. She started with the noise they had heard in the theater. The singing that had led them to the cottage and the mysterious woman who had aged decades during their conversation. She told Shazad's mom about the three questions they had been limited to, how the woman was protecting the theater, and the way she had walked out on them, casually abandoning them in the Himalayas. Joey chimed in, explaining that they'd nearly passed out from oxygen deprivation and frozen to death, but Shazad carried them to safety. No one said anything about the Staff of Sorcero.

"When we ended up in the desert, he saved us again by taking us here," Leanora said. "He wasn't happy about it, but he did it. We didn't want to intrude. We just didn't see any other way."

Through it all, Shazad's mother listened with rapt attention. "Is this true?" she asked her son when the story was over.

"We save things in our family," Shazad said. "I couldn't just save myself. What else could I do?"

His mother looked at him. "You could have told me the truth. It's a good explanation, but it's not an excuse for sneaking around. Lying to your brother. Lying to your father. Lying to *me*. You know better than that."

"I do know, and I'm sorry. It's just . . . you and Dad were so upset about how things went with the wand. And you told me Joey and Lea couldn't come here unless it was to bring the magical artifacts from the theater. I didn't want to show up with them empty-handed. We weren't going to stay. I wasn't even going to show them around! We just wanted to get in and get out, so I hid them. I didn't want to make you angry."

"I have a right to be angry. I was angry. I was livid."

A ray of hope appeared in Shazad's eyes. "Was?"

Shazad's mother's lips tightened into a hard line. "I see

now you didn't have a choice," she said with some difficulty. Her stern facade cracked ever so slightly, and Joey saw Shazad breathe a little easier. He was not yet forgiven, but it was a start. "I also understand more than you know," his mother went on. "You three don't have any idea who you met in that cottage, do you?"

"Do *you*?" Joey asked.

"I think so. Three sisters, three questions, and three cryptic answers that left you at a crossroads? It was fate that brought you here. Or should I say, the Fates."

"The Fates?" Leonora leaned forward. "Like in Greek mythology?"

"Not just Greek myths," Shazad's mother replied. "They appear in many stories. So many it's hard to know which ones are true, but it's possible there are elements of truth in all of them. They're ancient powers. Old magic. The Vikings called their three Fates the Norns. They were also referred to as the Weird Sisters, from the Norse word 'wyrd,' meaning 'fate.' If you've read your Shakespeare, you know Macbeth met three 'Weird Sisters' who told him he would be king."

"The Weird Sisters," Joey repeated, wheels turning in his head. "J. K. Rowling used that name for a witch's rock band in the Harry Potter books! Holy cow, I just got that reference. We read *Macbeth* in school, but I never made the connection before now." His mind was reeling. He thought about the Greek myths he'd learned reading Percy Jackson. The three Fates spun out the thread of life, creating it, deciding what it would become and when it was time to cut the line. It was just like the cards he had drawn from Redondo's deck— the women with the thread, knitting needles, and shears. "We really did meet the Fates, didn't we? But this wasn't like *Macbeth*. They didn't tell us our future."

"What did they tell you?" Ali asked, fascinated by the conversation's unexpected turn.

"They've been protecting us," Shazad said. "Protecting the theater. They're the ones keeping everybody out, not us. But we have only one week left. After that, anyone can get into the Majestic. The Invisible Hand has an office right across the street. They're just waiting for an opening."

"Then we haven't a moment to lose," Shazad's mother said. "Maybe now you'll listen to reason, now that fate itself is forcing your hand. Move the magical items out of the theater while there's still time," she urged. "What are you waiting for?"

Joey looked at Shazad and Leanora, unsure how to proceed. He knew Shazad wanted to do what his mother said, but Leanora clearly wasn't ready for that. Neither was he, for that matter. They still hadn't gotten a chance to talk about everything that had happened in the cottage. Their hesitation did not go unnoticed.

"I'm curious," Shazad's mother began, addressing Joey and Leanora, "why aren't you two *asking* us to help you empty the theater? You know you're running out of time, but still you resist. What aren't you telling me?"

Shazad answered for them. "There's something else, Mom. If those were the Fates we met up on the mountain, they didn't tell us what to do or where to go, but you could say they put us on a path." Shazad got up and took the storage tube off his shoulder. He crossed the room to an empty table and took out the Secret Map of the World. "We were given this."

Everyone crowded around the table as Shazad spread out the map and held it down. His mother looked at the map the same way Joey and Leanora had looked at the gallery outside the library. "Jorako is on this map," she said, staggered by a sight Joey assumed she had never seen before.

"Not just Jorako," Shazad said. "Other places too. Look." He pointed out Transylvania, Waywayanda, and more. In the process, he showed his mother how to scroll the map and zoom in and out.

"This is an extraordinary piece of magic," she said, astounded. "The Fates gave you this?"

"To go with what they couldn't tell us," Joey said. "They said something about the Lost Kingdom, the Caliburn Shield, and the Imaginary Vortex. Does that mean anything to—"

Shazad's mother put a hand on Joey's shoulder. "Did you say the Caliburn Shield?" She held her breath. Excitement bloomed in her eyes.

"You know what that is too?" Joey asked.

Shazad's mother chuckled, suddenly almost giddy. "Wait here." She left the table and went to a nearby shelf. Walking down a row of books, she ran her fingers over their spines, searching for a specific title. Eventually, she found what she was looking for: a giant, leather-bound book the size of an old photo album. She lugged it back to the table, dropped it down, and opened it up to the middle. "There, the Caliburn Shield," she said, tapping at a picture of a medieval king holding a sword and shield. Joey read the caption beneath the picture. It wasn't just any old king.

"That's King Arthur," he said.

Shazad's mother nodded. "It certainly is. Caliburn is another word for Excalibur, the legendary sword in the stone. I'm sure you know that story. Everyone does."

"I saw the Disney movie," Joey said, recalling an old animated film. The remark earned him disapproving looks from Leanora and Shazad. "I mean, I don't know how historically accurate it was, but I liked it."

Shazad's mother smiled, humoring Joey a bit. "There are many stories, just like with the Fates. Excalibur is one of the most famous magical weapons ever forged. However, those of us who have truly studied Arthurian legend know of other gifts Arthur received. Lesser-known objects, lost to history. Until now." Shazad's mother flipped through the book, energized by the hunt. Any anger or disappointment she had felt toward Shazad seemed now to be a distant memory. She stopped turning pages at a more detailed image of the shield. It was round with twelve swords painted on its face. They were arranged in a circle like spokes on a wheel, pointing in toward a center ring. "This shield . . . This is important. It's ancient magic. Power that could rival the wand."

Joey scrunched up his face, confused. "I don't understand. You have stuff in the next room that's way older."

"Older, yes, but not necessarily more powerful." Shazad's mother waved at the gallery outside the library. "Those relics out there, they're enchanted items—things that were infused with magic long ago. The Caliburn Shield comes from a pivotal point in magical history. If it's anything like other Arthurian relics, it could be a lightning rod for magical energy—able to channel it on an ongoing basis. It could bring new magic into the world. Do you have any idea how rare that is?"

"An infinite supply of magical energy?" Joey imagined the possibilities. "I get the appeal. But wait . . . What others?" He looked back toward the gallery outside. "Do you guys have King Arthur's sword out there and I missed it?"

Shazad shook his head at Joey. "I think you would have noticed that. As far as we know, only one other Arthurian relic has ever been found. It wasn't the sword, and my family never had it. I was supposed to get it for us, but you already know how that turned out."

Leanora furrowed her brow. "What are you talking about? The wand? The one Joey threw away?"

Joey sighed. "I'm never gonna live that down, am I?"

"That wand belonged to Redondo," Leanora said. "Before that it was Houdini."

"What about before that?" asked Shazad's mother.

Leanora's face went blank. "I don't know."

Shazad's mother raised an eyebrow. "Care to hazard a guess?"

Leanora realized what she was saying before Joey did. "You don't mean . . ." She trailed off, unable to finish her sentence.

"What am I missing?" Joey asked, impatient to understand what everyone else seemed already to know. "Whose wand was it?"

"Who helped Arthur become king in that movie you saw?" Shazad asked. He spun his mother's book around to face Joey, displaying a picture of an old wizard with a long white beard and pointy hat.

Joey's hands shot to his head. "I gave up *Merlin's* wand?" He nearly crumpled to the ground like a broken marionette. Joey looked at Shazad in disbelief. "You knew about this?"

189

"I couldn't tell you," Shazad said. "I knew it would only make you feel worse. What would have been the point of that?"

"Exactly, what's the point?" Ali asked. "The wand's already gone. Back to the shield. You think this map can lead us to it?"

"That and more," Shazad's mother said, tracing the crimson lines on the map with her finger. She went from city to city, like an Indiana Jones plane in a travel montage, crisscrossing the globe until she arrived at a blurry patch of land in southern England.

Shazad gasped. "How did I not see this? If the Caliburn Shield is Arthurian legend, the Lost Kingdom must be—"

"Camelot," his mother said, finishing his thought.

The room grew especially quiet as the weight of the revelation sank in.

"Whoa," Joey said, eloquently breaking the silence.

"Whoa indeed," Shazad's mother agreed.

"What about the Imaginary Vortex?" Leanora asked. "What is that?"

His mother pursed her lips, thinking. "I'm not sure." She leaned back over the map, scrutinizing the faded section on the southern tip of England. "Things get fuzzy here in this area."

"You think they're connected?" Shazad asked.

"There's only one way to find out for sure," Joey said. All eyes turned to him. "I mean, we're going, right? We can't pass this up."

"You're right," Shazad's mother said, staring at the map. "We certainly can't."

"Really?" Shazad asked. "You want to come with us?"

"Come with you?" Shazad's mother laughed out loud. "Don't be ridiculous. You're staying here. Your father and I will go."

"What!" Shazad nearly fell over. "You expect me to stay here?"

"You were expecting something different? Please. You're obviously grounded."

"Grounded! But you said—"

"I said you had a good explanation for doing what you did. And I forgive you. But there still have to be consequences, especially for the lying." Shazad's mother turned to Joey. "Also, not to rub salt in your wounds, but we can't risk losing Camelot and the shield the way you lost the wand.

191

Better to leave this quest to more experienced hands."

Ouch again, Joey thought. There was nothing he could say to that, but Leanora was indignant.

"You can't keep us here," she declared.

"On the contrary, that's exactly what I'm going to do."

"Shazad!" Leanora hit him in the shoulder. "Say something! This is *our* quest!"

Shazad looked up at his mother with pleading eyes, but it was plain to see her mind was made up. He grimaced, resigned to defeat. "Not anymore it's not. We're getting the boot." As he spoke, he started rolling up the map and stole a furtive glance at Leanora's feet. Joey caught it, but Leanora didn't.

"You're giving up?" Leanora said. "Just like that?"

"What do you want me to do? Change her mind? You don't know my mom."

"This isn't fair!" Leanora railed.

"No, it's not," Shazad said, stuffing the map back into the tube. "Believe me, I don't like it any more than you do. If it were up to me, I'd go out to the gallery, grab the magic carpet, and fly us all out of here, but I can't do that, can I?"

"Shazad's right," Joey told Leanora. "*He* can't do that.

We're getting *booted*." Joey nudged her magic kicks with his toe. "Get it?"

"Ohhh," Leanora said without a trace of subtlety. "Got it." She tapped her feet, and the Winged Boots of Fleetfoot once more sprouted wings. She was gone in a flash. The sound of glass shattering out in the gallery made everyone jump, and a second later she was back, holding the magic carpet.

Shazad's mother was taken aback, but the momentary flash of shock she must have felt quickly gave way to warning. "Shazad, stop this right now or so help me, I will see to it you never touch another magical object as long as you live. I will call your father in here, and you will be banished from Jorako. All of you. Shazad!"

Ali's jaw was on the floor. Joey was equally shocked as Shazad slung the map over his shoulder and flapped out the carpet. It hovered in the air, waist-high. "I'm sorry, Mom. I'm not going to argue with you, but I can't stay here and do nothing. Not when I've got a second chance." He climbed onto the carpet. Joey and Leanora were right behind him.

"What are you talking about? A second chance to do what?"

Shazad pulled back on the front edge of the magic carpet, bringing it up into the air, away from his mother. "I know it's hard to believe right now, but I'm going to make you proud," he called out. "You'll see!"

"Shazad, no!" his mother shouted. "COME BACK!"

Ali shouted, "Take me with you!"

But they were already gone. Joey held on tight as they went hurtling through the halls of the house, reaching the courtyard in seconds. Leanora *whoop*ed as they swung around the floating sculpture, riding the magic carpet out into the night. Joey gritted his teeth, holding on for dear life as they huddled close together, soaring through the sky.

9

The Devil's Teeth

"That was amazing!" Leanora exclaimed, her voice a mixture of shock and elation. "I can't believe you did that!"

"Me neither," Shazad said. His eyes were wide as the moonlit dunes raced by beneath them. "My mother definitely couldn't believe it."

Leanora nodded in agreement. "I take back what I said before. She *is* going to kill you."

"Maybe. Probably. Then again, maybe not."

Joey scoffed at Shazad's optimism. "Are you kidding? Did you see your mother's face back there? You're dead!"

"I don't know." Shazad chewed on the inside of his cheek, thinking it over. "I might be all right. I don't think I'm even responsible for my actions right now."

Joey's eyebrows went up. "That sounds nice," he said

sarcastically. "Who *is* responsible then—Leanora?" Joey threw her a playful grin. "Technically speaking, she's the one who stole the magic carpet."

"Shazad wanted me to get it!" Leanora protested. "That wasn't my idea!"

"It wasn't my idea, either," Shazad said. "It wasn't any of us—it was fate." Shazad looked straight ahead as he spoke. Joey couldn't tell if he was serious, or just working overtime to rationalize what he'd done. Either way, he was flying pretty fast for someone who claimed not to be worried about the consequences of his actions. "You heard my mother. Fate's forcing our hand. She said so herself!" Shazad's voice went up an octave with each new sentence. Joey had a feeling if he kept talking, pretty soon only dogs would be able to hear him.

Leanora chuckled. "I know what your mother said, but I don't think this is what she had in mind."

Shazad shrugged as if to say it was over and done with and there was no use dwelling on it now. "No one expects fate to tap them on the shoulder. I'll be fine as long as we don't mess this up."

Joey turned to look back at the oasis, which had already

vanished from sight. Wind whistled through his hair, and he gripped the carpet hard enough to fray the edges. They had to be going at least fifty miles per hour. "Is your family gonna come after us?" Joey figured the quickest way to mess things up would be to get caught.

"Don't worry. We'll be gone before they catch up."

"Where are we going?" Joey asked.

"What kind of question is that?" Leanora replied. "We're going to Camelot, of course."

"But where are we going *now*?" Joey clarified. "Don't we need to go through Jorako to get out of here?"

"Ordinarily, yes, but while you were sleeping I was studying the map and I found another way." Shazad banked a hard right, taking the carpet off in a new direction. "If you zoom in close enough on the map, you can see the ends of those red lines connecting the different cities. I did that and a message appeared."

"What message?" Leanora asked.

Shazad recited the note from memory:

Walk through the sand to a dangerous land, but danger lies beneath.

Be not afraid; courage serves those who have
strayed beyond the devil's teeth.

"Okay. Creepy," Joey said. "Any idea what it means?"

"I know what it means," Shazad said, somehow willing the carpet to go faster. "I wasn't going to use it before, but we don't have the luxury of being picky now."

"Why exactly weren't you going to use this . . . whatever it is?" Leanora wanted to know. "You still haven't said where we're going."

"I don't want you to worry," Shazad said. "It's better this way, though. I think we're supposed to be here."

"*Where?*" Joey and Leanora asked in unison.

"The Devil's Teeth."

They came upon a ring of pointed rocks in the desert. Cone-shaped peaks, big and small, grew up out of the sand like stone fangs, creating an uneven circle thirty feet in diameter. The ground fell away beyond the jagged rock border to form a deep pit with loose sand at the bottom. Joey tried not to imagine a many-tentacled monster lurking underground, but it wasn't easy to keep his imagination in check. Moonlight bathed the area in a supernatural, haunted glow that turned his blood into cold fish oil. The place was downright creepy, and it wasn't just the name. Everything about the Devil's Teeth said "Stay Away."

"Uhh . . . What are we doing at the Sarlacc Pit?" Joey asked as Shazad brought the carpet to a halt at the edge of the rocks.

"I know it looks bad," Shazad admitted, ignoring Joey's Star Wars reference. "I've always been scared of this place. Ever since I was little, my parents warned me and Ali never to come here. That's dry quicksand inside that ring. You go in, you don't come out."

"And we're here because . . . ?" Leonora asked.

"We're going through."

Everyone was quiet for a moment.

"Through the quicksand," Joey said, his tone revealing a clear lack of enthusiasm.

"We'll come out in the next location on the map," Shazad said. "That's why we have it. The red lines connecting the cities are shortcuts around the world, going through magical places—magic gates that are somehow still open! This one's been here all this time, right in our backyard, and we never knew it." He broke into an off-kilter laugh, amused that such an extraordinary find had gone unnoticed by his family for generations. "I guess it makes sense we never figured out what this was. How could we? Who in their right mind would ever go in there?"

"I was just wondering that myself," Joey said. "For a guy who doesn't like risks, this feels like a major risk. All of this is a major risk."

Shazad moved the carpet out over the center of the pit. "Desperate times . . ."

"Whoa!" Joey grabbed hold of the carpet to keep from falling off. "Can we talk about this?"

"What's to talk about? We have to get out of here."

"You said it yourself. People go in there and they don't come back out."

"Not here they don't," Shazad stressed. "They don't drown in the sand. They come out somewhere else."

"You're sure about that?" Joey pressed.

"I'm sure about one thing." Shazad stood up on the carpet, careful not to tip it over. "I didn't get the wand. I lost the staff. I am getting that shield." He gripped the strap of the map tube with one hand and gave a casual salute with the other. "See you on the other side."

"Shazad, wait!" Joey shouted as Shazad took a step back and dropped off the carpet. He fell into the pit and vanished under the sand instantly. Joey and Leanora held tight to the carpet, looking over the edge for some sign of him, but there was nothing. The sand at the bottom of the pit appeared completely undisturbed. It was as if Shazad had never been there at all.

"That was dramatic," Leanora said, clearly impressed. "I feel like we're seeing another side of Shazad."

"Tell me about it," Joey agreed. "You think he's all right?"

"He better be. We're up next." Leanora took a breath and stood up slowly. She had her arms out as if balancing on a surfboard. "If he can do it, so can we. Are you coming?"

Joey grimaced. "Do I have a choice?"

"I don't think so. It's fate, remember?" Leanora threw Joey a wink.

He made a noise that was half grunt, half laugh. "Good ol' fate. I'll be right behind you. I need to make a call first."

"Don't take too long. We've got work to do." Leanora leaped off the carpet and straightened out with her hands at her sides. It looked like she was doing a pencil dive into a swimming pool. A second later she was gone and Joey was alone.

Joey got out his phone. It was three thirty a.m. where he was. Checking the world clock, he saw that it was nine thirty p.m. back home and six thirty p.m. in Los Angeles. He would have called his parents, but Shazad had already tucked them in (so to speak), and they would have kept him on the phone forever. He called Janelle instead.

"Hello?" Joey asked once the phone stopped ringing. "Janelle, can you hear me?" Reception was spotty, but Joey thought he heard her pick up. He grabbed the edge of the carpet and tried to move it around in search of a better signal.

"Joey! Yes, I can hear you." Janelle's voice solidified, and Joey breathed a sigh of relief. "What's going on? Are you here yet?"

"Not yet," Joey said in a tone that suggested there was more to the story. "I'm actually not gonna make it out there today."

"Why not?" Janelle lowered her voice, sounding concerned. "Is everything okay? Your last text had me worried."

"I'm okay," Joey said. "I think."

"You think? Where are you?"

"Shazad's place. Jorako. Nearby anyway."

"No way!" Leanora sounded jealous. Joey thought she might feel differently if she could see the quicksand pit beneath him. "I thought you guys couldn't go there! What's it like?"

"It's . . . I don't even know where to begin. It's amazing, but that's not why I'm calling. Listen, Janelle, I'm gonna be off the grid for a little while. I need a favor. You have to text my parents as me. I'll give you the number. Tell them I lost my phone and that you're letting me use yours to stay in touch."

"What do I do when they call my phone because they want to talk to you?"

"Just say you can't talk. Stall them."

"For how long? When are you getting here?"

"I don't know. Soon, I hope. We're going on a quest."

"A quest? What are you—" She broke off, exasperated. "Joey, we're supposed to be working out here. I need your help!"

"I think this *will* help," Joey told her. "I'll explain more when I see you, but right now I gotta go. Everyone's waiting for me. Think you can you handle my mom and dad while I'm gone?"

Janelle grumbled reluctantly. "I can do that. As long I drop a comic book or movie reference every other text, they won't suspect a thing."

Joey laughed, knowing she was right. "You rock, Janelle."

"I know. Just don't take too long. There's only so much I can do. Speaking of which, are Shazad and Leanora going to let you bring the mask when you're done questing?"

"Well, I've got it with me," Joey said, not quite answering the question.

"Good. Everyone here wants to know what this big break-through I found is. I don't know what to tell them."

"You'll think of something. You're a genius."

"Just hurry up. We're saving the planet this week, remember?"

"That's the plan," Joey agreed, but at the moment he was thinking about something better than the mask—Camelot and the Caliburn Shield. "Wish me luck."

He hung up and looked down at the Devil's Teeth. Shazad and Leanora had jumped in like it was nothing, but it felt like a bigger deal to him. Maybe it was because he had to do it alone. Or maybe it was because he'd had too much time to think about it. It occurred to Joey that everything he knew about magic centered on belief. Every magical thing he could do depended on the ability to banish doubt and fear from his mind. It was something he was having trouble with at the moment. He was hung up on the message from the map. Part of it, anyway. "Be not afraid," Joey whispered into the night. "Courage serves those who have strayed beyond the Devil's Teeth." He wondered what would happen if he jumped into the pit with anything less than total confidence. Would the magic gate still be there for him? Assuming it was there to begin with and his friends weren't suffocating under the sand?

"Stop it," Joey told himself. "Don't think like that."

Joey forced himself to stand. He balled up his fists. It was possible that people who had stumbled into the pit by accident and went under while trying to claw their way out ended up drowning in quicksand. But it was equally possible that people who went in willingly and took a leap of faith ended up somewhere entirely different. It was a choice. Redondo had once told Joey "magnificence is a decision." Right now he had a decision to make. Dive in or bail out? Joey looked around at the barren desert landscape. "Who am I kidding?" He took a deep breath and let it out slowly, relaxing his muscles. Relaxing everything. A second later he was falling through the air, thinking only of Camelot and of seeing his friends again.

10

Vampire Tourism

It was like skydiving in a sandstorm. Joey buried his face in the crook of his arm as he fell for hundreds of feet. The pit seemed to have no bottom, but it did have air. Joey could tell because he heard the wind whipping sand around his body like a tornado. He felt it too. A million grains of sand attacked him, stabbing at his skin like tiny little pins. Joey gritted his teeth, hoping it would be over soon. After a few seconds with no end in sight, he realized he couldn't tell if he was actually falling, or if it just felt that way because of the rushing wind flying up past his body. Keeping his head down, he cracked his eyes open for a peek. As soon as he did that, the falling stopped. Much to Joey's surprise, he saw that his feet were firmly planted on the ground. The swirling sands around him thinned out, dissipating into twinkly stardust. A gentle breeze carried it off into oblivion, and his journey was complete.

Moving slowly, Joey lifted his head up from his elbow and took stock of his surroundings. He was standing on a cobblestone street in the middle of an intersection. At first glance, he thought he'd gone back in time a few hundred years, but then he saw a row of streetlights glowing in the night. He spit out a mouthful of sand, finding humor in the fact that unwanted time travel had become a legitimate concern for him, however fleeting. You never could tell what a new piece of magic would do. Fortunately, Joey wasn't stuck in the past. It was just a sleepy little town—somewhere in Europe, if he had to guess. Looking around, Joey decided that "town" was too generous, and perhaps too busy a word for where he was. "Village" felt more appropriate. The place had an old-world quality, like something out of a folktale. Aging, Tudor-style houses with steeply pitched roofs and dark brown wooden framework tilted over the winding, narrow streets. Every structure appeared to be handcrafted from wood and stone. They were crammed in on top of one another, none of them seemed to have any right angles, and many of them were ready to fall apart. It was quiet as a crypt.

The doors were all shut and the curtains were drawn inside every window. Even with the streetlights, the road ahead disappeared into darkness.

And I thought the Devil's Teeth looked haunted.

"Joey, over here," Shazad said behind him.

Joey turned around and saw his friends standing under a dim, flickering lamppost where the cobblestones gave way to dirt road. They were looking at the map, aided by the light from a glowing pendant around Leanora's neck. Joey went to join them.

"We were beginning to wonder if you were coming," Leanora said once he got there.

"I had to psyche myself up for the jump," Joey admitted. "That was weird. I felt like I was falling forever, but then I looked down and I was already on the street. How long was I standing over there? With my head ducked down like that?"

Shazad smirked. "A little while."

Joey made a face. "Thanks for telling me." He imagined himself standing out in the street with his head covered up, thinking he was still falling. It was embarrassing, not to mention unsafe. "We're lucky we did this in the middle of the night. I could have gotten hit by a car—or a runaway mule cart," he added with a nod toward the village. "Where are we, anyway?"

"See for yourself." Leanora slid over to give him a better view of the map. Joey leaned in as she held her glowing stone pendant over their location.

"Transylvania?" Joey blurted out in disbelief. "Is that even a real country?"

"Why does everybody say that?" Leanora wondered aloud. "It's not a country; it's a region. This is Romania. I've been here with my family plenty of times performing. We've been all over Europe. You'd be surprised how many people think Transylvania is fictional. It's a real place. Dracula was made up, not Transylvania."

"I thought Dracula was a real guy," Joey said. "Wasn't he based on Vlad the Impaler?"

"*Based on*," Leanora stressed. "Maybe. Vlad Țepeș was a fifteenth-century Wallachian prince. He had a reputation for cruelty, with impalement being his favorite method of execution. He was the second son of Vlad Dracul, and Bram Stoker used the name for Count Dracula. Whether or not he was the inspiration for the character, I couldn't tell you, but he wasn't a vampire."

"You seem to know a lot about this," Joey said.

"I told you, I've been here before. Depending who you're talking to, you have to watch what you say about vampires. Not everyone's thrilled with their history and culture getting swallowed up by ghost stories, but it's hard to avoid. For every person who wants to remember Vlad Ţepeş as a national hero, there's someone else selling guided tours of Bran Castle to people on vacation."

"Vampire tourism," Joey said. "We're sure that's all there is to it? 'Cause I didn't bring any garlic with me."

"I think we'll manage," Leanora said.

"I hope so," Joey said. "We're sure we didn't go back in time, either?" he asked, only half kidding. He gestured to a pair of horse-drawn carts and wagons, one loaded up with barrels and the other with hay. "I've never been to Romania before, but this looks pretty medieval."

"Romania has beautiful cities," Leanora said sternly. "This is just a rural village. I'm sorry, not every place can be as cosmopolitan as Hoboken."

Joey put his hands up. "I'm not judging. I'm just saying, if you don't like ghost stories, maybe don't have the Brothers Grimm design your village. And you can make fun of Hoboken if you want, but it's more sophisticated than you think. It's practically the sixth borough of New York City."

"Can we focus?" asked Shazad. "We've got a long road ahead of us. Relatively speaking."

"I'm just getting my bearings," Joey said. "What's the plan?"

"I'll show you. Hold this." Shazad offered one end of the map to Joey, giving himself a free hand to lay out the route he wanted them to take. Tracing the red lines on the map, Shazad went from Jorako to Transylvania to a place called Celestia, which was somewhere in Brazil, and finally to southern England, which was just as faded and hard to read as it had been back in the library.

"Not the quickest way to get where we want to go," Joey said.

"Are you sure?" Shazad countered. "Don't forget, a minute ago you were in North Africa, over two thousand miles away."

"That's true," Joey admitted. "What I mean is it's not the most direct route. Also, who knows what we're going to run into on the way? Can't we skip all that and go straight to England?"

"We could, but how are we going to get there?" Leanora

asked. "We left the flying carpet back in the desert—not that we could have used it out in the open, anyway. You want to find the nearest airport?"

Joey grimaced. Another good point. They didn't have any money or passports, either. "So how do we get to Brazil?"

"Through the woods. Look here." Shazad zoomed in on their location on the map, finding a castle in the woods that surrounded the village. The red line that connected Transylvania to Celestia started there.

"The Dead Woods," Joey said, reading the name off the map. "Gotta love the names of these places."

"It's just a name," Leonora said. "Probably."

"Sure," Joey replied. "It's a totally normal, totally innocent name. I like it, actually. It's got a nice ring to it." His eyes had now adjusted to the darkness. He could make out a dense forest that bordered the village and a mountain range beyond the trees. "I see the woods. I don't see the castle. Are we sure we're in the right place?"

Shazad hiked his shoulders. "The map says we are."

Leonora pointed up at the rocky peaks in the distance. "Those are the Carpathian Mountains up there. This forest must be the Dead Woods."

"Ever heard of this place before?" Joey asked.

"No," Leanora said. "I've heard of Hoia Forest in Romania. It's supposed to be the most haunted forest in the world, but that's here." She zoomed out on the map and pointed to an area that was hundreds of miles to the west.

"Is that where Dracula's castle is?" Joey asked.

"No, that's Bran Castle, outside Braşov—here." She scrolled to another area on the map, several hours to the south. "But that wasn't even Vlad Ţepeş's castle really. I told you, it's just for the tourists."

"What are we looking for, then?" Joey asked. "Is there another message?"

"There is," Shazad said. "We're not sure what it means yet. I'm assuming we'll understand better once we get there." He scrolled back to the castle in the Dead Woods and centered the map view on two lines written in elaborate cursive:

> 100 doors in the dungeon. The Count gave his prisoners a chance . . .
> A long life of exile and mercy, or a short one impaled on a lance.

214

"The Count, huh?" Joey looked at Leanora. "Let's hope you're right about the vampires."

"Don't worry. That's all superstition."

Joey nodded, unsure but very much wanting to believe Leanora.

"We trusted the map enough to follow it into a pit of quicksand," Shazad reasoned. "That worked out fine. We're all here. I say we stick with it."

"I'm with you," Leanora said.

They both looked at Joey as if he might need more convincing. He *pff*ed at that, putting on a brave face. "Don't get the wrong idea. I'm not backing out. I might have a few questions, but I'm not going anywhere except with you guys."

"What are we waiting for, then?" Shazad smiled and rolled up the map. "Let's go."

Joey, Shazad, and Leanora followed the main road out of the village, headed for the dark unknown of the forest. They walked under the streetlights as long as they could, which is to say, not very long at all. Once they reached the edge of town, they were forced to make do with the light from Leanora's glowing pendant. Fortunately, she was able to intensify its brightness, creating a magical flashlight, which

Joey thought was a neat trick. Leanora called the pendant a sunstone. There was an actual ray of sunshine trapped inside it, which charged up during the day and could be rationed out at night. They had to use it sparingly and make sure it lasted until morning. The road split near a farm outside the village. On one side, a dirt path bordered a field where a flock of sheep slept peacefully. On the other, a paved road wound around the corner, most likely leading off to more populated areas. Joey and the others followed the dirt path toward a forest gate. The field had a fence to keep the sheep from wandering into the woods and getting lost. Shazad unlatched the gate and went into the forest. Joey followed him in. He wasn't worried about getting lost. They had the map.

But the map was hard to follow through the untamed forest. For one thing, it was darker in the woods. The thick canopy of trees blocked out any light from above. Out on the street, the moon had been covered with clouds, but even that weak light was better than nothing, and the moon's absence made for slow going on the trail. That was the other problem. There was no trail. Joey, Shazad, and Leanora struggled with uneven terrain that was crowded with trees and overgrown plants. The earth seemed to rise and fall at random, keeping them off-balance, staggering through the night. After a while Joey began to wonder if the rocks and roots were jumping up to trip him on purpose. It didn't help that he flat-out couldn't see where he was going. Shazad was using the map and its compass to keep them on track, which meant he was the one who got to hold Leanora's pendant—otherwise he wouldn't be able to see which way the compass needle was pointing. Joey and Leanora did their best to follow in Shazad's footsteps, but he was stumbling just as much as they were.

The hike got easier as dawn approached, as the morning light made everyone more sure-footed. Joey's stomach rumbled, looking for breakfast. He had worked up an appetite in the night, but he didn't bother mentioning it. They weren't likely to find any food in the forest. They were in the middle of nowhere, which presented a bigger problem. "Where's the castle?" Joey wondered aloud. "I was hoping it would be there when the sun came up. Even if it was way out there, up on the mountain."

"That would have been nice," Leanora agreed. "I'd like to have an idea how close we are. Or how far."

Shazad was standing alone at the crest of a small hill. He was looking back and forth between the map and the land beyond the ridge. "The map says the castle's just up ahead." Joey heard uncertainty in Shazad's voice, like he was worried they were lost but didn't want to say so out loud. Joey and Leanora joined him on the hilltop. There was nothing but trees, trees, and more trees as far as the eye could see.

"Are you sure we're going the right way?" Leanora asked.

"The map says—"

"I know what the map says, but castles are big and hard to miss. There's nothing here."

"Exactly. It's hidden," Shazad decided. "What? You thought this would be easy? It's out there. I can feel it. Come on."

Shazad tucked the map under his shoulder and started down the hill, trying to find the easiest path through the trees. The look on his face was so determined, Joey and Leanora could do little but fall in line behind him. What else were they going to do? Turn back? Not likely. Shazad was right. They had come this far, and it made sense that the castle would be hidden. If not, someone would have surely discovered the castle—and the magic gate to the next city on the map—long ago. Joey had no idea how they were going to find it, but he knew only a fool would bet against Shazad, who was as focused and driven as Joey had ever seen him. The more Joey thought about it, the more he realized Shazad's mind-set presented another kind of problem. It was obvious why Shazad was so hot on finding Camelot. He wanted to impress his parents. He was going to blow them away with his monumental accomplishment. Joey remembered his exact words before jumping into the Devil's Teeth:

I didn't get the wand. I lost the staff. I am getting that shield.

Joey had to say something.

"Should we talk about what's going to happen if we find Camelot?"

"*When* we find Camelot," Shazad said.

"Sure. When we find it," Joey agreed. "What happens then?"

Moving swiftly, Shazad climbed over a large fallen tree that was blocking their path. "What's going to happen is, no one's going to give me grief about losing the wand ever again."

Coming up behind him, Joey struggled with the same tree that Shazad had effortlessly scrambled over. "I wouldn't mind that, but what happens specifically? With the shield?"

Shazad turned. "What do you mean? The shield is an Arthurian artifact. It has to be protected."

"Protected where?" Leanora asked, bounding over the tree in her magic boots. "In Jorako?"

Shazad cast his eyes skyward and pretended to momentarily lose strength in his legs. "Here we go."

Leanora frowned. "I don't think that's why the Fates stepped in to give us this quest, do you?"

"I don't know. Maybe the Fates are giving me another chance to get things right," Shazad replied.

"This is a chance for all of us," Leanora said. "You realize that whoever—or whatever—it was that gave us this map has been guarding the Majestic Theatre for us, and they're going to stop guarding it soon. We're looking for a magic shield, Shazad. Something with the power to protect what we have in the theater once the candle burns out."

"We don't know that. We don't know what the shield does yet," Shazad replied.

"It might do that and more," Joey said. "It might be just the thing Janelle and I have been searching for. Something to provide all the energy the world needs." He tapped the backpack on his shoulder. "This mask is going to run out of magic one day. If your mother's right, the shield won't."

Leanora's face contorted. "We're not going to turn the

shield into some kind of environmentally friendly battery, Joey."

"Why not?"

"A hundred reasons," Shazad replied. "We've talked about this. People need to believe in magic for it to work—and they *don't* believe. The world's been trained not to believe. They put their faith in technology. You can't introduce magic as part of some new tech and expect to change the world."

"Why not?" Joey asked again. "Most people don't have any idea how technology works. They still trust it to do things that used to be considered impossible. That's faith. That's belief."

"Even if you're right, it's too high profile. Too public," Shazad said. "The Invisible Hand would come after the shield if we used it the way you want. Not just them, either. We're talking about something that could be the most powerful object on the face of the earth. People, good and bad—governments, good and bad—from all around the world are going to want that power. It needs to be somewhere safe, or it's going to do more harm than good."

"Unbelievable," Joey said, throwing up his hands. "We still can't agree on anything."

"Let's stop talking about it," Leonora advised. "We have to actually find Camelot and the shield for any of this to matter. We'll deal with it then."

"And if we can't find it?" Joey waved a hand at the empty woodlands. "Then what?"

Leonora shook her head, done with the conversation. "We'll jump off that bridge when we come to it."

As they moved on, the forest grew dense. With every step, the space in between the trees was increasingly overtaken by pricker bushes. A torrent of thorny branches seemed to rise up in waves, reaching out to snag Joey's clothing and scrape at his skin. The tightly packed thicket was impenetrable in some places, forcing the group to change course more than once. Joey wove in and out of dead ends as if navigating a labyrinth. The more turns he and his friends had to make in search of an open path, the more the distance between them expanded. As Joey worked his way through the maze, he felt himself getting turned around and losing his way, but he pressed on, telling himself he would regroup with Shazad and Leonora after they cleared the brush. Soon everyone was walking alone. At first they called out to each other often, to keep from straying too far apart, but the calls grew less and less frequent, then eventually stopped altogether. In time Joey's sole focus in life became the frustrating task of fighting his way through the forest. He was sweaty, scratched up, and bleeding. He wanted out.

"Guys?" Joey shouted. "I made a decision. I hate the Dead Woods!"

He got no answer from his friends, but the woods, which up to that point had been actively resisting him, extended an olive branch by removing several hundred branches from his path. Joey pushed a cluster of pointed barbs out of his face and found an open fairway on the other side. A clear track of land stretched out before him like a park promenade. It was a hundred feet long, but Joey could see an opening at the far end. He was elated. It was almost too good to be true, but he didn't doubt it for a second. "Guys, I found something! Over here. I think I found the way out!"

Again no one answered him.

"Shazad? Leanora? Can you hear me?" Silent seconds stretched into minutes as Joey waited anxiously for a reply. He heard nothing but thrashing in the bushes. Joey whirled around and scanned the forest, unable to pinpoint where the noise was coming from. Was it a wild animal? His friends?

Someone else? He wanted to hightail it out of there, but he couldn't leave Shazad and Leanora behind. At the same time, he was worried if he went to search for them, he'd never find his way back to this spot. He was almost out of the briar patch! It was hard to resist, but he did it. Joey was turning around to go look for Shazad and Leanora when the rustling noise stopped and his friends' voices drifted through the woods. They were talking over each other, their words overlapping in such a way that Joey couldn't make out what they were saying, but one thing was clear—the sound was coming from up ahead.

"They're already out," Joey whispered to himself.

Relieved, he sprinted down the open path, chasing his friends' voices and calling their names. It felt good to be running free after the arduous hike, but halfway down the lane, he had to slow to a jog. The passageway narrowed as he moved through it, like a shrinking hallway of branches. Joey wondered if it was actually getting smaller, or if it was just a matter of perception. He called out to his friends and heard them call back to him, but now it sounded like he was ahead of them. He stopped and backpedaled a few steps, bumping right into a pricker bush.

"What the?" Joey turned around and found that he had nowhere to go. A tight nest of thorns now occupied the space he had just run through. They formed a sturdy, instant barricade. "No way. I was just there! That's imposs—"

Rather than waste time finishing his sentence, Joey spun back around, praying the same impossible situation wasn't unfolding behind him. He was relieved to find the trail out of the forest was still clear, but it definitely looked smaller than it had a moment ago. Joey squandered precious seconds staring as the branches grew before his eyes.

"I think I'm in trouble here," he said, moving forward again tentatively.

"Joey!" Leanora shouted. Her voice was coming in clearer now. "Don't stop! Keep going!"

Joey did as he was told, charging into the dry white branches. They broke off against his body and scratched his face as he barreled toward the rapidly closing exit. He didn't make it. Before he reached the finish line, the passageway closed off completely and he was trapped with nowhere to go.

"I'm stuck!"

"No, you're close!" Shazad told him. "This way! Follow my voice!"

Joey gritted his teeth and forced himself to keep moving forward. He felt like he was caught in a spider's web of spiky branches. The world was closing in on him, and he started to lose his cool. Joey called out for help and his friends called back again. They sounded nearby. He wondered if it was really them, or just a trick to lure him deeper into the forest. Were the Dead Woods cursed? Were they trying to kill him? Joey was running out of steam, but Shazad and Leanora shouted more encouragement.

"Joey, we can hear you! You're almost there! Don't give up!"

He had no choice but to push and believe. Tapping into a life-or-death adrenaline reserve—the kind of thing that allows mothers to lift cars off their children in emergency situations—Joey found the strength to keep going. He stomped into the thicket with renewed vigor, squeezing his body through one gap after another. It was painful, but he was making progress and building momentum, not to mention confidence. Near the end, the forest seemed to give a bit, loosening its hold on Joey. He picked up speed, storming through the bushes until finally he burst into the clearing—right at the edge of a cliff.

"Ahh!" Joey pulled up short and tried to stop, but his

ankle was snared in a tangle of branches. He fell forward, headfirst over the ledge. A hand caught him by the collar just before he went tumbling to his death.

"Got you!"

Joey gagged as his shirt dug into his throat. It was a welcome sensation considering the alternative. Choking, he looked back over his shoulder and saw Shazad holding on to him and Leanora holding on to Shazad, anchoring everybody to the ledge. It was their voices he had heard after all. Joey exhaled as they pulled him back to safety. "I hate the Dead Woods," he said again, once he caught his breath.

"We all do," Leanora said. "Trust me."

Joey saw that Leanora and Shazad were just as scratched up as he was, but Leanora looked particularly upset. There was an edge in her voice and her cheeks were flushed. "What did I miss?" he asked. "What happened?"

Leanora looked back into the pricker bushes, packed tight like a knot of barbed wire. She wiped her eyes, and Joey realized she was angry and sad at the same time. "I lost something in there. One of my necklaces."

"No," Joey said, feeling awful for her. He knew they couldn't go back for it. The branches he broke getting out of the pricker bushes had regrown behind him, bigger and stronger. There was no way back into the forest, and even if there were, they couldn't risk it. There was no guarantee they'd get out a second time. "Which one did you lose?"

"The one my grandmother gave me. The mental protection amulet. It must have caught on a branch and snapped off. I didn't even know it was gone until I got out."

Everyone was quiet for a moment.

"This is why the shield belongs in Jorako," Shazad said. "Out here, things get lost. You lost your necklace. I lost the staff. Joey lost the—"

"Shazad," Joey cut in. "Not a good time."

Shazad noticed how upset Leanora was getting and abandoned the topic. "The good news is we found the castle," he said.

Joey lifted his chin. The fog was thick on this side of the pricker bushes, but within it, he could see the shadowy outline of a large black stone castle. It sat across a wide chasm on the opposite cliff. "What's the bad news?"

"The bridge," Shazad said, pointing. "And I use that term loosely."

Joey's eyes fell on a shaky rope bridge that was tied to a rocky outcropping a few feet away. His spirits fell immediately after seeing it. "Is that the only way across?"

Shazad gestured to the vertical drop-off beyond the edge of the cliff. "Unless we can fly."

Joey groaned. The bridge was one step up from a tightrope at best. Two thick lines ran out across the abyss serving as handrails, with straps tied to short wooden planks that were spaced out every couple of feet. "Sure would be nice to have a magic carpet right now. Tell me again why we didn't take that with us?"

"We had to leave it," Shazad said. "My parents have ways to track their belongings. They'd catch up to us if we had the carpet."

"I'm starting to wish they would." Joey peered over the edge to see what he had almost fallen into. It was like looking into a cloud. The chasm was so filled with fog that he couldn't see the bottom. Joey kicked a stone into the mist. He didn't hear it hit the ground. "Did I miss something? Is there even a ground down there? And how long is that bridge?" he complained. "For all we know, it goes on forever." The rope bridge disappeared into the fog after about ten feet. The other side of the canyon was as much a mystery as the ground below.

"It can't be that far," Leanora said. "The castle's right there."

Joey stared at the ancient turrets and towers rising up out of the mist. "All right," he said, trying to find the courage to act. "Let's get this over with."

Trading one danger for another before he got too comfortable, Joey clenched his fists and walked up to the start of the bridge. With great effort, he forced his hands to open and grab hold of the ropes. His feet were another story. They didn't want to move. Shazad and Leanora stood behind Joey silently, not rushing him. No doubt they were just as nervous as he was. "Suck it up," Joey muttered under his breath, knowing the longer he waited, the harder it would be to begin. There was no going back. He had a wall of thorns behind him and a mysterious void in front. The only way out was through.

Joey took a deep breath and held it as he stepped onto the bridge. The ropes stretched and the bridge dipped as he walked across the planks. His stomach tied itself into the shape of a pretzel, but he crept forward, sliding his hands inch by inch over the rope. He was holding on tight enough to get friction burns. The rope felt old, like it could snap at any moment, and the whole bridge swayed when he leaned too heavily to one side or the other. Joey moved slowly, doing his best to keep his back straight and his weight perfectly centered. He breathed sparingly, deluding himself that having less air in his lungs made him that much lighter, and every little bit helped. The more Joey thought about it, the more he was glad he couldn't see how high up he was. He didn't want to know.

Joey felt the bridge strain under Shazad's and Leanora's weight as they followed him out. He grimaced, wishing they had opted to cross one at a time, but it was too late now. Shazad and Leanora were already on the bridge. Joey wasn't going to ask them to turn around and wait for him to reach the other side. He didn't even know if they'd be able to tell when he got there. They couldn't see the other side from the safety of the cliff. For all Joey knew, his friends wouldn't be able to hear him over there, either. As he journeyed deeper into the mist, something shifted. The air felt strange. It was colder and murkier. It smelled different too. Not better or worse, just different. The fog grew so thick, Joey couldn't see more than two feet in front of him. He glanced back over his shoulder to check on his friends, but it was no better in the other direction. Shazad and Leanora were just shadows in the mist.

Joey kept moving forward, careful not to upset the delicate balance of the bridge and wondering if he was still technically in Romania. The hazy crossing felt otherworldly. It reminded Joey of Redondo's "Off-Broadway" realm in between realities. As he closed in on the castle in the distance, he thought about who it might belong to. Was this the real Dracula's castle? Was he entering the *real* Transylvania? Joey's mind cycled through the possibilities. Transylvania, as he had always imagined it from stories, could be another dimension, like Redondo's sanctuary, or the mirror world, or it could be a magical place, hidden inside the "normal world" like Jorako. Joey gave the matter a lot of thought as he inched forward one wood plank at a time. He was happy to occupy his mind with something other than the weak and wobbly bridge under his feet.

"If the bridge snaps, don't let go of the rope!" Shazad shouted out of the blue, his voice quivering a bit.

"Don't say that!" Leanora shot back. "Don't even think it!"

Joey grunted. *Like we're not all thinking it.* He stretched out his leg to step over a missing plank and warned the others to watch out for it. Joey hoped he wouldn't come across any more gaps in the bridge, and he really hoped he wouldn't create one himself. In the movies, whenever someone had to cross a bridge like this, there was always one spot where it broke underneath their foot. Then there was a big tense moment as they nearly fell through but somehow managed to hang on and climb back up. Movie-star action heroes always made it back onto the bridge and finished their journey, but Joey knew if it happened here, the force of someone falling down would snap the rope like a string of dental floss. Even if the bridge didn't break, it would twist wildly and dump everyone into the canyon. Joey pressed on, tapping each plank with his toe before committing his full weight to it. He was like a person walking through a minefield, testing the ground with every step and hoping not to blow up. His caution paid off when the end of the bridge at last came into view. Joey shouted out the good news to his friends, resisting the urge to speed up. *Slow and steady,* Joey told himself. He couldn't afford to get sloppy. The stakes were too high. When he finally stepped off the bridge onto the rocky crag, he collapsed with relief as all the tension that had built up inside him drained out at once. He was so happy he nearly kissed the ground, but he decided against it, thinking it would have been overly dramatic. Also, germs.

Leanora and Shazad arrived a few minutes later. They were just as thrilled as Joey was to be back on land. The moment their feet hit solid ground, their bodies deflated as if someone had uncorked an air valve at their ankles. Joey leaned his head back against a rock, closed his eyes, and got comfortable. His friends did the same. The three of them sat in the shadow of the castle, recuperating. No one said anything for a while. They were too mentally exhausted after their harrowing walk across the bridge. Later, after Joey's heartbeat returned to normal, he opened his eyes and looked around. The sun had gone away completely, and it wasn't hiding behind a cloud. It was nighttime on this side of the bridge. Somewhere in the forest, a wolf howled at the large, bright full moon hanging in the sky. The sound jolted everyone back to full-alert mode.

"Velcome to Transylvania," Shazad joked in his best Dracula voice.

Everyone laughed. "Nice place to visit," Joey said. "I wouldn't want to live here."

"I don't think anyone lives here," Leanora said, looking up at the dark, Gothic castle above them. "Not for a long time."

"Good." The rock Joey was using as a headrest was next to a flagstone path that led up to the open drawbridge door. It was lined with torches, but none of them were lit. "The lights are off, and no one's home." Joey's neck started to itch. "So why do I get the feeling we're being watched?"

Leanora waved Joey off. "We're fine. You've seen too many horror movies."

"I don't watch horror movies. Not my thing."

"How come?" asked Shazad. "Too scary?"

Joey nodded. "Basically."

"That explains it," Leanora said. "If you don't like scary movies, you're in the wrong place."

Joey's stomach lurched as a man stepped off the bridge, shrouded in fog. He was a shadowy figure, dressed all in black, with skin as white as a sheet.

"I think you're right," Joey said. "Let's get out of here. Now."

11

To the Batcave

Shazad leaned forward, squinting in confusion. "Is that a vamp . . . ?" He trailed off, unable, or perhaps just afraid to say the word out loud.

Leanora acted quickly. "Close your eyes," she said, snatching the glowing pendant back from Shazad and springing to her feet. Joey did as he was told, turning away as she held up the magic stone. Joey had thought it was useful back in the forest, but it really came in handy as blinding light flared up like a tiny star being born. The glare was so intense it sizzled the hair on the back of Joey's neck. Leanora's pendant gave them instant daylight—for a few seconds anyway.

"Ahhh!" The man in black with the pale face (Joey wasn't ready to call him a vampire yet, either) cried out and turned away, hissing.

Joey opened his eyes and the light was already gone. He tried to get a look at the man who was staggering around, reeling from the flash, but there wasn't time. "Move!" Leanora ordered, pushing everyone up the stone path toward the castle. "I don't think I can do that again."

Joey didn't need to be told twice. He ran with his friends up the path, across the lowered drawbridge, and up to the main gate of the castle. Two massive wooden doors with large iron knockers blocked their entry. The doors were fifteen feet tall and had to weigh a thousand pounds each. Wasting no time, Joey, Shazad, and Leanora chose a door and pulled back on its handle with all their might. The ancient hinges protested and the base of the door scraped against the ground, but working together, Joey and his friends cracked the door wide enough to slip inside.

"This is great—we're running *into* the haunted castle," Joey said.

"It's not haunted," Leanora argued.

"Tell *him* that!" Shazad said.

Outside, the man in black was coming up the path.

"Close the door! He can't come in unless we invite him," Leanora said.

"I thought that was all superstition," Joey said, throwing his weight into the door.

"Not now," Leanora told him.

"This is probably his house," Shazad said as they pushed the door into place. "I don't think he needs an invitation."

"Lock him out, then," Leanora said, spotting a crossbar on the inside of one of the doors. She tapped her stone pendant to give Shazad and Joey more light as they pushed a rusty iron bar into position. "He'll have to break this door down if he wants to come after us."

"Aren't vampires super strong?" Joey asked.

"He's not a vampire. He can't be," Leanora said, still struggling with the idea. Joey looked at her skeptically. "Okay, he might be a vampire," she admitted.

Joey grunted as if to say, *That's what I thought.* "Let's get out of here. Shazad, where do we go?"

"Down," Shazad said instantly. "We go down. One hundred doors in the dungeon. Look for stairs."

They entered the castle's great hall, but it was difficult to see anything. The only light they had came from Leanora's pendant. "I can make it a little brighter," Leanora said, holding the sunstone up like a lantern. "Not too much. The stone's running out of light."

"Don't waste it in here," Shazad said, circling the empty room. "There's nothing here but tapestries. Let's try outside." They darted across the hall and out into the courtyard, where moonlight illuminated the grounds. On a wall near the base of a broken tower, a sketchy-looking door sat behind a half-lowered portcullis. The heavy metal grate with spiky bottoms struck everyone as dungeonesque.

"That looks promising," Shazad said.

"Promising. Right," Joey muttered. "Not the words I'd use."

They ducked under the portcullis and went down a handful of steps, stopping at an iron door at the end of a short tunnel. Shazad pulled the door open, revealing pitch-black darkness on the other side. Everyone paused at the threshold, waiting for someone else to make the first move. They had already seen one vampire, and there was no telling what might be hiding in the shadows ahead. "Hello?" Shazad called out. "Anyone in there?"

Or anything? Joey thought. After a few seconds, they heard something. It was a shuffling and scratching noise. *Please don't be rats. Or zombies.* Joey stepped back as Leanora inched forward with the sunstone, and a cloud of bats streamed out into the tunnel.

Everyone screamed as flying rodents filled the cramped space, rushing past them like a waterfall of black leathery wings. Fortunately, none of them transformed into vampires and tried to drink anyone's blood. In fact, they didn't seem very interested in Joey and his friends at all. They just wanted out. But there were so many of them. Too many. Joey knew that bat colonies could number in the millions and the tunnel wasn't big enough for that. The bats were getting hung up at the portcullis. Some of them squeezed their way through the grate and escaped, but they weren't getting out fast enough and they kept coming. Soon Joey, Shazad, and Leanora would be overrun.

Hugging the walls, Joey worked his way back to the portcullis and pushed with all his might to raise it up. It was far too heavy for him to lift on his own, but fortunately, whatever gear or pulley system it had was still functional. The gate went up with a series of loud click and clacks, and the relentless wave of bats passed out into the night, flying away in a crooked arc.

"Is that all of them?" Joey asked when the tunnel was finally clear.

Leanora let out a deep breath. "I think so." At that exact moment, a lone bat flew out, startling everyone like a jump scare in a monster movie. Thankfully, nothing followed it. "Hopefully, that's the last of them."

"What's in there?" Shazad asked as Leanora shined the sunstone pendant into the open door. There wasn't much to see. A flight of stone steps wound down around a corner, descending into darkness.

"Could be the way to the dungeon," Leanora said. "It certainly has that feel."

There was a pounding noise behind them as the door to the great hall burst open. The man who was chasing them stepped into the courtyard and locked eyes with Joey. He bared his teeth, and Joey swore he saw fangs. "Guys! He's back!"

"I told you he didn't need an invitation," Shazad said.

"Come on!" Leanora said, placing a foot on the staircase and waving for Joey and Shazad to join her.

Joey started back down the tunnel toward Leanora, but stopped himself halfway there. "Wait." He ran back to the portcullis and pulled down until its spikes dug into the earth. He heard a latch snap into position somewhere, locking the iron gate in place.

"Did you just lock us in?" Shazad asked.

"I hope so. Locking us in means locking him out." Joey fell in line behind Shazad and Leanora. They hurried down the steps, going deeper and deeper in a tight spiral with only the dying light from Leanora's pendant to guide them. At the bottom of the staircase was a long hallway lined with cells. Leanora shined her light into each one as they moved down the corridor. The chambers were all empty. There were no creatures lurking in the shadows or skeletons chained to the walls, and Joey was thankful for that. At the end of the hall was an arched doorway framed out with decorative stonework. A gargoyle figurehead sat on top, watching from the peak of the arc. Joey half expected the thing to say "Boo!" as they passed underneath it, but the ugly stone beast stood still.

Beyond the doorway was a spacious cavern. It was so big Leanora's pendant couldn't possibly light the whole place, but Joey could sense its size, even in darkness. The ground under his feet was made up of rough, bumpy, natural stone.

Joey imagined a massive cave underneath the castle—like the Batcave, only without the cool cars and supercomputers.

"Can you give us any more light?" Shazad asked Leanora. As soon as he asked the question, her sunstone began to flicker and dim. "I guess not," he said. His timing would have been funny if the situation weren't so dire.

"The flare used too much sunlight," Leanora said, her voice rising with concern. "There's almost nothing left."

"I've got this. It's not much, but—" Joey fumbled for his phone, but dropped it in his haste to get it out. "Great," he muttered.

"What was that?" asked Shazad.

"My phone. It's got a flashlight on it."

Everyone got down on their hands and knees to look for Joey's phone. "Found it!" Leanora called out a few feet away.

"Is the screen cracked?" Joey asked, but a second later he didn't care about the answer. He put a hand on the wall to get up, and the whole cave lit up as if someone had flipped a light switch. "Whoa!" Joey moved his hand, and the lights went out again. "Where did that come from?"

"What? What happened?" asked Shazad. "What's wrong?"

243

"Nothing! What do you mean what happened? You didn't see that?"

"See what?" Leanora asked.

"The light! It was everywhere! How could you miss it?" Shazad and Leanora assured Joey they had not seen any light. Leanora hadn't even opened Joey's phone. "I didn't just imagine it." Joey felt around for the "light switch" and found it again. In an instant, the whole cave was illuminated with a supernatural, bluish hue. "There! It's back. I can see— OH MY GOD!"

"What?" Leanora shouted, spinning around with her necklace, trying to see. "Is someone here?"

Joey couldn't answer. He was too much in shock.

"Talk to us!" Shazad ordered. "Joey, are you okay?"

"I'm fine," Joey managed to say after a few seconds. "It's just this thing I picked up. I—gah!" Joey shook his hand out in disgust and wiped it off on his jeans, trying in vain to get it clean. "It's dark again now. I dropped it."

"Dropped what?" Leanora said.

"Let me have my phone. I'll show you." Leanora passed him the phone. He turned it on and shined its flashlight on the floor, revealing what he had unintentionally picked up—a human hand severed at the wrist. The hand was greenish black. Its fingers were curled like a claw, and sawed-off radius and ulna bones stuck out at the end. It was withered, dry, and completely bloodless, which was a blessing. The hand looked like it had been cut off the arm of Frankenstein's monster.

"That's disgusting," Shazad said.

Leanora made a gagging noise. "You touched that?"

"I know. It's gross." Joey sniffed his fingers and cringed. "What is it?"

Leanora knelt down next to the hand, inspecting it but not touching it herself. "You said you could see when you were holding this?"

Joey nodded. "Just for a second, but yeah. It was like I was wearing night-vision goggles."

Leanora twisted her lips, showing her distaste. "It's a Hand of Glory. Made from the severed left hand of a thief. It gives light to the holder but leaves everyone else in darkness." She got up, leaving the Hand of Glory on the floor. "It's a vile thing. Black magic."

A loud banging noise echoed through the cave. The sound echoed with a metallic clang and was followed by a terrible *click-clack*ing that could only be the portcullis going up.

"I guess you didn't lock it," Shazad said.

Everyone looked at the hand on the floor, then back up at Joey. "You already touched it once," Leonora said.

"She's got a point," Shazad said, gently nudging him toward the hand.

Joey shuddered. "This is pretty foul, but at the same time, I like being able to see." He screwed up his courage and grabbed the Hand of Glory by the wrist. The blue light returned immediately. Joey looked around in wonder, trying not to think about the object in his hand. The cave was bigger and deeper than he'd expected, a giant hole under the earth. "This place is *huge*." Fifty feet above Joey's head, stalactites hung down from the ceiling, along with thousands of sleeping bats. "There's so many bats. . . . It's a good thing they didn't all wake up before. We'd still be back in the tunnel waiting for them to clear out. You guys really aren't getting this?"

"No," Shazad said.

"What do you see?" Leonora asked. "Are the hundred doors down here?"

"Right now I'd settle for one." Joey scanned the cave for a long second. "There, I see them! In the back of the cave. Across the bridge."

"Not another bridge," Shazad complained.

"Don't worry. This one's legit." Directly ahead of them, a natural stone bridge ran out and down to the floor of the cavern. Joey described the sturdy rock formation, assuring his friends it wouldn't be a problem. They told him that was easy for him to say. He was the only one who could see anything. They were still in the dark. Behind them, the clicking noise had stopped clacking. In its place they now heard footsteps. The vampire was coming. "We have to move," Joey said. "Take my phone. Just don't drop it like I did. And stay close. As long as you can see me, you'll be okay." Leanora took the phone, and Joey led the way across the bridge.

The footsteps in the distance made Joey want to run, but he couldn't do that. The bridge was strong and wide, but the path over it was a bumpy road riddled with potholes and jagged protrusions. If Joey went too fast, he was likely to turn his ankle or catch a toe and go tumbling down into who knows what. It was worse for Leanora and Shazad, who couldn't see a fraction of what he saw. Joey had to go at a pace that allowed his friends to watch where they put their feet. The bridge covered half the distance of the cave and started out pretty high up. As its arc bent down to touch the ground, it got steeper and passed over a river of mystery sludge. All the more reason to exercise caution. At first Joey thought it was water down below, but it was too thick and viscous for that. Whatever it was didn't move like water. It was the wrong temperature, too. Hot air rose off the slow-flowing, bubbling slime.

"What is that stuff down there?" asked Shazad. "Oil? Tar?"

"It smells terrible," Leanora said, wrinkling her nose. She was right. The air smelled like rotten eggs.

"I don't know what it is," Joey said. "It looks like purple lava."

"It's purple?" Shazad asked.

"I think so." Joey held up the gruesome Hand of Glory. "This hand gives everything I see a bluish tint. I don't know if it's because of that, or if that gunk down there really is purple. I still can't believe I'm touching this thing. I can't wait to get out of here."

"You're sure this is the way?" Leanora asked.

"It's the only way I can see," Joey said. "There's definitely doors ahead—lots of them. I can't say for sure they lead anywhere good. For all I know, they're just more cells."

"We have to trust the map," Shazad said. "We can't go back."

"No turning back," Joey groused. "We should get T-shirts that say that. It's like our motto for this trip."

They arrived at the bottom of the bridge. It dead-ended in a little island surrounded by more of the steaming purple sludge. From there, a stepping-stone path led to the back wall of the cave, which was covered with doors from top to bottom in ten rows of ten. Iron scaffolding, ladders, and platforms had been erected in front of the doors and anchored into the rock, providing access to every portal. But Joey and his friends had to cross the boiling river of slime to get there. Joey checked behind them. The vampire had entered the cave carrying a torch.

"Come on," Joey said, his heart speeding up. "Keep the light on me and step where I step. We're almost there." Acting fast, before he lost his nerve, Joey stepped over the strange, scalding liquid onto the first stone. He knocked a few pebbles into the purple ooze as he adjusted his feet, balancing his weight. The tiny pebbles frizzled as they went under and little sparks of blue flame flared up where they sank. Joey's throat tightened. It was a preview of what would happen to him if he fell into the muck. His whole body would melt like an ice cube in a bowl of soup. He had to be careful. Ahead, some of the stepping-stones were large, as big as rafts, and some of them were small, the size of coffee-table books. He pressed on, knowing he never would have found the courage to do this if he weren't being chased by a monster.

Once again he had to go slow. Every time Joey took a step forward, he had to wait for Leanora to move onto the stone he had just left, then turn around and shine the light back for Shazad to follow. If Joey went too far, too fast, Leanora wouldn't be able to see him. He had to stay within range of the flashlight on his phone. It was a nerve-racking trip across the river, every bit as bad as the rickety bridge. If anything, being able to see the danger around him made it worse.

Fortunately, the vampire didn't seem to be going any faster than they were. Joey kept checking over his shoulder as the creature continued its pursuit. He couldn't see the vampire from his angle below the bridge, but he saw the torchlight advancing at a surprisingly slow pace. Joey wondered why he didn't turn into a bat and fly ahead to cut them off. Also, he thought vampires were supposed to be superfast and strong. Either none of that stuff was true, or he was just toying with them. Joey got the feeling the creature was doing the menacing slow walk that bad guys did in movies when they knew their victims couldn't escape. He really hoped that one of the doors up ahead was an exit.

Joey kept moving forward, stone by stone, thinking about what would happen if they ended up trapped in the back of the cave. Nothing good. Leanora's sunstone pendant was tapped out, and they had no holy water, wooden stakes, or crucifixes to speak of. Shazad had his cape and Leanora had her boots and the firestone, but all Joey had was a deck of cards and a mask that didn't do much unless he hooked it up to a laser. He told himself he'd have to pack better next time—if there was a next time. Joey's fears mounted, and he nearly slipped stretching to reach a faraway stone. He realized he was too preoccupied with what might happen next. He had to focus on what was happening now, or he'd die before the vampire got the chance to kill him.

One thing at a time, Joey. Just a little farther . . .

He made it to the other side of the river without any more close calls. Clinging tight to the Hand of Glory, Joey climbed over a series of boulder-size rocks and came down in a smoothed-out clearing in the rear of the cave. A small circle of white stones had been arranged in the center of the floor. Beyond that, a hundred doors filled the wall, towering above him. Joey ventured into the circle, and twenty torches on the scaffolding burst into flame, lighting up the doors as bright as day.

Leanora and Shazad came over the rocks looking frayed and spent, but their faces lit up when they saw the torches blazing in the darkness. "We have to hurry," Shazad said, breathless. "That . . . *thing* is still on the bridge, but it's coming. It'll be here any minute."

"Which one of these doors is the way out?" Leanora asked, sounding harried. Her momentary flash of relief was already gone.

"We have to choose," Joey guessed. On a hunch, he held up the Hand of Glory, and the doors all swung open. There was a terrible clattering of steel as dozens of swords, spears, lances, and knives appeared in every doorway but one. The weapons were all clustered together, floating in the shadows.

They shook their sharp edges and points as if they were alive and adamantly wished for Joey and his friends to be otherwise. But one door was different. Down at their level, right in front of them on the cavern floor, lay salvation. Less than ten feet away, golden light poured out of an open door as if it were the gateway to paradise. "I say we take that one," Joey said. "All in favor?"

"I don't know," Leanora said, scrunching up her face. "This is too easy. Don't you think?"

Joey snorted. "You're joking, right? None of this has been easy. Also, I like easy. We don't have enough easy in our lives. Let's get out of here!" Joey went for the door, but as soon as he left the circle of stones, every single door slammed shut. Then they started moving. Joey's heart sank as the doors shuffled position on the wall like tiles in a mix-and-match memory game.

"I told you," Leanora said. Joey just grumbled, hating that she was right.

"Either of you have eyes on the right door?" Shazad asked. "I already lost it."

"I can hardly see to begin with," Leanora complained.

"Quiet!" Joey hissed. "I'm trying to concentrate." His eyes

were glued to the wall, darting up, down, left, and right, tracking the door with the golden light as it tried to hide itself in the crowd. He blocked out everything, afraid to lose focus for a second. If Joey was right about the way this shell game worked, he was going to get only one chance to pick the correct door.

> *100 doors in the dungeon. The count gave his*
> *prisoners a chance . . .*
> *A long life of exile and mercy, or a short one*
> *impaled on a lance.*

The real Count Dracula, assuming there was one, had probably thought of this as good sport. His prisoners could either choose to rot in a cell, or run the gauntlet to these doors. One of them was a way out. The others were a death sentence. A hundred doors. One chance. Now it was Joey's turn. His fingers squeezed the wrist of the monstrous severed hand hard enough to grind the bones inside. Sweat beaded up on Joey's forehead. His nose itched, but he couldn't scratch it. His eyes stung, but he couldn't blink. He heard footsteps behind him, but he couldn't turn around. He had to stay focused. The doors sped around the wall, moving in every direction. Meanwhile, the world was creeping in, trying to distract Joey. He couldn't keep this up much longer. He blinked involuntarily. He couldn't help it. Panic gripped his heart as he wondered if that tiny, momentary lapse was all it took to lose the count's game. Was the door he was following with his eyes still the right one, or had he lost track of it? He'd find out soon enough. At last everything stopped moving and settled into place. Joey marked the position of one door in his mind. "I think I've got it. Let's go before it's—"

"Too late," Leanora said, tapping his shoulder.

Joey turned around. The vampire was right behind him. And he had Shazad. The torch he had been carrying lay at his feet, bathing him in flickering light, not that Joey needed it to see. Thanks to the Hand of Glory, he got a good look at the vampire, much better than the quick, fleeting glance he'd gotten by the bridge. Joey's mouth went dry at the sight of him. It was as if the classic 1930s Bela Lugosi version of Dracula had stepped out of a movie screen. He had slick black hair and a pale white complexion. He wore a high-collared black cape over a black tuxedo with a clean white shirt. A gold medallion with a red ruby in the center hung around his neck. Shazad's neck was dangerously exposed. The vampire held him fast, with one of Shazad's arms bent painfully behind his back.

"I was watching the doors," Shazad said. "I didn't even hear him come up behi–ahh!" He winced as the vampire twisted his arm in a direction it didn't want to go.

"Stop!" Joey pleaded. "Don't hurt him."

The vampire said nothing.

"What do you want?" Leanora asked.

The vampire's cold eyes narrowed. He studied them a moment before saying anything. When he finally spoke, it was with the same heavily accented, deep baritone voice that Shazad had used earlier as a joke. "I vant to know how you found this place. Vat are you doing here?"

"We were just leaving," Joey said. "Let him go and we're gone. History. If you want, we'll even play your game with the doors. I already started," he added, holding up the Hand of Glory. "Just let us go, please."

"My game?" the vampire repeated, looking over the doors and the severed hand as if seeing it all for the first time. "I think not. You're not going anywhere until I get answers. Vy are you here? Vat are you looking for?"

"Just the way out," Joey said. "That's all, really."

"We're only passing through," Leanora said. "Whatever magic items you've got in this castle, we're not after them."

"Vat *are* you after?"

Joey hesitated. He was desperate to get away, but at the same time his gut told him the less they said about what they were up to the better. "It's nothing to do with you. It doesn't matter. Just let him go, and you'll never see us again. I promise."

The vampire bared his sharp, terrible teeth. "I don't like repeating myself. If you need incentive to talk . . ." He opened his mouth, moving closer to Shazad's throat, but he didn't bite him. The vampire spun Shazad around and gripped him by shoulders. Shazad tried to get away, but the red ruby in the vampire's medallion lit up and Shazad stopped struggling. His arms fell to his sides, lifeless. "Vat are you doing here?" the vampire asked again.

"We're on a quest," Shazad replied. His voice was monotone and tired. Entranced. "A quest for Camelot."

"Camelot?" The vampire closed his mouth and lifted his chin. "King Arthur's Court? Here?"

Shazad shook his head in a zombielike motion. "Not here. This castle's just on the way."

257

The vampire seemed taken aback by the revelation. Joey and Leanora watched helplessly as the hypnotized Shazad spilled their secrets.

"How do you know this?" the vampire probed.

"Don't tell him, Shazad!" Leanora shouted. "Fight it!"

Shazad twitched, seeming to hear her. "We've got . . ." He paused, straining against the vampire's influence, but it was no use. The red light in the vampire's medallion intensified, and Shazad was overpowered. "I've got a map."

"A map." The vampire's eyes fell on the tube-shaped container Shazad had slung over his shoulder. He pushed Shazad away, ripping the map tube off him in the process. Shazad stumbled and fell to the ground right next to the burning torch. He rubbed his head, shaking off the vampire's control. Leanora helped him up and asked if he was okay. He said he was. Meanwhile, Joey watched the vampire take the map out of its container, silently freaking out. What were they going to do now? They couldn't lose the map. How would they complete their quest without it? For that matter, how would he get home before his parents found out he was missing? Joey briefly considered snatching the map back and running away, but that was no good. The way the vampire was looking at the map, Joey knew he wouldn't give it up easy. But something about the situation rubbed Joey the wrong way.

Why was the vampire so interested in the map? And why all the questions? Why didn't he just swoop in and attack, trying to drink everyone's blood? From the looks of the castle, no one else had been there in years. Joey and his friends were likely the vampire's first shot at a decent meal in forever, but he didn't seem to care. He didn't seem hungry at all. A funny feeling gnawed at Joey. Inconsistencies started jumping out at him. The vampire's outfit was too polished. Too put-together and perfect. Everything else in the castle was a dusty ruin, so why did he look so good? And why hadn't the sunstone killed him, or at least hurt him really bad? Leanora had said there was an actual ray of sunshine trapped inside it. Sunlight was death to vampires—everyone knew that. Also, weren't vampires were supposed to be able to hypnotize people with their eyes? This guy used a magic object to make Shazad talk.

Not just any object, Joey thought. *A red crystal . . .*

He caught himself scratching at an itch on his neck again, and all at once he tumbled to a realization. He knew exactly who he was dealing with.

The vampire's eyes widened as he looked over the map. "This is incredible. . . . Where did you get this?" His accent was slipping. Joey smirked.

"Why do you care?"

The vampire looked up from the map with a hard stare. "I'm asking the questions here."

"I noticed. I also noticed you didn't ask who we are."

"I don't care who you are."

"Or maybe you already know. Lea, is there something on my neck?"

Joey pulled down his collar, and Leanora shined the phone light at him. "It's covered in paint," she said, confused.

"That's what I thought. Light up your firestone. Hit her."

"Her?" Shazad asked.

"Hard and fast," Joey said. "She's no vampire."

The faux-vampire's eyes widened, anticipating an attack. He reached for something inside his jacket, but Leanora got there first, swinging a fiery, red-orange fist. As always, her punches sent their targets reeling, and Count Fake-ula went flying back into a large rock, hitting it with an ugly *splat*. The splat was the sound of black paint splashing across stone in the shape of a person. Underneath the impromptu mural, their true enemy was curled up in a ball on the cavern floor, unmasked. It was Scarlett, the red lady of the Invisible Hand. She was clutching her side, her face a picture of pain worth a thousand words. "I think you broke my ribs."

"Look at that," Shazad said, taken aback.

Leanora chuckled, pleased with her handiwork. "I told you there's no such thing as vampires."

"Yeah. You told me," Joey said as Leanora took back the map. Scarlett reached out to stop her, but lifting her arm was agony and she had to abandon the effort. "Get her jacket off," Joey said. "Grab her brushes before she can use them for something besides a Halloween costume." Leanora stripped Scarlett's coat off, taking away her brushes and her hypnotic crystal.

"Give those back or you are entering a world of hurt," Scarlett said, but her voice was strained and the threat rang hollow.

"Sounds like you're already there," Leanora said, tossing the coat to Joey.

"The question is, why are you here?" Joey asked. "How did you find us?"

Scarlett stood up, bracing herself against the wall. She let out a snicker behind an unhinged, eerie smile. "I'm here because you're here. I marked you, Joey Kopecky. I can follow you anywhere."

"How?" Shazad demanded. "How can you even find this place without our map?"

"Wouldn't you like to know?"

Joey scowled. "You know what I'd like? To never see these things again." He took out one of Scarlett's brushes and threw the rest of them into the purple sludge, jacket and all.

"NO!" Scarlett shouted as her trendy red coat sailed through the air to land on a stepping-stone. She sighed with relief when she saw they hadn't been lost.

"You're lucky," Joey said. "I couldn't hit that target again if I tried."

Scarlett gave Joey a look of death. "You're going to pay for that."

"Then I guess I'd better keep this," Joey said, taunting her with the brush in his hand. "If I were you, I'd go get the other ones. They look pretty hard to replace."

Scarlett bit back an insult rather than gamble that Joey wouldn't be able to use her own brush against her. Struggling with the torch and her injury, she climbed back over the rocks to go collect her magic items. Joey had a feeling they were her most prized possessions and, without them, she was nothing. He really wished they had gone into the steaming purple slime.

"Time to go," Shazad announced.

Joey pointed behind him to the wall of doors. "Third level, second door from the left." They took off running and were there in a flash. When they got there, Leanora reached for the doorknob, but Joey stopped her.

"Not that one," he whispered.

She turned to him, confused. "You said the second door."

"I know what I said. That was just in case she follows us." Joey nodded toward the stepping-stones. Scarlett was almost at her brushes.

"Pretty smart," Shazad said.

"We'll see," Joey replied, moving past Leanora to the third door on the platform. He tried the handle, but it wouldn't open. It was locked. He pulled harder. "I don't get it."

"Use the hand," Leanora told him.

"What?"

"A Hand of Glory can open any lock," she said. "Touch it to the door."

Joey held up the repugnant, green-black hand. "For someone who didn't want any part of this thing, you know an awful lot about it."

"I know stuff about things," Leanora said. "We've established that. Can we go now?"

"Love to." Joey touched the hand's dead fingers to the door and heard a dead bolt turn. "Here goes nothing." He pulled back on the door, hoping he wasn't about to get rushed by a stampede of sharp metal objects. Fortunately, a warm fuzzy feeling washed over him as golden light poured out of the open door instead. Joey smiled and dropped the Hand of Glory like it was a microphone.

"Say goodbye to Transylvania, guys. We are out of here."

12

Painted into a Corner

Joey couldn't see anything. He doubted Leanora or Shazad could, either. In the cave, before the blue light, it had been so dark he couldn't see his hand two inches in front of his face. He had the same problem now in the space beyond the dungeon door, but for a different reason. It was too bright. Joey squinted hard, barely able to open his eyes. He kept moving forward, trusting that he would end up someplace good. Or, at the very least, someplace better.

His faith was soon rewarded as the light softened and a vision of emerald green emerged behind it. He felt the earth grow wet and mushy beneath his feet. He was back in the forest, but the creepy, black twisted trees of the Dead Woods had been replaced by a vibrant jungle overflowing with plant and animal life. He heard birds chirping, along with other animal sounds he couldn't recognize. He was surrounded by towering trees. Thick vines hung down all around and sunlight poured in from above. It was hot, humid, sticky, and wonderful.

"We made it," Joey said, eyeing a red bird with bright blue and yellow tail feathers perched overhead. Monkeys watched from the trees, making chittering noises as he and his friends materialized in the jungle. "The next stop on the map was in Brazil. This must be the Amazon rain forest. It's got to be."

Leanora spun around, taking a quick look behind her.

"What is it?" Joey asked immediately. "Something back there?" He had learned in school that the Amazon rain forest was possibly the most biologically diverse place on the planet. That meant tropical birds and monkeys, but it also meant crocodiles, jaguars, anacondas, tarantulas, brightly colored poisonous frogs, and more. The happy feeling Joey got from leaving Transylvania faded as he realized they weren't at all prepared for what they might find in the largest jungle on Earth. They didn't even have any bug spray.

"It's nothing," Leanora said. "I wanted to shut the door behind us, but . . ." She motioned to the space behind her.

266

There was nothing there. It was as if they had stepped out from behind a tree.

Shazad took out the map, confirming their location. "I guess all these passages are one-way."

"No going back," Joey said, the familiar sentiment resurfacing. "Not that we'd want to anyway."

"Look ahead," Shazad said, pointing.

Joey turned around. It was hard to see at first, camouflaged in the jungle, but an old, abandoned village ran up the side of a hill in the distance. Joey could tell it was abandoned because it was completely overgrown and empty. Creeping ivy and vegetation covered every inch of every house and hut. From far away, it looked like the entire village had a thick layer of lime-colored fur.

"Gives new meaning to the phrase 'going green,'" Joey said.

"Is that Celestia?" asked Leanora.

"No," Shazad said, studying the map. "Celestia's upriver. That's where we need to go."

"We should rest in that village first," Leanora suggested. "Find some cover and figure out our next move."

Joey looked quizzically at Leanora. "I thought we just did."

"Joey, you left the hand."

This confused Joey even more. "You didn't want to keep that, did you? I know it was a magical item, but it was disgusting. I don't want to carry that thing around. Not even in my backpack. You said yourself it was vile."

"It is, but what about the doors in the dungeon? Scarlett can use the hand to follow us."

Joey made a sour face. "I don't think she'll try the doors with the keys. She won't have to. She's got me."

"What are you talking about? How did you know that was her back there?" Shazad asked him.

"And what was that with the paint on your neck?" Leanora checked Joey's neck and shoulder for multicolored splotches of paint, but his skin was clean again. It was time for Joey to come clean too.

"I've been seeing it ever since Scarlett hit me with her paintbrush outside the theater."

Leanora gasped. "All this time? That was a month ago."

"Not all the time," Joey said. "It comes and goes. I thought it was just my mind playing tricks on me. I'd scratch an itch and find paint under my fingernails. Then I'd glimpse Scarlett, but only for a second. I was never sure. I just thought she got in my head."

"More like she got under your skin," Leanora said.

Joey gave a grim nod. "For a second I saw her on the mountain, but I thought it was just the lack of oxygen. I realize now, the paint materializes when she's close by. It shows up when she's watching me."

"You're just now telling us this?" Leanora asked.

"I just figured it out. I didn't even think it was real until Ali said he saw paint on my neck when I was a camel."

"Ali saw it?" Shazad put his hands on his head, reeling at the implications. "Scarlett said she can follow you anywhere. If that's true . . . If she's able to track you and just show up wherever you are, she could have followed us to Jorako. If my brother saw the paint, she must have been there too!" He covered his face, afraid of what he had done. "If the Invisible Hand finds Jorako because I took you there, I'll never forgive myself."

"I wasn't in Jorako when Ali saw the paint," Joey said. "We were still in the desert. Anyway, she's not going to Jorako. After what we just did, she's going to stay on us. Especially now that she knows about the map—and Camelot."

Shazad winced. "I wish I didn't tell her all that."

"You couldn't help yourself," Leanora said. "You wouldn't

have told her anything if I still had my grandmother's necklace." She shook her head in disgust. "Of all the things to lose in the forest."

"It could have been worse," Joey said. "You could have lost the firestone. That thing's saved us a bunch of times, including just now."

Leanora nodded. "True," she said, finding comfort in the stone around her neck.

"So they know what we're going after now," Joey said. "It doesn't change anything. Even if Scarlett didn't know about Camelot, she'd still be following us to find out what we're up to. The way we're hopping around the world, going through lost magical places . . . I must be leaving a pretty interesting trail."

Leanora's face turned sad again. "That does change things, Joey. If she can follow you anywhere, it puts everything at risk." She paused a moment, trying to choose her next words carefully. "There's no way to say this nicely, so I'm just going to say it. You should probably sit the rest of this trip out."

Joey blinked. The suggestion hit him like a bucket of ice water. "Are you kidding?"

"I wish I were," Leanora said. "I don't like it any more than you do, but . . ."

"She's right, Joey," Shazad agreed. "I hate to say it, but she's right."

"You too?" Joey whipped his head around to look at Shazad. "I can't believe what I'm hearing. I thought we were past you guys telling me to leave this stuff to the professionals."

"That's got nothing to do with it," Leanora assured him. "No one's doubting your ability, Joey. It's just this situation. You have to admit, it's a problem."

"Well, I don't want to be a bother," Joey said, getting testy. "I'll just go home. Let's see if my parents can pick me up." He took out his phone and acted like he was making a call. "Hi, Mom? Dad? You think you guys can come get me? I'm in *South America*." He dropped his hand, having made his point. He couldn't leave the group even if he wanted to. Or so he thought.

"My mom and dad can pick you up," Shazad told him.

"What?" Joey gaped at Shazad. "How?"

Shazad took out the Tiger's Eye crystal. "I still have this. It's my mother's. You remember, she has the other one. The

Tiger's Eye is a two-way seeing crystal. There's no sound, but the jewels have a connection. You can write a message and turn the crystal so she can read it."

Joey was quiet for a moment. He felt like he'd been punched in the gut. "What message?"

"That you need help. It's the truth. You don't want that paint on your neck. Maybe they can help you get it off." Shazad closed his fist around the Tiger's Eye, hiding it from sight. He held his hand out toward Joey, ready to drop the stone in his palm. "They'll be able to home in on your location as long as the eye can 'see.' If you cover it up, it goes dormant. To turn it on, all you have to do is hold it in the light."

Joey made no effort to take the stone. "Are we really talking about this?"

"Joey, it's Grayson Manchester tracking your phone all over again," Leanora said.

"No, it's not," Joey protested. "I told you, I've got location services turned off. That's a sacrifice, by the way. You know how many apps I can't use because of that?"

"Joey," Leanora said, trying to get him to focus. "The Invisible Hand can track you everywhere you go. That puts all of us in danger. I don't want to do this without you, but what are our options here?"

Joey looked down at his hand. He was gripping the paintbrush he had stolen from Scarlett hard enough to snap it in half. He cursed the moment she had tagged him with the paint, and he cursed himself for not doing a better job of throwing the rest of her brushes into the purple lava back in Transylvania. Most of all, he cursed the fact that Leanora was right. It killed him to admit it, but he couldn't ask his friends to keep going with the Invisible Hand hot on their tail like this. Still, he didn't want to give up. There had to be another way. "We're supposed to be working together," Joey said, his voice faltering.

The question no one wanted to ask was, working toward what? Not one of them knew what they were going to do when they found Camelot. They all still wanted different things. Tears welled in Joey's eyes. He tried to blink them away before anyone noticed. "This trip was supposed to be about finding our way together. All of us."

"It should also be about doing the right thing for all of us." Leanora put a hand on Joey's shoulder. "I know it's hard, but can you do that?"

Joey backed away from Leanora's touch, feeling hurt. He racked his brain, trying to think of another way out of this, or a hole in Shazad's and Leanora's logic, but they were right. As long as he had that paint on his neck, he was a danger. The problem wasn't him. It was the situation, and it had to be dealt with.

"Joey, say something," Leanora said.

He was staring at his shoes, dejected. Leanora's voice brought his eyes up. He looked at his two friends and nodded. "I can do it."

An hour later, Joey was alone in the village. The minutes crawled by as he sat there waiting on ancient, leaf-covered steps. He reached for his phone more than once, but stopped short of turning it on each time. Back home, he would have scrolled through social media, or occupied himself with a game, but he couldn't do either one in this place. Unless he found somewhere to plug in his charger, the phone was for emergencies only. As Joey sat there waiting, his mind turned back to his empty stomach. He hadn't eaten anything since Jorako. The more Joey thought about it, the hungrier he got. He had to do something to occupy his mind. Joey decided to pass the time checking out Scarlett's magic paintbrush. He tore the ivy off the side of one of the buildings, exposing the stone wall underneath. It became his canvas. He didn't have any paint, but he didn't think he needed it. He had never seen Scarlett use any. The brushes just provided whatever color she wanted, on demand. Anyway, Joey didn't need much in the way of art supplies. He wasn't planning to paint a masterpiece that would require a full artist's palette. He was just going to mess around with the brush and try it out. That was the plan, anyway. The brush had other ideas.

Joey addressed the wall, and the brush took over. His movements were surprisingly involuntary as he painted. It was as if he was being remotely controlled by some unseen creative force or impulse. Colors flowed from the bristles, changing in between strokes, putting together an image comprised of geometric shapes and sharp angular lines. It wasn't Joey's style, but it did look familiar to him. He didn't know what he was painting, but he trusted the brush, and found the picture in the process. When he stepped back and looked at the finished product, a prophetic vision decorated the wall. He, Shazad, and Leanora were on horseback, dressed in armor. Joey had the wand in his hand and held it forward like a sword as they rode into battle. The ghostlike image of a king with a golden crown watched over them, standing next to a blue-robed wizard with a long white beard. Joey recognized them as King Arthur and Merlin, despite the abstract style of painting. Behind them, a castle floated on a hunk of rock in the distance. Joey took this to be Camelot. He wondered if he'd ever get the chance to see it in person. There were other magicians in the picture. More ghosts. Joey couldn't identify most of them, but he thought one might be Houdini, and one of them was definitely Redondo the Magnificent. Joey was shocked by what he had painted. Where had it come from? What did it mean? Looking at the picture of Redondo, Joey realized how much he missed him. He wished the old man were there to explain everything, but then he remembered explanations weren't Redondo's style. "He'd probably tell me to figure it out myself," Joey said under his breath, the trace of a grin on his lips. "Find your own way, young Kopecky," he added in Redondo's voice.

Thinking of Redondo prompted Joey to take out his magic deck of cards. He drew three off the top to see what his future held. The pictures on the cards were as strange as ever: a stage curtain with THE FINALE written underneath it. A castle in the clouds dubbed THE LOST KINGDOM, and a wild cat with a gem-stone for an eye—the EYE OF THE TIGER. Joey couldn't say for sure what the cards meant, but they all felt very final. Like his part in this adventure was coming to an end.

He wondered how much longer he'd have to wait there by himself. He scratched an itch on his neck and found paint under his fingernails. "Not much longer, I guess." He turned around and saw a large, empty frame at the edge of the abandoned village. It hovered a foot off the ground as if hung on an invisible wall. The bright gold frame stood out against the green of the jungle. There was nothing inside it, but Joey knew there soon would be. His mouth went dry. The jungle swayed around him. He felt an odd, dizzy weight-lessness as the moment of confrontation approached, but he told himself to suck it up and stood his ground. "Here we go," Joey said, glancing quickly at the scene he had painted on the wall. "Showtime."

Joey watched as the leaves rustled beyond the gold frame and a figure in red appeared. Scarlett pushed her way through the trees and stepped out of the frame, looking fashionable as ever in her designer coat and dark sunglasses. She seemed surprised to find Joey waiting for her.

"So, that's how you do it," he said, trying to sound casual. "These brushes really are amazing."

Scarlett took her sunglasses off. Her eyes narrowed into slits at the sight of Joey holding one of her brushes. Joey watched her jaw muscles flex as she clenched her teeth, but she didn't let her anger off the leash. Instead, her features relaxed into the superior smile of someone who had the upper hand and knew it. "That they are," she said. "Art has the power to transport you anywhere, anytime. All I have to do is think about you and start painting. Inspiration strikes, and I end up painting a picture of exactly where you are in the world. After that, I just add myself into the scene, and voilà!" She flared her fingers, presenting herself as if she were an eagerly anticipated guest of honor. "Here I am. I see you've been doing a little painting yourself," she added, examining Joey's artwork. "I hope you don't need me to tell you who that brush belonged to."

"I'm guessing Picasso?" Joey noted the exaggerated boxy figures and shapes he had painted. "He was a cubist, right?"

"He was more than that," Scarlett said in a pretentious tone. "Picasso cofounded the cubist movement, yes, but he was a little bit of everything. The man had many styles. Personally, I prefer his blue period. His work is a gift, even with your uninspired hand holding the brush."

Joey looked at the picture he had made. It was his handiwork, and at the same time, it wasn't. He didn't really like it. Joey would have preferred a more straightforward image. He was tired of everything being so warped and unclear. "Picasso's okay, I guess. I'm more of a Jim Lee fan myself. I also like Bryan Hitch."

Scarlett squinted at Joey. "Who?"

"They're comic book pencillers," Joey said. His explanation earned an eye roll from Scarlett. "They're more than that, actually," he added, matching her know-it-all attitude. "Jim Lee cofounded Image Comics, and Bryan Hitch's work inspired the whole Marvel movie aesthetic."

Scarlett turned up her nose at Joey's commercial taste in art. "Generational talents, I'm sure." She was unimpressed by his favorite artists, but the information gave her fresh insight into his mind. "Comic book heroes . . . ," she mused, viewing his artwork in a new light. "Is this how you see yourself, then, you and your friends? Knights in shining armor riding to the rescue?"

Joey said nothing. There was definitely a bit of wannabe

hero in him, but the way she said it made him feel slightly ridiculous.

"It is," she decided. "I can see it is." Scarlett had a smug, condescending smile on her lips. "Art brings out what's in here," she told Joey, patting her chest. "It can betray your innermost thoughts. Your fondest desires. An artist's work says things they might never have the courage to say out loud." She waved a hand at his painting, dismissing it. "I feel bad for you if this is the limit of your imagination. This is a child's view of the world."

"What would you paint?" Joey asked. "What's your heart's desire? Assuming you have one."

"I want the same thing all artists want. The freedom to express myself."

"And the Invisible Hand gives you that?"

"I do as I please, when I please. No apologies. No explanations. My work speaks for itself." She twirled a finger, and Joey's shoulder started to itch. "Her work" was all over his neck. He scratched at it, unable to restrain himself. "You're going to give yourself a rash," Scarlett said, warning Joey to stop. "You can't scratch it off. It won't wash off, either. Not until I'm done with you."

"When's that gonna be?" Joey asked. "Why are you here now, anyway? Wouldn't it be smarter to wait until we found Camelot and skip to the finish line?"

Scarlett threw her head back with a laugh. "You think we're going to let you *reach* the finish line? That's not going to happen. We're going to find Camelot, not you." She started toward Joey, motioning with her hand to fork over the paintbrush. "I'll take that back now."

"Sure." Joey gripped the brush at both ends. "Just tell me how many pieces you want it in."

Scarlett froze in place. "You break that brush and I'll break you." She opened her coat, showing off her full collection of brushes. "You and your friends should have destroyed these when you had the chance. That opportunity won't come again." Her eyes swept the village. "Where are they, by the way?"

"My friends? They left."

Scarlett raised a skeptical eyebrow. "You expect me to believe that?"

"Believe what you want. It's the truth."

"They abandoned you?" Scarlett studied Joey, suspicious. "That doesn't sound very nice. I thought you three were a team. Thick as thieves."

"We are. That's why I agreed to stay behind. I'm not leading you to Camelot. They've got a better chance of getting there without me—or you. We shouldn't have told you where we were going, but you shouldn't have told us you can track me anywhere. Looks like we both said too much."

Scarlett looked around, trying to spot Shazad and Leanora in the jungle. Her face was locked in a frown, stung by the unwelcome truth of Joey's words. "If they really are gone, we're going to have a problem. And, by *we*, I mean *you*. These friends of yours must not be very good friends to leave you here waiting for me. Don't they know what I'm capable of?"

Joey gestured to his neck. "They've got an idea."

"That's nothing. Just a dash of paint so I can spot you in a crowd. You're going to show me where the other two went. We're going to follow them, and if they don't give me the map, I'm going to use more colors. Different techniques. I'm going to take my time and get creative with you. I might even hang you in my gallery when I'm done."

"Why do you want the map so bad? What's in Camelot?"

"Didn't you just chide me for saying too much? I'm not going to make the same mistake twice. This conversation is over." Scarlett held out her hand. "Give me the brush. I won't ask again."

"How about I give you something else?" Joey took a plastic water bottle out of his backpack. An inch of liquid sloshed around at the bottom, but it was the wrong color for water.

"What's that?"

"What's it look like? It's a plastic water bottle. I know, I shouldn't have it. Plastic's bad for the environment. My friend Janelle is always going on about sustainability and conservation. She gives me a hard time about this bottle, but I bought it a while ago. Way before I knew her. What am I supposed to do, just throw it out? That's wasteful too. I'll give it to you instead."

"Are you finished?" Scarlett asked, losing patience. "I can see it's a water bottle. What's in it?"

"This?" Joey jiggled the bottle. "Snake venom."

"What would I want with snake veno—OUCH!" She jumped, clutching at her ankle, a look of shock on her face. A shiny golden snake slithered through the grass, up to the steps to where Joey was.

"What would you want with snake venom? Funny you should ask." Joey cupped a hand beside his mouth. "We got her!" he shouted. Shazad came out of a leaf-covered building, holding his cape in front of him. He draped the cape over the body of the snake, then pulled it quickly away to reveal Leanora, transformed back into herself.

Joey commended him. "Perfect."

Leanora patted her chest and examined her hands, then nodded her approval as well.

"What is this?" Scarlett demanded. "What have you done?"

"Good question," Shazad replied. "You might be wondering what kind of snake just bit you. It was a golden adder. They used to plague the deserts of Africa, but they're gone now. Extinct, which is fortunate since they're so extremely poisonous."

"Not fortunate for you, though," Leanora told Scarlett.

"Not at all," Joey agreed. "There's only one place in the world you can get the cure for that bite." He held up the water bottle. "Here."

Scarlett looked flushed. Sweat beaded on her forehead. The golden adder's venom worked fast. "Give it to me."

"Hang on," Joey said, pulling the water bottle back. "It's not that simple. You can't just drink this and be okay. That's not how it works. You see, when an animal is injected with small doses of a particular snake's venom, they produce antibodies against that venom. Those antibodies are then harvested from the animal, and an antidote for the snakebite is made from *that*. The antidote is called antivenom. That's what you need right now. I don't know if you have someone who can do all that for you back at the Invisible Hand's HQ or not. Maybe you have some magic home brew you can make, but I'm betting you're gonna need this venom as an ingredient either way. Antivenom can only be used to cure snakebites if it's made from the venom of the same kind of snake that bit you."

Scarlett wiped the sweat from her forehead. Joey wondered what she was feeling right now. Probably enough to know something was wrong with her. They were bluffing about the poison. It was fast acting, but it wasn't going to kill her. At most, Scarlett would get dizzy, nauseous, and spend a few hours hunched over the toilet bowl vomiting, but she had no way of knowing that. Joey could see the fear in her eyes. They had her convinced.

"What do you want?" she asked.

"First take off that mind-control crystal you've got there.

Throw it into the woods." Scarlett hesitated at first, but she had no choice. She took the red ruby brooch off the front of her coat. "Throw it far," Joey said. She did as she was told. "Good. Now all you have to do is get this junk off my neck and stop following us. Leave us alone."

Scarlett shook her head. "I can't do that. You know I can't. Even if the snakebite kills me, DeMayne would just send someone else. Especially now that he knows what you're up to. He understands the value of what's in Camelot better than anyone. The Caliburn Shield? He knows all about it."

"What does he know?" Leanora asked. "What does the shield do?"

Scarlett's face twitched as she realized she had said too much after all. "I don't . . . That is, he . . . DeMayne doesn't tell me everything."

"Hey!" Joey barked. He could tell she was lying. "Are you gonna talk or am I gonna pour this out?"

Scarlett's shoulders sank. "It does the same thing any shield does," she said, giving in. "It protects its owner from harm. You can use it to keep DeMayne out of the Majestic Theatre."

"What about Camelot?" Leanora asked.

"What about it? Use your imagination. The Lost Kingdom could be full of powerful relics. Enough to shift the balance of power between us permanently. DeMayne has been comfortably in control of the world's supply of magic for the last twenty years. Probably more. He won't allow you to threaten that, and he won't leave you alone. Not ever. You're too dangerous."

Shazad scrunched up his face. "How are we dangerous? We don't even have the wand."

"Is it something else?" Leanora wanted to know. "Something we have inside the theater?"

Scarlett said nothing. Her eyes burned with silent rage.

"Just FYI, you're going to start losing feeling in your extremities soon," Joey warned Scarlett. "Paralysis comes after that. I'm no artist, but I do know it's hard to paint when you can't move. I should also tell you that antivenom can only neutralize the venom in your body. It stops it from causing any further harm. It can't reverse what's already been done." He shook the water bottle again. "Pretty important to get this stuff into your system before any permanent damage occurs. Once you start throwing up, it's already too late."

It was another bluff, but it was well timed. Scarlett made

a face like she threw up a little bit in her mouth and started pinching her fingertips, testing them for numbness. She was desperate and ready to break. "Tell us why DeMayne thinks we're dangerous," Joey ordered.

"Because!" Scarlett blurted out, exasperated. "You're not like your parents. You might actually do something."

"What?" Shazad was shocked and offended. "My family's been a thorn in the Invisible Hand's side for generations. We've dedicated our lives to finding and preserving magical objects. Keeping them away from people like you!"

Scarlett was unmoved. "So?"

"My family shares magic with the world," Leonora said, equally insulted. "Don't tell me we don't do anything."

"You don't," Scarlett said matter-of-factly. "I'm sorry, it's the truth. In the great game, you Nomadiks have been crawling along one tiny space at a time for so long it's like you're not even playing. You're always moving, but you never go anywhere. As for your family," she added, turning to Shazad. "You just take game pieces off the board. You're not a thorn in our side. You're nothing. I'll let you in on a little secret. We know where Jorako is. We've always known."

Shazad scowled. "You're lying."

288

"We know where to look," Scarlett said, hedging her claim a bit. "If we spent a year or two combing the Sahara, armed with magical protections, we'd find it. But who wants to do that? There's no point. Yes, you've managed to keep a few relics away from us over the years, but you don't get everything, and you don't do anything with what you find. It's a wash. You don't bother us, and we don't bother you. For now anyway. It's the same with the Nomadiks. Your family isn't beyond our reach. You're just not worth our time. You work a little magic here and there, and we allow it because you're not pulling a big lever. You're not leaving your mark on the world like we are. But you three . . . we've been watching you. Especially *you*." She pointed to Joey. "Young and idealistic. Rebellious. Disruptive. Out to change the world. Given the chance, you just might do it. That's why you're dangerous. And that's why DeMayne's going to nip your new Order in the bud."

"What's he going to do?" Joey asked. "Kill us?"

"He will if you push things too far. Or you stop being useful."

"How are we useful?" Shazad asked.

Scarlett snickered. "Are you kidding? You're like a magnet

289

for lost magical relics. First Houdini's wand and now that map? It's as if there's some special force connecting you three with the world's most powerful magic objects." Joey looked at Shazad and Leanora, thinking about the Fates that sent them on this mission. Scarlett picked up on it. "There is, isn't there? I'm not surprised. You've been active a month, and already you're knocking on Camelot's door. You think DeMayne is going to stand by and let you find it? Or lose it like you lost the wand? You don't know him like I do."

"We're *going* to find it," Joey promised. He held up the venom. "You want this? Tell DeMayne to back off. And get this paint off me. Now."

Scarlett swallowed hard, as if forcing down a spoonful of dirt. Her complexion had turned a pallid shade of gray. Unable to look him in the eye, she nodded, agreeing to his terms. Scarlett took out a brush and beckoned him to come closer. Joey handed the venom off to Shazad. "If she tries anything, dump that." Shazad gave a nod, and Joey stepped forward. He was wary, but he pulled down on his collar, exposing his paint-covered neck. He didn't like showing his throat to an enemy like this, but he didn't have a choice. Joey held his breath as Scarlett touched the bristles of the brush to his collarbone. She held her arm steady. It didn't look like she was doing anything, but Joey felt the colors swirl on his skin. Looking down, he saw the paint being drawn away, sucked back into the brush.

"Is it working?" he asked his friends, eager for confirmation.

"It's working," Shazad told him. "The paint's almost gone."

But before the last drop went away, Scarlett got creative. With a few quick flicks of the wrist, she painted a fresh design on Joey's shoulder—the symbol of the Invisible Hand. Joey jumped back, but it was too late. The mark was upon him, and it was alive. The black hand symbol clutched down on his shoulder, and a searing pain burned through his right side. "AHH!"

"Shazad!" Leonora shouted. "The venom!"

Shazad took the cap off the water bottle and went to pour it out.

"STOP!" Scarlett commanded. Something about her voice made everyone freeze. "Don't do it," she told Shazad. "One drop of that hits the ground, and I'll kill him right in front of you."

Joey fell to his knees. The pain was excruciating. His

friends could only watch as he suffered, helpless to do anything about it.

"If he dies, you die too," Shazad warned Scarlett. He spoke quickly, sticking with the story about the poison, but he was clearly rattled by what was happening to Joey. Shazad held the water bottle sideways. The small supply of venom teetered precariously at the edge, ready to spill out. "You think I'm kidding? I'll dump it all right now!"

"Then it'll be two lives lost for nothing," Scarlett shot back. "If I fall, DeMayne will send someone else. You can count on it. The only difference is they'll be chasing two people instead of three. It will be your fault. Can you live with that? You can stop this, but you better do it fast."

Joey couldn't speak. He couldn't breathe. He couldn't think. The pain was too great. A not-so-invisible hand was digging sharp fingernails into his skin, plunging into his shoulder like five sharp knives.

"All right!" Shazad said, capping the water bottle. "Let him go."

Scarlett grinned. She watched Joey writhe on the ground a moment longer, then flicked the brush like a wand. Joey's pain vanished instantly. Remaining on his knees, he clutched his shoulder, gasping for air. Shazad tossed Scarlett the water bottle and she caught it with her free hand.

"You tricked me," Joey said, breathless.

"Now you're catching on," Scarlett taunted. "That's what I do. I'm an artist, but I'm also a magician." Keeping her paintbrush pointed at Joey like a sword, she bent down and reclaimed the brush he had stolen from her back in the cave.

"Joey, are you okay?" Leanora asked, going to his side.

"No, he's not," Scarlett answered.

"What did you do to me?" Joey asked.

Scarlett smirked. "I wouldn't worry about it."

"Tell me!" Joey demanded.

"I *am* telling you," Scarlett replied. "Don't worry about it. You'll make it worse. See? It's spreading already." Joey checked the mark on his shoulder. The paint was under his skin like a tattoo, but it was growing. Scarlett bared her teeth in a predatory smile. "Look at that. We're collaborating now, you and me. The more you worry about what I've done, that more that paint will bleed out like an infection. The more parts of you I paint over, the more you belong to me. You're a living, breathing work of art now, Joey. Congratulations."

"No," Joey said, feeling terrified and dizzy. The jungle

seemed to pulse around him and tilt as the gravity of his ever-worsening situation sank in. Joey had hoped to lose Scarlett in the jungle, but instead she had strengthened her hold on him. He rubbed his shoulder in a futile effort to wipe the painted hand away, but Scarlett was telling the truth. The mark got bigger as lines of black paint dripped across Joey's arm and chest. Scarlett had her hooks him, and she wasn't letting go.

Using her firestone, Leanora charged up her fist. "Get that mark off him. Now."

Scarlett pointed her brush at Leanora, ready to strike her next. "That attitude won't get you what you want. It will only get you something worse. Give me the map and I'll take it off. That's the deal. It's the only one you're going to get, and you should be grateful for it. Grateful you're dealing with me and not Ledger DeMayne."

"We're supposed to trust you?" Shazad asked, incredulous. "After what you just did?"

"You can trust me to hurt your friend like he's never hurt before unless you do as I say. I turned off his pain; I can turn it back on." She donned her sunglasses with a shaky hand and sneered. It looked to Joey like she was putting up a front. Scarlett was trying to project strength, but she was still sick. Before he could say anything, she pointed the brush back at him.

"Nnngg!"

Once again the painted hand dug into his shoulder. It hurt even more the second time around. Joey's muscles locked up and his head jerked to the side. He looked like he was being electrocuted and felt worse. No one knew how to help him. Joey saw Shazad and Leanora trade agonized looks, forced to watch him suffer. Shazad took the map tube off his shoulder but stopped short of surrendering it. Joey shook his head.

Don't do it! Don't give it to her!

He couldn't speak. Shazad couldn't decide. Joey's torment continued, but after a few seconds, Scarlett's arm wavered slightly. She shifted her weight. Joey was sure it was to keep from falling over as the venom worked its way through her system. The pain he felt subsided momentarily. Just enough for him to get a couple words out.

"Don't . . . She's weak," he rasped. "Snakebite . . ." Joey wanted to tell his friends that Scarlett was pushing herself to the limit. As far as she knew, she'd been given a lethal dose of poison. They could take her. They could grab the brushes and try to fix him without her help. Unfortunately, he couldn't say any of that. The pain came back hard and strong, and Joey's powers of speech deserted him again. Fortunately, Leanora understood him well enough without any more talk. She charged at Scarlett with a red, glowing fist.

Scarlett let go of Joey and got her brush up in time to paint a brick wall between herself and Leanora's furious attack. The wall was no match for the power of a firestone punch. Leanora smashed it to pieces, but it had served its purpose, which was not to stop Leanora, but simply to slow her down. When the dust settled, Scarlett had fallen back to a safe distance and was making her escape.

"That's enough for now, I think," she said, stepping through the picture frame she had used to enter the jungle. "Even the best artists need a break from the canvas now and then. I'll take your advice, Joey," she said with a wave. "We'll see you at the finish line."

Scarlett dashed into the greenery and disappeared. The frame disappeared with her before anyone could follow, not that Joey was in any shape to chase after her. He turned around and sat on the ground, leaning against the newly formed and half-broken brick wall for support. Leanora kicked the wall in frustration, knocking a sizable chunk of bricks loose.

"That went well," said Shazad, dripping with sarcasm.

Joey grunted. *Yeah. Just like we drew it up.*

He stared at the black hand on his shoulder, watching it slowly expand to cover his unblemished skin. He tried telling himself not to be afraid, but it wasn't easy. Scarlett was gone but she was still with him. Joey wondered if he'd ever be rid of her now. He was a work-in-progress as far as Scarlett was concerned. Sooner or later, she'd be back to finish him off.

13

Where the River Goes

Joey's arm was going numb. The paint had spread to fully cover his shoulder and tricep area. He couldn't feel anything where his skin was painted black. The limb was still good below the elbow, and he had the use of his hand, but the arm itself hung dead at his side as if tied to his body by a rope.

He tried with limited success to will the black mark to stop growing while the others built a raft. Celestia, the next stop on the road to Camelot, was upriver, and the river was the only way to get there. Once again, Joey wished they still had the magic carpet. Instead, they were forced to make do with what nature provided. Leanora used her firestone to chop down trees with the edge of her hand, and Shazad tied the wood pieces together with vines. It was a big job, made harder by the fact that Joey wasn't able to help. He still had one good arm—one and a half, really—but he was in a bad place mentally and in no shape to contribute.

Everyone was being pretty cool about it. No one blamed Joey for what had happened. Confronting Scarlett had been a good idea, and it had almost worked, too. They almost got the paint off Joey's neck. And even though the plan had failed, it wasn't a total loss. They'd managed to find out what the Invisible Hand knew about Camelot and the Caliburn Shield, and they'd slowed Scarlett down in the process.

"She's going to be puking her guts out the next couple of hours, with or without an antidote," Shazad told the group after she left. "A golden adder bite is no joke."

"At the very least, we bought ourselves some time," Leanora said. "We got that mind-control ruby away from her too. That's good."

"Yeah, that thing," Shazad said, frowning. "Any luck finding it?" he asked Joey. "It's got to be around here somewhere."

"I haven't seen it." Joey had gone looking, but had come up dry. Given enough time to search the jungle, he would have surely come across it, but they weren't sticking around, and Joey's time was running out. Joey knew he wasn't long for this mission. The painted mark on his arm seemed to be a little bit bigger every time he looked at it. He told himself not to think about it, but that was easier said than done. He thought about the pain he had felt when Scarlett was torturing him. He didn't want to feel that again, and he worried the pain would be worse now that the mark covered more of his body. That kind of thinking made the mark grow even larger still. Scarlett had said Joey belonged to her now. It was hard to argue with that. She was in his head, under his skin, and everywhere in between. She could do more than track his movements now. She could hurt him. Joey just hoped she couldn't bring the pain from a distance. If Scarlett had to be there in person to cast her spell, that gave him some breathing room, however minimal. Joey supposed he'd find out for sure if shooting pains suddenly came out of nowhere, striking his body like lightning on a sunny day. He knew he had to do whatever it took to get the paint off, and that meant he needed Shazad's parents after all.

The plan was to get Joey out of the jungle and back to civilization. The next stop on the map was in England. He could call for help there. Shazad assured Joey that once his parents saw what condition he was in, they would do whatever they could to help him. Shazad was a little fuzzy on what that entailed, but he was confident they'd figure something out.

They better, Joey thought. Unfortunately, even if Shazad's parents were able to help him, they couldn't help with what he really wanted, which was to stay with Shazad and Leanora. Joey was being sent home, like a problem child getting bounced from a tour through Willy Wonka's chocolate factory. Previously, they had ditched the magic carpet because Shazad's parents could track it. Soon they would have to do the same with him. He wouldn't make it to Camelot with his friends. His adventure was over.

When the raft was completed they got on board and shoved off, following the river and the next cryptic clue on the map:

> *A tower waits in a secret river you find at the*
> *end of the day,*
> *Stay your course and take the high road, the stars*
> *will show you the way.*

No one knew exactly what that meant, but they all trusted it would make sense when they reached their destination. It helped that the moving X on the map confirmed they were headed in the right direction. Joey settled in and tried to get comfortable. He had a hunch they would be on the raft all day and into the night. Using long branches as make-shift paddles, Shazad and Leanora steered the raft into a narrow offshoot of the Amazon. The map was like a GPS system, guiding them through another mysterious, hard-to-reach corner of the world. As they floated downstream, the jungle soon became thicker and wilder. Once again, there was something in the air. Some kind of magic. Joey could feel it. He glimpsed strange animals on the banks of the river—things he had never seen before. There were tiger-size cats with bright green and red stripes moving in between the trees, and birds with two sets of wings gliding through the air like X-wing starfighters. "Something's happening, guys. We're crossing over into another place. Like with the Dead Woods and Transylvania."

"I think you're right," Leanora said. She pointed out a monkey that was fighting with a tree over a variety of fruit that Joey didn't recognize. The tiny creature was trying to get its hands on what looked like a banana, except the banana was blue. The tree branch it grew on kept pulling back, and the vines surrounding it swatted at the monkey like whips, keeping it at bay. "I was going to say we should try to get our hands on some of that fruit, but on second thought, I think I'll pass."

"Yeah, who knows if it's safe to eat. It's not even safe to go near it," Joey said as the tree successfully fended off the monkey, knocking it into the river. There was no doubt about it, they had entered some kind of lost, magical place. Again.

"I don't understand," Leanora said. "How does this keep happening without us using a magical object? This isn't like when you went through the magic mirror back in the theater. There's no sand pit or door this time, either. We're just here. How does that work?"

"Maybe it's the place itself," Shazad theorized. "Back in Romania, something happened when we went through those pricker bushes. We ended up on the edge of Transylvania, and once we crossed the bridge, we were all the way there. It feels like that now. Like we're moving through lost pockets of magic in the world."

"But how is it no one else ever found these places if all you have to do is get here?" Leanora asked.

"This place is pretty hard to get to," Joey said. "The Amazon's gigantic. A lot of it is still unexplored. Those pricker bushes back in the Romanian forest were no picnic, either. Maybe people do find these places, but they turn around when the going gets rough. Or they never live to tell about it." Joey immediately regretted saying the last part. Worries spread the paint on his shoulder. He didn't need to add to them.

"That's got to be it," Shazad agreed. "We didn't turn back when we went through the pricker bushes or when we came to the bridge. Or here. We're going up this river against all reason and common sense. No supplies, no preparation . . . nothing but the fact that we think this is the way. We *believe* it's the way. That's the heart of it. And we do have a magical object." Shazad tapped the map tube on his shoulder. "We have the map to help us believe." Joey and Leanora looked quizzically at Shazad, not quite understanding what he meant. Picking up on their confusion, he elaborated. "We called the forest in Romania the Dead Woods because that's what the map said it was. I don't know what they call it back in that village we went through, but I bet it's something else.

Something modern. Less creepy. Knowing the name of the place—its old name—changed it for us."

"What are you saying?" Leanora asked. "We turned the forest's magic on because we knew its name?"

"We knew its *real* name," Shazad stressed. "To know something is to believe it. My parents taught me knowledge can unlock mysteries. That's what happened back there, no doubt in my mind. All three of us believed we were going through the Dead Woods to Transylvania because of the map. Right now we all believe Celestia's up ahead, and we're going to find it for the same reason. That's the key. We have to believe in it to get there."

"My parents used to talk about a place like this," Leanora said. "A magic place you can't find unless you believe in it. I grew up hearing stories about a secret country with thousands of people. A place where all the fantastic and unbelievable things in the world . . . all the wonders of imagination . . . they all have a home."

"You think that's where we're going?" Shazad asked. "Were they talking about Camelot?"

"I don't know. They never called it by name." Leanora gave the matter some thought. "It could be."

Hearing Leanora say that rankled Joey. "You know, back when we first met I asked you about secret magical cities. You told me people didn't live in places like that anymore. You said Jorako was the only one left, remember?"

Leanora looked away. "That's what I thought at the time."

"At the time you acted like I was clueless for even asking the question. Now you say your family's been looking for some lost magic kingdom your whole life?"

Leanora looked embarrassed. "We never found it, Joey. We never found anything like this. I didn't even believe that story." She seemed to surprise herself with that admission. "Wow."

"What is it?" Joey asked.

Leanora covered her mouth, stunned by the unwelcome realization. "I never thought about it before, but maybe I'm the reason why we never got there."

"Don't get carried away," Shazad said. "It's more likely someone was working against you, just as the Invisible Hand is working against us. Don't you think, Joey?" He flashed Joey a look, telling him to drop it.

Leanora cracked a weak smile, buoyed by Shazad's support. Joey nodded along. They still had to find Celestia, and they weren't going to get there poking holes in each other's confidence.

"Shazad's right," Joey said. "Don't talk like that. We're all true believers if we made it this far."

"Exactly," Shazad said. "We should be looking forward. Not back."

Leanora agreed and Joey nodded, but his heart wasn't in it. He didn't have much left to look forward to.

The day dragged on forever. Evening approached and Joey's energy waned, but he got a boost as they neared their destination. In keeping with Shazad's theory, he and his friends never would have made it if not for the map. They never would have known they were there because there was nothing to see but an empty dock where the river came to an end.

"This is it," Shazad said, as they climbed off the raft onto the rickety wooden landing. He and Leanora had to help Joey up.

"There's nothing here," Leanora said, once they were all back on solid ground. The raft drifted away from the dock, abandoned. They let it go. Joey and his friends knew they couldn't go back the way they'd come. There was only one acceptable direction, and that was forward. At the moment the way forward eluded them, even with the Secret Map of the World as a guide.

"I don't know what to tell you," Shazad said, examining the map. "We're in the right place. There should be a tower right here in front of us." He looked around at the empty space, frustrated. "There has to be something we're not seeing. You don't build a dock in the middle of the jungle for no reason."

"Maybe it's invisible?" Leanora offered, stepping forward to inspect the landscape beyond the dock. There was a wide-open clearing in the jungle before them. Leanora walked through it waving her arms, hoping to feel out the unseen structure's walls, but there was nothing but empty space.

Joey knelt down to examine the ground. The clearing had been pressed completely flat. It was as if a giant foot had stomped down on the jungle floor, but the area wasn't in the shape of a footprint. Joey could see the edge of the clearing where the flattened land gave way to healthy vegetation. It ran out in perfectly straight lines and turned at right angles.

"Something very heavy was here," Joey said to himself. "Recently." All at once, it hit him. A charge ran through

Joey's body. He jumped up, shouting, "Leanora! Get back here! NOW!"

She ran to the foot of the dock in seconds with the help of her magic boots. "What is it? What's wrong?"

Joey breathed a sigh of relief. "I forgot you had those boots on. It's all right. Nothing's wrong. We're safe."

"From what?" asked Shazad, looking around. "There's nothing here."

"Not yet. We're early." Joey's statement drew confused looks from Leanora and Shazad. "Don't forget what the map said about this place . . . a secret tower in a secret river you find at the end of the day?" He motioned to the darkening sky. "It's not the end of the day yet. We have to wait."

They didn't have to wait long. When twilight set in, the stars came out, and something else came with them. Twinkling stardust lit up the air inside the clearing, swirling around to form a gigantic slab of black rock. Joey could see it taking shape. It made him think of a skyscraper-size domino without any white dots. Its blank sides were perfectly flat and smooth with one glaring exception. Three-quarters of the way up the tower—about 150 feet up in Joey's estimation—there had been some kind of explosion. The smooth shaft had been blown apart by an unknown force. Scattered fragments of all shapes and sizes hung in the air, with the intact top of the tower suspended in the sky above them. Joey and his friends backed up, afraid the debris would rain down on their heads when the stardust solidified, but in the end nothing fell. The giant black obelisk arrived with a heavy thud and the earth shook, but the exploded tower was frozen in time, forever in midblast.

"Just when you think you've seen it all," Joey said, but he didn't really mean it. These days he never thought anything like that.

14

Star Maps

"Good thing I wasn't still standing *there*," Leanora said, thanking Joey for the heads-up. Everyone agreed the tower would have crushed her like a grape. It was more than two hundred feet tall, counting its disconnected top section, and had to weigh at least a million pounds. They approached slowly, wondering what to do next. There was no door that they could see, but the tower was lined with stairs that ran around the exterior of the mysterious structure. They appeared to go all the way to the top. Joey, Shazad, and Leanora had no idea what they would find there, but there was nowhere for them to go but up. "We better get moving," Shazad said. "Before it gets too dark to see."

Joey nodded grimly. If they lingered too long, they'd be hiking up the staircase with only Leanora's pendant and his phone to light the way. They started the long walk up without delay.

The higher they climbed, the slower they went. Not because they were tired, although Joey's legs did grow weary, but because the steps were so narrow. They jutted out from the tower wall, just wide enough to fit one person at a time. There was no banister to hold on to. Everyone had to walk up in a single-file line, hugging the wall the whole way. As night fell and the ground shrank away beneath them, it got downright scary on those steps, especially for Joey with his painted arm hanging awkwardly as dead weight. Trying hard to look on the bright side, he noted the steps were at least clean and clear with nothing to trip on. Joey had expected Celestia to be buried under a mountain of vines and weeds. The village they had passed through earlier had been completely reclaimed by the jungle, but the tower had none of that. There wasn't so much as an errant leaf on the staircase. Joey attributed this to the tower disappearing and reappearing on a daily basis. Nothing got a chance to grow in.

They reached the end of the line just as the sky turned black. Technically speaking, it wasn't the top of the tower, but it was as far as Joey and his friends were concerned. They could go no farther. Whatever had blown Celestia apart had completely destroyed a whole section of the building. Chunks of rock were cast about everywhere, ranging in size from great big boulders to tiny pebbles. Half the rubble hung in the air defying gravity, and the rest was scattered across a broken, uneven stone surface. The true top of the tower floated above the children's heads, impossible to reach. Fortunately, there was no need to try. In the center of the blast site was a cube-shaped room the size of a log cabin.

"I can't tell you how glad I am to see that," Joey said as he came off the steps. The journey up the long staircase had been hard enough. He couldn't imagine going back down in the dark if the rooftop had been empty. The room on the roof had an open door with a soft white light glowing inside. As they moved toward the featureless, cube-shaped room, they saw that it was untouched by the explosion that had wrecked everything else.

"Amazing," Leanora said, running her hand over the smooth walls. "Not a single scratch. You think someone blew up this tower to get to this room? Is that possible?"

"Anything's possible," Joey said.

"Hello?" Shazad called out, poking his head in the door. "Anyone in here?"

No one answered. They went inside. The room was empty, save for a painting of a starry sky set inside a decorative frame. It hung suspended in the air, just like the picture frame Scarlett had used to enter the jungle. The light was coming from the stars in the painting.

"Look at this," Shazad said, pointing up above them. "Another map." Joey looked up and saw a faded mural of constellations painted on the ceiling. It had a blue-green background dotted with stars and a clear line running through golden images of zodiac signs. Shazad was right; it was a map of the stars.

"Take the high road," Joey began.

"The stars will show you the way," Leanora said, finishing the line.

As soon as they said the words, the light in the room intensified. The painting was large and rectangular in shape, glowing like the screen of a twelve-foot smartphone. The children moved in for a closer look. Joey walked around behind it. The same incredibly detailed image he saw on the front had been reproduced on the back. "It looks so real,"

314

Leanora said, reaching out to touch it. She gasped as her hand went into the canvas and quickly retracted it. "Cold!" she said, shaking her fingers out. "This isn't a painting—this is it. This is what we're here for."

"Let me see," Joey said, his curiosity piqued. He put a hand on the picture frame and leaned his head in for a look. Sure enough, Leanora was right. And she wasn't kidding about the cold. It was freezing inside the frame, even worse than the top of Mount Everest, and with much less oxygen. The whole universe stretched out before Joey's eyes. Nothing but stars, stars, and more stars as far as the eye could see. His fingers tightened around the frame. Joey was afraid if he fell in, he'd end up a human block of ice, drifting from one galaxy to the next on a never-ending journey. A shiver ran through his body that had nothing to do with the subzero temperature. He looked to his right and saw Shazad there, staring into space alongside him.

"Take the high road," Shazad said again. "Doesn't get much higher than this."

They pulled their heads out and looked at each other. There was nothing on the other side of the picture frame but the infinite void of deep space. There was no bridge or path to follow. There wasn't even gravity. All they could do was jump in and hope for the best. Joey checked his arm. Black paint was dripping down past his elbow. "We should get moving," he said, putting on a brave face. "The sooner the better."

As they stepped up and balanced their feet on the inside of the frame, Joey reminded himself that the scene at the Devil's Teeth had not looked any better than this. The same went for the door in Dracula's dungeon. That door had looked good only because the other doors were all teeming with swords. The truth was, they hadn't known for a fact that any of the other portals were safe when they had gone through them. They just trusted the map, believing that it wouldn't steer them wrong.

On the count of three, they jumped through the frame together. With a whoosh, the room was gone, replaced by an infinite field of stars. The vastness of space swirled in Joey's vision as he fell forward, landing hard on a brilliant beam of solid light.

"What the?"

It took a second for Joey's brain to process what his eyes were seeing. When the moment passed, he stood up giggling in wonder. Joey had seen his share of miracles and then some, but this was truly special. The endless black sky was flecked with pinpricks of white light, and he stood on a luminous bridge that ran clear across the cosmos. Joey looked back the way he and his friends had come. Just like with all the other portals, the doorway had vanished behind them. That was the deal. You couldn't see the path until you were on it, and once you were there, you couldn't go back.

Joey, Shazad, and Leanora wandered around, marveling at the view and testing the starlight platform beneath their feet. Not only was it strong and sturdy, but it gave off heat. The icy cold they had each felt before was gone. The bridge had warmth, air, and gravity. Three things that were very hard to come by in their present location.

Joey walked to the edge of the bridge and looked down into the vacuum of space. He imagined if he fell from this perch, he would go tumbling through the universe just as he had feared, but as long as he stayed on the light bridge he was safe. Constellations were visible in the sky, their detailed outlines drawn around them in a bluish-white glow. Joey saw Perseus, Hercules, and Orion. The zodiac signs of Cancer, Leo, Gemini, and Scorpio were there too. The sight of them boggled the mind. It was enough to make Joey forget all about his blackened arm for a moment. Even Shazad and Leanora, who had grown up with magic, had never seen anything like this.

"You guys," Joey said, stunned. "We're in space—outer space!" he added, as if clarification were necessary. "We're standing on a constellation!" Joey stomped his feet on the light bridge, punctuating the impossible reality of the situation. "I wonder which one it is." He stepped back to get a look at the shape of the star line, but it was too big.

"I'll tell you where we are." Shazad unfurled the map, sharing Joey's excitement. His eyes widened. "Look at this!" He turned so Joey and Leanora could watch as a star chart materialized on the Secret Map of the World. A glowing picture overlaid the map with an image that was identical to the mural on the ceiling back in Celestia. Shazad pointed out a series of constellations that bridged the gap between England and Brazil. "Here we are," he said, finding the X that marked their location. "Ursa Major. We have to cross this distance here."

"This is awesome," Joey said, checking the map against the starscape. "I always thought Ursa Major looked more like a dog than a bear, but now I get it." He traced the route they had to travel, understanding now that the lines between the stars weren't just there for show. They were real. He didn't know how they were going to get back down to Earth, but he didn't waste his breath asking that question. There was only one possible answer. Trust the map. Trust and believe.

"Anyone care for a walk?" Leanora asked playfully.

"Don't you mean a *Star Trek*?" Joey corrected. Shazad and Leanora stared blankly at him, not getting the reference. "C'mon, guys! Really?" Joey made a disappointed face, lamenting the waste of a perfectly good pun. He told himself Janelle would have laughed.

They struck off down the starlit path together and walked all night long, or so they assumed. Day and night were relative terms in outer space, but it was a lengthy hike by anyone's estimation. Had they been anywhere else, Joey would have dreaded such a long walk, especially after riding the raft all day, but under the circumstances he didn't mind it one bit. The radiant path they followed was easy to travel, and the view was beyond special. Being up there put Joey and his friends in a very exclusive club. Not even astronauts ever got to see anything like this.

They went from constellation to constellation, walking right up to stars and turning to follow the gleaming bridge on to the next one. Everyone gawked as they passed stars that were larger than the earth itself. Giant balls of gas, constantly exploding with heat and light, were everywhere. Logic told Joey that he and his friends should have been struck blind or burned to a crisp before they got anywhere near a star, but logic didn't apply up here. They were magically protected as long as they were standing on the bridge. Their only concern was finishing the trip by morning. Because of the way Celestia showed up at night and disappeared during the day, there was a chance the whole bridge would vanish when the sun came up over the Amazon. Fortunately, they were making good time. *Very* good time. Whatever magic protected them out in space also enabled them to walk at what was essentially warp speed. The distance between each star was literally astronomical, but they covered it easily, traveling light-years with every step. Joey loved it. A shortcut around the world that skirted the edge of the galaxy. The inherent paradox made it even more magical for him. Of all the secret passageways they had found using the map, this one was by far the best.

We saved the best for last, Joey thought.

He realized that with every step he took, his part in the quest was coming closer to an end. Joey's spirits sank, and Scarlett's dark mark crept down his arm toward his wrist. He tried to ignore it, but Leonora wouldn't let him.

"Joey," she said, pointing at his arm. "It's getting worse."

"It's fine," he said, playing it off. His arm wasn't fine, but he didn't want to talk about it. The more he thought about Scarlett's curse, the worse it got.

"Hang in there," Shazad told Joey. He checked their progress on the map. "We're almost in England. As soon as we get there, we'll call my parents. They'll take care of you. You just have to wait until we . . . you know."

"Until you guys leave," Joey said in a sullen voice. "Without me."

His friends got quiet.

"We don't have a choice." Leonora's voice was heavy with regret. "We have to keep going. You heard what Scarlett said about Camelot. It could change everything. We can't let them stop us from getting there."

"I know," Joey said.

"We'll never make it if we stay together," she continued. "Scarlett can track you *and* hurt you. Badly."

"I know," Joey said again, getting testy. "You don't have to tell me that." He shook his limp arm as best he could. It flopped around like a stocking full of sand.

"Sorry," Leanora said, chastened.

Joey closed his eyes and let the frustration pass. "No," he said, admonishing himself. "I'm sorry. I'm not angry at you. I'm angry at the situation. I hate it."

"Of course you do," Shazad said, trying to sympathize. "I'd be angry too. No one's asking you to like it, but we're splitting up to protect you. We care about you, Joey. Scarlett could show up right now and torture you to death. I don't want to see that."

Joey groaned. He didn't want to see it, either, but he couldn't help picturing the scenario Shazad had just described. The black paint spread down to his hand. He wiggled his fingers while he still could, but he felt them going numb. "Can we stop talking about this? It isn't helping."

Leanora grimaced. "I wish there was something we could do."

"Just don't forget me when you guys make it to Camelot."

Shazad looked at Joey sideways. "We're not going to forget about you. What kind of talk is that?"

Joey shrugged. "I don't know. I'm not going to be there. Assuming your parents can fix me and you guys find the shield, what happens then? You still want to keep it in Jorako? After everything we found out?"

Shazad said nothing. Joey took his silence as a confirmation.

"That's what I thought."

"No," Leanora said, looking at Shazad in disbelief. "Really? Even after Scarlett said the Invisible Hand knows where Jorako is?"

"She didn't say they know where Jorako is. She said they could find it," Shazad said. "If she was telling the truth—and that's a big if—then it's all the more reason to take the shield there. To protect my family and the magic we've saved."

"If she was telling the truth, it doesn't matter what's in Jorako," Leanora countered. "They haven't gone after your collection because they don't care about it. It's a write-off to them. Acceptable losses. You don't bother them, and they don't bother you."

Shazad scoffed. "I'm sure we bother them plenty. You've been to my home. You've seen the things we've kept out of their hands."

"I don't think it matters though," Leanora said. "They're still as strong as they ever were."

Shazad took umbrage at that. "If my family's work doesn't matter, then neither does yours. Scarlett said the Invisible Hand *lets* your family go around putting on shows, hiding magic in plain sight. They don't care because no one believes it's real."

"Not yet," Leanora said. "Maybe something in Camelot can change that."

"So what, your family gets the shield?" Shazad asked in a challenging tone. "I don't think so."

Joey sighed. "Here we go again. Is it always going to be like this? The three of us fighting over some magical object?"

"You're the one who brought it up," Leanora said.

"Not so we could argue. It's a bigger conversation. We have to deal with it, but this isn't the time or the place. Look at me. I can't go on like this. I know that. I'm willing to drop out so you guys can reach Camelot, but you've got to promise not to cut me out. Get the shield and bring it back to the theater. We'll settle this at the Majestic, all three of us. We're in this thing together, right? Even when we're not together. All for one, one for all."

"Where'd that come from?" Shazad asked.

Joey reddened. "The Three Musketeers. It's their motto. What, too much?"

"No, I mean where'd *that* come from?" Shazad asked, pointing into space.

Everyone looked up. An object the size of a small moon was barreling toward them. It looked like a fireball, white-hot at the front, with tongues of powder-blue flames trailing off the back end. Only it wasn't fire; it was ice. A giant ball of ice, gas, and dust.

"It's a comet," Joey said in a slightly dazed voice. He was hypnotized by the sight of the massive celestial object. It was breathtaking. Another once-in-a-lifetime sight for the mental scrapbook.

Frozen particles that were traveling with the comet hit the light bridge, making a *tink-tink-tink* sound, like ice in a cosmic hailstorm. The noise jolted Joey out of his reverie. Apparently, the magic protections that shielded them from the stars didn't apply to things like comets. It was going to hit them for real. Everyone came to the same conclusion at once and ran, but there was nowhere to run to. There was no exit at the end of the bridge. No escape. Shazad had said they were close to England, but Joey couldn't see any way to get there. The starlight bridge went on forever, disappearing into the blackness of space.

The comet smashed into the bridge, hitting with all the force of a planet-killing meteor. The impact threw everyone into the air. Joey went sliding across the bridge and came to a halt just short of the edge. Shazad wasn't so lucky. When Joey got up, he saw his friend hanging on by his fingertips.

"SHAZAD!"

Joey ran as fast as he could and knelt down to pull Shazad up, but he didn't have any leverage. He had to lie flat on his belly and grab Shazad by the belt with his one good arm.

"Forget about me!" Shazad yelled. "Get the map!"

"What?" Joey said, turning his head to look down the bridge. The map was there in its tube, balanced half on the bridge and half off. The strap that had held it to Shazad had snapped, and the map was about to fall. Joey wanted to run and save it, but he had to save Shazad first. Joey strained with all his might, but Shazad was too heavy. Even worse, as long as Joey was holding on to Shazad, he couldn't hold on to the bridge. Joey felt himself sliding right up to the precipice, about to go over. Leanora swooped in just in time to save them both. Together, she and Joey dragged Shazad back to safety. As soon as they got him up, he scrambled after the map.

"Don't let it fall. Don't let it fall!"

Leanora chased after him. Joey stayed where he was. His friends didn't know it yet, but it no longer mattered if they saved the map or not. The comet's collision with the starlight bridge had created a tidal wave of solid light. Joey watched it rise up a mile high—a solar tsunami headed straight for them, moving like a runaway mountain. He couldn't speak. Leanora and Shazad didn't even have time to turn around. They never knew what hit them.

15

End of the Road

Joey blinked his eyes open. He was lying flat on his back and staring straight up at a white ceiling. A soft pillow had been placed beneath his head. He realized he was in bed, and for a very pleasant second he thought everything he had been through over the last couple days had been nothing but a dream. Then it dawned on him that he wasn't in his bed, and the memories drifted back in bits and pieces. The pleasant feeling Joey had briefly enjoyed faded away, replaced by burning questions. He had no idea where he was or how he had gotten there. The last clear memory he had was the light wave hitting his body up in space. After that he had nothing but broken fragments. Joey closed his eyes and thought back, retracing his steps. Images ran through in his mind like flashback scenes in a movie:

He was sprawled out on the ground. There was grass in his face, pushing up against his nose. Someone turned him over and picked him up. They were shouting. . . . Who was it? Joey couldn't make out any faces. They were all masked by shadows. He didn't see them. Strangers carried him off. Where to? And was he alone?

Where were his friends?

Joey opened his eyes back up. He tried to get out of bed, but he couldn't sit up. He looked down and saw his arm was wrapped in thick red linen, all the way up to the finger-tips. Using his left hand, he tugged on his collar and looked under his shirt. His shoulder and upper chest had been ban-daged too. It was the kind of wrap job Joey had seen on major league pitchers who were icing up their shoulders and arms after baseball games. Only his arm wasn't cold. It was warm and tingly. Joey took that as a good sign. Whoever had picked him up was trying to help him. With some effort, he sat upright and saw Leanora and Shazad sleeping on a couch across the room. Relieved, Joey quietly got out of bed. He turned the blinds on a nearby window and looked out upon green fields.

Joey was baffled. He could see that everyone had made

it back to Earth in one piece, but that was the limit of his knowledge. He inspected the immediate area with a keener eye. He wasn't in a hotel room, and it wasn't a room in a house, either. His first thought was that he was in a mobile home, but those words didn't do the place justice. This was a luxury trailer. The kind of place a movie star would hang out in on set or a rock star would use to travel from one tour date to the next. Anything that was too short to fly but too long to drive without all the comforts of a five-star hotel. Joey spotted some handbills on a nearby desk. They were printed on rough parchment paper. He picked one up and read it. The tiny poster advertised a performance by the Nomadiks. A magic show. One night only. The date, time, and venue had yet to be filled in. Joey felt safer now that he knew who it was that had gathered him up and treated his wounds. The question was, how had Leanora's family found him and the others—and where were they? "What's going on here?" Joey whispered to himself.

On the couch, Shazad and Leanora began to stir. "Hey," Joey said, waving from the window.

Shazad stretched and looked around, thoroughly confused. "Where are we?"

Joey held up the mini poster. "Ask Leanora."

"Me? Why m—" Leanora broke off midsentence, recognizing the room. "My parents' trailer? What are we doing here?"

Shazad did a double take at Leanora. "This is your parents' trailer? Really?"

"I know, right?" Joey said. "Not what I pictured, either."

Leanora fixed a pointed look on the two boys. "What exactly did you two picture? Horse-drawn carriages and covered wagons?"

"No," Joey said a little too quickly. The truth was, that was pretty close to how he had envisioned Leanora's life on the road, but he didn't want her to know that. "I didn't think you had any kind of trailer," he said, trying to cover. "I figured your family used magic to go from place to place. Like with your doorknob."

Leanora seemed to accept that explanation. "No," she said, her expression relaxing. "My father says it's important to see the world, not just hop from one city to the next. We have to appreciate the spaces—and the people—in between. They all deserve magic. So, we drive."

"How did we get here?" Shazad asked, joining Joey at the

window. "The last thing I remember is almost falling off the bridge."

"Nothing after that?" Joey asked.

"After that . . . we were trying to get the map." Shazad took in a sharp breath as an unwelcome memory crystalized in his brain. "The map!" he exclaimed, putting both hands on his head. He looked around the room, hoping to spot it. This time, it was nowhere to be found. "I lost the map!"

Shazad collapsed back onto the couch. Everyone was quiet as he hunched over, covering his face with his hands. Leanora and Joey looked at each other, not knowing what to say. Joey had actually forgotten the map was gone until the moment Shazad had mentioned it. The loss hit him hard too.

Leanora put a hand on Shazad's shoulder. "It's not your fault," she said weakly.

Shazad scoffed at that, pulling his shoulder away. "No? I was holding it. Whose fault is it?"

"It wasn't you," Joey said. "We got hit by a comet! After that, a giant wave of light rushed us. I think it was the bridge itself. It must have taken a while to build up, but when it came down, it came down hard. That was probably always going to be the way we got down to Earth, but we didn't know it was going to hit us. We couldn't have known. The map didn't give us any clue about that."

"That's what I'll tell my parents, then." Shazad pushed an angry tear away with the heel of his palm. "It was the map's fault. It didn't specifically tell me not to drop it while I was out in space."

"If it's gone, it's gone. Don't beat yourself up about it," Joey told Shazad. "It doesn't do any good. I know. If anyone knows how you feel right now, it's me. At least you didn't do it on purpose."

"It doesn't matter how it happened. All that matters is it's gone. This is on top of losing the staff!" Shazad leaned his head back on the couch and looked up at the ceiling in a daze. "What a disaster. This trip is over. *I'm* over. What are we going to do now?"

"I don't know," Leanora said. She had a shell-shocked expression on her face too. "I don't think there's anything we *can* do."

"It could be worse," Joey said.

Shazad snorted. "That's what you said when Leanora lost her necklace. There's no bright side this time, Joey."

"Don't be so sure." Joey gestured to his arm, which was wrapped up like a birthday present. "At least you have your health."

Everyone got quiet when they looked at Joey's arm, suddenly remembering what he was going through. "Right," Shazad said. "Sorry."

"Don't worry. You're going to have your health too," Leanora told him. "Soon. Those are special bandages. I broke my arm when I was nine years old and my parents wrapped my arm up just like you are now. I was good as new an hour later."

Joey's eyebrows went up. "I like the sound of that. Will it work on what I've got?"

Leanora shrugged. "I suppose it's like any magic item. It depends on you."

Joey nodded. "Think happy thoughts," he told himself.

"Let's find out where everyone is," Leanora said, getting up. "And how we got here. I'd like to get that story."

He and Shazad followed Leanora to a spiral staircase that led down to a floor with a living room, an entertainment center, and a full kitchen. "This trailer is practically the size of my apartment," Joey said. "I can't believe this is how you guys get around. How much do you charge for tickets?"

Leanora made a face at Joey. "Don't be ridiculous. Our shows are free. Every audience is a chance to make people believe in magic. You think we'd turn someone away just because they couldn't afford a ticket?" She shook her head as if Joey should have known better. "We have other ways of getting money."

"Like what? A goose that lays golden eggs?" Joey joked.

Leanora smiled. "Something like that."

Joey's eyebrows went up, realizing she was serious. "That must be nice," he said. "Still, I would have thought you guys kept a lower profile out on the road."

Leanora opened the trailer door and held it for Joey. "Have a look out here."

They stepped outside, and Joey saw that from the exterior, the Nomadiks' luxury trailer looked like a plain old tractor trailer.

"Just a big boring truck." Leanora smiled, letting the door swing shut with a bang. "Not the kind of thing that gets a second look from anyone."

"Not bad," Joey said, impressed by the illusion.

"It's a glamour charm," Shazad said, opening the door to look back inside. "That's a magical object used to disguise

335

the appearance of something," he added for Joey's benefit. "This is a good one. One of the best I've seen."

"What about the rest of these?" Joey asked. "More magic camouflage?" The truck was parked on the shoulder of a country road miles from anywhere. A trail of rusty RVs and broken-down jalopies were lined up behind it.

"That's right." Leanora walked up to one of the cars. Actually, it was not so much a car as it was a dumpster with wheels. It was dented all over, and a clear plastic garbage bag had been duct-taped over a broken window. Inside, the car was stuffed with so much random junk it looked like the driver had just robbed a garage sale. "This one's a Maserati," Leanora announced. She opened the door, and Joey gawked at the spotless interior of a sleek, stylish sports car. He stuck his head inside. It still had that new-car smell.

"You see?" Leanora said. "We take precautions too. Even when it hurts. Believe me, this car's not nearly as much fun to drive when it looks like this."

"You know how to drive?" Joey asked. "And your parents let you?"

"Why not? With the glamour on, it looks like there's an

old lady behind the wheel. Not that anyone would see me out here."

Leanora motioned to the wide-open fields. Rolling hills and pastoral meadows ran out in every direction. The landscape was empty except for a large circus tent that had been erected nearby. As Joey turned to look at it, he saw a man and a woman coming toward them. He could only assume he was looking at Leanora's mom and dad. "How do your parents feel about you disappearing for the last two days?" he asked her.

Leanora took a breath. "I'm about to find out."

Joey and Shazad waited on the side of the road as Leanora went to meet her parents halfway. There was a brief reunion out on the field and a conversation Joey couldn't hear, but it was clear that Leanora was not in trouble. She and her parents hugged it out and walked back toward the trucks together.

"In my house, that would have gone differently," Joey said.

Shazad nodded, looking grim. "It will definitely be different when my parents get their hands on me."

Leanora and her parents returned holding hands, a happy trio. Her father was tall and well built. He wore black pants and a loud, multicolored shirt. He had black hair, blue eyes, and a stubbly beard. Her mother wore a patterned folk dress and a single jeweled pendant around her neck. She had long dark wavy hair like her daughter and mysterious, hypnotic eyes. "Joey, Shazad," Leanora began. "These are my parents. Dimitry and Natasha Valkov."

Shazad stood up a little straighter. "It's nice to meet you," he said.

"And you," Leanora's father said with an accent slightly thicker than Leanora's. He offered his hand, and the boys took turns shaking it. "It's about time we got to meet Lea's friends."

"Yes, I was wondering when she was going to bring you by," Leanora's mother agreed. "I didn't expect it to happen like this."

Joey thought that was an odd comment, since they had not been allowed to visit before now, but he let it slide. "Sorry to drop in on you like this," Joey said. "Thanks for putting us up."

"You should not be up. Especially you," Leanora's father said, noting Joey's bandages. "We were letting you rest."

"I appreciate that—and this," Joey said, gesturing with his

arm. He was able to move it a little, which was a big improvement. "I feel like I'm getting better. Can these bandages heal me all the way?"

"Those are the Bandages of Panacea. They can heal just about anything," Leanora's mother said. "Of course, I've never seen anything like this," she added, examining Joey's arm. "What happened to you?"

"It's a long story," Joey said.

"You should lie back down," Leanora's father told him. "Rest."

"Thanks, but I don't think I could sleep any more."

"What about food?" Leanora's mother asked. "Can you eat?" Joey's empty stomach growled audibly, answering the question for him. Shazad and Leanora's stomachs made similar noises.

Leanora's father laughed. "Is there a pack of wild dogs nearby? Come. We are eating. The whole family. Join us."

He led the way to the tent. As they approached, the smell of food nearly lifted Joey off his feet like a cartoon character. He didn't know what was on the menu, but it didn't matter. He was starving. He could have eaten a rock at that point. Inside the tent, it smelled delicious. Tables had been set up, and the rest of Leanora's family was eating, drinking, and laughing. Joey estimated the tent held somewhere between twenty and thirty people. There were children younger than Leanora, older cousins, aunts, uncles, and grandparents. There was also more food than anyone there could hope to eat. Leanora pointed out various dishes with growing excitement. Joey's mouth watered over the blini, which were thin pancakes that looked like French crepes. They were folded in triangles, filled with strawberry jam, and not to be confused with the syrniki, which were cottage-cheese-based pancakes topped with yogurt and caramelized fruit. Joey thought he could eat about a hundred of each, but he had to save room for the buterbrody: open-faced sandwiches layered with different types of cheese, sausage, smoked fish, and various flavorful spreads. There were dozens upon dozens of them, and that was just the tip of the iceberg. The breakfast feast was so plentiful Joey could hardly keep track of it all.

"What's all this for?" Leanora asked her parents.

"We're celebrating," her mother replied.

"I'm afraid we don't have much to celebrate right now," Shazad said.

"Don't be silly," Leanora's father said, shaking Shazad by the shoulder. "We found you, didn't we? Also, we have guests. That's reason enough."

Three chairs opened up at a table in front of Joey, Leanora, and Shazad. "Here, sit," Leanora's mother said, ushering the children into their seats. "We'll make you plates. Lea, introduce your cousins. Dimitry, come." As Leanora's mother dragged her father off in the direction of the food, Leanora introduced Joey and Shazad to the other people at the table. As she spoke, Joey reached for a basket filled with black bread in the center of the table. Shazad and Leanora did the same. Joey slathered fresh butter on a hearty slice and took a bite. It was heaven. He quickly lost track of who was who as Leanora rattled off the names of first cousins, second cousins, and second cousins once removed.

"Sometimes forcibly removed," one of them joked. Everyone laughed. Even Shazad, despite his sour mood.

"Are we in England right now?" Joey asked the table in between bites.

"Wales," answered one of Leanora's cousins with a nod. "We've been here all month, touring the countryside, putting on shows. Lucky for you."

"Is that how you found us?" Joey asked. He remembered Shazad's mother had said that Leanora's family was somewhere in England at the moment. "You just happened to be in the right place, at the right time?"

"That's some coincidence," Shazad said.

"Maybe it was fate," Leanora said.

"It wasn't fate," one of her cousins said, dismissing the idea out of hand. "We knew you were going to be here. We canceled our show to go looking for you all day yesterday."

"What are you talking about?" Shazad said. "How did you know we'd be here?"

"We told them," Shazad's mother said behind him.

Shazad shook in his seat at the sound of his mother's voice. Leanora's parents had returned to the table with generous helpings of food—and both of Shazad's parents.

Shazad turned around in his seat, his eyes the size of quarters. His mother and father were dressed in khaki pants and white shirts. They looked to Joey like archaeologists on a dig. Both of them had stern looks on their faces.

Shazad scrambled out of his chair and stood up straight like a soldier who had been called before a superior officer. His father stepped forward to face him. Shazad was tall, but his father was even taller and had a larger, more powerful frame. He had thick black hair and a neatly trimmed black beard with touches of gray around the chin. He was painfully silent and was giving Shazad a hard stare. It was uncomfortable for Joey to watch. He couldn't imagine how Shazad felt.

"Do you know how worried we were?" his father asked after what felt like forever. His voice was soft and somehow all the more threatening for it.

"I'm sorry." Shazad choked on the words. "I didn't mean . . . I didn't think—"

His father closed the distance between them with a great sweeping stride and wrapped Shazad up with both arms, clutching him tight. He was on the verge of tears and had a hard time speaking. "We found the carpet at the Devil's Teeth! We were afraid that . . ." He trailed off, unable to finish his sentence. Instead, he hugged Shazad even tighter. "Thank goodness you're all right."

"Don't ever do that to us again," Shazad's mother said, giving Shazad a hug of her own once his father finally let go.

"I don't understand," Shazad said, clearly shocked to find out he wasn't being yelled at, punished, or killed. "How are you here? How did you know we'd be here?"

"Please," Shazad's mother said. "Give me some credit. I saw the map too. I knew you were looking for Camelot. We've been scouring the area ever since you ran out of the house. We didn't know for sure where you'd end up, or if you'd even make it here, but it was all we had to go on. So we came."

"Your parents contacted us early yesterday morning," Leanora's father said. "They told us the three of you had taken on some kind of quest?"

"Don't ever do that again," Shazad's mother said one more time for good measure.

"We won't," Shazad said, his spirits sinking once more. "We can't. It's over."

"What do you mean?" his mother asked.

"Our quest," Joey said. "It's over. I lost the map."

"What?" everyone exclaimed at once, staggered by the news. Shazad was more surprised than anyone.

Joey gave Shazad a subtle look telling him to go with it. He could take the heat for losing the map. He was fine with it. His parents weren't in the tent. No one there could punish him.

Shazad's father turned his intense, penetrating eyes on

344

Joey. "Aren't you the same boy who lost Houdini's wand?"

"No," Shazad said before Joey could answer. "I mean, yes, he is. Dad, this is Joey. And this is Leanora," he added, pausing to introduce everyone. "Guys, this is my father, Ahmad ibn Jabari ibn Amon al-Hassan."

"Mr. Hassan is fine. It's nice to meet you both," Shazad's father said with a genuine but rushed friendly tone. He was understandably impatient to get back to the matter at hand. "Can one of you *please* tell me what's going on?"

"What's going on is Joey didn't lose the map," Shazad replied.

"Shazad," Joey said. "You don't have to do this."

"Yes I do. Thank you, Joey, but I have to take responsibility. I lost the map. I was holding it. It was my fault." He looked up at his parents, ready to face the consequences of his actions. "Joey's just trying to keep me out of trouble. The map's gone because I couldn't hold on to it. No other reason. I'm sorry."

"It wasn't his fault," Joey said. "It could have been any one of us."

"It was all of us," Leanora said. "We got the map together. We lost it together. That's the truth."

345

Shazad's father looked at all three children, making eye contact with each of them one by one. Joey saw appreciation for their solidarity and friendship in his expression. "I think you'd better tell us everything," Shazad's father said.

They told the story together, recounting their quest for Camelot, starting with the trip through the Devil's Teeth and the journey into Transylvania. Both sets of parents were amazed by their descriptions of the hidden magical gates and enraged by their accounts of the confrontations with the Invisible Hand. Shazad and Leanora left out the things Scarlett had said about their families but described in detail what she had done to Joey. They finished the tale with how they had outwitted Scarlett, discovered Celestia's doorway to the stars, and walked across the universe before falling back to Earth.

"Unfortunately, that's the end of it," Shazad said. "We don't know where to go from here. Not without the map. It was fuzzy in England, but I was hoping it would clear up once we got here. Now we'll never know."

"You said you've been looking for us since yesterday," Joey said, hoping to find a silver lining. "I don't suppose you saw anything out there . . ."

"That looked like Camelot?" Leonora's mother asked. She looked at Joey sideways. "Sorry, no," she said with a smile.

Joey looked down, disheartened. "That's too bad. I really wanted to find it."

"It's the end of the road," Leonora said, disappointed. "No map. No shield. No Camelot. Nothing."

"We don't need Camelot, Lea," her father said to her. "We just need this." He drew Leonora and her mother close to him. "Family. This is what matters."

"My family doesn't even know I'm here," Joey said. "They think I'm in a lab with Janelle, trying to save the planet. I should call them. What day is it again?"

"Wednesday," Shazad's mother answered.

Joey fished around in his pocket for his phone. "I need to text Janelle and tell her I'm coming to California. Can you guys get me there in a hurry?" Leonora's mother told Joey he was approved for travel as soon as his arm was fully healed. He thanked her, flexing his fingers a little bit, grateful that he was on the road to wellness. "That's it, then. While I'm there you guys can divvy up what we've got in the theater," he told Shazad and Leonora.

Shazad looked at Joey, stunned. "Are you sure? Even after what Scarlett said?"

Joey shrugged. "What else can we do? The theater's going to be unprotected soon. At least with your families, it's got a chance. You can split everything between you."

"Split up what?" Leanora's father asked. "What are we talking about here?"

"The magic items in the theater," Joey said. "What Redondo left us. I thought you guys wanted them."

Leanora's mother looked lost. "This is the first I'm hearing about it."

"What?" Shazad said. He and Joey looked back and forth between Leanora and her parents, thoroughly confused.

"The stuff in the theater," Joey said again. He pointed at Shazad and his parents. "They wanted to protect the items from the Invisible Hand," he said, sounding unsure. "You guys wanted to use them to amp up your shows and fight the Invisible Hand. Didn't you?"

Everyone turned to Leanora for an explanation. She was turning red.

"Not exactly," she admitted, now that she was busted. "Bringing the items back from the theater . . . that's what *I* wanted to do. I thought if I could do that, I could convince my parents to go bigger with our shows. No more low profile. I wanted us to make a difference in the world."

Leanora's father smiled, understanding everything. "Our Lea is a fighter," he explained. "That is not our way. We aren't looking to make a 'big splash,'" he said, making air quotes with his fingers. "We just want to do what we love. Make magic. Play for the people."

"But you sent her to get Houdini's wand," Shazad said.

"Ha!" Leanora's father looked at his wife. "He thinks we could have stopped her!"

"You don't want to use the items the children have in the theater?" Shazad's mother asked Leanora's mom and dad.

"Better you should keep them," Leanora's mother replied. "If the Invisible Hand is going to come for them, they'll be safer with you. We have plenty of magic in our family. Enough for us, and more important, enough to share. We do make a difference," she told her daughter. "We don't need Camelot for that. We just need one another. If we can open the eyes of one person in the audience every night and light them up inside, that has an impact. That matters."

"I don't get it," Joey said. "Leanora said you've been

looking for lost magical cities like the places we found on the map. You've been looking for Camelot too, haven't you?"

"Of course," Leanora's father said. "The world is a magic place full of wonder. We want to see as much as we can. But the quest to find such places is not a race you win. It's not about the destination. It's the journey. We look for magic wherever we can find it, and we do find it every day. In little, small miracles. Tiny moments that astound and amaze. We share those moments onstage with the people we meet, and when they leave our shows, they take magic with them. Inside." He tapped his chest. "They pass it on to others, each in their own way. I've seen it. They make their own brand of magic and we help them do it. We give the world magic every day, and we're not alone." Leanora's father gestured to the Hassans. "Our friends here do the same good work in their own way."

"Thank you, Dimitry," Shazad's father said. A look of mutual understanding and respect passed between both sets of parents before Shazad's father turned his attention back to the children. "Our family saves magic items, but only that which is worth saving. There are magical artifacts in the world that serve no good purpose: Pandora's box, the Casket of Ancient Winters, Fabergé eggs . . . Even after everything you've been through, you haven't had to face anything like them."

"Did you say Fabergé eggs?" Joey asked. "Weren't those, like, jeweled Easter eggs?"

"Given as gifts to the Russian tsars in the last century," Shazad's mother confirmed. "But some of them were much older than that. If I told you what was inside them, you wouldn't sleep."

"I think the less said about them the better," Leanora's mother said.

"It's enough to say that some things exist only to unleash evil and suffering," Shazad's mother agreed. "We make sure lost items like that stay lost, and when we have to, we eliminate them. We've done this for generations."

"I thought you just collected things like a museum," Leanora said.

"We collect benevolent magic items, because their power is required to wipe out malignant dark magic," Shazad's father explained. "The Invisible Hand claims to have a similar mission, but we all know that's not true. They hoard magic. We do the real work of protecting magic. Virtuous, life-giving magic. That matters too. We do what we can, and we hope it's enough to keep the world turning, but I know one thing for certain: whatever magic items you have in the theater will be safe with us. I give you my word. All of you."

Joey thought carefully about what Leanora's and Shazad's parents were saying. They were noble sentiments, and there was definitely some truth to their words. Redondo had once told Joey about the vital importance of magicians and why they kept magic a secret. Joey had appreciated the idea at the time, but that explanation wasn't enough for him anymore. He understood that Leanora's family spread magic around, changing the world for the better, but it was progress by inches. They weren't pulling a big lever, and from the sound of it, they didn't want to. Shazad's family was the same. They protected magic and kept it out of the wrong hands, but their work didn't change the world. They just kept everything the same. Scarlett had told them the truth. It was up to them. Joey, Shazad, and Leanora were the ones who were going to change the game. They were going to find Camelot and open the world's magical floodgates. They were going to use the Caliburn Shield to protect the Majestic Theatre, or even better, he and Janelle would find a way to use it to give the world magic for real. But none of that was going to happen now. It was over. They weren't the Order of the Majestic. They were failures.

"I know what you're thinking," Leanora's father told Joey. "Magic can change the world. We can do more. Lea tells us this. She tells us all the time. That we have to fight the Invisible Hand." He *pff*ed his dismissal. "They aren't as powerful as you think they are. They don't understand magic. What it's for. What it's worth. The Invisible Hand can't keep magic from the world. They can try to control it, but it's always going to be there. Those of us who go looking for it—really go looking for it—are always going to find it."

"I wanted it to be us who found it this time," Shazad told his parents. "I wanted to find Camelot and make you proud."

"That was your mistake," Shazad's father said. He went down on one knee and looked his son in the eye. "You don't need to do anything to make us proud of you. We're *already* proud of you. We always have been."

"If Camelot is lost, then it's lost," Shazad's mother said. "So be it. I'd rather it happen this way than lose it to the Invisible Hand—or worse, lose you."

Shazad nodded, holding back tears. His parents pulled him into another hug. There was a lot of hugging going on. It was all very touching and made Joey think about his own parents. He felt guilty that he hadn't spoken to them since Monday, and also for asking Janelle to stand in for him via text. His mom and dad were probably driving her crazy trying to get him on the phone. Sure enough, when he turned his phone back on, he had a dozen text messages from Janelle. The most recent one read:

Your parents are blowing up my phone. WHERE ARE YOU???
Srsly, U OK?

Joey put the phone away. "I think it's time for me to go." He jiggled his arm. "How long do I need to wear this?"

"That depends," Leanora's mother said. "How does it feel?"

Joey lifted his arm, bending it at the elbow as much as the tight wrapping would allow. "It feels great, actually. I mean, it's a little stiff, but I couldn't move it at all before this. It was deadweight."

"Good. Let's see how we did." Leanora's mother removed the bandages, starting with his hand and working her way up the arm. With every length of enchanted red linen she

354

peeled away, more healthy pink skin was found underneath. Joey's spirits soared as he wiggled his fingers and twisted his wrist around with newfound appreciation. Leanora's mother asked him to keep still, and also to take his shirt off so she could unwind the wrapping from his shoulder. When she was finished, Joey didn't have a single mark on him. He was cured.

"Wait a minute—what's that?" Leanora asked, pointing out a black dot on his collarbone the size of a mole. No sooner had she asked the question than a torrent of black paint gushed out of the dot, covering every inch of his arm and half of his chest.

"No," Joey said, crushed. His arm was numb again. So was most of his torso. He wasn't better; he was worse. A horrible thought took root in his brain. *They can't fix me. They can't help me!* For all he knew, no one could.

"What am I going to do?"

Leanora's mother studied Joey's blackened arm with a frown. "Put your shirt back on," she told him. Joey couldn't move his right arm, so she had to help him cover up. "I was afraid of this. If these bandages can't remove this curse, we're going to need the item that put it there to fix this."

"We need the paintbrush," Leanora said, a determined look on her face.

"How are we going to get that?" Shazad asked.

"We need to find Scarlett," Leanora replied.

"That's great," Joey said. "What happens if she finds me first?"

"You don't have to wonder," Scarlett announced. Joey spun around and saw her standing by the entrance to the tent. She was painting large blue waves with white caps in the air. Like everything else she painted, it was a re-creation of someone else's work; a famous Japanese print Joey had seen many times before. However, what Scarlett lacked in originality she made up for in effectiveness. The wave came crashing down with the force of a battering ram, knocking everyone off their feet. Tables and chairs went flying and a boat inside the wave ripped through the room, collapsing half the tent. As the water drained out into the field, Joey flopped around, coughing up salt water and trying to stand. Scarlett dragged him out of the tent and into a frame outside the door.

16

The Imaginary Vortex

The tent was gone. Joey's friends were gone. He was disoriented and had no idea where he was. All he knew was that he was soaking wet and Scarlett was pulling him by the collar through another empty field, this one scattered with medieval ruins. "Did you like that?" she asked him. "That was *The Great Wave off Kanagawa* by Katsushika Hokusai. I mean, he's no comic book artist, but I think his work is pretty powerful." Joey whipped his head back and forth, looking for a way out. The picture frame he had just been forced through was still there behind him. In a desperate move, Joey wrestled free of Scarlett's grip and tried to run back to it. Rather than chase after him, she took careful aim with her brush and gave him a jolt of pain that stopped him dead in his tracks. For a second, half of Joey's body was on fire. He dropped as if he'd been shot. The pain was gone before he hit the ground. Scarlett told him it was just a taste. A little something to make him behave. "We can do this the easy way or the hard way," she said. "It's up to you."

Joey watched the picture frame fade into nothingness, taking with it any hope of escape. He balled a fist with his one good hand, but it was no use fighting. He couldn't fight her head-on. Not as long as she held that brush. He pushed himself up and agreed to come quietly.

Scarlett told Joey to head for the ruins, and he did as he was told. She followed behind him, keeping her paintbrush trained on him like a pistol.

"What is this place?" he asked.

"Just keep walking."

Joey tried to figure out what the ruins were on his own. The foundation of an old castle or some kind of defensive barrier were the only things that came to mind. Ancient stone walls had been built in a wide circle, three hundred feet in diameter. There were eight chunks of wall, each of them ten feet high, spaced evenly around the circle with gaps in between them that were big enough to drive a truck through. Scarlett directed Joey to a path that led to the top of one of the sections of wall. Inside the circle of stone, the ground dropped down another twenty to thirty feet, but it wasn't a sudden drop-off. The other side of the wall went down in steps like seats in an amphitheater.

DeMayne was there, sitting on the top step, facing the open field. He turned his head as Joey arrived. "There you are, Joey. Glad you could join us." He wasn't alone. There were about fifty people inside the circle with him, also sitting on the steps.

"Who is this?" Joey asked. "The rest of the Invisible Hand?"

DeMayne tilted his hand from side to side as if to say, *Yes and no.* "Not in the way you're thinking. They're with me, but they're not magicians. Just some locals who are helping out. Norms, if you'll excuse the term." He stood up and dusted himself off. DeMayne was dressed in another one of his fantastic custom-made suits. "With the Hassans and the Nomadiks in the area, I thought it couldn't hurt to have a little extra muscle on hand."

Joey took a closer look at the people on the steps. They were civilians. Old men and women from the local villages, adult tourists his parents' age, teens, and even little kids.

They all had shovels, bats, sticks, and rocks in their hands. Everyone had some kind of weapon and looked ready to use it. Not because they were angry. They weren't itching for a fight. They looked blank and empty, like machines waiting to be turned on. Their eyes were jet-black with the white parts completely filled in.

"What did you do to them?" Joey asked.

DeMayne held up his hand. "You see this?" He wiggled his fingers, showing off a black ring on his right hand. "The Ring of Ranguul. I took it off a small-time con man ages ago. The fool didn't even know what he had. If I shake someone's hand wearing this ring, they become very susceptible to suggestion. It doesn't always work on fellow magicians, but people like them?" He nodded to the local townspeople assembled on the steps. "They'll do whatever I say. I've been out here shaking hands all morning. I felt like a politician running for office, but it was worth the effort. Believe me, I've got their vote." He gestured to the helpless and hypnotized people in his thrall. "These 'sheeple' will die before they let anything happen to me, or let you get away. I tell you this just to let you know that you're not in a position to help yourself, so don't get any ideas."

Joey looked at the black-eyed men, women, and children. They weren't muscle. They were cannon fodder. A brainwashed mob to be used as a human shield in case Joey's friends came to rescue him.

"You're a monster," he said, appalled.

"Oh, don't worry," DeMayne said. "Nothing's going to happen. First of all, if you tried to run, Scarlett would strike you down before you took a single step. Second, I don't need these people to take care of your little friends. Scarlett and I handled them easily, I'm sure you remember. I'm not really worried about their families, either. They're academics and performers. Not real players in our game."

"So why have these people here at all?" Joey asked.

DeMayne shrugged. "Why not? It never hurts to have an insurance policy. People surprise me sometimes. You certainly surprised me, Joey. Managing to keep us out of the Majestic? I'm still not sure how you did that, but don't worry, we'll get to the bottom of it soon enough. I'm incredibly patient—and persistent. However, the Majestic Theatre and its contents have been bumped to number two on my list of priorities after the last few days. Scarlett told me what you've been up to. It's very exciting stuff. I don't usually get personally involved in the acquisition of magical objects, but three times now I've made an exception in your case. You should be flattered."

Joey nodded. "I'm so flattered," he said, his voice full of disdain.

DeMayne's lips flattened into a tight smile. "I'm going to miss your sarcastic little quips. This will likely be the last time we meet. After today, I expect I won't have any more use for you."

DeMayne let the subtle threat hang there a moment, giving Joey time to think about all the different ways he could have meant it. "All right, enough preamble," he said, clapping his hands together. "Let's get down to business. Where's this map I've heard so much about?"

"He didn't have it," Scarlett said. "None of them did."

DeMayne raised an eyebrow. "You let them keep it?" He had a smile on his face, but it was all pretense. There was anger underneath.

"I didn't let them keep anything. It wasn't there."

"The map's gone," Joey said. "We lost it. In space."

"In space," DeMayne repeated. "You don't say. This is getting to be a habit with you, Joey. First you drop Houdini's wand down a black hole, and now this? You've got to take better care of our things."

"They're not *your* things," Joey said. "And they never will be. At least this one won't. You missed your shot," he added, looking at Scarlett. "You had your chance to get the map, and you blew it."

Scarlett made Joey pay for that one. He'd known she would. He was deliberately provoking her, which was arguably the worst possible move he could make, and yet he had to do it. The pain that followed was ten times worse than he remembered. Probably because the black mark on his skin was ten times bigger. His whole body convulsed as she tortured him with her paintbrush once again. He tried to ignore the pain and block it out, but that was impossible. It took everything he had just to think straight. He screamed at the top of his lungs, hoping someone would hear him. DeMayne had let it slip that Shazad's and Leanora's families were both in the area. They were somewhere close. Joey knew they'd come for him. He just had to give them a chance to find him. As he flailed around, tumbling down the steps, he felt like Luke Skywalker being electrocuted by the Emperor. DeMayne didn't have a change of heart and save him like

Darth Vader had saved Luke, but he did surprise Joey by making Scarlett stop.

"That's enough," he said, pushing her paintbrush down and away from Joey. "Don't punish him for your mistakes. He's right. You had a chance to get the map and he out-maneuvered you." Scarlett opened her mouth to protest, but DeMayne put his hand up, heading her off. "I know, you salvaged the situation. You came back with valuable information, and now with Joey, which in the end is all we need. Still, it's a shame about the map. It sounded like an exciting find." He walked down the steps to where Joey was lying on the ground, trying to catch his breath. "I would have liked to have it, but we don't need it to find what you were looking for."

Joey sat up. "Camelot? You know where it is?"

"Do I know where it is?" DeMayne repeated. "I've known for ages." He gestured to the open circle of land, presenting the vast expanse as if it were something grand. "We're here."

Joey looked at the vacant field, bordered by the ruins. "I don't see anything."

"That doesn't mean it's not there. Joey, you've led us on a wild ride. You could have avoided a great deal of trouble if you'd accepted my offer a month ago. You would have saved us all some time and spared yourself a lot of pain. The fact is, we were always going to end up here, no matter what. I want to show you something."

DeMayne produced a compact metal box. He popped the lid open and took a pinch of bright red powder from inside. "This is fairy dust. It has many interesting applications, but it has to be used sparingly. They're not making any more of it." He pocketed the box, sprinkled the powder into his open palm, and blew it into the empty, circular field. A strong wind that Joey couldn't see or feel took hold of it and whipped it around in a swirling upward spiral. Joey watched as the red powder spread out, changing the color of the air like an inkling of dye that had been dropped into a clear glass of water. The fairy dust twisted up into the clouds, revealing the funnel of a massive, stationary tornado in the center of the ruins. The whirling crimson storm was awesome in its size and scope, powerful enough to rip up whole forests and scatter them about like twigs. Fortunately, it didn't seem to be going anywhere. "Impressive, isn't it?" DeMayne asked Joey. "This is the Imaginary Vortex."

Joey stared, dumbstruck. "How did you know this was here?"

"That's what I do. I know things other people don't. The vortex is hidden by a glamour charm. It's a manifestation of one of the most powerful warding objects in the world. It has a special effect on people like us. Magic users. For those of us who are aware of its existence, there's another level of sorcery at play. If you know it's there and still dare to venture in, it will turn you away permanently. You lose your imagination. The ability to believe in the impossible. You'll never work magic again. Scary, I know, but the bigger the curse, the bigger the treasure. Behind all this is the Lost Kingdom of Camelot. You're going to give it to me."

"Am I?" Joey eyed DeMayne with a healthy dose of skepticism. "Exactly how am I supposed to do that?"

"By using the only thing that makes you the least bit special," DeMayne told him. "The wand. Call the wand and vanish the vortex." He folded his arms. "I'll wait."

Joey's face twisted into a mask of confusion. "What?"

"You heard me," DeMayne said, nonchalant. "Use the wand. Wipe this monstrosity away."

Joey shook his head. "I don't understand."

"I know you don't. I can teach you. That's something Redondo never did. It's not too late for you to join us, you know. You can have these secrets . . . this power without having to constantly look over your shoulder and see if we're there behind you." DeMayne nodded to Scarlett, and she gave Joey a little sting of pain to help make his point. "Wouldn't it be nice to never feel that again? You have a choice, Joey. Why choose the hard road?"

Joey didn't know what to say. "What you're asking me to do . . . I don't even know what you're talking about. I don't have the wand."

"But you do," DeMayne replied. "In a way. You have a connection to it. It's yours. You can call it wherever it is, and it will come to you."

"That can't be right," Joey said. "You told me the wand was lost. That anybody could find it."

"I know what I told you. I lied. I do that. The wand has only one master at a time, and like it or not, that's you. You've always had the power to call it. Why do you think we haven't killed you yet? Scarlett's been following you for a month now. She could have taken you out at any time, but she didn't because you still have value to us. That's why we're here."

Joey was floored by what DeMayne was telling him.

Could getting the wand back really be that simple? It had to be a trick.

"It's no trick," Scarlett told Joey, seeming to read his mind. "The wand is out there, waiting for you. Make the call. You know you want to do it. In the jungle, you painted yourself wielding the wand like a knight of the round table. Deep down you know you can get it. You just have to believe."

Joey thought about what they were telling him. It made sense in an unbelievable sort of way. "That's why you were watching me but never did anything. You were waiting to see if I'd work this out on my own."

"Which obviously didn't happen, so here we are." DeMayne held out his hands. "Even my patience has its limits."

Joey weighed his options, wondering if he could turn the situation to his advantage. If they were telling the truth, the wand could be his way out. Joey could use it to get rid of Scarlett and DeMayne and then see what was behind the red tornado. He could have Camelot, the shield, and the wand. He could be the conquering hero, but he couldn't use the wand if he was busy being tortured by Scarlett. Or worse, killed. Wand or no wand, the Invisible Hand had the edge on him. "I'll do it on one condition," he said. "You have to get this paint off my arm first."

DeMayne smiled. "I don't think so."

"I'm right-handed," Joey complained. "If you want this to work, I'm gonna need my right hand."

DeMayne studied Joey, considering his point. "Fine," he said after some deliberation. "Scarlett, give the boy a hand." She waved her paintbrush with a swish and a flick. The black paint under Joey's skin shifted from the right side of his body to his left. Joey sighed in disappointment. DeMayne snickered. "You think I'm going to let you summon the most powerful magic object in the world without protection?"

"It was worth a shot."

"I wasn't born yesterday. Get to work."

"No," Joey said. "I wasn't born yesterday, either. The wand can have only one master at a time, right? That's *my* insurance policy. You need to kill me to own the wand, but you need me alive to find it. The second I have it in my hand, I become expendable. I'm not loving that idea. I can live without Camelot. We'll find another way to change the world." He nodded toward the Imaginary Vortex. "I can't go in there without the wand, but you can't, either. It's a wash."

A crease appeared in DeMayne's forehead. He was visibly frustrated by Joey's lack of cooperation. "You know what doesn't come out in the wash?" He patted Joey's blackened arm. "This."

"AHHH!!" Joey screamed as the pain rocketed through his body. This time DeMayne let Scarlett go on a little longer before he told her to stop.

"Your insurance policy has a very high premium," DeMayne taunted. "Don't misunderstand me, Joey. This is not a request. I'm not asking you to call the wand. I'm telling you. You're right. I can't kill you until I have it, but I can let Scarlett hurt you so bad you'll wish you were dead. And then we can nurse you back to health and do it again. And again, and again, until you listen to reason."

Joey locked eyes with DeMayne. He wanted to say something really clever and cutting, like a character in one of his favorite movies would do, but he couldn't speak and nothing snappy came to mind. He felt like he was going to melt into the ground. The best he could muster up was a defiant stare. He wasn't going to play ball, and DeMayne knew it. His courage was rewarded with more enthusiastic torture from Scarlett.

"I'm actually glad you're being so stubborn," she told him. "It gives me an excuse to pay you back for the snakebite in the jungle. Did you think I was going to let that go? I threw up fourteen times in the last twenty-four hours. Did you think I was going to forget?"

"This is pointless," DeMayne told Joey as Scarlett put him through the wringer. "You really think you're going to change the world? Set magic free? Think again. We like the world the way it is—ours. It's *our* playground. I invited you in, but clearly you don't play well with others. Do you realize what it is you're trying to fight? How hopeless your situation is? *I'm* going to control whatever's left in Camelot. Anything in there belongs to me. No one else. If you don't want to curse the day magic entered your life, you'll give me the wand now. While I'm still in a mood to ask nicely."

"This is you . . . being . . . *nice?*" Joey struggled to say.

"This is me being very nice," DeMayne continued. "I could go after your family. Your mother and father . . . your friends at school . . . that cute little girl Janelle who's trying to use magic as part of some next-generation power grid. We know all about it. We could do so much more. This can get so much worse. You told me last time we met that we only think of ourselves. That's true, but if you force us to consider others, we will do so. Is that what you want?"

"NO!" Joey shouted in agony. DeMayne's words had introduced a whole other level of trauma. He was talking about hurting Joey in ways that would never fully heal, and Joey knew he wasn't bluffing. He couldn't let DeMayne hurt the people he cared about, but he couldn't give him the wand, either. Joey didn't know what to do. Only one thing was certain. He couldn't take much more of this.

Fortunately, the moment was interrupted by the sound of a honking horn. Joey's pain eased up as Scarlett and DeMayne both paused to see what was going on. Joey crawled up the steps in time to see a car driving up to the ruins. It was a beat-up old junker being driven by a blue-haired lady who could barely see over the steering wheel. She looked like she was ninety-nine years old. The man sitting next to her was at least 112.

The car came to a halt at the edge of the ruins and the doors opened. Leanora and Shazad stepped out. "Get away from him," Leanora said. "Now."

"How do you like that? It's the cavalry," DeMayne said,

amused. "Welcome to Camelot. How did you two find us so fast?"

Shazad held up an orange gemstone the size of a walnut. He didn't say anything. He had a stunned look, taking in the sight of the Imaginary Vortex.

DeMayne's eyes narrowed, trying to identify the object in Shazad's hand. "What have you got there?"

Joey cleared his throat and picked up an identical gemstone that was sitting on the steps next to him. "You could ask me the same question."

17

Eye of the Tiger

"It's activated by the light." Joey held up the jewel, letting it sparkle in the sun. "Like anything else, you've also got to believe."

He still had the Tiger's Eye from when Shazad had given it to him back in the Amazon village. Joey had pushed Scarlett to attack him, knowing it would hurt, but also knowing it would give him the chance to remove the gemstone from his pocket without anyone noticing. He wasn't able to take it out while he was standing across from Scarlett and DeMayne, but when he was thrashing about on the steps, he could do it on the sly. Shazad had told Joey that his parents could home in on the jewel's location as long as it was out in the open. He'd hoped Shazad would remember he still had it and that his parents would have the other gemstone with them. Fortunately, that hope had been well placed.

Joey didn't come out and say all of this to Scarlett and DeMayne. They didn't need to be told the details to guess at the connection between the two stones. "Clever," DeMayne admitted, giving Joey credit. "Just not very smart," he added. "You never learn, do you? There's no reason to think this is going to go any better for you than it did outside the Majestic Theatre."

"Actually, there is," Leanora said. "We didn't come alone. We just have the fastest car." A motorcade of trucks and cars blasted through the trees behind her. The cavalry had truly arrived now.

DeMayne's face fell flat. "How very annoying." He looked at Scarlett next to him. "I guess this is happening. Let's get it over with."

Once again, DeMayne donned the Armor of the Ages. Joey watched the invincible suit of armor cover his body just as it had outside the Majestic. DeMayne couldn't be hurt as long as he was wearing the armor, but he still hid behind the innocent, sending his horde of hypnotized people out first.

Shazad's and Leanora's parents exited the newly arrived vehicles, followed by half of Leanora's family. "What is this?"

Leanora's father asked, gaping at the Imaginary Vortex.

"And who are *they*?" Shazad's father added as the black-eyed men, women, and children charged up the steps of the ruins and stormed across the field.

"They're not magicians," Leanora's father replied, studying their appearance. "These are local people."

"Look at their eyes; they're enchanted," Shazad's mother said. DeMayne's unwitting infantry ran headlong toward them, ready to fight. "We can't hurt them."

One of the children threw a rock. Many others followed, sailing through the air like arrows on a medieval battlefield. Grasping the amulet around her neck, Leanora's mother put up a translucent golden force field just in time. The rocks bounced harmlessly off it, but Joey could see the magical barrier wouldn't last long. The first wave of stones had left it riddled with spiderweb cracks like a big broken windshield.

The spellbound people pounded on the force field with sticks, shovels, and more rocks. Basically, anything they could pick up and use as a weapon. Leanora's mother barked out orders in Russian, most likely telling the rest of the Nomadiks to go easy on them once the fighting started. "These people aren't our enemies," she said, switching back to English. "They don't know what they're doing. We have to help them."

"Too bad they don't feel the same way about us," Leanora's father said, bracing for the wave of people to come crashing in. The force field soon came down, shattering into pieces, and the fight was on.

Shazad's and Leanora's parents set their sights on DeMayne. All four of them took him on at once using various magical items, but none of their attacks had any effect. They couldn't touch him in that armor. Joey wondered if anything could. He stood up, wanting to help, but Scarlett sat him back down.

"Wait there," Scarlett told Joey, turning the pain back on. "This will be over in a minute."

Joey's perspective of the fight shifted to a jerky, flailing view. As he rolled around on the steps suffering, he saw the Nomadiks trying to subdue the locals through nonviolent means, which wasn't easy. Leanora's family had to pull their punches, but their opponents were out for blood, swinging shovels, rakes, and hoes.

Joey saw Leanora going after Scarlett. She was speeding around in her elven-made boots and using her firestone to battle the subjects of famous paintings throughout history: Mona Lisa, Degas's dancers, and Whistler's mother (who was surprisingly strong and lively for her age). Through it all, Scarlett made time for Joey and had no trouble keeping him pinned down in agony while fighting Leanora.

Joey flipped onto his back, staring up at the clear blue sky, a vision interrupted only by the massive crimson funnel of the Imaginary Vortex. The pain got so bad he actually thought he might die, when Shazad appeared at his side.

"Try to hold still," Shazad said, wrapping the red Bandages of Panacea around Joey's left hand.

"What . . . what're you doing?" Joey forced the question out in grunts. "Bandages . . . didn't work."

"Yes they did," Shazad said, working his way up Joey's arm undeterred. "Sort of. Scarlett didn't show up until you took this thing off. You were able to move your arm when you had it on, too. It didn't cure you, but it blocked the magic. That's worth another try, don't you think?"

Shazad was right. Joey was convinced, and since all magic hinges on belief, the bandage started working almost immediately. He felt the pain go away inch by inch as Shazad wound the bandage around his arm and shoulder. When he finished, Joey felt warm and tingly again. His arm was still pretty much useless, but the pain was gone. Joey could think straight again.

Leanora raced over to Joey and Shazad, breathless from her clash with Scarlett, which was still ongoing. "Did it work? Is he okay—are you okay?" she added to Joey.

Joey nodded weakly. "I'm getting there."

"We still need the brush," Shazad said.

Leanora turned to face Scarlett with fire in her eyes, not to mention burning inside her fist. "I'll get it." A second later, she was back on the field, trading blows with Vincent van Gogh's self-portrait. Joey heard Scarlett order him to bring her Leanora's ear.

"What is this place?" Shazad asked Joey as the fighting went on around them. "What is *this*?" He waved at the red tornado in the center of the ruins. "Did DeMayne say 'Welcome to Camelot' when we got here?"

"That's what he said." Joey tilted his head toward the swirling magic whirlwind behind them. "This is what that old lady Fate was talking about—the Imaginary Vortex. Camelot's on the other side of it."

Shazad's face lit up. "Really? Can we go through it?"

"No. It'll zap your imagination away. Kill your ability to do magic."

Shazad's eyes widened in alarm. "Let's get away from it, then. Can you stand?" Joey noticed Shazad didn't ask him if he could fight. He stuck out his hand, and Shazad helped him up. "Why did they bring you here?" Shazad asked.

"They wanted me to get rid of the vortex."

"Get rid of it how?"

Before Joey could answer, another piece of artwork attacked. This time, it was the couple from *American Gothic*— the famous portrait of a farmer and his wife standing in front of their house with a pitchfork. Only the pitchfork wasn't in the farmer's hand anymore; it was sailing through the air, right at Shazad.

"Look out!" Joey shouted, pulling Shazad out of the way in time to keep him from being impaled. The sharp tines of the pitchfork clattered harmlessly on the stone steps, right where Shazad had been. "These guys aren't messing around," Joey said.

They looked over at Leanora, who was outnumbered by Scarlett and her art-based minions eight-to-one. "I'd better give her a hand. Wait here. We'll be back with the brush."

Shazad grabbed the pitchfork by the handle and ran back into the fray. Joey wanted to help, but he was still weak from his ordeal. His arm was coming back to life, but it would be a while before he could move it, and even longer before he could throw a punch. He was forced to watch from the steps as his friends put themselves in harm's way for his benefit.

Neither one of them was able to get close enough to Scarlett to steal her brushes. Not with the living paintings blocking their path. Leanora dodged twirling kicks from Degas's dancers. They attacked, one after the other, in a graceful, choreographed attack pattern. Shazad was locked in mortal combat with Mona Lisa, who inexplicably turned out to be a kung-fu master. Joey wondered if that was a creative choice by Scarlett. If so, it was the first original thing he had seen her do. Using the pitchfork like a bo staff, Shazad defended himself against a flurry of kicks and punches. Leanora went on offense, tearing through three dancers and Vincent van Gogh with a single firestone punch, reducing them to puddles of wet paint. Following her example, Shazad found an opening and stabbed through Mona Lisa, wiping the smile off her face. She liquefied just like the other paintings, but Shazad and Leanora still had to deal with *American*

Gothic, Whistler's mother, and whatever Scarlett decided to paint next.

Meanwhile, Shazad's and Leanora's parents were getting their butts kicked by DeMayne. They were no match for him in his armor. Shazad's mother wrapped DeMayne up with a golden lasso, binding him tight. He broke free. Leanora's father swung two morning stars. One burned with a smoldering red glow as if it had just been forged by a blacksmith, and the other one looked like it was carved out of ice. Neither one left so much as a dent in the armor. Shazad's father took out a small fife and played a tune that controlled DeMayne's movements for a moment, but the moment didn't last. DeMayne lowered the visor on his helm and blocked out the influence of the song. After that he delivered a one-two punch to Shazad's father, knocking the fife out of his hands and the wind out of his lungs. All the attacks on him amounted to nothing. It was the battle outside the Majestic all over again.

DeMayne flipped his visor back up. "Honestly, people, what are we doing here? I can't remember the last time it came to blows between us. You've all gone out of your way to avoid me for years! Why make a mistake like this now?"

"*You* made the mistake," Leanora's father said, swinging his morning stars at DeMayne. "You threatened our children."

DeMayne turned his shoulder into the attack, letting his armor absorb the impact. "Blah, blah, blah," he said, shooting out his leg with a lightning-fast back kick that sent Leanora's father reeling. "I can see it's no use talking to you. This 'fight,' if you want to call it that, accomplishes nothing." He drew the Sword of Storms from its scabbard. "I'm done with it."

Holding the broken sword with both hands, DeMayne called on hurricane-force winds to blow everyone away. Shazad's and Leanora's parents, the brainwashed townspeople, and the other Nomadiks went rolling across the field. DeMayne kept the pressure on as they tried to stand their ground, aiming the winds to push the trucks back and flip the cars into them.

"Leave them alone!" Joey shouted.

"I'd love to," DeMayne called back over the roaring winds. "You can stop this, Joey! Call the wand before someone gets hurt! Do it now!"

Joey realized in that instant that he should have called the wand the second Shazad had bandaged his arm. He was protected against Scarlett's curse, and he cursed himself for not acting sooner. He was going to try to summon the wand when the farmers from *American Gothic* surprised him. The old man ripped his backpack off, and his wife grabbed him by his good arm. "Get his bandages off, Pa," she said in a crotchety old voice.

"Yes, Ma," the farmer replied, and went to work unraveling Joey's magical protections. Joey struggled, but it was too late. His fingers were exposed and Scarlett's black paint spread out to his extremities once again.

"Just keeping you honest, Joey," DeMayne shouted. "Better hurry!"

He turned up the volume on the sword, uprooting trees and flipping Leanora's parents' trailer onto its side. Joey wanted to fight back, but he didn't have any weapons, and now his arm was vulnerable again. He looked around for something that could help him. The only thing he saw was his backpack lying on the ground. The zipper was open and the Finale Mask was sticking out. Joey didn't have a laser to hook it up to, but he knew it had plenty of power all by itself. He had always been afraid to try it on. If he could just get to it . . .

"Get your pitchfork, Pa," the farmer's wife told her husband as Joey tried to free himself from her grip. "I'll hold him."

"Yes, Ma," her husband droned, and went off to collect his prized possession. Shazad had lost it at some point during the fight and was now engaged in hand-to-hand combat with Whistler's mother. It was a wild and oddly welcome sight. With Whistler's mother occupied and the farmers focused on Joey, Leanora was finally free to go after Scarlett.

"What's wrong? Run out of famous paintings to fight for you?" Leanora taunted. "Too bad you can't think of anything yourself."

"I don't need to come up with anything new," Scarlett countered. "I have an endless appreciation for the classics."

She took out the Jackson Pollack brush and started shooting blasts of paint at Leanora. Fortunately, Leanora's winged boots helped her dodge them easily.

"I've been waiting for you to get out that brush," Leanora said.

"Come and get it," Scarlett said, firing off a fresh salvo.

The farmer picked up his pitchfork just as Whistler's mother spun around with a vicious roundhouse kick that caught Shazad in the face, dropping him. She climbed on top of his body and pinned him to the ground. Staying true to her namesake, she whistled for the farmer's attention. A high-pitched, piercing noise cut across the battlefield. The farmer turned and saw Shazad trapped and helpless. "Hang on, Ma."

The farmer stalked toward Shazad, pitchfork in hand, as Leanora made her move on Scarlett, who was trying in vain to splatter her with weaponized bursts of paint. Leanora ran at Scarlett, using the Winged Boots of Fleetfoot to take three steps up into the air. She flipped over Scarlett, snatching a brush away from her in the process.

A few feet away, the farmer stood over Shazad. He raised the pitchfork high above his head, ready to stab it down in a killing blow. "This is for Mona."

Leanora snapped the paintbrush in half.

It wasn't the Jackson Pollock brush that had cursed Joey's arm. It was a brush that had once belonged to Grant Wood, the artist who had painted *American Gothic*. The farmer and his pitchfork melted into a swirling, colorful mess just in time to save Shazad's life. The farmer's wife dripped away into nothing behind Joey, turning him loose as well. He sprang into action.

"Scarlett!" DeMayne barked out, while struggling to keep the Sword of Storms under control. "He's going to get the wand. Don't let him use it on us!"

"I'm not getting the wand," Joey said, grabbing the Finale Mask off the ground with his one good hand. He lunged for DeMayne as Scarlett raised her brush in his direction. Before she could hurt him, Leanora hit her hard with the firestone, knocking her back to the steps of the ruins. Joey charged into DeMayne, holding the mask out in front of him. "This is for you! One-point-twenty-one gigawatts—in your face!"

DeMayne managed to lower the visor on his helm just before Joey got to him, but it didn't save him. Power surged through the mask into DeMayne, and he staggered back as if he'd been hit by a charging rhino. He dropped the Sword of Storms. It sank into the ground with a *thunk*, and the winds stopped blowing. DeMayne fell, and Joey fell on top of him, holding the mask in place. His unwavering belief activated the latent energy inside the mask, bringing about the finale of DeMayne's precious armor. The magical power grid DeMayne had been so quick to mock now lit him up like a Christmas tree. Green energy poured out of the mask, eating away at his black iron shell like a toxic acid.

Joey spent the next sixty seconds getting payback for the torture he had endured, eradicating the Armor of the Ages. DeMayne was screaming for Joey to get off him, but that just fueled his fire. He pushed down harder, determined to see this through to the end. If he had to use up every ounce of power in the mask, then that was what he was going to do. A fracture appeared in the Finale Mask, right between the eyes. Joey didn't let up for a second. The mask split in two, releasing a shock wave that knocked Joey off DeMayne. He landed flat on his back.

When it was over, DeMayne tried to get up, but he didn't have the strength to stand. The armor was too heavy for him, but that problem didn't last. As he fell to one knee, the armor cracked and broke apart, crumbling into dust. He coughed and coughed, waving the black cloud away. The black iron armband that had once housed the Armor of the Ages slipped off his wrist and rolled across the ground. It came to a stop next to the Sword of Storms, useless and devoid of magic. The armband clinked against the sword, which was still lodged in the earth and vibrating with energy, waiting for someone to turn it off.

DeMayne stared in a daze at what was left of his

armor. He was much less intimidating now that he wasn't wearing it. Kneeling there in his fancy three-piece suit, covered in dust, he looked like the world's best-dressed chimney sweep. "What happened?" he asked Joey. "What did you do?"

Everyone else was wondering the same thing, Scarlett most of all. Joey locked eyes with her across the field. She looked scared. Joey was pretty sure she had never seen anyone take on Ledger DeMayne and win. *You're next*, he thought. She still had the paintbrush that had caused him so much pain. She was about to use it again, but Joey didn't give her the chance. He dashed forward and grabbed the Sword of Storms by the hilt. "Not this time."

He aimed the jagged edge of the sword at Scarlett and sent a wind strong enough to topple a house right at her. The brush flew from her hand and into the Imaginary Vortex. Joey kept the winds focused on Scarlett, pushing her in after it. She tried to stand her ground, but it was like trying to hold back the ocean.

"Sorry, Scarlett!" Joey shouted as he drove her to the brink. "I'm done suffering for your art!"

"NO!" Scarlett screamed as she slid back toward the

vortex. "Please, stop! I'll leave you alone. I swear! The brush is gone. You're safe! You don't have to do this!"

Oh yes I do, Joey thought. She was practically begging him for mercy, but Joey wasn't moved by her pleas. He wasn't going to let her hurt anyone else the way she had hurt him. He kept the sword aimed at her, holding on with all his might.

Bye, Scarlett, Joey thought as the violent red storm swallowed her up. *Now we see you . . . now we don't.*

He didn't get to enjoy the moment after she was gone. The temperamental Tempest Blade bucked in his hands, and he nearly shot his friends into the vortex after Scarlett. "Joey, watch out!" Leanora yelled.

He thought she was telling him to watch where he pointed the sword, but it turned out she was trying to warn him about DeMayne. He barreled into Joey and tried to steal the sword out of his hands before Joey used it on him. Joey nearly lost his grip on it, but now that Scarlett's magic ability was gone, so was her curse. Joey got two hands on the hilt and wrestled with DeMayne for control of the blade.

"Give me that—it's mine!" spit DeMayne. He sounded like a petulant child. Joey didn't waste time arguing with him. He just fought to hold on with all his might. He wasn't letting go of the sword for anything. "You're going to pay for this," DeMayne told him through gritted teeth. "You're going to *pay*. Everything I told you before? It's going to happen. Your family, your friends . . . they're *dead*. You hear me? They're de—AHHHH!"

DeMayne's voice broke into a scream as Joey threw his weight on top of the sword, pointing it down at the ground. The unstoppable winds pouring out of the blade shot them both up into the air and sent them rocketing backward— right into the heart of the Imaginary Vortex.

18

Go the Distance

Joey held on to the Sword of Storms as he went flying through the air, leaving the ground far behind. He grew dizzy and disoriented as the whirlwind spun him out of control, but he held on to the sword as if his life depended on it. DeMayne did the same, shouting at Joey as the vortex whipped them around in a mad orbit.

"What have you done?" he railed. "You've killed us! Worse than killed us! You're mad!"

Joey couldn't argue with that. He felt sick. They climbed higher and higher with each turbulent revolution, but the vertigo-inducing ride had nothing to do with the nauseous feeling in Joey's stomach. His imagination was about to be removed from his brain! For all he knew, it was already happening. DeMayne was right; it was a fate worse than death.

What did I do? Joey asked himself as the magical storm cast him about wildly. *What was I thinking?*

It was a question that had no answer. Joey had not been thinking when he used the sword to push himself into the vortex. He had just acted. On the one hand, he was protecting the people he cared about. DeMayne couldn't go after Joey's friends and family if he couldn't do magic anymore. On the other hand, the price Joey would have to pay to keep everyone safe was unbearable. Life as he knew it was over. The loss of imagination was more than the loss of magic; it was the loss of who he was. His personality, his sense of humor . . . everything about him! It all started with imagination. Joey thought about his favorite things: Star Wars, *The Avengers*, Harry Potter, Indiana Jones . . . Would he ever enjoy them again? Would he ever enjoy *anything* the way he had before? Who would Joey be when he came out of the Imaginary Vortex? Would he still be himself, or just an empty shell of what he used to be? He had no idea.

Also on the list of things Joey didn't know was *if* he would ever make it out of the Imaginary Vortex. There was no guarantee he was going to survive it. The whirlwind had carried Joey and DeMayne so far up they couldn't see the ground.

If it spit them out now, they would surely both fall to their deaths. Joey didn't want to live without his imagination, but he didn't want to die, either. Not if he could help it. What he wanted was to get down, but how? No sooner had the question entered Joey's mind than his sneakers grazed against hard red dirt.

What the–

It turned out Joey wasn't as high up as he thought. He had just lost all sense of direction. The wind seemed to loosen its grip on him and DeMayne, lowering them to the ground and pushing them along in a straight line. They bounded up and down in high arcs like astronauts on a moonwalk. Each jump was a little smaller than the last as they made a bumpy descent, both of them still holding tight to the sword.

DeMayne tried to pull the blade away from Joey one last time. He was bigger and stronger, but he had no leverage while they were flying through the air. That evened the odds. "Out of your mind," DeMayne muttered. "You're out of your mind. Throwing away the wand was one thing, but THIS! Sending us in here! Give me that sword," he spit, struggling with Joey. "At least I don't need magic to kill you with it!"

Joey put a foot on DeMayne's chest and straightened out his leg, kicking him away as he pulled back on the sword. They broke apart and tumbled to the ground. As Joey rolled to a stop, he lost control of the blade. DeMayne landed two feet away. Three at the most. The sword was closer to him, and he was the one who came up with it. He got up fast, filled with rage at what Joey had done to him. Joey watched his arm go back, ready to stab him through the heart with the broken tip of the blade.

"Wait!" Joey blurted out. "Stop!"

"Stop?" DeMayne repeated. "Did you just tell me to stop?" An unhinged, broken laugh leaked out of his mouth. "Joey, the way I feel right now, I might not ever stop."

"But the sword! It's still going!"

"What?"

"The sword's still working!" Joey shouted, pointing up at DeMayne. "Look! See for yourself!" DeMayne paused and studied the blade in his hands. Sure enough, the Sword of Storms was still going strong. All around, blood-red air rushed past them, sparkling with the fairy dust DeMayne had blown into the vortex, but not so much as a speck of glitter touched them. The sword had created a pocket of clean air inside the vortex—a protective whirlwind to counter its magic and keep it at bay. "The vortex didn't take away our imagination," Joey exclaimed. "We've still got it!" He was delirious with relief, despite the fact that DeMayne was about to hack him into tiny pieces.

Or so Joey thought. DeMayne's rage cooled instantly once he realized he was safe from the effects of the vortex. He looked at his hands, as if checking for signs of infection. Satisfied with what he found, he turned his attention back to the sword, waving it around to determine the limits of its reach. It was much easier to handle inside the vortex. "Fascinating," he said. "This sword always did have a mind of its own."

"It's protecting us?" Joey asked.

"More likely, it's protecting itself," DeMayne corrected. "But I'll take it. The result is the same either way. Today is your lucky day, Joey."

"How's that?"

"First off, I'm not going to kill you." DeMayne brushed himself off and straightened out his tie. "I'm not going to let anything happen to you in here. I still need you to get me the wand, don't forget. We're back where we started, you and I."

"A little past that, I think." Joey gestured at the raging storm that surrounded them. The vortex was bigger on the inside. It went on for miles like a Martian landscape in a sandstorm. Joey realized it was another gateway. The red tornado was taking them to another realm, just like the famous twister that had carried Dorothy's house to Oz.

"How do we get back?" DeMayne wondered aloud. He wasn't really asking Joey what to do, but Joey had an answer for him anyway.

"We can't go back," Joey said. "Only forward. That's how these things work." He looked around, his eyes settling on the hazy outline of a castle in the distance. DeMayne saw it too.

"All right, then." DeMayne motioned with the sword in the direction of the castle. "Lead the way."

They stalked through the windy landscape together, protected by the magic of the sword. Conflicting emotions warred inside Joey as DeMayne urged him on with the sword at his back. Joey wanted to reach Camelot, of course, but he wanted to go there with his friends, not DeMayne. He knew no good could come out of the Invisible Hand finding the Lost Kingdom. If he had a chance to stop it from happening, he had to act, but he didn't know what to do. Joey thought about summoning the wand and using it against DeMayne, but something stopped him. Calling the wand back was what DeMayne wanted him to do, which felt like a very bad idea. There was no telling what kind of tricks he had up his sleeve, even here. *Especially here,* Joey thought. DeMayne probably didn't even have to kill Joey to take ownership of the wand inside the vortex. All he had to do was push him out into the imagination-stripping storm to remove him from his position as master of the wand. If Joey meant to use the wand against DeMayne, he would get one shot. That was it. He didn't want to think about what would happen if he missed.

Another thought occurred to Joey. It was less attractive than fighting, but more certain of success, depending on how he chose to look at it. Joey had the power to keep DeMayne from getting the wand just by taking two steps to his right. If he moved beyond the sword's protective boundaries, he would lose the ability to do magic and the wand would stay wherever it was, lost in space. But DeMayne would still find Camelot—even without the wand—and Joey didn't have the guts to throw himself into the storm a second time. He had made a split-second decision to push himself and DeMayne into the vortex. It had been a rash impulse; otherwise he wouldn't have done it. The more time he had to think about the idea, the less likely he was to do it again.

Then he saw Scarlett. After that, the plan was off the table completely. They came across her sitting on the ground by herself, looking traumatized. Joey watched from safety as she tried to use her brushes. Nothing happened. The vortex had permanently disarmed her. "Keep going," DeMayne said without breaking his stride. Scarlett was only a few feet away, but she couldn't see them through the cyclone. "Poor thing," he added, making a heartless *tsk-tsk* noise as they passed. "She appears to have lost her muse."

Joey was shocked by DeMayne's total lack of empathy. "You don't want to stop?"

"What for?" DeMayne asked. "Don't tell me you feel sorry for her. I can assure you, if your positions were reversed, she wouldn't shed a single tear for you."

"I'm not sorry," Joey said. "I'm just surprised." Scarlett had a dead-eyed, defeated stare as she gave up trying to make magic with her art. Joey actually did feel a little sorry for her, in spite of himself. "You're just going to leave her there by herself?"

"Where we're going, she can't follow," DeMayne said without looking back. "Believe me, I know. She's not the first person we've lost to this place. I'm just glad it's not me this time."

"That's your philosophy, isn't it? Me, me, me."

"There's nothing I can do for her," DeMayne told Joey as Scarlett broke down behind them. "She's not one of us anymore, thanks to you. If you want to feel bad about that, go ahead, but don't expect me to go back and try to help her find her lost magic. I've got more important things to do. As far as I'm concerned, the number of people that currently have magic are the only people who should have it. I'm not under any obligation to share with anyone. No one ever shared with me. If you want magic, earn it. If you want to keep it, fight for it. Some people win. Some people lose. Scarlett lost. That's life."

"I get the feeling that with you, a lot more people lose than win," Joey said.

DeMayne shrugged. "That's the nature of any game. Your generation doesn't understand that. You want everybody to win, but everybody *can't* win. If they do, the game doesn't matter. If everybody gets a trophy, none of them mean anything."

"That's the problem with *your* generation," Joey countered. "You think life is some all-or-nothing, winner-takes-all game. Whoever dies with the most toys wins. That's old. That's over. You don't get it. Things like this sword, the wand . . . they aren't trophies. Magic is more than that."

"You're going to tell *me* what magic is?" DeMayne said. "Really?"

"Magic is a chance to change the world, but you're too selfish to take it. The world is falling apart in a million different ways and you won't lift a finger to help. You're having too much fun playing your game. I know you think you're winning, but if we don't do something soon, it's gonna be game over—for everybody."

"I've been hearing that kind of talk for longer than you've been alive," DeMayne replied, unconcerned. "The truth is, this world will last much longer without magic than it would with it. The little people out there . . . the norms? They can't understand things like this." DeMayne motioned to the magical windstorm raging around them. "God only knows what they'd try to do with this kind of power. By keeping magic under control, I keep the world turning, even if it's just for a little while longer. I'm not a villain, Joey. I'm actually the hero of this story. I may not be the hero you want, but I'm the hero you need."

"Yeah, you're a real man of the people," Joey said. "Except you already told me you want to make the world your playground, remember?"

"What's wrong with that? I'm not allowed to enjoy my work?" DeMayne let out a small laugh. "I'm working my tail off here, Joey. Sure, I'm one of the lucky people who gets out of bed happy every morning. I love what I do for a living, but no one ever gave me anything. I've worked hard to get where I am."

They broke through the vortex and came out the other side. A towering white castle stood before them. DeMayne grinned like a wolf that had just cornered a rabbit.

"I deserve this."

19

The Lost Kingdom

Camelot was the polar opposite of Dracula's dark castle in Transylvania. Crafted entirely out of white stone, decorated with gold trimming, and topped with royal-blue spires, it was a grand, inspiring sight that filled Joey with a sense of hope and fascination. King Arthur's castle looked like something out of a fairy tale—a larger version of Cinderella's castle from Disney World, only this was a real magic kingdom. Joey and DeMayne approached the gates of the city in awe. The doors were shut tight and looked to be every bit as strong as the day they were first hung on their hinges. All of Camelot looked brand-new, as if the castle had been magically protected against the ravages of time. All was quiet and still. The castle appeared to be deserted.

The Sword of Storms stopped humming in DeMayne's

hand, turning itself off without a fight. DeMayne looked down at the sword, stunned. Joey got the sense that the feisty relic had never gone to sleep on its own before. He wondered if something about Camelot had caused it to shut down. The sword's magic wasn't required to protect them anymore; that much was certain. The savage winds of the Imaginary Vortex raged around the castle, but they kept a respectful distance. Something inside Camelot gave it shelter from the storm. Joey had an idea what it was.

A boulder stood between them and the gates of the castle. It was fractured at the base where someone had driven a black iron spike into it. A series of cracks splintered out from the point of impact, and a dark energy glowed inside the stone. Joey and DeMayne looked it over together. Joey, showing greater interest than DeMayne, was the one to find the thin slit on top of the rock. An opening just big enough for a sword.

"Look at this," he said, feeling the gap with his fingers. "This is the stone. *The* stone! As in, the sword in the stone."

"It was," DeMayne half agreed, crouching down to examine the spike. "Not anymore." The black iron spike was hard for Joey to look at. It seemed to pulse as if it had a heartbeat. White smoke wafted out of the cracks in the rock like evaporation coming off dry ice. It drifted away from the castle, fading into invisibility. "Now it's something else. This is what powers the vortex."

Joey looked back at the vortex and saw a small, hooded figure emerge from within. It was a young woman dressed in black robes. Joey recognized her instantly. "I was wondering if she was going to show up."

DeMayne stood up, holding the Sword of Storms in a defensive stance as the woman approached. "Who's this? Another friend of yours?"

"I don't know if we're friends exactly. The last time I saw her, she left me for dead in the Himalayas."

"Don't be so dramatic," the young woman told Joey once she reached the stone. "Everything worked out, didn't it?" As she spoke, her soft, waifish features gave way to that of a more mature, middle-aged woman. She gave Joey a congratulatory pat on the shoulder. "I knew you'd find your way." She turned to face DeMayne, aging as she moved. DeMayne wrinkled his nose in disgust as she withered into an elderly woman, close to death. "I didn't expect *you* to be here with him," the old woman said, shaking a gnarled, accusatory finger. "You weren't invited, Ledger DeMayne."

"How do you know me?" DeMayne asked. "Who are you?"

"This is Fate," Joey said. "Or the Fates, depending on how you look at it."

"Really." DeMayne cocked an eyebrow. He had a suspicious smile on his face. "I don't believe in fate."

The old woman met DeMayne's gaze and held his eyes for a few seconds before she finally gave in and returned his smile, minus several teeth. "Fair enough," she croaked. "Neither do I." She pulled down the hood of her cloak, hiding her face for a moment, and threw it back to reveal her most substantial transformation yet. In the blink of an eye, she became someone completely new. A young woman with dark brown skin, hazel eyes, and hair that fell down around her shoulders in thick white braids. Beneath her robes she wore a stylish green and gold outfit with a golden saber on her hip.

"What the—" Joey sputtered, flabbergasted. The old woman was now a very young, dashing, and formidable buccaneer. She looked like a pirate from some kind of fantasy world, and who was to say she wasn't? "What's going on here?" Joey asked. "Why do you keep changing the way you look?" He figured she was using a glamour charm, but what for, he had no idea. What was she hiding? Who was she?

"I'm not changing my image," the woman said. "I'm changing your perception of it. Adjusting your memory. You see me as one thing but remember me as another. This, however . . . this is my true face."

"You're not Fate, then?" Joey asked.

"I never said I was Fate. My name is Hypnova. I'm a Secreteer. At least I was. I'm not with the Order anymore. Not for a long time."

"What Order? The Order of the Majestic?" Joey asked hopefully.

Hypnova shook her head. "The Clandestine Order of Secreteers."

Joey waited for Hypnova to elaborate, but she failed to offer up any more details. *Am I supposed to know what that is?* he wanted to ask.

Joey checked to see if DeMayne knew what Hypnova was talking about, but he had already bailed on the conversation. By the time Joey had turned his head, DeMayne was already at the gates of Camelot. Hypnova paid him no mind.

"The Secreteers are the guardians of all things fantastic

and unbelievable," she explained to Joey. "Sworn protectors of a land created long ago as a refuge for magic—for imaginary forces that were hidden away to ensure their survival."

"Okay," Joey said, struggling to take everything in. "That sounds good. But you said you're not a Secreteer anymore?"

"No."

"So you're not doing that job anymore, then? What's going on? Why are we here? What do you want with me?"

"I want the same thing you want," Hypnova told Joey. "I'm here because the world needs to change, and that starts here. Today. With you."

A few feet away, DeMayne was trying to force the castle doors open. They wouldn't budge. Undaunted, he aimed the Sword of Storms at the gates, intending to blow them down. Again, the sword refused to obey. Frustrated, DeMayne banged on the doors with the bottom of the hilt, ordering them to open for him. "You can't get in that way," Hypnova called out, a taunting edge in her voice. DeMayne turned to look at her with murder in his eyes, but she wasn't scared. "Think about where you are," she told him. "The Caliburn Shield is in there, keeping the vortex away. It keeps *everything* away. The castle is impenetrable. It has been for centuries."

"So how do we get in?" DeMayne barked at Hypnova. "If you know so much, you must have a plan."

Hypnova smiled. "I do. And you're not part of it." She looked at Joey. "An Arthurian relic blocks our path. It's going to take another one to remove it."

Joey understood what she was asking.

"The wand," Joey said, his heart sinking. "I can't call it." He gestured to DeMayne. "He'll do anything to get his hands on it. He'll kill me. . . . He said he'd kill my family if I don't give it to him."

"What if he doesn't remember you?" Hypnova asked.

Joey blinked. "What?"

Hypnova smiled. "What if I made him forget? He can't hurt you if he doesn't remember who you are."

"Is that a threat?" DeMayne said, storming back over to where they stood. "I don't know who you are or where you came from, but I—"

"That's right, you don't," Hypnova said, cutting him off. "And you won't. You won't remember either one of us if I have my way, and I rather think I will." She twirled her finger, and a winding trail of smoke spun out. It zeroed in on DeMayne's forehead, hitting him like a dart and stopping him cold. His indignant scowl melted away, along with, Joey suspected, any angry feelings he had toward Joey and Hypnova. DeMayne stood there slack-jawed and stone-still, as if awaiting instructions. Hypnova walked up to him, patted him on the cheek, and told him he was no longer needed. DeMayne nodded with a zombielike stare, and she sent him on his way. Clutching the Sword of Storms to his chest like a knight laid to rest in his tomb, DeMayne marched into the vortex and vanished from sight.

"Holy cow," Joey said, staggered by DeMayne's abrupt and seemingly voluntary exit. "He's just going to leave? You're gonna *let* him leave? Just like that?"

"We have bigger concerns than him."

"Bigger than the guy who secretly runs the world?"

Hypnova looked at Joey as if to say, *Seriously?*

"The Invisible Hand doesn't run the world. They're just a network of superpowered criminals. Gangsters and thieves. Liars and tricksters."

"Don't forget killers," Joey added.

"Yes, that too," Hypnova admitted. "They're dangerous people running around doing whatever they want, but the world is full of people like them. The world is also bigger than they are and extends beyond their reach. You're about to find that out."

Hypnova walked toward the castle and motioned for Joey to follow. "Yeah, but still," Joey said, trailing after her. "You didn't have to let him go with the sword. We could have kept that. We could have taken away his ability to do magic. That would have been a good thing."

"Forget about DeMayne. He's not important right now. Don't look back. Focus on what's ahead." They stopped outside the castle doors. Joey looked up at them and then back at the vortex, still thrown by DeMayne's sudden departure.

"He really isn't going to remember me?"

"Nothing about you. Or this place. Not even the Majestic Theatre."

"Wow." Joey had no reason to doubt Hypnova. He had seen the empty look in DeMayne's eyes, and he had relished it. If Joey was officially off the Invisible Hand's radar, that meant his family and friends were too. The relief he felt was indescribable. Now it was not only in his power to summon the wand, but it was safe to do so. This was going to change everything.

With the moment upon him, Joey wasn't 100 percent

sure what to do, so he just went with his gut. He held out his right hand, thinking he might will the wand back into being with some kind of dazzling, magical light show, but it didn't come. After a few seconds of nothing happening, he lowered his arm and thought about what else he could do. An idea popped into his head as he thought about where Redondo always kept the wand. Joey reached into his sleeve and pulled out the wand like it was nothing. Just like Dorothy with her ruby-red slippers, he had the power with him all along.

A rush of energy surged through Joey's body as if he had just chugged a gallon of soda. He didn't know if it was magic energy from the wand, or just the excitement of holding it again that filled him with such warmth. Once again, Joey had the power to bring imagination to life—unlimited possibility in the palm of his hand. He had the power to change the world.

"Well?" Hypnova asked Joey. "Are we going in or not?"

Joey grinned and pointed the wand at the castle doors, but he stopped short of opening them. "Wait," he said, drawing his arm back. "Not yet."

Joey thought about how he had used the wand in the

past. First he had to focus on something he wanted. Then he had to think of a command. He needed a word or phrase that felt right and lined up with the image in his mind. After that it was easy. All he had to do was believe. Saying the words out loud made it real. A real spell with real magic. All of this Joey had known instinctually from the moment he had first picked up the wand. He sized up the heavy doors of Camelot. Magic had sealed them shut ages ago, but his magic was stronger, or at the very least, equal to the task. He could do this. But he had to do something else first.

"What are we waiting for?" Hypnova asked.

Joey waved the wand and said, "The Three Musketeers." There was a flash of light, and Leanora and Shazad appeared beside him. "We're in this together."

20
The Secret History
of the World

"Joey!" Leanora threw her arms around him, hugging him tight. "You're okay!"

After she let him go, Shazad put a hand on Joey's shoulder and gave it a hearty shake. "You had us worried. It's good to see you—back to your old self, too!"

Leanora stepped back to examine Joey's arms. "Scarlett's curse?"

"Gone now," Joey said, holding up his unmarked hands and moving them around freely. "So is she."

Leanora smiled. "Thank goodness." She looked past Joey to the castle. "Oh my God. Is this . . . ?"

"It sure is. Camelot. We're here."

While Leanora was staring at the castle, Shazad was staring at the wand in Joey's hand. Leanora noticed it too. "And is that . . . Houdini's wand?" she added, even more amazed.

Joey nodded.

"It's Merlin's wand," Shazad said, now looking up at the castle.

"I still think of it as Redondo's wand," Joey said.

"It's *your* wand," Hypnova told him. "It answers to you. You couldn't have called it here otherwise."

Leanora and Shazad turned toward Hypnova. "Who are you?" Shazad asked her.

"This is Hypnova," Joey said, introducing her. "She's the one who sent us on our magical mystery tour."

"I thought it was Fate," Leanora said.

"Nope. It turns out the Fates aren't the Fates. Or even a single Fate. She's a Secreteer."

Shazad and Leanora looked at Joey with blank stares. "You're going to have to explain that," Shazad said.

"What's a Secreteer?" Leanora asked Hypnova. "What do you want with us?"

"This isn't about what I want. It's what I need," Hypnova said. "Actually, I needed Joey, but he needed you, which means we all needed each other."

"For what?" Shazad asked, suspicious.

"For this," she said, motioning to the castle. "For Camelot."

"Hypnova can't open this door," Joey said. "Only I can." He held up the wand like a magic key.

Shazad held up a finger. "Can you give us a second?" he asked Hypnova.

She smiled. "Take all the time you need."

The three children went into a huddle. "Are we okay with this?" Shazad whispered. "Are we sure we want her in there with us? Can we trust her?"

"I don't think we could keep her out if we tried," Joey said. "She's all right, though. She got rid of DeMayne for us."

"She did?" Leanora asked. "Got rid him of how? Where is DeMayne?"

"In there," Joey said, pointing to the vortex. "She wiggled her finger and he walked right in."

"Really?" Shazad's eyebrows went up. "That's it, then? He's done? No more Invisible Hand?"

"Don't get your hopes up. He'll be back, I'm sure. But he won't be back here, and he won't come back to the theater, either. He won't even remember us. Hypnova saw to that."

"Really!" Shazad said again, incredibly pleased. He turned around and looked at Hypnova, suddenly a big fan. "In that case, glad to have you with us!"

"Any friend of Joey's . . . ," Leanora said happily, feeding off Shazad's excitement. "What are we waiting for?" she asked Joey. "Let's go in."

"We're going," Joey said. "I just need to think of the right words first." He decided to go with an oldie but goodie. "Let's see if you remember this one." Joey held the wand aloft and shouted, "OPEN SESAME!"

The gates of Camelot swung open, and a rush of wind flew out, startling Joey. "Seriously, enough with the wind!"

"This wind I don't mind," Shazad said. "Look at that." The gust that had blown out of the castle had pushed the vortex back a good ten feet in every direction. "The shield must be stronger than the vortex."

"It's not just the shield," Leanora said, placing a hand on the castle wall to feel its power. "This whole place is magic. Scarlett told us it could open the floodgates."

"That's why we're here," Hypnova said. "These doors haven't opened in a thousand years." She looked at Joey and stepped aside to let him go first. "After you."

They went inside together. It was empty, just as Joey had expected.

"What are we going to find in here?" Joey asked.

"The past, the future . . . and hope," Hypnova said. "At least that's my hope."

Joey looked sideways at her. "How about we lose the riddles? Now that we know you're not Fate, you can just talk normal."

Hypnova nodded, accepting the criticism. "Sorry. Force of habit. I've been keeping secrets so long, my default state is to be cryptic. Don't worry. I'm going to tell you everything. Would you like to know what happened here? What happened to magic? Why it went away?"

Joey's eyes lit up. "Yes, please."

Hypnova led them deeper into the castle. "Follow me."

They passed under a great stone arch, entering the castle's map room. Inside, a global atlas had been painted on the floor, covering it completely. They moved across it like armies in a giant game of Risk, and Joey noticed the map displayed parts of the world that had not yet been discovered in King Arthur's day. It also had things that didn't exist, like an island the size of Texas between America and Europe.

"This map has an extra continent," Shazad said, studying the curious landmass.

"Yes, it does," Hypnova replied. "That's partly what we need to talk about." She looked around the room, which was lined with columns and centrally located with passageways leading out on all sides. "This way," she said, choosing a direction.

Hypnova directed the group up a flight of stairs to a chamber with a large round table. It had enough chairs to seat twenty people.

"Whoa," Joey said, stopping at the edge of the room. He looked at Leanora and Shazad. "You realize what this is? Where we are?"

Joey's friends nodded quietly. They were just as wonderstruck as he was. No one said the words out loud. They didn't need to. Everyone knew they were looking at a legendary piece of history. It was something everybody knew about, whether they believed the story or not. Finding Camelot was special, but actually seeing this and being in this room took it to another level. They were in the place where King Arthur and his Knights of the Round Table once met. Joey, Shazad, and Leanora approached the table in reverent awe.

Hypnova pulled out a chair and sat down like it was the kitchen table. "Let's stop here a moment. I owe you a story."

"You want to sit *here?*" Joey looked at the chair in front of him. It was sturdy enough, ancient and new all at once. Hypnova's chair had barely creaked. Still, sitting at King Arthur's Round Table felt improper to Joey. As if he would be disregarding some unseen velvet ropes to sit down on an off-limits museum exhibit. "Are you sure?"

"Sit," Hypnova told Joey. "You've earned it. All of you."

That was all anyone needed to hear. Just the pretense of permission was enough to get them moving. Joey, Shazad, and Leonora each took their place at the table, buzzing with excitement as they sat down. Joey was practically bouncing in his chair. It was just like the picture he had painted with the three of them dressed up as knights and him wielding the wand. Now the wand was back in his hand and they were sitting at King Arthur's Round Table! All that was missing were the horses and the armor.

"I'm going to tell you a secret," Hypnova began. "Something very few people know. I'm aware that magicians never reveal their secrets, but I'm not a magician and I'm not a Secreteer anymore, either. That's why I'm going to share with you the secret history of the world. The map I gave you earlier and your understanding of this place . . . everything about it, is incomplete."

As she spoke, Hypnova took out a small golden box, similar to the one DeMayne had used to hold his fairy dust. Hypnova's box contained a powder as well, but hers was deep purple. She took a pinch and sprinkled it into an open palm. "One thousand years ago, magic was everywhere."

She blew into her hand, and a lavender cloud flared up. It stretched and spread out, filling the air, eventually settling into a specific shape. Joey recognized it as the world atlas from the map room. The image rotated over the table like some kind of dust hologram.

"The world didn't always look the way it does today," she said, somehow manipulating the purple cloud and causing it to zoom in on the landmass between Europe and North America. "Once upon a time, a transatlantic continent existed. The ruler there fancied himself more than a king. He was an emperor, and he controlled magic in his land with fanatical vigilance." The purple powder swirled into the form of the emperor in question. He was making a fist. "This man saw magic as chaos and danger. More than that, he believed it to be unnatural and wicked—that no one should have such power."

The dust took the shape of a mighty army.

"He used military might to confiscate magical objects in his country, but he couldn't outlaw magic completely. That would have made him vulnerable to magic users in other lands. They were many in those days, including elves, dwarves, fairies, and giants. The emperor mistrusted other magical races especially. They were better at magic than men were and would always have an unfair advantage in his mind. What to do?" Hypnova's voice was bitter. "What to do?"

The dust cloud reformulated into the shape of the emperor and another man standing just behind him, whispering in his ear.

"The Emperor's Hand, a sorcerer himself, had a plan to control magic beyond the kingdom's borders. To consolidate power in 'the right hands.' He agreed that magic was a necessary evil. He couldn't eliminate magic for his emperor, but he came close. He was able to cast spells that weakened magic's influence in this world and blocked it out.

"Over a number years and a long, bloody campaign, these two men essentially conquered the world. Magical creatures were hunted to extinction. Survivors retreated to safety in forgotten realms and closed the doors behind them. Old roads that once led to places beyond your wildest imaginings were lost forever. Some shadows of them still remain," Hypnova allowed. "You passed through their remnants on your way here, but for the most part, they're gone."

"I don't understand," Joey said. "This guy . . . the Hand . . . how did he block out magic? What did he do?"

The cloud of powder over the table morphed into a spinning globe.

"He left three dark marks around the world." As Hypnova spoke, tiny explosions of dust erupted at key points on the globe, including Camelot. "Forbidden magic. Unspeakable magic. He poisoned Earth in places where magic was strong. Where magic users naturally gathered. One of them is nailed into the stone outside this castle. Camelot was the last kingdom to fall. King Arthur was slain. Excalibur was broken and corrupted with more dark magic. It became the Sword of Storms. The Tempest Blade. And this place . . . this powerful touchstone of magical energy was hidden away from the world on the other side of a magic gateway. Unreachable behind the Imaginary Vortex."

Joey, Shazad, and Leanora were riveted by Hypnova's tale.

"Why don't we know any of this?" Joey asked.

"You know some of it," Hypnova said. "You know of King Arthur. You've heard legends of mythical creatures and stories of magic."

"I never heard this part," Leanora said.

"Me neither," Shazad agreed. "An eighth continent in the middle of the Atlantic? Where did it go? Why isn't it there now?"

"Because ages ago, a small group of heroes, including Merlin, a young apprentice, and the first Secreteer, infiltrated the transatlantic continent and fought back. They meant to cripple the emperor's power by stealing his kingdom, but he wasn't there. The Emperor's Hand had betrayed him. He had banished his master to a realm of nothingness, where he could finally have the peace and order he had always desired. The Emperor's Hand was the true enemy. The power behind the throne."

The shape-shifting powder played out the scenes as Hypnova described them, starting with an eclectic band of heroes, moving through the Hand's traitorous turn, and finishing on the very familiar image of a greedy, grabbing hand—the symbol of the Invisible Hand.

"It was them," Joey said, realizing it had been the Invisible Hand's scheming power grab that had cost the world its magic. "I knew it."

"It wasn't them yet," Hypnova told him. "It was just him. The Emperor's Hand was one man, and he was defeated. Merlin and the others fought bravely and stole the heart of the emperor's kingdom. It was itself a magical land. They broke off the capital city to create a safe haven for magic. A home for all the world's unique, extraordinary things."

Joey didn't know what it meant to "steal the heart of a kingdom," but Hypnova's magic powder painted a picture for him. He watched as an image of the lost continent materialized before him and his friends. A ripple of energy ran through the land, and a section of the kingdom literally broke off and floated away.

"A new country was born," Hypnova said. "A secret country. The Clandestine Order of Secreteers was born with it. They swore to protect their new home at all costs. To protect magic and imagination. History was rewritten to include none of this. Memories were adjusted and the stories passed into legend. Parts of them anyway. The rest of the emperor's kingdom sank into the ocean. You've heard that story too, I expect."

"Atlantis?" Joey asked.

Hypnova nodded. Joey and the others watched as her magic powder depicted the ocean swallowing up the transatlantic continent. After that it settled down on the table.

"What about the Emperor's Hand?" Shazad asked. "What happened to him?"

"He escaped," Hypnova said. "And he learned a valuable lesson: not to draw so much attention to himself. Unfortunately, that's all he learned. He went on being the same miserable excuse for a person he always was, stealing magic items from others and keeping them for himself. His own actions had caused there to be less magic in the world, so naturally he wanted more of it. He found other conniving, selfish people who were willing to follow him, and the Invisible Hand was born."

"So that's how they got started," Leonora said. "I'm assuming Merlin founded the Order of the Majestic to fight them?"

"Sadly, Merlin died. You have to understand, what he did . . . evacuating a continent, hiding a piece of it away, sinking the rest . . . it was too much. For anyone." She looked at Joey. "That wand of yours is one of a kind. It can do almost anything, but it takes its toll. If you push it too far, there's a price. Merlin paid the ultimate price. He did so willingly, because that's what it took to free the world from a tyrant. Merlin's apprentice founded the Order of the Majestic to honor his sacrifice. Her name was Kadabra, and she dedicated her life to preserving the world's remaining supply of magic. Finding magic objects that survived the emperor's purge, searching for ways to reach lost magical realms . . . She's the one who started the Secret Map of the World. The Order spent centuries on that, continuing her good work."

Joey, Shazad, and Leanora traded troubled looks. No one wanted to be the one to tell Hypnova they had lost the map.

"In the old days—the very old days—the Order kept magic alive and free for all, but times change. The modern world pushed magic to the fringes, and the Invisible Hand grew in power. Harry Houdini tried to change that. They killed him. Redondo tried to carry on in his place. They broke him. He had potential, but he never made it this far. He never got the chance to come here."

Joey took Redondo's magic deck out of his pocket and showed them to Hypnova. "Were you really the one who gave Redondo these cards? He said an old woman told him he'd inspire a new age of magic. Was that you in disguise?"

"No. That was someone else," Hypnova said. "She's gone now, but she lived long enough to give me back my purpose. After the Secreteers cast me out, I was lost, but she inspired me, just as Redondo inspired you. For years I thought the wand was wasted on Redondo, but now I see he was just another step on the path to you. It's the three of you. You're going to set imagination free and give the world back its magic."

"How?" Joey asked.

Hypnova rose from the table and motioned for Joey, Shazad, and Leanora to do the same. "Follow me."

Continuing to act as their guide, she took them through a series of chambers to the throne room of Camelot. It was large and empty, as was the throne itself. Long, vertical banners hung on the wall displayed King Arthur's coat of arms: three golden crowns on a field of blue. A gleaming silver shield rested on the floor, leaning up against the legs of the King Arthur's royal seat. Hypnova picked it up.

"I give you the Caliburn Shield, one of the three great Arthurian relics—the others being Excalibur and that wand," she said with a nod to Joey. "The Imaginary Vortex surrounding this castle was created to hide Camelot and eat away at its magic. This shield protected it. It has the power to create an impenetrable force field around a person, place, or thing. The only way you can bypass its defensive barrier is by using one of its sister objects, as we did, or if you have touched the inside of the shield."

Hypnova turned the shield around and pressed her palm against it. Then she held it up for Joey, Shazad, and Leanora to do the same.

"Why didn't you tell us this back on the mountain?" Joey asked. "Why all the mystery?"

"I told you, I spent my life keeping secrets. Old habits die hard. Also, I had to test you. I gave you time with the candles to see if you would find your way and figure things out. You didn't, so I had to give you a nudge. I wanted to know if you would go the distance or give up. I'm risking my life by telling you these secrets. The Clandestine Order will find out what I have told you. They'll kill me if they can." Joey, Shazad, and Leanora were all startled to hear that. "Don't worry. I'll be ready for them," Hypnova added with a wink.

"Why would they want you dead?" Leanora asked.

"Because I'm telling secrets I swore to take with me to my grave. Secrets that have kept their home safe for generations."

"I don't understand," Shazad said. "Why take the risk?"

"Because," Hypnova replied. "Everybody deserves magic. It's worth the risk. I'm not worried. I've seen the extent of your will now. I believe you'll do what's necessary. Imaginary forces still exist in the world. Imaginary places. You have seen some of them, but there's more. So much more. This is just the beginning. You came here to find Camelot, but we can do more than that. We can set it free."

"Why us?" Joey asked. "You know all these secrets. You knew how to get here. You had the map. Why didn't you just do this yourself?"

"I could get through the vortex unscathed, but I couldn't destroy it. I needed to get into the castle for that." Hypnova held up the shield. "To get this. I couldn't do that without your help. We needed each other. No one can break the spells that hide magic from the world alone."

Joey nodded. "Redondo told us the most powerful magic can't be created alone."

Hypnova gave Joey the shield. "Like you said, we're in this together."

They went outside, back to the sword in the stone, which was now the spike in the stone. Joey had slipped his arm through the straps on the inside of the shield. He wanted to take it off and throw it at the stone, smashing it with a well-aimed throw worthy of Captain America, but he didn't have the arm strength for that. He walked up to the stone, took off the shield, and looked back at his friends. "You guys want to get in on this?"

Shazad and Leanora joined him at the rock, and everybody took a section of the shield, holding it by its metal edge.

"All for one . . . ," Leanora began.

"One for all," Shazad said.

Together they raised the shield as high as they could and brought it down hard. It cleaved through the stone like it was made out of snow, going all the way down to the black iron spike at its base. The shield hit the spike with a metallic clang. The rock blew apart, and *whoosh*—the vortex blew away.

They were back on the windswept battlefield, surrounded by crumbling ruins, only now there was a perfectly intact medieval castle in the center of them. Shazad's and Leanora's families spun around in surprise, elated to see their children returned to them safe and sound. They were mixed in with the formerly brainwashed locals who were already struggling to make sense of what had happened to them. Now they were scratching their heads, trying to deal with the impossible scene that had just played out before their eyes.

"That's it," Hypnova said. "There's no turning back now. The world is going to notice this."

Joey scanned the faces of the people all around, gawking at the sight of a castle suddenly appearing out of thin air. "We can't change the world by trying to make people believe in magic," he said. "We have to make people believe in magic so that we can change the world. This is gonna go a long way toward making people believe."

"Well said," Hypnova replied. "And that belief will enable magic to live. Where I come from, we save the world, but we don't change it. It's time for something different. The world needs to change. If we want that to happen, we have to make it happen. We need you to lead the way. The Order of the Majestic."

Hypnova bent down to pick up a broken piece of the Finale Mask. "I'd hang on to this. There's still a bit of magic left in there. Might come in handy." She gave the fragment to Joey. "Remember, magic is an energy powered by belief. That doesn't make it less powerful. That makes it more powerful. You decide how strong it is. It's like imagination. You decide if it you want to make it real."

A tinny, whistling sound drew everyone's attention to the iron spike on the ground. The shield had left a tiny ding in its side, and white smoke poured out of it like steam escaping a kettle. Hypnova nudged the spike with her toe, and it broke apart, dissolving into ashes. "One marker down," she said.

"Two to go," Leanora said, finishing her thought.

"How are we supposed to find them?" Shazad asked. "We lost the map."

"Did you?" Hypnova's eyebrows went up at first, but she took the news in stride as the children explained what had happened to it. "That's unfortunate, but don't worry. I memorized it."

She took another pinch of purple powder and blew it out again, this time directly at Joey, Shazad, and Leanora.

Joey nearly hacked up a lung, coughing inside a smoky purple haze. His throat closed up and his eyes stung, but as he pounded his chest, trying to catch his breath, he felt something else happening between his ears. A picture formed in his mind. It was the map. He saw it clearly, as if he were holding the map in his hands. Just as Hypnova had taken away DeMayne's memories, she had given him a new memory to keep.

The last thing Joey saw before the smoke cleared was a fuzzy outline of Hypnova pulling the hood of her cloak back up. Their eyes met, and Joey knew that she understood he had seen the map in his mind's eye. "Something to remember me by until next time," she told him, her eyes lighting up under the hood. "Goodbye, Joey. I look forward to working with you."

Joey rubbed his eyes, and when he looked up, all was calm. The purple smoke had vanished and Hypnova had gone with it. Something else was missing too. "The shield!"

Shazad said, noticing its absence before anyone else. "Where's the shield?"

"Hypnova took it," Leonora said. "I saw her. I couldn't stop her. I couldn't even breathe."

"She didn't take it," Joey said. "She traded us for it."

"What are you talking about? What tra—" Shazad stopped and touched a hand to his temple. "Did she give us the map? In our heads?"

Everyone confirmed the image of the Secret Map of the World had been burned into their brains. They suddenly knew every inch of the map as if they had studied it all their lives. Joey figured that, plus making Ledger DeMayne forget about him and the theater, made for an even exchange. Better than even.

The astonished crowd of locals closed in around Joey, Shazad, and Leonora, assaulting them once again, but this time with questions about the castle.

"Where did this come from?"

"Were you kids in there?"

"How did *we* get here? *What happened?*"

Joey didn't know what else to tell them, so he just shrugged and told the truth. "Magic happened." What else could he say? "Don't worry, you're safe," he added in his most soothing, reassuring voice. "It's over now." But that part wasn't the truth. Nothing was over. Joey felt the wand in one hand and the broken piece of mask in the other. What had happened in Camelot was just the beginning.

21

The Journey Continues

A couple hours later, Joey finally arrived in California, but not before placing a phone call to his mother. He decided he couldn't put it off any longer. In his mom's last text to Janelle, she had threatened to call the police and file a missing persons report on him. Joey called her back and she answered on half a ring. He told her he had found his phone and apologized profusely for not calling. His mother wanted to know what was going on and demanded an explanation for why he had refused to call home, despite getting a million and one texts telling him to do so. "I was going to get on a plane and fly out there if I didn't hear from you today!"

Joey apologized again and told her he had been buried with work in the lab with Janelle. His mother told him that was no excuse. In fact, there was no excuse. She didn't understand why Joey couldn't find five minutes for a phone call in three days. "Forget five minutes; you could have taken *one* minute!" she scolded. "We were worried! It was like you fell off the face of the earth!"

You don't know the half of it, Joey thought.

"I'm sorry, I got caught up. Exciting things are happening out here." It was a true statement. As Joey spoke with his mom, people were snapping pictures of Camelot with their phones, posting to social media, and making calls of their own. "Anyway, I was just doing what you told me to do."

"What are you talking about?"

"Don't you remember? You said you wanted us to get the world off fossil fuels by Wednesday. That way I could come home early. Well, we had a breakthrough."

There was silence on the other end of the line. "Are you serious?"

"We might even make the news," Joey said. *Just maybe not the front page,* he thought, eyeing the castle and enjoying the budding excitement around its appearance. "Either way, I'm done here. I'm ready to come home."

There was more silence on the other end of the line. Joey checked his screen to make sure the connection was still good.

"Mom, you there? Did I lose you?"

"No, I'm here. That's . . . that's good. I'm glad."

Joey smiled. He was glad too. His mother's voice still had an edge, but it was softening, which meant he was off the hook.

"Don't go thinking you're off the hook," she told him. "We'll talk about all this other stuff later, but first things first. Let's change your flight."

Joey smiled. "Okay, Mom. Whatever you say."

He spent the next ten minutes listening as his mother rattled off flight options with LAX departure times and Newark arrivals. He mixed up the time zones when picking a flight back and nearly gave away the fact that he wasn't in California just yet. He had to remember that England was six hours ahead of New Jersey and California was three hours behind. He covered up by saying he was messed up from working around the clock, and they arranged for him to fly back at eight p.m., West Coast time.

Joey knew he was getting ahead of himself, telling his

mom that he and Janelle had a big breakthrough in the lab, but he didn't feel like he was overpromising anything. It was going to happen. He believed that without question. Shazad and Leanora didn't give Joey any pushback about him bringing the remnants of the Finale Mask with him to Caltech. After everything they had just been through, they were past that. Leanora's family had another magic doorknob like the one she had left in the theater. After things had settled down, they used it to send Joey to California. Better late than never.

By the time Joey found Janelle on campus, the discovery of Camelot was a global news story. Just as Joey had said, it was something that would go a long way toward changing the world into a place where people were willing to believe in magic. After all, there was no explaining Camelot away. People were forced to reckon with the magical nature of King Arthur's castle. It was not a situation where the ruins of an undiscovered city were found deep in an unexplored jungle. This was an ancient castle—fully intact—materializing out of thin air in a place that had been empty the day before. Joey knew there would still be plenty of doubters out there. People who thought the sudden appearance of Camelot was some kind of prank or stunt, or that there had to be some rational explanation for why everyone had "just missed" the castle all these years. But the truth was undeniable. With the vortex gone, a major source of magic had been returned to the world, and that had a ripple effect that ran all the way to Janelle's research lab at Caltech.

Joey told her everything that had happened, and he wasn't the least bit surprised when she was able to fire the laser using the mask as a power source. She did it on the first try and was able to repeat the experiment on demand. The training wheels were officially off her imagination, and that was going to have a major impact on the world too. Maybe even bigger than Camelot's return. The broken fragment of the mask generated only a quarter of the power the whole mask had put out, but it was still a big leap forward—especially since Janelle's lab partners were able to fire the laser too. Some of them, anyway. There was no doubt about it, magic was making a comeback. Joey wondered if the appearance of Camelot had made it easier for people to believe in new ideas, or if there was literally more magic in the world as a result of Camelot's liberation.

Maybe it was a bit of both.

Sure enough, the experiment did make the news. It wasn't as sensational as a fantasy castle dropping out of the sky, but a group of students discovering a brand-new source of clean, renewable energy was still a very big story. It was presented as a temperamental new element called Finalium. Janelle had picked the name on a whim. It didn't always work, but some people were able to get it to generate incredible amounts of power. The university faculty was popping champagne and congratulating Joey and Janelle. "Finalium" had the potential to be the next big thing in alternative energy, and they were just getting started.

When the time came to go home, Joey had to fly back to keep up appearances with his parents. It was tedious going through airport security and sitting through a six-hour flight, especially when he could have used magic to make the trip in seconds, but he had to take baby steps in bringing magic back. It was bad enough he had been out of contact for three days. He wasn't ready to show his parents what he'd really been up to, and they weren't ready to see it. Joey also doubted they would be on board with what he and his friends were going to do next.

Back at the Majestic Theatre, Joey looked at the NATL building across the street. In the past, the mere thought of the NATL office and the people who worked there had filled him with dread, but no longer. There was no one inside looking out the windows watching and waiting for him. There were no threats coming out the front door. If DeMayne was inside, it didn't matter. Joey was a stranger to him now. After the Imaginary Vortex had collapsed, DeMayne had left Camelot in a stupor, leaving Scarlett to fend for herself. She'd run off, leaving her coat and brushes behind. No one chased after her. Joey knew from the look on her face she wouldn't be coming back. She was broken, her magic spark of imagination gone. *Good riddance,* Joey thought. The brief touch of sympathy he had felt for her was fading faster than Hypnova's mark on the theater door. Joey paused to look at it before he went inside. There wouldn't be a new mark coming to replace it after this one disappeared, but that was fine. Joey entered the Majestic feeling energized and safe just the same.

He didn't care that Hypnova had taken the Caliburn

Shield. Shazad and Leanora didn't mind, either. Based on what Hypnova had told them about the other Secreteers, they had a feeling she needed it more than they did. Besides, they wouldn't have even known about the shield if not for Hypnova, and they had other, more pressing concerns than simply collecting rare magical items.

Joey and his friends had found their way. They knew what they had to do now, and all three of them were finally in agreement. There were other magical impediments like the spike that had powered the Imaginary Vortex still out there in the world. As the Order of the Majestic, it was their job to find and destroy them. It wasn't just about beating the Invisible Hand, or convincing the world to believe in magic. It was about locating the things that had ended the age of magic and taking them out. Setting magic free. That was what they intended to do, and thanks to Hypnova, they knew exactly where to look.

Joey found Shazad and Leanora in Redondo's office. It would always be Redondo's office as far as Joey was concerned, but his friends were doing some redecorating. They

444

had taken the picture frames down off one of the walls and were painting a mural on it using Scarlett's magic brushes. They had been entrusted to Shazad's family for safekeeping after the battle of Camelot, but his parents were more open to loaning out the items in their collection these days. They also had an open invitation to the Majestic Theatre. As soon as Hypnova's mark wore off, they could come visit anytime. Leanora's family, too.

Joey came up behind Shazad and Leanora, taking in their work. "What do you think?" Leanora asked him. "We're almost done." They had painted a perfect re-creation of the Secret Map of the World. It took up the entire wall.

"Not bad," Joey said, nodding enthusiastically. "Seriously. I'm impressed."

"It's easy when you have the right tools for the job," Shazad said, adding some finishing touches on the wall.

"We got tired of picturing the map in our heads while we were talking about where to go next," Leanora added. "Now we don't have to."

"This is great," Joey said. "Can we zoom in on stuff? Will it move like the paper map did?"

"It should," Leanora said. "We'll find out for sure after it dries."

"Or, we could find out right now," Shazad said, stepping back from the wall. He pointed to the spot where he had made his final brushstroke. Shazad had painted something that wasn't on the map before. It was an island that didn't exist, and it was already moving.

"What is that?" Joey asked as the island drifted slowly away from mainland China toward the Philippines.

"It's an island that won't stay still," Shazad said, setting down his brush. "It's part of the reason I asked Leanora to paint this with me. This island here's been bugging me. I kept glimpsing it here and there whenever I thought about the map, but not all the time and never in the same place. I'm not the only one, am I? You guys must have seen it too."

Joey searched the memory of the map that Hypnova had implanted in his head. He didn't know why he hadn't seen it before, but now that he knew where to look, the island was right there. Now that he believed, he could see it. He couldn't miss it. Joey saw something else, too. The image wasn't complete. He grabbed a brush, addressed the canvas, and labeled the roaming island. The words floated alongside the mystery island as it moved out to sea.

"What the heck is the Imagine Nation?" Leanora asked, reading the name off the wall.

"I don't know," Joey said. "Maybe we should go find out."

Acknowledgments

Lost Kingdom is my seventh novel, but a first for me, creatively speaking. I've never written a book like this before.

Usually, I plot out my books with super detailed outlines before I start working on them. I try to figure out everything that's going to happen, chapter by chapter and scene by scene. It takes me months to do this. Sometimes more.

I didn't do it that way this time.

Instead, I thought I about how much my stories always change from the first draft to the final. That outline I spend so much time obsessing over? It's not carved in stone. First of all, that would take forever. Second, I think it's impossible to know every detail of a story before you start writing it.

There are some ideas that only show up when you are "in the story" yourself, thoroughly immersed in the characters' world. The longer I do this, the more I realize that writing a book is like following a path that only reveals itself to you as you walk it.

So, I tried something new with this one. At the risk of sounding pretentious, I fully surrendered myself to the magic of storytelling. Like Joey, Shazad, and Leanora, I decided to trust and believe that I would be able to find my way as I went. It was stressful at times, and it took a little while longer, but it all worked out in the end. I want to thank you for coming along for the ride, and some other special people who made the trip possible:

For every book I write, my agent, Danielle Chiotti, is an amazing partner who is with me every step of the way. Without her, these stories go nowhere.

My editor, Liesa Abrams, has been a trusted guide on my storytelling adventures for almost ten years now. If not for her, I'd be lost on the trail, wandering around in circles.

Samira Iravani helped me make this journey more authentic and real. Art director Karin Paprocki and artist Owen Richardson designed an amazing cover to help me put my best foot forward. I'm so lucky to have their talent and energy elevate my work. The same goes for publisher

450

Mara Anastas, production editor Rebecca Vitkus, copy-editor Penina Lopez, and proofreader Stacey Sakal. Thank you to them, and everyone at Simon & Schuster/Aladdin.

Finally, I have to thank my family. My wife, Rebecca, and our two boys . . . They're my own personal Order of the Majestic. They keep my life filled with fantastic, unbelievable moments, and I couldn't do this without them.

MATT MYKLUSCH

is the author of the Jack Blank Adventure series and other books for children (including grown-up children like himself). He lives in New Jersey with his wife, Rebecca; his boys, Jack and Dean; assorted pets; and other forms of magic. Find him online at MattMyklusch.com.